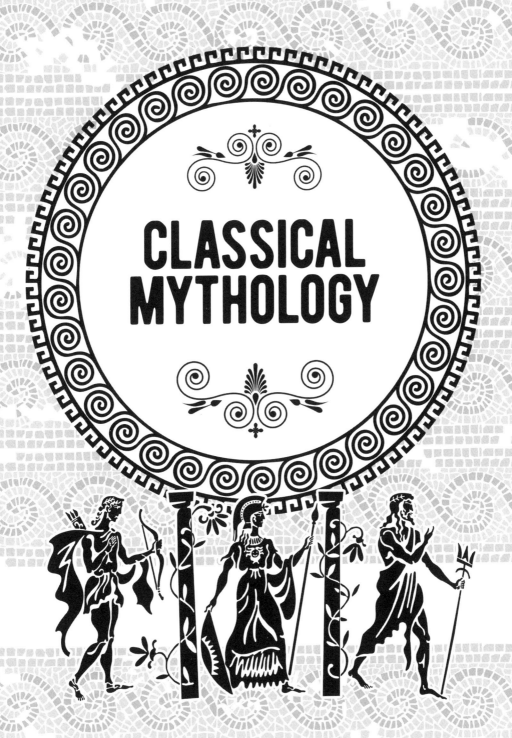

CLASSICAL MYTHOLOGY

CLASSICAL MYTHOLOGY

MYTHS AND LEGENDS OF THE ANCIENT WORLD

Nathaniel Hawthorne, M.M. Bird,
Mrs. Guy E. Lloyd et al.

SIRIUS

SIRIUS

This edition published in 2023 by Sirius Publishing, a division of
Arcturus Publishing Limited,
26/27 Bickels Yard, 151–153 Bermondsey Street,
London SE1 3HA

ISBN: 978-1-3988-3015-8
AD006079UK

Printed in China

Contents

Introduction

The Oedipus complex of psychoanalysis. The Trojan Horse computer virus. Nobel and poet laureates. What do these all have in common?

Greek and Roman myths. Or rather, the ideas contained within those myths, myths that are thousands of years old.

They reach us across time, from an era without writing, when songs and poems held memories and beliefs. Before the invention of writing, singers and poets played a vital role, telling and retelling the stories that helped to create a society and hold it together.

This is why so many myths are located in a specific time and place. Turn to the first story in this collection – *Pluto and Proserpine* – and you see that it is no fairy tale that happened once upon a time and far, far away. No, in this telling it happened in Sicily, by the groves of Enna – where there stood an important temple honouring Proserpine's mother, Ceres.

Yet that is only one telling of the story. Ceres, after all, is a Roman goddess. The Greeks knew her as Demeter, and a temple was built for her at Eleusis – where, so it was believed, she had rested in her search for her missing daughter.

Such variations are common, even inevitable. Different societies need different traditions. And as societies develop, so too do the myths they tell. Jason's quest for the golden fleece was already an old story by the eighth century BCE, when *The Iliad* and *The Odyssey* were first recorded in writing; some scholars suggest it reflects the moment when sheep farming reached Greece. Fifth-century BCE Athens was the cradle of democracy and a centre of the arts and philosophy, and seems to have had no need for the story – we find only two images from that era referencing the myth. Yet the myth must have retained its resonance, for in the third century Apollonius of Rhodes wrote the epic *Argonautica*, making use of a variety of sources, some of which no longer exist. Today we consider his to be the 'standard' version of those that have reached us.

How did it do so? How indeed have any of these myths, from societies so

unlike our own, reached us? Via the Roman Empire and the Islamic world.

As the Roman Empire rose, it subsumed Greece, absorbing its culture and traditions, and subsequently spreading these across the regions it controlled in Europe, Africa and Asia. And when the empire gradually collapsed, centuries later, it left traces: its architecture, its art and its writing. Texts survived, often in translation, thanks to Arab scholarship.

In the Middle Ages, Christianity and Islam clashed, bringing the two worlds into contact. And when Constantinople fell, scholars fled to Europe, bringing their libraries with them – one more factor spurring the Renaissance.

Ovid's *Metamorphoses*, a poem in fifteen books, was particularly influential: it references almost 250 different myths, offering alternatives to the subjects of Christianity. Artists across the centuries were inspired, from Titian to Rubens, Michelangelo to Caravaggio – and their achievements also reflect the influence of Greco-Roman art.

At the same time as rediscovering its writings, Europeans were also digging up and rediscovering its art, especially its statues. The *Apollo Belvedere*, for example, was found near Rome and quickly recognised as a masterpiece: Dürer reversed its pose for his Adam in his engraving *Adam and Eve* in 1504, while Michelangelo was also one of several artists to sketch it.

Why were these statues so important? The Greeks, and later the Romans, had aimed to portray the human body in all its complexity, creating a sense of movement, of living, breathing bodies, even while using the materials of bronze and marble. The artists of the Renaissance and beyond strived to achieve a similar dynamism on the two dimensions of a flat canvas.

The poets who flourished during the Renaissance also owe much to the classical myths. Dante combines myth with classical allusions, and Ovid is an obvious source for Shakespeare. Nor can the impact of *The Iliad* and *The Odyssey* be underestimated. The debt to English literature alone is clear enough: George Chapman's translation of *The Iliad* inspired John Keat's sonnet 'On First Looking into Chapman's Homer'; 'Ulysses' (the Latin variant of Odysseus) is both a poem by Tennyson and one of the most important works of modernist literature by James Joyce.

Joyce had first been introduced to Ulysses as a child, via Charles Lamb's adaptation for children *The Adventures of Ulysses*. Lamb was not the only writer who considered it important to introduce children to the myths that have impacted Western thought. Nathaniel Hawthorne was similarly inspired,

and many of his versions are included here. Among his fellow authors is Francis Storr, a Classical scholar celebrated for his translations of Sophocles. These are master storytellers, whose compelling versions make the myths accessible even to audiences unfamiliar with the Classical world – or, it must be said, the sometimes tedious conventions of the poetry. The oral origins of the Homeric epics are sometimes all too obvious, featuring the repetition that is so necessary for memory and performance: Odysseus is always *crafty*; Agamemnon, *the king of men*; and Dawn, *early born* and *rosy-fingered*.

Some of the authors have been faithful to the sources, while others have added their own flourishes. The same has been true for storytellers across the centuries. Myths have always been – and always will be – open to reinterpretation and re-creation. In 1943, when France lay under Nazi rule, Jean Anouilh revived the myth of Antigone to attack the Vichy government in his play of the same name, while Sartre reinterpreted the myth of Electra to explore the moral compromises of occupation in his play *The Flies*.

In any era, myth can carry the meanings we need it to hold.

The stories that were first told by peoples now long gone are still enabling us to tell our own.

Caroline Curtis

Pluto and Proserpine, from 'The Loves of the Gods' by Giulio Bonasone.

Pluto and Proserpine

H.P. Maskell

In the very heart of Sicily are the groves of Enna—a land of flowers and rippling streams, where the spring-tide lasts all through the year. Thither Proserpine, daughter of Ceres, betook herself with her maidens to gather nosegays of violets and lilies. Eager to secure the choicest posy, she had wandered far from her companions, when Pluto, issuing, as was his wont, from his realm of shadows to visit the earth, beheld her, and was smitten by her childlike beauty. Dropping her flowers in alarm, the maiden screamed for her mother and attendants. 'Twas in vain; the lover seized her and bore her away in his chariot of coal-black steeds. Faster and faster sped the team as their swart master called to each by name and shook the reins on their necks. Through deep lakes they sped, by dark pools steaming with volcanic heat, and on past the twin harbors of Syracuse.

When they came to the abode of Cyane, the nymph rose up from her crystal pool and perceived Pluto. 'No farther shalt thou go!' she cried. 'A maiden must be asked of her parents, not stolen away against her mother's will!' For answer the wrathful son of Saturn lashed his foam-flecked steeds. He hurled his royal scepter into the very bed of the stream. Forthwith the earth opened, making a way down into Tartarus; and the chariot vanished through the yawning cave, leaving Cyane dissolved in tears of grief for the ravished maiden and her own slighted domain.

Meanwhile Ceres, anxious mother, had heard her daughter's cry for help. Through every clime and every sea she sought and sought in vain. From dawn to dewy eve she sought, and by night she pursued the quest with torches kindled by the flames of Ætna. Then, by Enna's lake, she found the scattered flowers and shreds of the torn robe, but further traces there were none.

Weary and overcome with thirst, she chanced on a humble cottage and begged at the door for a cup of water. The goodwife brought out a pitcher of home-made barley wine, which she drained at a draught. An impudent boy jeered at the goddess, and called her 'toss-pot.' Dire and swift was the punishment that overtook him. Ceres sprinkled over him the few drops that remained; and, changed into a speckled newt, he crept away into a cranny.

Too long would be the tale of all the lands and seas where the goddess sought for her child. When she had visited every quarter of the world she returned once more to Sicily. Cyane, had she not melted away in her grief, might have told all. Still, however, on Cyane's pool the girdle of Proserpine was found floating, and thus the mother knew that her daughter had been carried off by force. When this was brought home to her, she tore her hair and beat her breast. Not as yet did she know the whole truth, but she vowed vengeance against all the earth, and on Sicily most of all, the land of her bereavement. No longer, she complained, was ungrateful man worthy of her gifts of golden grain.

A famine spread through all the land. Plowshares broke while they were turning the clods, the oxen died of pestilence, and blight befell the green corn. An army of birds picked up the seed as fast as it was sown; thistles, charlock, and tares sprang up in myriads and choked the fields before the ear could show itself.

Then Arethusa, the river nymph, who had traveled far beneath the ocean to meet in Sicily her lover Alpheus, raised her head in pity for the starving land, and cried to Ceres: 'O mourning mother, cease thy useless quest, and be not angered with a land which is faithful to thee. While I was wandering by the river Styx I beheld thy Proserpine. Her looks were grave, yet not as of one forlorn. Take comfort! She is a queen, and chiefest of those who dwell in the world of darkness. She is the bride of the infernal king.'

Ceres was but half consoled, and her wrath was turned from Sicily to the bold ravisher of her daughter. She hastened to Olympus, and laid her plaint before

Jupiter. She urged that her daughter must be restored to her. If only Pluto would resign possession of Proserpine, she would forgive the ravisher.

Jupiter answered mildly: 'This rape of the god lover can scarce be called an injury. Pluto is my brother, and like me a king, except that he reigns below, whereas I reign above. Give your consent, and he will be no disgrace as a son-in-law.'

Still Ceres was resolved to fetch her daughter back, and Jupiter at length agreed that it should be so on condition that Proserpine, during her sojourn in the shades, had allowed no food to pass her lips.

In joy the mother hurried down to Tartarus and demanded her daughter. But the fates were against her. The damsel had broken her fast. As she wandered in the fair gardens of Elysium she had picked a pomegranate from the bending tree, and had eaten seven of the sweet purple seeds. Only one witness had seen her in the fatal act. This was Ascalaphus, a courtier of Pluto, who some say had first put it into the mind of the king to carry off Proserpine. In revenge for this betrayal, Ceres changed him into an owl, and doomed him ever after to be a bird of ill-omen who cannot bear the light of day, and whose nightly hooting portends ill tidings to mortals.

But Ceres was not doomed to lose Proserpine utterly. Jupiter decreed that for six months of each year her daughter was to reign in dark Tartarus by Pluto's side; for the other six months she was to return to earth and dwell with her mother. Joy returned to the mother's saddened heart; the barren earth at her bidding once more brought forth its increase. Soon the fields were smiling with golden corn, and the mellow grapes hung heavy on the vines, and once again that favored land became the garden of the world.

Pan and Syrinx

Mrs. Guy E. Lloyd

Long ages ago in the pleasant land of Arcadia, where the kindly shepherds fed their flocks on the green hills, there lived a fair maiden named Syrinx. Even as a tiny child she loved to toddle forth from her father's house and lose herself in the quiet woods. Often were they forced to seek long and far before they found her, when the dew was falling and the stars coming out in the dark blue sky; but however late it was, they never found her afraid nor eager to be safe at home. Sometimes she was curled up on the soft moss under the shelter of a spreading tree, fast asleep; sometimes she was lying by the side of a stream listening to the merry laughter of the water; sometimes, sitting over the stones upon the hillside, she would be watching with wonder and delight the lady moon, with her bright train of clouds, racing across the sky as if in hot chase.

Years passed on, and Syrinx grew into a tall and slender maiden, with long fair hair and great gray eyes, with a look in them that made her seem to be always listening. Out in the woods there are so many sounds for any one who has ears to hear—the different notes of the birds, the hum of the insects, the swift, light rustle as some furry four-legged hunter creeps through the underwood. Then there is the pleasant, happy murmur of the breeze among the leaves, with a different sound

Left: Pan spying of the nymph Syrinx who is seated on a rock, combing her hair by Marcantonio Raimondi.

in it for every different tree, or the wild shriek of the gale that rends the straining branches, or the bubbling of the spring, or the prattle of the running stream, or the plash of the waterfall. Many are the sounds of the woods, and Syrinx knew and loved them all until:

'Beauty born of murmuring sound,
Had passed into her face.'

'Have a care, Syrinx,' her playfellows would say sometimes. 'If you wander alone in the woods, some day you will see the terrible god Pan.'

'I should like well to see him,' the maiden made answer one day to an old crone who thus warned her. 'The great god Pan loves the woods and everything that lives in them, and so do I. We must needs be friends if we meet.'

The old woman looked at her in horror and amazement. 'You know not what you say, child,' she made answer. 'Some aver that none can look upon Pan and live, but of that I am none so sure, for I have heard of shepherds to whom he has spoken graciously, and they never the worse for it. But of this there is no doubt—whoever hears the shout of Pan runs mad with the sound of it. So be not too venturesome, or evil will come of it.'

Now Syrinx might have taken warning from these wise and kindly words. As it was, she treasured them, and only wondered what this god could be like, the sound of whose shout made men run mad. She feared to see him, and would have run swiftly away if she had caught a glimpse of him, and yet she went continually to the far and silent groves whither, so the shepherds said, Pan was most wont to resort.

It chanced one day that Syrinx had wandered farther than was her wont; she had been in the woods since daybreak, and now it was high noon. She was tired and hot, and lay down to rest on a bank beneath a tall ash tree that was all covered with ivy, and resting there she soon fell fast asleep. While she slept the wild things of the woods came to look upon her with wonder. A doe that was passing with her fawn stood for a moment gazing mildly upon the maiden, and the fawn stooped and licked her fingers, but at the touch Syrinx stirred in her sleep and both doe and fawn bounded away among the bushes. A little squirrel dropped lightly from a tree and sat up close beside her, his tail curled jauntily over his back, his bright eyes fixed upon her face. The little furry rabbits first peeped at her out of their holes, and then growing bolder came quite close and sat with their soft paws tucked down and their ears cocked very stiffly, listening to her quiet breathing. And last of all, stepping noiselessly over the grass, came the lord of all the wild things, the great god Pan himself.

His legs and feet were like those of a goat, so that he could move more quickly and lightly than the wild gazelle, and his ears were long and pointed—ears like those of a squirrel, so that he could hear the stirring of a nestling not yet out of its egg. Softly he drew nigh to the maiden, and there was a wicked smile in his bright dark eyes. But as he bent to look into her face she stirred, and he leapt lightly back and sat himself down a little space from her, leaning on his arm among the brushwood till he was half hidden from her. Beside him lay a great bough torn from the tree by some winter storm; Pan drew this to him and began to cut from it a piece of wood whereof to fashion a dainty little drinking-cup. And lying there, cutting at the wood, Pan began to whistle low and sweetly to himself, just as though he had been some shepherd or huntsman resting in the shade.

At first the soft notes made for the half-awakened maiden a dream of singing birds and rippling water; then her drowsy eyes unclosed and she became aware of a bearded face turned half away from her and bent over some sort of work. For a time she lay still, and Pan forebore to glance at her, but cut away at the piece of wood he was fashioning, and whistled to himself as though he had not marked the maiden.

Presently, broad awake, Syrinx raised herself upon her elbow and gazed full upon the stranger, who glanced round at her in a careless, friendly way, and nodded to her with a kindly smile.

'Thou hast slept well, fair maiden,' said Pan, in a low, gentle voice, that sounded like the far-off murmur of a winter torrent.

And Syrinx, reassured by the gleam of the merry dark eyes, made answer:

'Yea, fair sir, for I had wandered far, and was aweary.'

'How hast thou dared to wander so far from the haunts of men?' asked the sylvan god, 'Art thou not afeard of all that might meet thee here in the deep forest?'

'I fear none of the wild things of the wood,' answered Syrinx simply, 'for none has ever done me hurt. If thou art, as I judge thee, a hunter, thou knowest that it is through fear alone that the beasts of the forest do harm to man. But I move ever quietly among them, and do not startle them, and they go on their ways and leave me in peace.'

'Thou art passing wise,' said Pan; 'there are few indeed of thy years who have attained to thy knowledge. When a man perceives a rustling in the brushwood he flings his spear at the place; while women, for the most part, scream and flee. But the fearless may walk quiet and unharmed through the depths of the forest.'

'There is one fear in my heart, kind stranger,' said Syrinx earnestly. 'There be shepherds who say that in these forest paths they have seen and spoken with the great god Pan himself. But some say that it is death to see him, and all say that men run mad at the sound of his shout. How thinkest thou? Hast thou ever caught a glimpse of him?'

There was a merry twinkle in those dancing eyes as the stranger made answer: 'Nay, maiden, I have never seen him of whom thou speakest; but cast away thy last fear, for sure I am that the sight of him is not death to any living thing. He loves and cares for all that hath life; and as for his shout, that is only heard in battle, for he never cries aloud save in wrath, and then indeed it brings confusion to his enemies or to those who withstand him, but to his friends it brings courage and triumph.'

Syrinx heaved a sigh of relief, and lay back again, one arm under her head, her long fair hair rippling over her shoulder, and her beautiful gray eyes fixed upon the face of the stranger.

Pan gazed upon her, and crept a little nearer through the brushwood.

'Sure I am that thou art as wise as thou art kind, fair stranger,' said the innocent maiden. 'There has ever been within me a secret thought that Pan, the lord of all the wild things of the wood, could not be fierce and cruel as men said, and ever have I been assured that could I meet and speak with him I should love him well.'

'Love, love, love, love,' said the deep soft voice of the great god Pan. 'Every tree, every flower, every bird, every beast lives for nothing else. Dost thou indeed understand what thou sayest, fair maiden?'

And the girl nodded her pretty head wisely, for she quite thought she did. 'Yea, kind stranger,' she answered, 'for when I look into the eyes of one to whom I have never yet spoken a word, I know at once whether his speech and company are like to be pleasant to me, or whether I would have him pass on and speak no word. When I lay half asleep but now, and listened to your merry whistling, I could feel within me that it was a sweet and a friendly sound, and good to hear. It was like the speech of the forest, which I have loved since I was a baby.'

Pan laughed gently to himself as he fashioned his wooden cup; but there was a new gleam in his downcast eyes, and when next he glanced at her Syrinx saw the change, and a vague uneasiness awoke in her. She looked at the sky, already beginning to glow with the radiance of the setting sun.

'It grows late,' she said; 'I must away, for I have far to go ere night-fall. Farewell, gentle stranger.'

'Nay, but stay a little longer,' said Pan gently. 'I know every path of the forest, and if the darkness falls upon thee I can guide thee safely, never fear.'

But the maiden feared the more, as she sprang to her feet.

'Nay, I must tarry no longer,' she said hastily; 'it is already over-late.' Tossing her hair back from her flushed face she sprang away down the slope like a frightened fawn.

Forgetting all but his wish to stay her Pan leapt up to follow her, and glancing back over her shoulder Syrinx saw his goat feet, and knew with whom she had been speaking. With a sudden start she plunged into the brushwood, and as she disappeared from his sight Pan, anxious only to bring her back, uttered a mighty cry.

The sound smote upon the ear of the terrified maiden, and her brain reeled. With one wild shriek of terror she turned and fled, and before even those swift goat's feet could overtake her she had plunged into the river, and was gone—a reed lost among the river-reeds.

And the great god Pan sat down upon the river bank sorrowful and baffled; and as he gazed upon the water, flushed with the light of the setting sun, he saw the very bank of water-reeds where Syrinx had disappeared. Slender and graceful they were, as the maiden who was gone, and they trembled as she had done when she looked behind and saw who was her pursuer, and their tufted heads, golden in the evening light, reminded Pan of the golden hair of Syrinx. He stepped forward to the edge of the water, and stooping, plucked a handful of the reeds. They snapped with a sharp crack in his strong fingers, and as he looked down at them he sighed deeply. His sigh came back to him with a low musical note, and Pan went back to the bank, and sitting himself down he scanned and fingered tenderly the hollow stalks. Long did he sit there with his newly found treasure; the sun went down, the crimson clouds turned to dark lines across the pale saffron sky, the full moon rose slowly from behind the hill, and still Pan bent over his handful of water-reeds, and breathed upon them this way and that, and cut and fashioned them with care.

Next day the shepherds were all abroad in the woods searching for Syrinx, but of her they found no trace; only, as they moved hither and thither, they heard sweet and strange and far-off music. It was as if all the sounds of the forest had been modulated and harmonized; now it swelled and grew loud and joyous, and now it died away in pitiful lamenting. It was Pan, playing upon the sevenfold pipe that he had made, and when at length he gave it to the sons of men, and taught them to play upon it too, he gave it the name of Syrinx, the beautiful and hapless maiden whom he had loved and lost.

The Fall of Phaeton *by Hendrick Goltzius.*

The Story of Phaeton

M.M. Bird

A fiery and high-spirited youth, Phaeton could not brook the taunts of his playmate Epaphus, who claimed divine descent from Isis. When Phaeton boasted that his father was Phoebus the Sun-god, Epaphus only laughed and called him a base-born pretender. So one day Phaeton, stung to madness by these taunts, went boldly to his mother Clymené and demanded that she should give him some clear proof that he was indeed, as she averred, the very son of Phoebus. Clymené lifted her beautiful hands to the Sun, who rode gorgeous in the Heavens, and swore by him that none other than Phoebus was the father of the boy. 'Nevertheless,' said she, 'if this doth suffice you not, and you seek other proof, travel yourself to his Eastern Mansion, which lies not so far remote from here, and ask him whether you are not his son.'

The ambitious youth hastened to follow her counsel; he longed to see his father, and to visit the Eastern Mansion where he abode. Through India he traveled in haste, never resting till afar off he saw the wondrous light that shimmered perpetually over the Palace of the Sun.

High it stood on columns of burnished gold ablaze with jewels. The folding doors were of silver, the walls of ivory, and Vulcan had wrought the precious metals in designs of wonderful beauty. The seas, the earth, the fair forms of the immortal gods, all graced the carven portals.

Phaeton, toiling up the steep ascent, saw at a great distance the dazzling god, seated high on an imperial throne, all sparkling with gems. The Hours, Days,

Months, and Years, were ranged on either hand. He saw Spring decked in flowers, Summer with her garner of grain, Autumn bowed beneath his burden of grapes and fruits, and hoary Winter shivering behind them. The all-beholding eye of the god perceived him from afar, and before he had spoken a word, a voice from the throne bade him welcome: 'What wants my son? For my son thou art.' Thus encouraged, the youth, though dazzled by the exceeding brightness, poured out his tale and proffered his petition.

The god was touched by his tale of wrong. Flinging aside the awful glories that surrounded him, he bade his son advance, and embraced him with tenderness.

'Make of me some request,' he said, 'and to convince thee that I am thy father, I swear by Styx to grant it, whate'er it be.'

The youth was transported with delight, and asked at once to be permitted to guide the Sun's bright chariot for one day.

Phoebus was grieved beyond measure at the young man's rash ambition, and bitterly repented of his oath; but even a god, when he has sworn by Styx, cannot take back or annul that awful oath.

'Ask of me some other proof,' he begged. 'Too vast and hazardous this task for thy strength and years. Not one of all the gods—not Jupiter himself, ruler of the sky—dares mount that burning chariot, save I alone!' He told him how with pain and labor the wild steeds climb up the arc of the sky—how from the topmost pinnacles of Heaven the Earth and Ocean lie so far beneath that even he himself is sometimes seized with giddiness and his brain reels. And when down the steep descent of the western sky the horses plunge headlong, it needs a strong and steady hand to check them in their course. He told him how, through all his daily task, the brave Sun has to front the opposing forces of the Bear, the Scorpion, and the Dog Star, and guide his steeds among their influences. Through a thousand snares his progress lies, with forms of starry monsters ready to devour him if he strays by a hair's breadth from the appointed way. And the very horses themselves, when their mettle is up, are a team that only a god may control. 'My son,' he besought him, 'do not require of me a fatal gift.'

But the fond father pleaded in vain. The bold youth was unaffrighted, and the oath was binding.

The time had come: Aurora heralded the new day. The golden chariot made by Vulcan was drawn forth; the spokes of the wheels were of silver, its seat was starred with gems.

The nimble Hours brought forth from their stalls the fiery steeds.

With last words of warning and advice, the father bade his son farewell, and watched him wend forth on his perilous journey. The youth leaped into the seat, he gathered up the reins, and gave his father such praise and thanks for his indulgence as cut him to the heart.

The horses neighed and pranced, breathing fire from their distended nostrils. They sprang out through the gates of Dawn and flew over the clouds, leaving the light breezes of Morn far behind them.

The youth was light; he could not poise or weight the chariot as did its accustomed rider. The bounding car was tossed to and fro, the sport of winds and currents. Wildly they hurtled headlong up the sky. The steeds perceived the lighter weight, the weaker hands. They plunged, and plunging, left the stated course.

The youth became confused; he looked around him, but could no longer recognize the track. He did not know which way to steer, nor would the horses have obeyed his hand. Wildly they careered and brought the heat of midday into far regions of the Heavens that were unused to its untempered rays. All around him monstrous threatening shades awoke and stirred in the Heavens as he vexed them with the heat. Far, far below the affrighted youth could see Earth and Ocean spread out. But as his chariot raced madly down the heights, the clouds were dispersed by his fierce rays, the high mountains began to smoke, the forests to burn; ripened harvests were devoured by fire, whole cities were turned to ashes. Pindus and Parnassus were steaming, the fountains of Mount Ida were dried up, and Ætna raged with redoubled heat. Even the towering Apennines and Caucasus lost their snows, and the huge Alps were one range of living flame.

The horrified youth beheld the universe burn around him, and he could scarce endure the sultry vapors that rose about him as from a furnace. Lost in clouds of whirling smoke and ashes, the steeds careered madly to and fro, he knew not whither. It is said that in that day the Moor began to change his hue and turn black, and Libya and all the deserts of Africa were then first drained of their moisture and left in great tracts of parching sandy waste. The great rivers, the Ganges, Euphrates, and the Danube, rose up in clouds of hissing steam, and the frightened Nile ran off and hid his head in the sands, and there for centuries and centuries it has lain hid.

Stern Neptune, in amazement and anger, thrice reared his head above the shrinking waves where his fishes all were dying, and thrice the fierce flames drove him back.

At length Earth, wrapped in her scalding seas, uplifting her scorching brows, appealed to Jupiter.

'See how fierce vapors choke my breath; see my singed hair, my withered face, the heaps of cinders that defile my fair body . . . Have pity.'

Jupiter heard her prayer. He mounted his high ethereal throne, called all powers, even the god whose son drove the chariot, to witness that what he did he was compelled to do, and launched a thunderbolt at the head of the despairing Phaeton.

Thus with fire the god of gods suppressed the raging fire. Lifeless from the chariot the boy fell like a falling star, and his charred body dropped to the earth far from his own land, far in the western world, beside the river Po.

The horses broke loose from their harness, the chariot was splintered into a thousand shining fragments and scattered far over the steaming earth.

And the story goes, that for the space of one whole day, from morn till eve, the world existed without a sun, lighted only by the lurid glare of the burning ruins.

Beside the waters of the river the Latian nymphs came round and gazed with awe upon the dead youth. His charred body they inclosed in a marble urn and wrote on it an epitaph:

'Here lies a youth as beautiful as brave, Who through the heavens his father's chariot drave.'

His mother Clymené, frantic with grief, ceased not to roam the world, followed by her weeping daughters, until at last she came to the banks of Po, and found there the sculptured urn. She hung above it, bedewing the marble with her tears, crying aloud the name so dear to her. Her daughters stood around, weeping and lamenting with her. All night long they kept their watch, and returning day found them still calling on their brother's name. Four days and nights they kept their stand, till at length, when for their weariness they would have sought rest, they found they could not move. Phaethusa's arms were covered with hardening bark and branching boughs; Lampetia stood rooted to the ground; Æglé, as she tore her hair, only filled her hands with leaves. While their faces were yet untransformed, they cried to their mother for help. But, alas! she was powerless. She tore the bark from their fair bodies, she stripped the leaves from their sprouting fingers, she clung to their hardening limbs in vain. Only blood came trickling where she tore away the leaves and bark, and in faint voices the maidens cried that she only wounded her daughters when she tore their trees.

Then the bark covered their fair faces, and they stood for ever dumb, waving green boughs in the sun, while tears of amber rolled slowly down the encrusting bark.

Arethusa

V.C. Turnbull

Lord of all waters was Oceanus, the ancient Titan god, whose beard, like a foaming cataract, swept to his girdle. Many fair daughters had he, of whom poets sing, yet the fairest of all was the nymph Arethusa. She had not lacked for wooers, but she shunned the haunts of men and abode on the Acroceraunian heights whence she had sprung, or when she descended to the plain hid herself in tangled bushes and overhanging alders. She loved the quiet woodland ways, and had vowed herself to the chaste huntress Diana, and in her train loved to fleet through the woods and over the plains of Achaia, chasing the flying deer.

Now it happened one day that Arethusa, wearied with hunting and with the great heat, wandered alone among the woods and meadows, seeking a place of rest. Presently she heard the ripple of waters, and soon she came to a river flowing between straight poplars and hoary willows. Swiftly and quietly it ran, making no eddies, and so pure were its waters that she could count the pebbles lying in its deep bed like jewels in an open casket.

Joyfully then the tired maiden unbound her sandals, and, sitting down upon the bank, dipped her white feet in the cool water. For a while she sat there undisturbed, and idly watched the growing ripples as she dabbled in the stream.

Left: Alpheus and Arethusa *by Antonie Waterloo.*

But while she thus rested and played, a strange commotion drew her eyes to the middle of the stream, and a fear fell upon her, for she knew that it could be none other than Alpheus, the god of that river. Quickly she sprang to her feet, and while yet she stood trembling and irresolute, a hollow voice cried to her from mid-stream. And (oh marvel!) the voice was not terrible like that of a god, but tender and full of pleading love.

'Whither dost thou hasten, Arethusa?' it said. And again: 'Whither dost thou hasten?'

But Arethusa, a maiden who cared nothing for love, would be wooed by neither god nor man.

Swiftly she fled from the enchanted spot, even before the young river-god had sprung from the stream with love and longing in his eyes. And now began that long chase of which the end was even stranger than the beginning. Arethusa, weary no longer, darted like a fawn from the river, and Alpheus, more ardent still as the maid was coy, swiftly followed her flying steps. Through woods and meadows, over hills and across valleys—yes, and past more than one city, fled pursuer and pursued. But now, as the day drew towards sunsetting, Arethusa's strong limbs wearied, her strength flagged, and her pace slackened, and in her sick heart she knew how vain a thing it is for a mortal to strive against a god. For no weariness weighed down the feet of Alpheus; straight and swift he ran as his own river. Now so near was he to the maiden that his long shadow fell across her feet; but no faster could she go, for the sun smote fiercely upon her, and her strength was failing. Louder and louder sounded the footsteps of the god. Now she could feel his hard breathing in her long hair; was there no escape? With her last strength she cried to her sovereign mistress: 'Help, O Huntress, thy huntress maiden! Aid her who so often carried thy bow and thine arrows in the chase!'

And the goddess answered her votary.

For at once Arethusa was wrapped in a dense cloud, so dense indeed that even the burning eyes of her pursuer could not pierce it. There, then, she crouched, like a hare on its form, while outside she heard the footsteps of Alpheus pacing round her hiding-place, searching and baffled. But he, having come so near his

Arethusa Chased by Alpheus *by Wilhelm Janson and Antonio Tempesta.*

prize, would not now give it up, and she knew that he would watch the cloud till she came forth. At the thought, beads of sweat gathered on her forehead and ran down to her feet. Faster and faster it poured; she was as ice that melts in the sun; and she realized with joy that the goddess was opening for her another way of escape. All her weariness and terror slid from her straightway; her tired limbs melted into a liquid ease, and it was no maiden but a laughing stream that shot from under the cloud and fled singing towards the western sea.

But Alpheus, noting the guile of the goddess, laughed aloud, for could he not at will become even as his own river? He changed even as he conceived the thought; and now the chase began once more, only this time river pursued stream, leaping from crag to crag, and rushing across wide wastes of marshy country.

And again Arethusa, finding herself in straits, cried aloud to her sovereign mistress Diana. And, behold, in answer to her prayer, the earth was suddenly rent asunder and a vast black chasm yawned in her path. Into it she plunged, and down, down, down she fell. And into it in pursuit plunged also Alpheus, who loved her so well that he was ready to follow her to the depths of the earth.

The darkness passed, and overhead was a beautiful green light, and on all sides a profound and solemn silence. Arethusa had left the land behind, and was pushing across the floor of the ocean. And behind her came the waters of Alpheus. Then into the maiden heart, which as yet had known not love, came something better than fear. From the lover who could follow her even hither why should she fly? On he came, undeterred and unpolluted by the brackish sea, his waters as fresh and pure as when they had first run laughing through the sunlit meadows of Arcadia . . . Arethusa sought no more to fly. Love had conquered—Love, the lord of gods and men, who mocks at maidens' vows and melts the coldest breast. So there, amid the alien waters of the sea, the two met in loving embrace, never again to part. And after this the gods brought them once again to the light of the sun. For, finding at length a way of escape through a fissure of the rocks, they rushed forth as that Arethusan Fount which springs up in the Sicilian island of Ortygia.

And now from their fountains
In Enna's mountains,
Down one dale where the morning basks
Like friends once parted
Grown single-hearted,
They ply their watery tasks.
At sunrise they leap
From their cradles steep
In the cave of the shelving hill;
At noontide they flow
Through the woods below
And the meadows of Asphodel;
And at night they sleep
In the rocking deep
Beneath the Ortygian shore;—
Like spirits that lie
In the azure sky
When they love but live no more.

Percy Bysshe Shelley (1792–1822)

Apollo and Daphne from Quatuor libri amorum *by Conrad Celtis.*

The Story of Daphne

M.M. Bird

Phoebus Apollo, the Sun-god, a hunter unmatched in the chase, had slain the awful Python with his shafts. To commemorate such a doughty deed, he instituted the Pythian Games wherein noble youths should strive for mastery. The prize was a simple green wreath, the symbol of victory. The laurel was not yet the leaf dedicated to the wreaths the gods bestowed upon the happy victors, but every kind of green was worn with promiscuous grace upon the flowing locks of Phoebus.

Flushed with pride in his new success against the Python, Phoebus saw Cupid, Venus' immortal son, bending his bow and aiming his feathered shafts at unwary mortals. A heart once pricked by one of those tiny darts felt all the bitter-sweet of love, and never recovered from the wound. Him Phoebus taunted. 'Are such as these fit weapons for chits?' he cried. 'Know that such archery is my proper business. My shafts fly resistless. See how the Python has met his just doom at my hands. Take up thy torch, and, with that only, singe the feeble souls of lovers.'

Cupid returned him answer that though on all beside Apollo's shafts might be resistless, to Cupid would justly be the fame when he himself was conquered. The mischievous boy flew away to the heights of Parnassus, and thence winged one of his sharpest arrows against the breast of the bold deity. Another and different shaft he took, blunt and tipped with lead, and this he aimed at the heart of a certain nymph of surpassing fairness, a shaft designed to provoke disdain of love in her chaste bosom. Her name was Daphne, the young daughter of Peneus. She

37

was a follower of Diana, the divine huntress. All her days she spent in the woods among the wild creatures, or scoured the open plains with swift feet. All her love was given to the free life of the forest: she roamed in fearless pursuit of beasts of prey, her quiver at her side, her bow in hand, her lovely hair bound in many a fillet about her head. Her father often blamed her. 'Thou owest it,' he said, 'to thyself and me to take a husband.'

But she, casting her young arms about his neck, begged him to leave her free to pursue the life she loved, and not set the yoke of marriage on her unwilling shoulders. 'No more I beg of thee,' she said, 'than Diana's fond parent granted her.'

Her soft-hearted father consented to respect her whim, but warned her that she would soon rue her unnatural wish.

As Daphne was one day hunting in the forest, Apollo perceived her. The arrow winged by Cupid had not failed of its effect, and the poison of love ran like fever through his veins. He saw the polished argent of her bared shoulder; he saw the disheveled hair that the wind had loosened from its snood; he saw the eyes, limpid and innocent as a fawn's, the beauty and speed of her feet as she fled down the forest glade, her taper fingers as they fitted an arrow to the bow-string. He saw and burned.

Swift as the wind the startled damsel had fled as she espied him, nor when he overtook her would she stay to hearken to his flattering words.

'Stay, nymph!' he cried. 'It is no foe who follows you. Why should you flee as the trembling doe from the lion, the lamb from the hungry wolf, the dove from the pursuing falcon? It is a god who loves and follows. It is a god you flee from, a god who loves, and will not be denied.'

Still she fled and still he followed; he the loving, she the loath, he pleading and she deaf to his prayers. As a hare doubles to elude the greyhound that is gaining on her, the flying maid turned back and sought thus to elude her pursuer. In vain she strove against a god. Terror winged her feet, but there is no escape from Love.

Right: Apollo chasing Daphne. The background right-hand side also shows the moment Daphne turns into a laurel tree. This engraving by Master of the Die was designed by Baldassare Tommaso Peruzzi.

He gained ground upon her, and now she felt his hot breath on her hair; his arm was just outstretched to clasp her.

The nymph grew pale with mortal terror. Spent with her long, hard race for freedom, she cast a despairing look around her. No help was to be seen, but near by ran the waters of a little brook. 'Oh, help!' she cried, 'if water gods are deities indeed. Earth, I adjure you, gape and entomb this unhappy wretch; or change my form, the cause of all my fear!'

Above: Daphne embracing her father, the river god Peneus, from the engravings by Master of Die, designed by Baldassare Tommaso Peruzzi. At the left, three nymphs bring jars.

Left: River gods consoling Peneus for the loss of his daughter Daphne, from 'The Story of Apollo and Daphne', from the engraving by Master of the Die, designed by Baldassare Tommaso Peruzzi.

The kind earth heard her frenzied prayer. The frightened nymph found her feet benumbed with cold and rooted to the ground. As Apollo's arms were flung about her a filmy rind grew over her body, her outflung arms were changed to leafy boughs, her hair, her fingers, all were turned to shuddering leaves; only the smoothness of her skin remained.

'Gods and men, we are all deluded thus!' For a maiden he clasped a laurel tree, and his hot lips were pressed upon the cold and senseless bark.

Yet Apollo is a gracious god, and presently, when his passion had cooled, he repented him of his mad pursuit and its desperate ending. The idea of the coy maiden, roaming the forest fancy-free, crept into his imagination, more delicate and lovely than when she lived in deed. So he vowed that the laurel should be his peculiar tree. Her leaves should be bound for poet's brow, should crown the victor in the chariot race, and the conqueror as he marched in the great triumph.

Secure from thunder should she stand, unfading as the immortal gods; and as the locks of Apollo are unshorn, her boughs should be decked in perpetual green through all the changing seasons.

And the grateful tree could only bend her fair boughs above him and wave the leafy burden of her head.

Left: Apollo standing at the left shooting a python with an arrow, from the engraving by Master of the Die, designed by Baldassare Tommaso Peruzzi. Above to the left are the muses, and at the right Cupid can be seen on a cloud, approaching Apollo.

Bella

Deucalion and Pyrrha

M.M. Bird

To the golden age of innocence, when the world was young and men a race of happy children, succeeded an age of silver, and then an age of brass. Last came an age of iron, when every man's hand was against his neighbor, and Justice fled affrighted to the sky. Then the sons of earth, the giants, no longer curbed by law or fear of the gods, waxed bold and wanton. Piling mountain upon mountain they essayed to scale the heavens and hurl its monarch from his throne. These Jupiter blasted with his red lightnings and transfixed with his winged bolts. But from their blood, as from seed that the sower scatters, there arose a race of men, a feeble folk, but no less godless and lawless than their sires. Then Jupiter, beholding the ways of men that they were evil and that none was righteous in his eyes, determined to destroy this world and people it with a new race unlike the first. He was minded at first to destroy it by fire, and made ready his artillery of thunderbolts, but then he bethought him that the vast conflagration might blaze up to heaven itself and scorch the gods on their golden thrones. So he dropped the bolts from his hand.

'Water,' he cried, 'as my poet has sung "is the best of all elements"; by water I will drown the world.'

Left: Deucalion and Pyrhha, *a 17th-century etching by Stefano della Bella, designed by Jean Desmarets de Saint-Sorlin.*

First he bound the North Wind that freezes floods by its icy breath, then loosed the South Wind that brings fog and darkness and horror on its wings. From his beard and eyebrows he rained showers, from his robe and mantle the unceasing floods streamed down and wreathing mists encircled his frowning brow.

He swept above the earth, wringing the waters from the high clouds, while peal on peal of thunder rolled about him.

The bearded corn bent before the driving rain, and the farmers lamented their ruined crops. But not alone in the skies was Jupiter content to open the watergates. He summoned to his aid the powers of Neptune. The ocean, the natural enemy of the fruitful earth, swelled with pride at this request, and rushed inland to meet the swollen torrents that gushed from the hills across the sodden plains. The floods gathered deep over the lowlands, the fields were drowned, the ruined grain was submerged. Sheep and cattle, peasants and their plows, trees and wild beasts, were all borne out upon the resistless waters. Even the houses, sapped by the water, fell into the angry flood, and all the household goods were swallowed up. Some climbed high cliffs to escape the general doom, others launched out in little boats and floated above the submerged chimneys of their homes or cast anchor among their vines. Hills and valleys were alike engulfed by the heaving waters; those who had sought safety on the hilltops died of starvation, and those in boats were swamped.

Jupiter, looking down from his starry heights, saw nothing but a lake of troubled waters where the blooming earth had been. The destruction was complete. Then he unloosed the North Wind, and set fierce Boreas to drive away the clouds. Neptune he commanded to lay his trident on the rough waves and smooth out their furrows. And he bade Triton, who appeared above the waves, give the signal for the waters to retire within their proper bounds. Triton blew a blast on his shell, and the note was borne from wave to wave, from marge to marge. The waters, obedient to the summons, ran off the shores. The streams shrank by slow degrees to their accustomed level, and the green shoulders of the earth rose up from out their watery shroud. The tops of the drooping trees emerged all matted with mud, the houses lay in heaps of reeking ruin, the whole world lay desolate and wore a sickly hue.

I have said that all men were evil, yet among this sinful race were two righteous found, and though they could not save others from destruction, they themselves were saved. In a far vale of Thessaly there lived an aged couple, who had fled there to escape from the wickedness of men, Deucalion and Pyrrha his wife. When the flood came they had seen a little skiff floating by their cottage door and had embarked in it. For many days the skiff had floated like a cork above the surging flood, and when the flood abated they found themselves stranded on the heights of Parnassus.

They were the sole survivors, and they blessed the gods for their deliverance, but as they looked upon the scene of desolation they were sad at heart. It was a silent world. No human voice to greet them, no sound of beast or bird. They were childless and without hope of children, and if one of them were to die, how could the other live on?

Yet in their misery they forgot not to pay their reverent vows to Jupiter, the God of Deliverance, and then together made their way down from Parnassus and sought the now ruined shrine of Themis. The roofs were green with moss and slime; no fire burned on the deserted altar.

They fell prostrate and implored the goddess: 'O righteous Themis, if the gods can be moved to love or pity by our prayers; if the miseries of men can touch them; if there is forgiveness and renewed favor to be found in them, tell how we may restore mankind, and by a miracle repeople all the world!'

The gracious goddess bowed to them and said: 'Depart! Veil your heads and cast each behind you the bones of your mighty mother.'

The pair stood amazed and dumb with wonder.

Pyrrha could not bring herself to obey the dire and seemingly impious command.

'Forbid it, Heaven,' she cried, 'that I should tear those sacred relics from their sepulcher!'

But Deucalion pondered in his heart the word of the goddess, ever seeking in it some hidden meaning not at first made clear. At length his eye brightened; he called Pyrrha to him and said: 'If I understand it right, there is an answer to the dark enigma that will free the goddess's word from taint of sacrilege. Our mighty mother is the earth; the stones are her bones. These we must cast behind us.'

With renewed hope and gladness Pyrrha heard his words, and though doubting still resolved to try.

Descending from the mountain to the plain that was strewn with stones, reverently they veiled their heads, and, taking up one stone after another, they flung them over their shoulders.

And as the stones fell to the ground a miracle was wrought. As each stone fell it visibly changed. At first but the imperfect rudiments of a form appeared, such as is seen in marble where the chisel has begun to chip it out, and the sculptor has not yet lavished on it his finished art. Then by degrees the stones seemed to swell and soften like ripening fruit, till at last the life-blood ran through the blue veins, while the bones kept their hardness and supported the new-formed frame.

By divine power each stone thrown by Deucalion turned into a man; while each that Pyrrha threw bloomed into a fair woman. Thus was the earth repeopled.

'Tis a marvelous tale, but if you doubt its truth go question the Egyptian rustics. They will tell you that when the Nile subsides they find in the slime rude stones shaped like a man's body, with a knob like a head and bosses like the beginnings of arms and legs. These are stones that Deucalion and Pyrrha threw, but such as fell at their feet instead of behind them, and only began to turn into men and women.

Iulio Bonasone . f

Epimetheus and Pandora

Nathaniel Hawthorne

Long, long ago, when this old world was in its tender infancy, there was a child, named Epimetheus, who never had either father or mother; and that he might not be lonely, another child, fatherless and motherless like himself, was sent from a far country to live with him, and be his playfellow and helpmate. Her name was Pandora.

The first thing that Pandora saw, when she entered the cottage where Epimetheus dwelt, was a great box. And almost the first question which she put to him, after crossing the threshold, was this: 'Epimetheus, what have you in that box?'

'My dear little Pandora,' answered Epimetheus, 'that is a secret, and you must be kind enough not to ask any questions about it. The box was left here to be kept safely, and I do not myself know what it contains.'

'But who gave it to you?' asked Pandora. 'And where did it come from?'

'That is a secret, too,' replied Epimetheus.

Left: A 16th-century depiction of Epimetheus opening Pandora's box, by Giulio Bonasone.

'How provoking!' exclaimed Pandora, pouting her lip. 'I wish the great ugly box were out of the way!'

'Oh, come, don't think of it any more!' cried Epimetheus. 'Let us run out of doors, and have some nice play with the other children.'

It is thousands of years since Epimetheus and Pandora were alive; and the world, nowadays, is a very different sort of thing from what it was in their time. Then, everybody was a child. There needed no fathers and mothers to take care of the children, because there was no danger or trouble of any kind, and no clothes to be mended, and there was always plenty to eat and drink. Whenever a child wanted his dinner, he found it growing on a tree; and if he looked at the tree in the morning, he could see the expanding blossom of that night's supper; or, at eventide, he saw the tender bud of tomorrow's breakfast. It was a very pleasant life indeed. No labor to be done, no tasks to be studied; nothing but sports and dances, and sweet voices of children talking, or caroling like birds, or gushing out in merry laughter throughout the livelong day.

It is probable that the very greatest disquietude which a child had ever experienced was Pandora's vexation at not being able to discover the secret of the mysterious box.

This was at first only the faint shadow of a Trouble; but every day it grew more and more substantial, until before a great while the cottage of Epimetheus and Pandora was less sunshiny than those of the other children.

'Whence can the box have come?' Pandora continually kept saying to herself and to Epimetheus. 'And what on earth can be inside of it?'

'Always talking about this box!' said Epimetheus at last; for he had grown extremely tired of the subject. 'I wish, dear Pandora, you would try to talk of something else. Come, let us go and gather some ripe figs, and eat them under the trees for our supper. And I know a vine that has the sweetest and juiciest grapes you ever tasted.'

'Always talking about grapes and figs!' cried Pandora pettishly.

'Well, then,' said Epimetheus, who was a good-tempered child, 'let us run out and have a merry time with our playmates.'

'I am tired of merry times, and don't care if I never have any more!' answered our pettish little Pandora. 'And besides, I never do have any. This ugly box! I am so taken up with thinking about it all the time. I insist upon you telling me what is inside of it.'

'As I have already said, fifty times over, I do not know!' replied Epimetheus, getting a little vexed. 'How, then, can I tell you what is inside?'

'You might open it,' said Pandora, looking sideways at Epimetheus, 'and then we could see for ourselves.'

'Pandora, what are you thinking of?' exclaimed Epimetheus.

And his face expressed so much horror at the idea of looking into a box which had been confided to him on the condition of his never opening it, that Pandora thought it best not to suggest it any more. Still, she could not help thinking and talking about the box.

'At least,' said she, 'you can tell me how it came here.'

'It was left at the door,' replied Epimetheus, 'just before you came, by a person who looked very smiling and intelligent, and who could hardly forbear laughing as he put it down. He was dressed in an odd kind of a cloak, and had on a cap that seemed to be made partly of feathers, so that it looked almost as if it had wings.'

'What sort of a staff had he?' asked Pandora.

'Oh, the most curious staff you ever saw!' cried Epimetheus. 'It was like two serpents twisting around a stick, and was carved so naturally that I, at first, thought the serpents were alive.'

'I know him,' said Pandora thoughtfully. 'Nobody else has such a staff. It was Quicksilver; and he brought me hither, as well as the box. No doubt he intended it for me; and most probably it contains pretty dresses for me to wear, or toys for you and me to play with, or something very nice for us both to eat!'

'Perhaps so,' answered Epimetheus, turning away. 'But until Quicksilver comes back and tells us so, we have neither of us any right to lift the lid of the box.'

'What a dull boy it is!' muttered Pandora, as Epimetheus left the cottage. 'I do wish he had a little more enterprise!'

For the first time since her arrival, Epimetheus had gone out without asking

Pandora to accompany him. He was tired to death of hearing about the box, and heartily wished that Quicksilver, or whatever was the messenger's name, had left it at some other child's door, where Pandora would never have set eyes on it. So perseveringly as she did babble about this one thing! The box, the box, and nothing but the box! It seemed as if the box were bewitched, and as if the cottage were not big enough to hold it, without Pandora's continually stumbling over it and making Epimetheus stumble over it likewise, and bruising all four of their shins.

Well, it was really hard that poor Epimetheus should have a box in his ears from morning to night, especially as the little people of the earth were so unaccustomed to vexations, in those happy days, that they knew not how to deal with them. Thus a small vexation made as much disturbance then as a far bigger one would in our own times.

After Epimetheus was gone Pandora stood gazing at the box. She had called it ugly above a hundred times; but in spite of all that she had said against it, it was in truth a very handsome article of furniture. It was made of a beautiful kind of wood, with dark and rich veins spreading over its surface, which was so highly polished that little Pandora could see her face in it. As the child had no other looking-glass, it is odd that she did not value the box, merely on this account.

The edges and corners of the box were carved with wonderful skill. Around the margin there were figures of graceful men and women, and the prettiest children ever seen, reclining or sporting amid a profusion of flowers and foliage; and these various objects were so exquisitely represented, and were wrought together in such harmony, that flowers, foliage, and human beings seemed to combine into a wreath of mingled beauty.

But here and there, peeping forth from behind the carved foliage, Pandora once or twice fancied that she saw a face not so lovely, which stole the beauty out of all the rest. Nevertheless, on looking more closely, she could discover nothing of the kind. Some face, that was really beautiful, had been made to look ugly by her catching a sideway glimpse at it.

The most beautiful face of all was done in what is called high relief, in the center of the lid. There was nothing else save the dark, smooth richness of the polished wood, and this one face in the center, with a garland of flowers about its brow. Pandora had looked at this face a great many times, and imagined that the mouth could smile if it liked, or be grave when it chose, the same as any living mouth. The features, indeed, all wore a very lively and rather mischievous expression, which looked almost as if it needs must burst out of the carved lips and utter itself in words.

Had the mouth spoken, it would probably have been something like this:

'Do not be afraid, Pandora! What harm can there be in opening the box? Never mind that poor, simple Epimetheus! You are wiser than he, and have ten times as much spirit. Open the box, and see if you do not find something very pretty!'

The box was fastened; not by a lock, nor by any other such contrivance, but by a very intricate knot of gold cord. There appeared to be no end to this knot, and no beginning. Never was a knot so cunningly twisted, nor with so many ins and outs, which roguishly defied the skilfullest fingers to disentangle them. And yet, by the very difficulty that there was in it, Pandora was the more tempted to examine the knot, and just see how it was made. Two or three times already she had stooped over the box, and taken the knot between her thumb and forefinger, but without positively trying to undo it.

'I really believe,' said she to herself, 'that I begin to see how it was done. Nay, perhaps I could tie it up again after undoing it. There could be no harm in that, surely. Even Epimetheus would not blame me for that. I need not open the box, and should not, of course, without the foolish boy's consent, even if the knot were untied.'

First she tried to lift it. It was heavy; much too heavy for the slender strength of a child like Pandora. She raised one end of the box a few inches from the floor, and let it fall again with a pretty loud thump. A moment afterwards she almost fancied that she heard something stir inside of the box. She applied her ear as closely as possible and listened. Positively there did seem to be a kind of stifled murmur within. Or was it merely the singing in Pandora's ears? Or could it be the beating of her heart? The child could not quite satisfy herself whether she had heard anything or no. But, at all events, her curiosity was stronger than ever.

As she drew back her head her eyes fell upon the knot of gold cord.

'It must have been a very ingenious person who tied this knot,' said Pandora to herself. 'But I think I could untie it, nevertheless. I am resolved, at least, to find the two ends of the cord.'

So she took the golden knot in her fingers, and pried into its intricacies as sharply as she could. Almost without intending it, or quite knowing what she was about, she was soon busily engaged in attempting to undo it. Meanwhile the bright sunshine came through the open window, as did likewise the merry voices of the children playing at a distance; and, perhaps, the voice of Epimetheus among them. Pandora stopped to listen. What a beautiful day it was! Would it not be wiser if she were to let the troublesome knot alone, and think no more about the box, but run and join her little playfellows and be happy?

All this time, however, her fingers were half unconsciously busy with the knot; and, happening to glance at the flower-wreathed face on the lid of the enchanted box, she seemed to perceive it slyly grinning at her.

'That face looks very mischievous,' thought Pandora. 'I wonder whether it smiles because I am doing wrong! I have the greatest mind in the world to run away!'

But just then, by the merest accident, she gave the knot a kind of a twist, which produced a wonderful result. The gold cord untwined itself as if by magic, and left the box without a fastening.

'This is the strangest thing I ever knew!' said Pandora. 'What will Epimetheus say? And how can I possibly tie it up again?'

She made one or two attempts to restore the knot, but soon found it quite beyond her skill. It had disentangled itself so suddenly that she could not in the least remember how the strings had been doubled into one another; and when she tried to recollect the shape and appearance of the knot, it seemed to have gone entirely out of her mind. Nothing was to be done, therefore, but to let the box remain as it was until Epimetheus should come in.

'But,' said Pandora, 'when he finds the knot untied, he will know that I have

done it. How shall I make him believe that I have not looked into the box?'

And then the thought came into her naughty little heart, that, since she would be suspected of having looked into the box, she might just as well do so at once. Oh, very naughty and very foolish Pandora! You should have thought only of doing what was right, and of leaving undone what was wrong, and not of what your playfellow Epimetheus would have said or believed. And so perhaps she might, if the enchanted face on the lid of the box had not looked so bewitchingly persuasive at her, and if she had not seemed to hear, more distinctly than before, the murmur of small voices within. She could not tell whether it was fancy or no; but there was quite a little tumult of whispers in her ear—or else it was her curiosity that whispered:

'Let us out, dear Pandora; pray let us out! We will be such nice pretty playfellows for you! Only let us out!'

'What can it be?' thought Pandora. 'Is there something alive in the box? Well!—yes!—I am resolved to take just one peep! Only one peep; and then the lid shall be shut down as safely as ever! There cannot possibly be any harm in just one little peep!'

But it is now time for us to see what Epimetheus was doing.

This was the first time since his little playmate had come to dwell with him that he had attempted to enjoy any pleasure in which she did not partake. But nothing went right; nor was he nearly so happy as on other days. He could not find a sweet grape or a ripe fig (if Epimetheus had a fault, it was a little too much fondness for figs); or, if ripe at all, they were over-ripe, and so sweet as to be cloying. In short, he grew so uneasy and discontented, that the other children could not imagine what was the matter with Epimetheus. Neither did he himself know what ailed him any better than they did.

At length, discovering that, somehow or other, he put a stop to all the play, Epimetheus judged it best to go back to Pandora, who was in a humour better suited to his own. But, with a hope of giving her pleasure, he gathered some flowers, and made them into a wreath, which he meant to put upon her head. The flowers were very lovely—roses and lilies, and orange-blossoms, and a great many more, which left a trail of fragrance behind as Epimetheus carried them along; and the wreath was put together with as much skill as could reasonably be expected of a boy. The fingers of little girls, it has always appeared to me, are the fittest to twine flower-wreaths; but boys could do it in those days rather better than they can now.

Meanwhile a great black cloud had been gathering in the sky for some time past, although it had not yet overspread the sun. But just as Epimetheus reached the cottage door, this cloud began to intercept the sunshine, and thus to make a sudden and sad obscurity.

He entered softly; for he meant, if possible, to steal behind Pandora and fling the wreath of flowers over her head before she should be aware of his approach. But, as it happened, there was no need of his treading so very lightly. He might have trod as heavily as he pleased without much probability of Pandora's hearing his footsteps. She was too intent upon her purpose. At the moment of his entering the cottage the naughty child had put her hand to the lid, and was on the point of opening the mysterious box. Epimetheus beheld her. If he had cried out Pandora would probably have withdrawn her hand, and the fatal mystery of the box might never have been known.

But Epimetheus himself, although he said very little about it, had his own share of curiosity to know what was inside. Perceiving that Pandora was resolved to find out the secret, he determined that his playfellow should not be the only wise person in the cottage. And if there were anything pretty or valuable in the box, he meant to take half of it to himself. Thus, after all his sage speeches to Pandora about restraining her curiosity, Epimetheus turned out to be quite as foolish, and nearly as much in fault, as she. So, whenever we blame Pandora for what happened, we must not forget to shake our heads at Epimetheus likewise.

As Pandora raised the lid the cottage grew very dark and dismal, for the black cloud had now swept quite over the sun, and seemed to have buried it alive. There had, for a little while past, been a low growling and muttering, which all at once broke into a heavy peal of thunder. But Pandora, heeding nothing of all this, lifted the lid nearly upright and looked inside. It seemed as if a sudden swarm of winged creatures brushed past her, taking flight out of the box, while, at the same instant, she heard the voice of Epimetheus, with a lamentable tone, as if he were in pain.

'Oh, I am stung!' cried he. 'I am stung! Naughty Pandora! why have you opened this wicked box?'

Pandora let fall the lid, and, starting up, looked about her, to see what had befallen Epimetheus. The thunder-cloud had so darkened the room that she could not very clearly discern what was in it. But she heard a disagreeable buzzing, as if a great many huge flies, or gigantic mosquitoes, were darting about. And, as her eyes grew more accustomed to the imperfect light, she saw a crowd of ugly little shapes, with bats' wings, looking abominably spiteful, and armed with terribly long stings in their tails. It was one of these that had stung Epimetheus. Nor was it a great while before Pandora herself began to scream, in no less pain and affright than her playfellow, and making a vast deal more hubbub about it. An odious little monster had settled on her forehead, and would have stung her I know not how deeply if Epimetheus had not run and brushed it away.

Now, if you wish to know what these ugly things might be which had made their escape out of the box, I must tell you that they were the whole family of earthly Troubles. There were evil Passions; there were a great many species of Cares; there were more than a hundred and fifty Sorrows; there were Diseases, in a vast number of miserable and painful shapes; there were more kinds of Naughtiness than it would be of any use to talk about. In short, everything that has since afflicted the souls and bodies of mankind had been shut up in the mysterious box, and given to Epimetheus and Pandora to be kept safely, in order that the happy children of the world might never be molested by them. Had they been faithful to their trust, all would have gone well. No grown person would ever have been sad, nor any child have had cause to shed a single tear, from that hour until this moment.

But—and you may see by this how a wrong act of any one mortal is a calamity to the whole world—by Pandora's lifting the lid of that miserable box, and by the fault of Epimetheus, too, in not preventing her, these Troubles have obtained a foothold among us, and do not seem very likely to be driven away in a hurry.

For it was impossible, as you will easily guess, that the two children should keep the ugly swarm in their own little cottage. On the contrary, the first thing they did was to fling open the doors and windows in hope of getting rid of them; and, sure enough, away flew the winged Troubles all abroad, and so pestered and tormented the small people everywhere about that none of them so much as smiled for many days afterwards. And, what was very singular, all the flowers and dewy blossoms on earth, not one of which had hitherto faded, now began to droop and shed their leaves, after a day or two. The children, moreover, who before seemed immortal in their childhood, now grew older, day by day, and came soon to be youths and maidens, and men and women by and by, and aged people, before they dreamed of such a thing.

Meanwhile, the naughty Pandora, and hardly less naughty Epimetheus, remained in their cottage. Both of them had been grievously stung, and were in a good deal of pain, which seemed the more intolerable to them, because it was the very first pain that had ever been felt since the world began. Besides all this, they were in exceedingly bad humour, both with themselves and with one another. In order to indulge it to the utmost, Epimetheus sat down sullenly in a corner with his back towards Pandora; while Pandora flung herself upon the floor and rested her head on the fatal and abominable box. She was crying bitterly, and sobbing as if her heart would break.

Suddenly there was a gentle tap on the inside of the lid.

'What can that be?' cried Pandora, lifting her head.

But either Epimetheus had not heard the tap, or was too much out of humour to notice it. At any rate, he made no answer.

'You are very unkind,' said Pandora, sobbing anew, 'not to speak to me!'

Again the tap! It sounded like the tiny knuckles of a fairy's hand, knocking lightly and playfully on the inside of the box.

'Who are you?' asked Pandora, with a little of her former curiosity.

'Who are you, inside of this naughty box?'

A sweet little voice spoke from within: 'Only lift the lid, and you shall see.'

'No, no,' answered Pandora, again beginning to sob, 'I have had enough of

lifting the lid! You are inside of the box, naughty creature, and there you shall stay! There are plenty of your ugly brothers and sisters already flying about the world. You need never think that I shall be so foolish as to let you out!'

She looked towards Epimetheus as she spoke, perhaps expecting that he would commend her for her wisdom. But the sullen boy only muttered that she was wise a little too late.

'Ah,' said the sweet little voice again, 'you had much better let me out. I am not like those naughty creatures that have stings in their tails. They are no brothers and sisters of mine, as you would see at once, if you were only to get a glimpse of me. Come, come, my pretty Pandora! I am sure you will let me out!'

And, indeed, there was a kind of cheerful witchery in the tone, that made it almost impossible to refuse anything which this little voice asked. Pandora's heart had insensibly grown lighter at every word that came from within the box. Epimetheus, too, though still in the corner, had turned half round, and seemed to be in rather better spirits than before.

'My dear Epimetheus,' cried Pandora, 'have you heard this little voice?'

'Yes, to be sure I have,' answered he, but in no very good humour as yet. 'And what of it?'

'Shall I lift the lid again?' asked Pandora.

'Just as you please,' said Epimetheus. 'You have done so much mischief already, that perhaps you may as well do a little more. One other Trouble, in such a swarm as you have set adrift about the world, can make no very great difference.'

'You might speak a little more kindly!' murmured Pandora, wiping her eyes.

'Ah, naughty boy!' cried the little voice within the box, in an arch and laughing tone. 'He knows he is longing to see me. Come, my dear Pandora, lift up the lid. I am in a great hurry to comfort you. Only let me have some fresh air, and you shall soon see that matters are not quite so dismal as you think them!'

'Epimetheus,' exclaimed Pandora, 'come what may, I am resolved to open the box!'

'And, as the lid seems very heavy,' cried Epimetheus, running across the room, 'I will help you!'

So, with one consent, the two children again lifted the lid. Out flew a sunny and smiling little personage, and hovered about the room, throwing a light wherever she went. Have you never made the sunshine dance into dark corners by reflecting it from a bit of looking-glass? Well, so looked the winged cheerfulness of this fairy-like stranger amid the gloom of the cottage. She flew to Epimetheus, and laid the least touch of her finger on the inflamed spot where the Trouble had stung him, and immediately the anguish of it was gone. Then she kissed Pandora on the forehead, and her hurt was cured likewise.

After performing these good offices, the bright stranger fluttered sportively over the children's heads, and looked so sweetly at them that they both began to think it not so very much amiss to have opened the box, since, otherwise, their cheery guest must have been kept a prisoner among those naughty imps with stings in their tails.

'Pray, who are you, beautiful creature?' inquired Pandora.

'I am to be called Hope!' answered the sunshiny figure. 'And because I am such a cheery little body, I was packed into the box to make amends to the human race for that swarm of ugly Troubles, which was destined to be let loose among them. Never fear! we shall do pretty well in spite of them all.'

'Your wings are colored like the rainbow!' exclaimed Pandora. 'How very beautiful!'

'Yes, they are like the rainbow,' said Hope, 'because, glad as my nature is, I am partly made of tears as well as smiles.'

'And you will stay with us,' asked Epimetheus, 'for ever and ever?'

'As long as you need me,' said Hope, with her pleasant smile, 'and that will be as long as you live in the world—I promise never to desert you. There may be times and seasons, now and then, when you will think that I have utterly vanished. But again, and again, and again, when perhaps you least dream of it, you shall see the glimmer of my wings on the ceiling of your cottage. Yes, my dear children, and I know something very good and beautiful that is to be given you, hereafter!'

'Oh, tell us,' they exclaimed; 'tell us what it is!'

'Do not ask me,' replied Hope, putting her finger on her rosy mouth. 'But do not despair, even if it should never happen while you live on this earth. Trust in my promise, for it is true.'

'We do trust you!' cried Epimetheus and Pandora, both in one breath.

And so they did; and not only they, but so has everybody trusted Hope, that has since been alive. And, to tell you the truth, I cannot help being glad (though, to be sure, it was an uncommonly naughty thing for her to do)—but I cannot help being glad that our foolish Pandora peeped into the box. No doubt—no doubt—the Troubles are still flying about the world, and have increased in multitude, rather than lessened, and are a very ugly set of imps, and carry most venomous stings in their tails. I have felt them already, and expect to feel them more as I grow older. But then that lovely and lightsome figure of Hope! What in the world could we do without her? Hope spiritualizes the earth; Hope makes it always new; and, even in the earth's best and brightest aspect, Hope shows it to be only the shadow of an infinite bliss hereafter.

Europa and the God-Bull, as shown in a preparatory study for a frescoed frieze by Annibale Carracci.

Europa and the God-Bull

Nathaniel Hawthorne

admus, Phoenix, and Cilix, the three sons of King Agenor, and their little sister Europa (who was a very beautiful child), were at play together near the sea-shore in their father's kingdom of Phoenicia. They had rambled to some distance from the palace where their parents dwelt, and were now in a verdant meadow, on one side of which lay the sea, all sparkling and dimpling in the sunshine, and murmuring gently against the beach. The three boys were very happy gathering flowers and twining them into garlands, with which they adorned the little Europa. Seated on the grass, the child was almost hidden under an abundance of buds and blossoms, whence her rosy face peeped merrily out, and, as Cadmus said, was the prettiest of all the flowers.

Just then there came a splendid butterfly fluttering along the meadow, and Cadmus, Phoenix, and Cilix set off in pursuit of it, crying out that it was a flower with wings. Europa, who was a little wearied with playing all day long, did not chase the butterfly with her brothers, but sat still where they had left her, and closed her eyes. For a while she listened to the pleasant murmur of the sea, which was like a voice saying 'Hush!' and bidding her go to sleep. But the pretty child, if she slept at all, could not have slept more than a moment, when she heard something trample on the grass not far from her, and peeping out from the heap of flowers, beheld a snow-white bull.

And whence could this bull have come? Europa and her brothers had been a long time playing in the meadow, and had seen no cattle, nor other living thing, either there or on the neighboring hills.

'Brother Cadmus!' cried Europa, starting up out of the midst of the roses and lilies. 'Phoenix! Cilix! Where are you all? Help! Help! Come and drive away this bull!'

But her brothers were too far off to hear, especially as the fright took away Europa's voice and hindered her from calling very loudly. So there she stood, with her pretty mouth wide open, as pale as the white lilies that were twisted among the other flowers in her garlands.

Nevertheless, it was the suddenness with which she had perceived the bull, rather than anything frightful in its appearance, that caused Europa so much alarm. On looking at him more attentively, she began to see that he was a beautiful animal, and even fancied a particularly amiable expression in his face. As for his breath—the breath of cattle, you know, is always sweet—it was as fragrant as if he had been grazing on no other food than rosebuds, or, at least, the most delicate of clover blossoms. Never before did a bull have such bright and tender eyes, and such smooth horns of ivory, as this one. And the bull ran little races, and capered sportively around the child; so that she quite forgot how big and strong he was, and, from the gentleness and playfulness of his actions, soon came to consider him as innocent a creature as a pet lamb.

Thus, frightened as she at first was, you might by and by have seen Europa stroking the bull's forehead with her small white hand, and taking the garlands off her own head to hang them on his neck and ivory horns. Then she pulled up some blades of grass, and he ate them out of her hand, not as if he were hungry, but because he wanted to be friends with the child, and took pleasure in eating what she had touched. Well, my stars! was there ever such a gentle, sweet, pretty, and amiable creature as this bull, and ever such a nice playmate for a little girl?

When the animal saw (for the bull had so much intelligence that it is really wonderful to think of), when he saw that Europa was no longer afraid of him, he

grew overjoyed, and could hardly contain himself for delight. He frisked about
the meadow, now here, now there, making sprightly leaps, with as little effort as
a bird expends in hopping from twig to twig. Indeed, his motion was as light as
if he were flying through the air, and his hoofs seemed hardly to leave their print
in the grassy soil over which he trod. With his spotless hue, he resembled a snow-
drift wafted along by the wind. Once he galloped so far away that Europa feared
lest she might never see him again; so, setting up her childish voice, she called
him back.

'Come back, pretty creature!' she cried. 'Here is a nice clover blossom.'

And then it was delightful to witness the gratitude of this amiable bull, and
how he was so full of joy and thankfulness that he capered higher than ever. He
came running and bowed his head before Europa, as if he knew her to be a king's
daughter, or else recognized the important truth that a little girl is everybody's
queen. And not only did the bull bend his neck, he absolutely knelt down at her
feet, and made such intelligent nods, and other inviting gestures, that Europa
understood what he meant just as well as if he had put it in so many words.

'Come, dear child,' was what he wanted to say, 'let me give you a ride on
my back.'

At the first thought of such a thing Europa drew back. But then she considered
in her wise little head that there could be no possible harm in taking just one
gallop on the back of this docile and friendly animal, who would certainly set
her down the very instant she desired it. And how it would surprise her brothers
to see her riding across the green meadow! And what merry times they might
have, either taking turns for a gallop, or clambering on the gentle creature, all
four children together, and careering round the field with shouts of laughter that
would be heard as far off as King Agenor's palace!

'I think I will do it,' said the child to herself.

And, indeed, why not? She cast a glance around, and caught a glimpse of
Cadmus, Phoenix, and Cilix, who were still in pursuit of the butterfly, almost at
the other end of the meadow. It would be the quickest way of rejoining them, to get
upon the white bull's back. She came a step nearer to him, therefore; and—sociable

creature that he was—he showed so much joy at this mark of her confidence, that the child could not find it in her heart to hesitate any longer. Making one bound (for this little princess was as active as a squirrel), there sat Europa on the beautiful bull, holding an ivory horn in each hand lest she should fall off.

'Softly, pretty bull, softly!' she said, rather frightened at what she had done. 'Do not gallop too fast.'

Having got the child on his back, the animal gave a leap into the air, and came down so like a feather that Europa did not know when his hoofs touched the ground. He then began to race to that part of the flowery plain where her three brothers were, and where they had just caught their splendid butterfly. Europa screamed with delight; and Phoenix, Cilix, and Cadmus stood gaping at the spectacle of their sister mounted on a white bull, not knowing whether to be frightened, or to wish the same good luck for themselves. The gentle and innocent creature (for who could possibly doubt that he was so?) pranced round among the children as sportively as a kitten. Europa all the while looked down upon her brothers, nodding and laughing, but yet with a sort of stateliness in her rosy little face. As the bull wheeled about to take another gallop across the meadow, the child waved her hand and said 'Good-bye,' playfully pretending that she was now bound on a distant journey, and might not see her brothers again for nobody could tell how long.

'Good-bye,' shouted Cadmus, Phoenix, and Cilix, all in one breath.

But, together with her enjoyment of the sport, there was still a little remnant of fear in the child's heart; so that her last look at the three boys was a troubled one, and made them feel as if their dear sister were really leaving them forever. And what do you think the snowy bull did next? Why, he set off, as swift as the wind, straight down to the sea-shore, scampered across the sand, took an airy leap, and plunged right in among the foaming billows. The white spray rose in a shower over him and little Europa, and fell spattering down upon the water.

Then what a scream of terror did the poor child send forth! The three brothers screamed manfully, likewise, and ran to the shore as fast as their legs would carry them, with Cadmus at their head. But it was too late. When they reached the margin of the sand, the treacherous animal was already away in the wide blue sea, with only his snowy head and tail emerging, and poor little Europa between them, stretching out one hand towards her dear brothers, while she grasped the bull's ivory horn with the other. And there stood Cadmus, Phoenix, and Cilix, gazing at this sad spectacle through their tears, until they could no longer distinguish the bull's snowy head from the white-capped billows that seemed to boil up out of the sea's depth around him. Nothing more was ever seen of the white bull—nothing more of the beautiful child.

This was a mournful story, as you may well think, for the three boys to carry home to their parents. King Agenor, their father, was the ruler of the whole country; but he loved his little daughter Europa better than his kingdom, or than all his other children, or than anything else in the world. Therefore, when Cadmus and his two brothers came crying home, and told him how that a white bull had carried off their sister, and swam with her over the sea, the king was quite beside himself with grief and rage. Although it was now twilight, and fast growing dark, he bade them set out instantly in search of her.

'Never shall you see my face again,' he cried, 'unless you bring me back my little Europa to gladden me with her smiles and her pretty ways. Begone, and enter my presence no more, till you come leading her by the hand.'

As King Agenor said this his eyes flashed fire (for he was a very passionate king), and he looked so terribly angry that the poor boys did not even venture to ask for their suppers, but slunk away out of the palace, and only paused on the steps a moment to consult whither they should go first. While they were standing there, all in dismay, their mother, Queen Telephassa (who happened not to be by when they told the story to the king), came hurrying after them, and said that she too would go in quest of her daughter.

'Oh, no, mother!' cried the boys. 'The night is dark, and there is no knowing what troubles and perils we may meet with.'

'Alas! my dear children,' answered poor Queen Telephassa, weeping bitterly, 'that is only another reason why I should go with you. If I should lose you too, as well as my little Europa, what would become of me?'

In this manner they went down the palace steps, and began a journey which turned out to be a great deal longer than they dreamed of. The last that they saw of King Agenor, he came to the door, with a servant holding a torch beside him, and called after them into the gathering darkness:

'Remember! Never ascend these steps again without the child!'

'Never!' sobbed Queen Telephassa; and the three brothers answered, 'Never! Never! Never! Never!'

And they kept their word. Year after year King Agenor sat in the solitude of his beautiful palace, listening in vain for their returning footsteps, hoping to hear the familiar voice of the queen and the cheerful talk of his sons entering the door together, and the sweet, childish accents of little Europa in the midst of them. But so long a time went by that, at last, if they had really come, the king would not have known that this was the voice of Telephassa, and these the younger voices that used to make such joyful echoes when the children were playing about the palace. We must now leave King Agenor to sit on his throne, and must go along with Queen Telephassa and her three youthful companions.

They went on and on, and traveled a long way, and passed over mountains and rivers and sailed over seas. Here and there, and everywhere, they made continual inquiry if any person could tell them what had become of Europa. The rustic people, of whom they asked this question, paused a little while from their labors in the field, and looked very much surprised. They thought it strange to behold a woman in the garb of a queen (for Telephassa, in her haste, had forgotten to take off her crown and her royal robes) roaming about the country, with three lads around her, on such an errand as this seemed to be. But nobody could give them any tidings of Europa—nobody had seen a little girl dressed like a princess, and mounted on a snow-white bull, which galloped as swiftly as the wind.

I cannot tell you how long Queen Telephassa, and Cadmus, and Phoenix, and Cilix, her three sons, went wandering along the highways and by-paths, or through the pathless wildernesses of the earth, in this manner. But certain it is that, before they reached any place of rest, their splendid garments were quite worn out. They all looked very much travel-stained, and would have had the dust of many countries on their shoes, if the streams, through which they waded, had not washed it all away. When they had been gone a year, Telephassa threw away her crown, because it chafed her forehead.

'It has given me many a headache,' said the poor queen, 'and it cannot cure my heartache.'

As fast as their princely robes got torn and tattered, they exchanged them for such mean attire as ordinary people wore. By and by they came to have a wild and homeless aspect; so that you would much sooner have taken them for a gipsy family than a queen and three princes, who had once a palace for their home, and a train of servants to do their bidding. The three boys grew up to be tall young men, with sunburnt faces. Each of them girded a sword to defend himself against the perils of the way. When the husbandmen at whose farmhouses they sought hospitality needed their assistance in the harvest-field, they gave it willingly; and Queen Telephassa (who had done no work in her palace, save to braid silk threads with golden ones) came behind them to bind the sheaves. If payment was offered, they shook their heads, and only asked for tidings of Europa.

'There are bulls enough in my pasture,' the old farmers would reply; 'but I never heard of one like this you tell me of. A snow-white bull with a little princess on his back! Ho! ho! I ask your pardon, good folks; but there never was such a sight seen hereabouts.'

At last, when his upper lip began to have the down on it, Phoenix grew weary of rambling hither and thither to no purpose. So one day, when they happened to be passing through a pleasant and solitary tract of country, he sat himself down on a heap of moss.

'I can go no farther,' said Phoenix, 'it is a mere foolish waste of life to spend it, as we do, in always wandering up and down, and never coming to any home at nightfall. Our sister is lost, and never will be found. She probably perished in the sea, or to whatever shore the white bull may have carried her. It is now so many years ago that there would be neither love nor acquaintance between us, should we meet again. My father has forbidden us to return to his palace, so I shall build me a hut of branches and dwell here.'

'Well, son Phoenix,' said Telephassa sorrowfully, 'you have grown to be a man, and must do as you judge best. But, for my part, I will still go in quest of my poor child.'

'And we two will go along with you!' cried Cadmus and Cilix.

But before setting out they all helped Phoenix to build a habitation. When completed it was a sweet rural bower, roofed overhead with an arch of living boughs. Inside there were two pleasant rooms, one of which had a soft heap of moss for a bed, while the other was furnished with a rustic seat or two, curiously fashioned out of the crooked roots of trees. So comfortable and homelike did it seem, that Telephassa and her two companions could not help sighing to think that they must still roam about the world instead of spending the remainder of their lives in some such cheerful abode as they had there built for Phoenix. But, when they bade him farewell, Phoenix shed tears, and probably regretted that he was no longer to keep them company.

However, he had fixed upon an admirable place to dwell in. And by and by there came other people, who chanced to have no home; and seeing how pleasant a spot it was, they built themselves huts in the neighborhood of Phoenix's habitation. Thus, before many years went by, a city had grown up there, in the center of which was seen a stately palace of marble, wherein dwelt Phoenix, clothed in a purple robe, and wearing a golden crown upon his head. For the inhabitants of the new city, finding that he had royal blood in his veins, had chosen him to be their king. The very first decree of state which King Phoenix issued was, that if a maiden happened to arrive in the kingdom, mounted on a snow-white bull and calling herself Europa, his subjects should treat her with the greatest kindness and respect, and immediately bring her to the palace. You may see by this that Phoenix's conscience never quite ceased to trouble him for giving up the quest of his dear sister, and sitting himself down to be comfortable, while his mother and her companions went onward.

But often and often, at the close of a weary day's journey, did Telephassa, Cadmus, and Cilix remember the pleasant spot in which they had left Phoenix. It was a sorrowful prospect for these wanderers, that on the morrow they must again set forth; and that, after many nightfalls, they would, perhaps, be no nearer the close of their toilsome pilgrimage than now. These thoughts made them all melancholy at times, but appeared to torment Cilix more than the rest of the party. At length, one morning, when they were taking their staffs in hand to set out, he thus addressed them:

'My dear mother, and you, good brother Cadmus, methinks we are like people in a dream. There is no substance in the life which we are leading. It is such a dreary length of time since the white bull carried off my sister Europa, that I have quite forgotten how she looked, and the tones of her voice, and, indeed, almost doubt whether such a little girl ever lived in the world. And whether she once lived or no, I am convinced that she no longer survives, and that therefore it is the merest folly to waste our own lives and happiness in seeking her. Were we to find her, she would now be a woman grown, and would look upon us all as strangers. So, to tell you the truth, I have resolved to take up my abode here; and I entreat you, mother, and you, brother, to follow my example.'

'Not I, for one,' said Telephassa; although the poor queen, firmly as she spoke, was so travel-worn that she could hardly put her foot to the ground. 'Not I, for one! In the depths of my heart little Europa is still the rosy child who ran to gather flowers so many years ago. She has not grown to womanhood, nor forgotten me. At noon, at night, journeying onward, sitting down to rest, her childish voice is always in my ears, calling, 'Mother! mother!' Stop here who may, there is no repose for me.'

'Nor for me,' said Cadmus, 'while my dear mother pleases to go onward.'

They remained with Cilix a few days, however, and helped him to build a rustic bower, resembling the one which they had formerly built for Phoenix.

When they were bidding him farewell, Cilix burst into tears, and told his mother that it seemed just as melancholy a dream to stay there in solitude as to go onward. If she really believed that they would ever find Europa, he was willing to continue the search with them even now. But Telephassa bade him remain there, and be happy, if his own heart would let him. So the pilgrims took their leave of him and departed, and were hardly out of sight before some other wandering people came along that way and saw Cilix's habitation, and were greatly delighted with the appearance of the place. There being abundance of unoccupied ground in the neighborhood, these strangers built huts for themselves, and were soon joined by a multitude of new settlers, who quickly formed a city. In the middle of it was seen a magnificent palace of colored marble, on the balcony of which, every noontide, appeared Cilix, in a long purple robe, and with a jeweled crown upon his head; for the inhabitants, when they found out that he was a king's son, had considered him the fittest of all men to be a king himself.

One of the first acts of King Cilix's government was to send out an expedition, consisting of a grave ambassador and an escort of bold and hardy young men, with orders to visit the principal kingdoms of the earth, and inquire whether a young maiden had passed through those regions, galloping swiftly on a white bull. It is therefore plain to my mind, that Cilix secretly blamed himself for giving up the search for Europa, as long as he was able to put one foot before the other.

Telephassa and Cadmus were now pursuing their weary way, with no companion but each other. The queen leaned heavily upon her son's arm, and could walk only a few miles a day. But for all her weakness and weariness, she would not be persuaded to give up the search. It was enough to bring tears into the eyes of bearded men to hear the melancholy tone with which she inquired of every stranger whether he could tell her any news of the lost child.

'Have you seen a little girl—no, no, I mean a young maiden of full growth—passing by this way, mounted on a snow-white bull, which gallops as swiftly as the wind?'

'We have seen no such wondrous sight,' the people would reply; and very often, taking Cadmus aside, they whispered to him, 'Is this stately and sad-looking woman your mother? Surely she is not in her right mind; and you ought to take her home, and make her comfortable, and do your best to get this dream out of her fancy.'

'It is no dream,' said Cadmus. 'Everything else is a dream, save that.'

But one day Telephassa seemed feebler than usual, and leaned almost her whole weight on the arm of Cadmus, and walked more slowly than ever before.

At last they reached a solitary spot, where she told her son that she must needs lie down, and take a good long rest.

'A good long rest!' she repeated, looking Cadmus tenderly in the face. 'A good long rest, thou dearest one!'

'As long as you please, dear mother,' answered Cadmus.

Telephassa bade him sit down on the turf beside her, and then she took his hand.

'My son,' said she, fixing her dim eyes most lovingly upon him, 'this rest that I speak of will be very long indeed! You must not wait till it is finished. Dear Cadmus, you do not comprehend me. You must make a grave here, and lay your mother's weary frame into it. My pilgrimage is over.'

Cadmus burst into tears, and for a long time refused to believe that his dear mother was now to be taken from him. But Telephassa reasoned with him, and kissed him, and at length made him discern that it was better for her spirit to pass away out of the toil, the weariness, the grief, and disappointment which had burdened her on earth, ever since the child was lost. He therefore repressed his sorrow, and listened to her last words.

'Dearest Cadmus,' said she, 'thou hast been the truest son that ever mother had, and faithful to the very last. Who else would have borne with my infirmities as thou hast? It is owing to thy care, thou tenderest child, that my grave was not dug long years ago, in some valley or on some hillside, that lies far, far behind us. It is enough. Thou shalt wander no more on this hopeless search. But when thou hast laid thy mother in the earth, then go, my son, to Delphi, and inquire of the oracle what thou shalt do next.'

'Oh, mother, mother,' cried Cadmus, 'couldst thou but have seen my sister before this hour!'

'It matters little now,' answered Telephassa, and there was a smile upon her face. 'I go now to the better world, and sooner or later, shall find my daughter there.'

I will not sadden you with telling how Telephassa died and was buried, but will only say, that her dying smile grew brighter, instead of vanishing from her dead face; so that Cadmus felt convinced that, at her very first step into the better world, she had caught Europa in her arms. He planted some flowers on his mother's grave, and left them to grow there and make the place beautiful when he should be far away.

Cadmus and the Dragon's Teeth

Nathaniel Hawthorne

After performing this last sorrowful duty, he set forth alone, and took the road towards the famous oracle of Delphi, as Telephassa had advised him. On his way thither he still inquired of most people whom he met whether they had seen Europa; for, to say the truth, Cadmus had grown so accustomed to ask the question, that it came to his lips as readily as a remark about the weather. He received various answers. Some told him one thing, and some another. Among the rest, a mariner affirmed that, many years before, in a distant country, he had heard a rumor about a white bull, which came swimming across the sea with a child on his back, dressed up in flowers that were blighted by the sea water. He did not know what had become of the child or the bull; and Cadmus suspected, indeed, by a queer twinkle in the mariner's eyes, that he was putting a joke upon him, and had never really heard anything about the matter.

Poor Cadmus found it more wearisome to travel alone than to bear all his dear mother's weight, while she had kept him company. His heart, you will understand, was now so heavy that it seemed impossible, sometimes, to carry it any farther. But his limbs were strong and active, and well accustomed to exercise. He walked swiftly along, thinking of King Agenor and Queen Telephassa, and his brothers, all of whom he had left behind him, at one point of his pilgrimage or

another, and never expected to see them any more. Full of these remembrances, he came within sight of a lofty mountain, which the people thereabouts told him was called Parnassus. On the slope of Mount Parnassus was the famous Delphi whither Cadmus was going.

This Delphi was supposed to be the very midmost spot of the whole world. The place of the oracle was a certain cavity in the mountain-side, over which, when Cadmus came thither, he found a rude bower of branches. It reminded him of those which he had helped to build for Phoenix and Cilix. In later times, when multitudes of people came from great distances to put questions to the oracle, a spacious temple of marble was erected over the spot. But in the days of Cadmus, as I have told you, there was only this rustic bower, with its abundance of green foliage and a tuft of shrubbery that ran wild over the mysterious hole in the hillside.

When Cadmus had thrust a passage through the tangled boughs, and made his way into the bower, he did not at first discern the half-hidden cavity. But soon he felt a cold stream of air rushing out of it, with so much force that it shook the ringlets on his cheeks. Pulling away the shrubbery which clustered over the hole, he bent forward and spoke in a distinct but reverential tone, as if addressing some unseen personage inside of the mountain.

'Sacred oracle of Delphi,' said he, 'whither shall I go next in quest of my dear sister Europa?'

There was at first a deep silence, and then a rushing sound, or a noise like a long sigh, proceeding out of the interior of the earth. This cavity, you must know, was looked upon as a sort of fountain of truth, which sometimes gushed out in audible words; although, for the most part, these words were such a riddle that they might as well have stayed at the bottom of the hole. But Cadmus was more fortunate than many others who went to Delphi in search of truth. By and by the rushing noise began to sound like articulate language. It repeated, over and over again, the following sentence, which, after all, was so like the vague whistle of a blast of air, that Cadmus really did not quite know whether it meant anything or not: 'Seek her no more! Seek her no more! Seek her no more!'

Cadmus sows the Dragon's Teeth which turn into Armed Men *by Hendrik Goltzius*

'What, then, shall I do?' asked Cadmus.

For ever since he was a child, you know, it had been the great object of his life to find his sister. From the very hour that he left following the butterfly in the meadow, near his father's palace, he had done his best to follow Europa, over land and sea. And now, if he must give up the search, he seemed to have no more business in the world.

But again the sighing gust of air grew into something like a hoarse voice.

'Follow the cow!' it said. 'Follow the cow! Follow the cow!'

And when these words had been repeated until Cadmus was tired of hearing them (especially as he could not imagine what cow it was, or why he was to follow her), the gusty hole gave vent to another sentence.

'Where the stray cow lies down, there is your home.'

These words were pronounced but a single time, and died away into a whisper before Cadmus was fully satisfied that he had caught the meaning. He put other questions but received no answer; only the gust of wind sighed continually out of the cavity, and blew the withered leaves rustling along the ground before it.

'Did there really come any words out of the hole?' thought Cadmus; 'or have I been dreaming all this while?'

He turned away from the oracle, and thought himself no wiser than when he came thither. Caring little what might happen to him, he took the first path that offered itself, and went along at a sluggish pace; for, having no object in view, nor any reason to go one way more than another, it would certainly have been foolish to make haste. Whenever he met anybody, the old question was at his tongue's end: 'Have you seen a beautiful maiden, dressed like a king's daughter, and mounted on a snow-white bull, that gallops as swiftly as the wind?'

But, remembering what the oracle had said, he only half uttered the words, and then mumbled the rest indistinctly; and from his confusion, people must have imagined that this handsome young man had lost his wits.

I know not how far Cadmus had gone, nor could he himself have told you, when, at no great distance before him, he beheld a brindled cow. She was lying down by the wayside, and quietly chewing her cud; nor did she take any notice of the young man until he had approached pretty nigh. Then getting leisurely upon her feet, and giving her head a gentle toss, she began to move along at a moderate pace, often pausing just long enough to crop a mouthful of grass. Cadmus loitered behind, whistling idly to himself, and scarcely noticing the cow, until the thought occurred to him, whether this could possibly be the animal which, according to the oracle's response, was to serve him for a guide. But he smiled at himself for fancying such a thing. He could not seriously think that this was the cow, because she went along so quietly, behaving just like any other cow. Evidently she neither knew nor cared so much as a wisp of hay about Cadmus, and was only thinking how to get her living along the wayside, where the herbage was green and fresh. Perhaps she was going home to be milked.

'Cow, cow, cow!' cried Cadmus. 'Hey, Brindle, hey! Stop, my good cow.'

He wanted to come up with the cow, so as to examine her, and see if she would appear to know him, or whether there were any peculiarities to distinguish her from a thousand other cows, whose only business is to fill the milk-pail, and sometimes kick it over. But still the brindled cow trudged on, whisking her tail to keep the flies away, and taking as little notice of Cadmus as she well could. If he walked slowly, so did the cow, and seized the opportunity to graze. If he quickened his pace, the cow went just so much faster; and once, when Cadmus tried to catch her by running, she threw out her heels, stuck her tail straight on end, and set off at a gallop, looking as queerly as cows generally do while putting themselves to their speed.

When Cadmus saw that it was impossible to come up with her, he walked on moderately, as before. The cow, too, went leisurely on, without looking behind. Wherever the grass was greenest, there she nibbled a mouthful or two. Where a brook glistened brightly across the path, there the cow drank, and breathed a comfortable sigh, and drank again, and trudged onward at the pace that best suited herself and Cadmus.

'I do believe,' thought Cadmus, 'that this may be the cow that was foretold me. If it be the one, I suppose she will lie down somewhere hereabouts.'

Whether it was the oracular cow or some other one, it did not seem reasonable that she should travel a great way farther. So, whenever they reached a particularly pleasant spot on a breezy hillside, or in a sheltered vale, or flowery meadow, on the shore of a calm lake, or along the bank of a clear stream, Cadmus looked eagerly around to see if the situation would suit him for a home. But still, whether he liked the place or no, the brindle cow never offered to lie down. On she went at the quiet pace of a cow going homeward to the barn-yard; and every moment Cadmus expected to see a milkmaid approaching with a pail, or a herdsman running to head the stray animal and turn her back towards the pasture. But no milkmaid came; no herdsman drove her back; and Cadmus followed the stray brindle till he was almost ready to drop down with fatigue.

'Oh, brindled cow,' cried he, in a tone of despair, 'do you never mean to stop?'

He had now grown too intent on following her to think of lagging behind, however long the way and whatever might be his fatigue. Indeed, it seemed as if there were something about the animal that bewitched people. Several persons who happened to see the brindled cow, and Cadmus following behind, began to trudge after her, precisely as he did. Cadmus was glad of somebody to converse with, and therefore talked very freely to these good people. He told them all his adventures, and how he had left King Agenor in his palace, and Phoenix at one place, and Cilix at another, and his dear mother, Queen Telephassa, under a flowery sod; so that now he was quite alone, both friendless and homeless. He mentioned likewise, that the oracle had bidden him be guided by a cow, and inquired of the strangers whether they supposed that this brindled animal could be the one.

'Why, 'tis a very wonderful affair,' answered one of his new companions. 'I am pretty well acquainted with the ways of cattle, and I never knew a cow, of her own accord, go so far without stopping. If my legs will let me, I'll never leave following the beast till she lies down.'

'Nor I!' said a second.

'Nor I!' cried a third. 'If she goes a hundred miles farther, I'm determined to see the end of it.'

The secret of it was, you must know, that the cow was an enchanted cow, and that, without their being conscious of it, she threw some of her enchantment over everybody that took so much as half-a-dozen steps behind her. They could not possibly help following her, though all the time they fancied themselves doing it of their own accord. The cow was by no means very nice in choosing her path, so that sometimes they had to scramble over rocks, or wade through mud and mire, and were all in a terribly bedraggled condition, and tired to death, and very hungry, into the bargain. What a weary business it was!

But still they kept trudging stoutly forward, and talking as they went. The strangers grew very fond of Cadmus, and resolved never to leave him, but to help him build a city wherever the cow might lie down. In the center of it there should be a noble palace, in which Cadmus might dwell and be their king, with a throne, a crown and scepter, a purple robe, and everything else that a king ought to have; for in him there were the royal blood, and the royal heart, and the head that knew how to rule.

While they were talking of these schemes, and beguiling the tediousness of the way with laying out the plan of the new city, one of the company happened to look at the cow.

'Joy! joy!' cried he, clapping his hands. 'Brindle is going to lie down.'

They all looked; and, sure enough, the cow had stopped and was staring leisurely about her, as other cows do when on the point of lying down. And slowly, slowly did she recline herself on the soft grass, first bending her fore-legs, and then crouching her hind ones. When Cadmus and his companions came up with her, there was the brindled cow taking her ease, chewing her cud, and looking them quietly in the face; as if this was just the spot she had been seeking for, and as if it were all a matter of course.

'This, then,' said Cadmus, gazing around him, 'this is to be my home.'

It was a fertile and lovely plain, with great trees flinging their sun-speckled shadows over it, and hills fencing it in from the rough weather. At no great distance they beheld a river gleaming in the sunshine. A home feeling stole into the heart of poor Cadmus. He was very glad to know that here he might awake in the morning without the necessity of putting on his dusty sandals to travel farther and farther. The days and the years would pass over him, and find him still in this pleasant spot. If he could have had his brothers with him, and could have seen his dear mother under a roof of his own, he might here have been happy, after all their disappointments. Some day or other, too, his sister Europa might have come quietly to the door of his home, and smiled round upon the familiar faces. But, indeed, since there was no hope of regaining the friends of his boyhood, or ever seeing his dear sister again, Cadmus resolved to make himself happy with these new companions who had grown so fond of him while following the cow.

'Yes, my friends,' said he to them, 'this is to be our home. Here we will build our habitations. The brindled cow which has led us hither will supply us with milk. We will cultivate the neighboring soil, and lead an innocent and happy life.'

His companions joyfully assented to this plan; and, in the first place, being very hungry and thirsty, they looked about them for the means of providing a comfortable meal. Not far off they saw a tuft of trees, which appeared as if there might be a spring of water beneath them. They went thither to fetch some, leaving Cadmus stretched on the ground along with the brindled cow; for, now that he had found a place of rest, it seemed as if all the weariness of his pilgrimage, ever since he left King Agenor's palace, had fallen upon him at once. But his new friends had not long been gone when he was suddenly startled by cries, shouts, and screams, and the noise of a most terrible struggle, and in the midst of it all a most awful hissing, which went right through his ears like a rough saw.

Running towards the tuft of trees, he beheld the head and fiery eyes of an immense serpent or dragon, with the widest jaws that ever a dragon had, and a vast many rows of horribly sharp teeth. Before Cadmus could reach the spot, this pitiless reptile had killed his poor companions, and was busily devouring them, making but a mouthful of each man.

It appears that the fountain of water was enchanted, and that the dragon had been set to guard it, so that no mortal might ever quench his thirst there. As the neighboring inhabitants carefully avoided the spot, it was now a long time (not less than a hundred years, or thereabouts) since the monster had broken his fast; and, as was natural enough, his appetite had grown to be enormous, and was not half satisfied by the poor people whom he had just eaten up. When he caught sight of Cadmus, therefore, he set up another abominable hiss, and flung back his immense jaws, until his mouth looked like a great red cavern, at the farther end of which were seen the legs of his last victim, whom he had hardly had time to swallow.

But Cadmus was so enraged at the destruction of his friends, that he cared neither for the size of the dragon's jaws nor for his hundreds of sharp teeth. Drawing his sword he rushed at the monster, and flung himself right into his cavernous mouth. This bold method of attacking him took the dragon by surprise; for, in fact, Cadmus had leaped so far down into his throat, that the rows of terrible teeth could not close upon him, nor do him the least harm in the world. Thus, though the struggle was a tremendous one, and though the dragon shattered the tuft of trees into small splinters by the lashing of his tail, yet, as Cadmus was all the while slashing and stabbing at his very vitals, it was not long before the scaly wretch bethought himself of slipping away. He had not gone his length, however, when the brave Cadmus gave him a sword thrust that finished the battle; and, creeping out of the gateway of the creature's jaws, there he beheld him still wriggling his vast bulk, although there was no longer life enough in him to harm a little child.

But do not you suppose that it made Cadmus sorrowful to think of the melancholy fate which had befallen those poor, friendly people, who had followed the cow along with him? It seemed as if he were doomed to lose everybody whom he loved, or to see them perish in one way or another. And here he was, after all his toils and troubles, in a solitary place, with not a single human being to help him build a hut.

'What shall I do?' cried he aloud. 'It were better for me to have been devoured by the dragon, as my poor companions were.'

'Cadmus,' said a voice—but whether it came from above or below him, or whether it spoke within his own breast, the young man could not tell—'Cadmus, pluck out the dragon's teeth, and plant them in the earth.'

This was a strange thing to do; nor was it very easy, I should imagine, to dig out all those deep-rooted fangs from the dead dragon's jaws. But Cadmus toiled and tugged, and after pounding the monstrous head almost to pieces with a great stone, he at last collected as many teeth as might have filled a bushel or two. The next thing was to plant them. This, likewise, was a tedious piece of work, especially as Cadmus was already exhausted with killing the dragon and knocking his head to pieces, and had nothing to dig the earth with, that I know of, unless it were his sword-blade. Finally, however, a sufficiently large tract of ground was turned up, and sown with this new kind of seed; although half of the dragon's teeth still remained to be planted some other day.

Cadmus, quite out of breath, stood leaning upon his sword, and wondering what was to happen next. He had waited but a few moments when he began to see a sight which was as great a marvel as the most marvelous thing I ever told you about.

The sun was shining slantwise over the field, and showed all the moist, dark soil, just like any other newly planted piece of ground. All at once, Cadmus fancied he saw something glisten very brightly, first at one spot, then at another, and then at a hundred and a thousand spots together. Soon he perceived them to be the steel heads of spears, sprouting up everywhere like so many stalks of grain, and continually growing taller and taller. Next appeared a vast number of bright sword-blades, thrusting themselves up in the same way. A moment afterwards, the whole surface of the ground was broken by a multitude of polished brass helmets, coming up like a crop of enormous beans. So rapidly did they grow, that Cadmus now discerned the fierce countenance of a man beneath every one. In short, before he had time to think what a wonderful affair it was, he beheld an abundant harvest of what looked like human beings, armed with helmets and breastplates, shields, swords, and spears; and before they were well out of the earth, they brandished their weapons, and clashed them one against another, seeming to think, little while as they had yet lived, that they had wasted too much of life without battle. Every tooth of the dragon had produced one of these sons of deadly mischief.

Up sprouted, also, a great many trumpeters; and with the first breath that

they drew, they put their brazen trumpets to their lips, and sounded a tremendous and ear-shattering blast; so that the whole space, just now so quiet and solitary, reverberated with the clash and clang of arms, the bray of warlike music, and the shouts of angry men. So enraged did they all look, that Cadmus fully expected them to put the whole world to the sword. How fortunate would it be for a great conqueror, if he could get a bushel of the dragon's teeth to sow!

'Cadmus,' said the same voice which he had before heard, 'throw a stone into the midst of the armed men.'

So Cadmus seized a large stone, and, flinging it into the middle of the army, saw it strike the breastplate of a gigantic and fierce-looking warrior. Immediately on feeling the blow, he seemed to take it for granted that somebody had struck him; and, uplifting his weapon, he smote his next neighbor a blow that cleft his helmet asunder and stretched him on the ground. In an instant those nearest the fallen warrior began to strike at one another with their swords, and stab with their spears. The confusion spread wider and wider. Each man smote down his brother, and was himself smitten down before he had time to exult in his victory. The trumpeters, all the while, blew their blasts shriller and shriller; each soldier shouted a battle-cry, and often fell with it on his lips. It was the strangest spectacle of causeless wrath, and of mischief for no good end, that had ever been witnessed; but, after all, it was neither more foolish nor more wicked than a thousand battles that have since been fought, in which men have slain their brothers with just as little reason as these children of the dragon's teeth. It ought to be considered, too, that the dragon people were made for nothing else; whereas other mortals were born to love and help one another.

Well, this memorable battle continued to rage until the ground was strewn with helmeted heads that had been cut off. Of all the thousands that began the fight, there were only five left standing. These now rushed from different parts of the field, and, meeting in the middle of it, clashed their swords and struck at each other's hearts as fiercely as ever.

'Cadmus,' said the voice again, 'bid those five warriors sheathe their swords. They will help you to build the city.'

Without hesitating an instant, Cadmus stepped forward, with the aspect of a king and a leader, and extending his drawn sword amongst them, spoke to the warriors in a stern and commanding voice.

'Sheathe your weapons!' said he.

And forthwith, feeling themselves bound to obey him, the five remaining sons of the dragon's teeth made him a military salute with their swords, returned them to the scabbards, and stood before Cadmus in a rank, eying him as soldiers eye their captain while awaiting the word of command.

These five men had probably sprung from the biggest of the dragon's teeth, and were the boldest and strongest of the whole army. They were almost giants, indeed, and had good need to be so, else they never could have lived through so terrible a fight. They still had a very furious look, and, if Cadmus happened to glance aside, would glare at one another with fire flashing out of their eyes. It was strange, too, to observe how the earth, out of which they had so lately grown, was incrusted here and there on their bright breastplates, and even begrimed their faces; just as you may have seen it clinging to beets and carrots when pulled out of their native soil. Cadmus hardly knew whether to consider them as men, or some odd kind of vegetable; although, on the whole, he concluded that there was human nature in them, because they were so fond of trumpets and weapons, and so ready to shed blood.

They looked him earnestly in the face, waiting for his next order, and evidently desiring no other employment than to follow him from one battlefield to another, all over the wide world. But Cadmus was wiser than these earth-born creatures, with the dragon's fierceness in them, and knew better how to use their strength and hardihood.

'Come!' said he. 'You are sturdy fellows. Make yourselves useful! Quarry some stones with those great swords of yours, and help me to build a city.'

The five soldiers grumbled a little, and muttered that it was their business to overthrow cities, not to build them up. But Cadmus looked at them with a stern eye, and spoke to them in a tone of authority, so that they knew him for their master, and never again thought of disobeying his commands. They set to work in good earnest, and toiled so diligently, that, in a very short time, a city began to make its appearance. At first, to be sure, the workmen showed a quarrelsome disposition. Like savage beasts, they would doubtless have done one another mischief, if Cadmus had not kept watch over them and quelled the fierce old serpent that lurked in their hearts when he saw it gleaming out of their wild eyes. But, in course of time, they got accustomed to honest labor, and had sense enough to feel that there was more true enjoyment in living at peace, and doing good to one's neighbor, than in striking at him with a two-edged sword. It may not be too much to hope that the rest of mankind will by and by grow as wise and peaceable as these five earth-begrimed warriors who sprang from the dragon's teeth.

And now the city was built, and there was a home in it for each of the workmen. But the palace of Cadmus was not yet erected, because they had left it till the last, meaning to introduce all the new improvements of architecture, and make it very commodious, as well as stately and beautiful. After finishing the rest of their labors, they all went to bed betimes, in order to rise in the gray of the morning, and to get at least the foundation of the edifice laid before nightfall. But, when Cadmus arose and took his way towards the site where the palace was to be built, followed by his five sturdy workmen marching all in a row, what do you think he saw?

What should it be but the most magnificent palace that had ever been seen in the world? It was built of marble and other beautiful kinds of stone, and rose high into the air, with a splendid dome and a portico along the front, and carved pillars, and everything else that befitted the habitation of a mighty king. It had grown up out of the earth in almost as short a time as it had taken the armed host to spring from the dragon's teeth; and what made the matter more strange, no seed of the stately edifice had ever been planted.

When the five workmen beheld the dome, with the morning sunshine making it look golden and glorious, they gave a great shout.

'Long live King Cadmus,' they cried, 'in his beautiful palace!'

And the new king, with his five faithful followers at his heels, shouldering their pickaxes and marching in a rank (for they still had a soldier-like sort of behavior, as their nature was), ascended the palace steps. Halting at the entrance, they gazed through a long vista of lofty pillars that were ranged from end to end of a great hall. At the farther extremity of this hall, approaching slowly towards him, Cadmus beheld a female figure, wonderfully beautiful, and adorned with a royal robe, and a crown of diamonds over her golden ringlets, and the richest necklace that ever a queen wore. His heart thrilled with delight. He fancied it his long-lost sister Europa, now grown to womanhood, coming to make him happy, and to repay him, with her sweet sisterly affection, for all those weary wanderings in quest of her since he left King Agenor's palace—for the tears that he had shed, on parting with Phoenix and Cilix—for the heartbreakings that had made the whole world seem dismal to him over his dear mother's grave.

But, as Cadmus advanced to meet the beautiful stranger, he saw that her features were unknown to him, although, in the little time that it required to tread along the hall, he had already felt a sympathy betwixt himself and her.

'No, Cadmus,' said the same voice that had spoken to him in the field of the armed men, 'this is not that dear sister Europa whom you have sought so faithfully all over the wide world. This is Harmonia, a daughter of the sky, who is given you instead of sister, and brothers, and mother. You will find all those dear ones in her alone.'

So King Cadmus dwelt in the palace, with his new friend Harmonia, and found a great deal of comfort in his magnificent abode, but would doubtless have found as much, if not more, in the humblest cottage by the wayside. Before many years went by, there was a group of rosy little children (but how they came thither has always been a mystery to me) sporting in the great hall, and on the marble steps of the palace, and running joyfully to meet King Cadmus when affairs of state left him at leisure to play with them. They called him father, and Queen Harmonia mother. The five old soldiers of the dragon's teeth grew very fond of these small urchins, and were never weary of showing them how to shoulder sticks, flourish wooden swords, and march in military order, blowing a penny trumpet, or beating an abominable rub-a-dub upon a little drum.

But King Cadmus, lest there should be too much of the dragon's tooth in his children's disposition, used to find time from his kingly duties to teach them their A B C—which he invented for their benefit, and for which many little people, I am afraid, are not half so grateful to him as they ought to be.

Orpheus and Eurydice

V.C. Turnbull

Orpheus with his lute made trees,
And the mountain-tops that freeze,
Bow themselves when he did sing;
To his music plants and flowers
Ever sprung; as sun and showers
There had made a lasting spring.

'Everything that heard him play,
Even the billows of the sea,
Hung their heads and then lay by.
In sweet music is such art,
Killing care and grief of heart
Fall asleep, or hearing, die.

William Shakespeare (1564–1616)

Left: Orpheus and Eurydice *by Agostino Carracci.*

Never was musician like Orpheus, who sang songs, inspired by the Muses, to a lyre that was given to him by Apollo. So mighty indeed was the magic of his music, that Nature herself owned his sway. Not only did rocks and rills repeat his lays, but the very trees uprooted themselves to follow in his train, and the savage beasts of the forest were tamed and fawned upon him as he played and sang.

But of all who hearkened enchanted to those matchless strains, none drew deeper delight therefrom than the singer's newly wed wife, the young and lovely Eurydice. Hour by hour she sat at his feet hearkening to the music of his voice and lyre, and the gods themselves might have envied the happy pair.

And surely some god did look with envious eye upon those two. For on an evil day, Eurydice, strolling with her maidens through a flowery meadow, was bitten on her foot by a viper and perished in all her beauty ere the sun went down.

Then Orpheus, terrible in his anguish, swore that death itself should not forever rob him of his love. His song, which could tame wild beasts and drag the ancient trees from their roots, should quell the powers of hell and snatch back Eurydice from their grasp.

Thus he swore, calling on the gods to help him; and taking his lyre in his hand he set forth on that fearful pilgrimage from which never man—unless, like Hercules, he was a hero, half man and half god—had returned alive.

And now he reached the downward path, the end whereof is lost in gloom. Deeper and deeper he descended till the light of day was quite shut out, and with it all the sounds of the pleasant earth. Downward through the silence as of the grave, downward through darkness deeper than that of any earthly night. Then out of the darkness, faint at first, but louder as he went on, came sounds that chilled his blood—shrieks and groans of more than mortal anguish, and the terrible voices of the Furies, speaking words that cannot be uttered in any human tongue.

When Orpheus heard these things his knees shook and his feet paused as if rooted to the ground. But remembering once more his love and all his grief, he struck his lyre and sang, till his dirge, reverberating like a coronach or funeral march, drowned all the sounds of hell. And Charon, the old ferryman, subdued by the melody, ferried him over the ninefold Styx which none save the dead might cross; and when Orpheus reached the other side great companies of pale ghosts flocked round him on that drear shore; for the singer was no shadowy ghost like themselves, but a mortal, beautiful though woebegone, and his song spoke to them as with a thousand voices of the sunlight and the familiar earth, and of those who were left behind in their well-loved homes.

But Orpheus, not finding Eurydice among these, made no tarrying. Onward he passed, over the flaming flood of Phlegethon, through the cloud-hung and adamantine portals of Tartarus. Here Pluto, lord of the under-world, sits enthroned, and round him sinners do penance for the evil that they wrought upon earth. There Ixion, murderer of his father-in-law, is racked upon the ever-turning wheel, and Tantalus, who slew his son, endures eternal hunger in sight of food and eternal fear from the stone ever ready to fall. There the daughters of Danaüs cease not to pour water into bottomless urns. There Sisyphus, who broke faith with the gods when they permitted him to return a little while to the upper world, evermore rolls up a steep hill a great stone that, falling back from the summit, crushes the wretch in its downward rush.

But now a great marvel was seen in hell. For as Orpheus entered singing, his melodies, the first that had ever sounded in that dread abode, caused all its terrors for a moment to cease. Tantalus caught no more at the fruits that slipped through his fingers, Ixion's wheel ceased to turn, the daughters of Danaüs paused at their urns, and Sisyphus rested on his rock. Nay, the very Furies themselves ceased to scourge their victims, and the snakes that mingled with their locks hung down, forgetting to hiss.

So came Orpheus to the throne of great Pluto, by whose side sat Proserpine, his Queen. And the king of the infernal gods asked: 'What wouldst thou, mortal, who darest to enter unbidden this our realm of death?'

Orpheus answered, touching his lyre the while: 'Not as a spy or a foe have I come where no living wight hath ventured before, but I seek my wife, slain untimely by the fangs of a serpent. Such love as mine for a maiden such as she

must melt the stoniest heart. Thy heart is not all of stone, and thou too didst once love an earthly maiden. By these places filled with horrors, and by the silence of these boundless realms, I entreat thee restore Eurydice to life.'

He paused, and all Tartarus waited with him for a reply. The terrible eyes of Pluto were cast down, and to Proserpine came a memory of the far-off days when she too was a maid upon earth sporting in the flowery meads of Enna. Then Orpheus struck again his magic strings and sang: 'To thee we all belong; to thee soon or late we all must come. It is but for a little space that I crave my Eurydice. Nay, without her I will not return. Grant, therefore, my prayer, O Pluto, or slay me here and now.'

Then Pluto raised his head and spoke: 'Bring hither Eurydice.'

And Eurydice, still pale and limping from her mortal wound, was brought from among the shades of the newly dead.

And Pluto said: 'Take back, Orpheus, thy wife Eurydice, and lead her to the upper world again. But go thou before and leave her to follow after. Look not once back till thou hast passed my borders and canst see the sun, for in the moment when thou turnest thy head, thy wife is lost to thee again and forever.'

Then with great joy Orpheus turned and led Eurydice from thence. They left behind the tortured dead and the gibbering ghosts; they crossed the flaming Phlegethon, and Charon rowed them once more over the ninefold Styx; and up the dark path they went, the cries of Tartarus sounding ever fainter in their ears; and anon the light of the sun shone faint and far where the path returned to earth, and as they pressed forward the song of the little birds made answer to the lyre of Orpheus.

But the cup of happiness was dashed from the lips that touched its brim. For even as they stood upon the uttermost verge of the dark place, the light of the sun just dawning upon their faces and their feet within a pace of earthly soil, Eurydice stumbled and cried out in pain.

Without a thought Orpheus turned to see what ailed her, and in that moment was she caught from him. Far down the path he saw her, a ghost once more, fading from his sight like smoke as her faint form was lost in the gloom; only for

a moment could he see her white arms stretched towards him in vain; only once could he hear her last heart-broken farewell.

Down the path rushed Orpheus, clamoring for his Eurydice lost a second time; but vain was all his grief, for not again would Charon row him across the Styx. So the singer returned to earth, his heart broken, and all joy gone from his life. Thenceforth his one consolation was to sit upon Mount Rhodope singing his love and his loss. And the Thracian women, worshipers of Bacchus, kindling at his strains, called to him to join in their wild rites. But when he turned from them with loathing, they fell upon him, tearing him limb from limb. And his head they cast into the river Hebrus, whose banks bore to the Ægean Sea that long-drawn wail: 'Eurydice, Eurydice!' And still as we hear the music of that sweet name we think of 'infinite passion, and the pain of finite hearts that yearn.'

But the gods, first punishing the Thracian women by turning them into trees, took the lyre of Orpheus and set it among the stars. And Orpheus himself, once more entering by the gate of death the regions of the dead, seeks and finds his beloved Eurydice. Now may they walk side by side, now Orpheus, if he goes before, may look back in safety upon the face of his loved one. For the sorrows of life are over and the pangs of death are past, and no shadow of parting can come between the singer and his love in the Elysium of the Blessed.

The Old Man of the Sea and Hercules beneath the Tree with the Golden Apples *by Harold Nelson. One of the terrible heads of the dragon guarding the apples can be seen at the top.*

Hercules and the Golden Apples

Nathaniel Hawthorne

PART I
Hercules and the Old Man of the Sea

Did you ever hear of the golden apples that grew in the garden of the Hesperides? Ah, those were such apples as would bring a great price by the bushel, if any of them could be found growing in the orchards of nowadays! But there is not, I suppose, a graft of that wonderful fruit on a single tree in the wide world. Not so much as a seed of those apples exists any longer.

And even in the old, old, half-forgotten times, before the garden of the Hesperides was overrun with weeds, many doubted whether there could be real trees that bore apples of solid gold upon their branches. All had heard of them, but nobody remembered to have seen any. Children, nevertheless, used to listen, open-mouthed, to stories of the golden apple tree, and resolved to discover it

when they should be big enough. Adventurous young men, who desired to do a braver thing than any of their fellows, set out in quest of this fruit. Many of them returned no more; none of them brought back the apples. No wonder that they found it impossible to gather them! It is said that there was a dragon beneath the tree, with a hundred terrible heads, fifty of which were always on the watch while the other fifty slept.

But it was quite a common thing with youths, when tired of too much peace and rest, to go in search of the garden of the Hesperides. And once the adventure was undertaken by a hero who had enjoyed very little peace or rest since he came into the world. At the time of which I am going to speak, he was wandering through the pleasant land of Italy, with a mighty club in his hand and a bow and quiver slung across his shoulders. He was wrapped in the skin of the biggest and fiercest lion that ever had been seen, and which he himself had killed; and though, on the whole, he was kind and generous and noble, there was a good deal of the lion's fierceness in his heart. As he went on his way, he continually inquired whether that were the right road to the famous garden. But none of the country people knew anything about the matter, and many looked as if they would have laughed at the question, if the stranger had not carried so big a club.

So he journeyed on, still making the same inquiry, until at last he came to the brink of a river, where some beautiful girls sat twining wreaths of flowers.

'Can you tell me, pretty maidens,' asked the stranger, 'whether this is the right way to the garden of the Hesperides?'

The girls had been having a fine time together, weaving the flowers into wreaths, and crowning one another's heads. But, on hearing the stranger's question, they dropped all their flowers on the grass and gazed at him with astonishment.

'The garden of the Hesperides!' cried one. 'We thought mortals had been weary of seeking it, after so many disappointments. And pray, bold stranger, what do you want there?'

'A certain king, who is my cousin,' replied he, 'has ordered me to get him three of the golden apples.'

'Most of the young men who go in quest of these apples,' observed another

of the damsels, 'desire to obtain them for themselves, or to present to some fair maiden whom they love. Do you, then, love this king, your cousin, so very much?'

'Perhaps not,' replied the stranger, sighing. 'He has often been severe and cruel to me. But it is my destiny to obey him.'

'And do you know,' asked the damsel who had first spoken, 'that a terrible dragon, with a hundred heads, keeps watch under the golden apple tree?'

'I know it well,' answered the stranger calmly. 'But from my cradle upwards, it has been my business, and almost my pastime, to deal with serpents and dragons.'

The maidens looked at his massive club, and at the shaggy lion's skin which he wore, and likewise at his heroic limbs and figure; and they whispered to each other that the stranger appeared to be one who might reasonably expect to perform deeds far beyond the might of other men. But then, the dragon with a hundred heads! What mortal, even if he possessed a hundred lives, could hope to escape the fangs of such a monster? So kind-hearted were the maidens, that they could not bear to see this brave and handsome traveler attempt what was so very dangerous, and devote himself, most probably, to become a meal for the dragon's hundred ravenous mouths.

'Go back,' cried they all; 'go back to your own home! Your mother, beholding you safe and sound, will shed tears of joy; and what can she do more, should you win ever so great a victory? No matter for the golden apples! No matter for the king, your cruel cousin! We do not wish the dragon with the hundred heads to eat you up!'

The stranger seemed to grow impatient at these remonstrances. He carelessly lifted his mighty club, and let it fall upon a rock that lay half buried in the earth near by. With the force of that idle blow, the great rock was shattered all to pieces. It cost the stranger no more effort to achieve this feat of strength than for one of the young maidens to touch her sister's rosy cheek with a flower.

'Do you not believe,' said he, looking at the damsels with a smile, 'that such a blow would have crushed one of the dragon's hundred heads?'

Then he sat down on the grass and told them the story of his life, or as much of it as he could remember, from the day when he was first cradled in a

warrior's brazen shield.

When the stranger had finished the story of his adventures, he looked around at the attentive faces of the maidens.

'Perhaps you may have heard of me before,' said he, modestly. 'My name is Hercules.'

'We had already guessed it,' replied the maidens; 'for your wonderful deeds are known all over the world. We do not think it strange any longer that you should set out in quest of the golden apples of the Hesperides. Come, sisters, let us crown the hero with flowers!'

Then they flung beautiful wreaths over his stately head and mighty shoulders, so that the lion's skin was almost entirely covered with roses. They took possession of his ponderous club, and so entwined it about with the brightest, softest, and most fragrant blossoms that not a finger's breadth of its oaken substance could be seen. It looked all like a huge bunch of flowers. Lastly, they joined hands, and danced around him, chanting words which became poetry of their own accord, and grew into a choral song in honour of the illustrious Hercules.

And Hercules was rejoiced, as any other hero would have been, to know that these fair young girls had heard of the valiant deeds which it had cost him so much toil and danger to achieve. But still he was not satisfied. He could not think that what he had already done was worthy of so much honour, while there remained any bold adventure to be undertaken.

'Dear maidens,' said he, when they paused to take breath, 'now that you know my name, will you not tell me how I am to reach the garden of the Hesperides?'

'Ah! must you go so soon?' they exclaimed. 'You that have performed so many wonders, and spent such a toilsome life—cannot you content yourself to repose a little while on the margin of this peaceful river?'

Hercules shook his head.

'I must depart now,' said he.

'We will then give you the best directions we can,' replied the damsels. 'You must go to the sea-shore, and find out the Old One, and compel him to inform you where the golden apples are to be found.'

'The Old One!' repeated Hercules, laughing at this odd name. 'And pray who may the Old One be?'

'Why, the Old Man of the Sea, to be sure!' answered one of the damsels. 'He has fifty daughters, whom some people call very beautiful; but we do not think it proper to be acquainted with them, because they have sea-green hair, and taper away like fishes. You must talk to this Old Man of the Sea. He is a seafaring person, and knows all about the garden of the Hesperides, for it is situated in an island which he is often in the habit of visiting.'

Hercules then asked whereabouts the Old One was most likely to be met with. When the damsels had informed him, he thanked them for all their kindness; most of all for telling him the right way; and immediately set forth upon his journey.

But, before he was out of hearing, one of the maidens called after him.

'Keep fast hold of the Old One when you catch him!' cried she, smiling, and lifting her finger to make the caution more impressive. 'Do not be astonished at anything that may happen. Only hold him fast, and he will tell you what you wish to know.'

Hercules again thanked her, and pursued his way, while the maidens resumed their pleasant labor of making flower-wreaths. They talked about the hero long after he was gone.

'We will crown him with the loveliest of our garlands,' said they, 'when he returns hither with the three golden apples, after slaying the dragon with a hundred heads.'

Meanwhile Hercules traveled constantly onward, over hill and dale, and through the solitary woods.

Hastening forward, without ever pausing or looking behind, he by and by heard the sea roaring at a distance. At this sound he increased his speed, and soon came to a beach, where the great surf-waves tumbled themselves upon the hard sand, in a long line of snowy foam. At one end of the beach, however, there was a pleasant spot, where some green shrubbery clambered up a cliff, making its rocky face look soft and beautiful. A carpet of verdant grass, largely intermixed with sweet-smelling clover, covered the narrow space between the bottom of the cliff and the sea. And what should Hercules espy there but an old man, fast asleep!

But was it really and truly an old man? Certainly, at first sight, it looked very like one; but on closer inspection it rather seemed to be some kind of a creature that lived in the sea. For on his legs and arms there were scales such as fishes have; he was web-footed and web-fingered, after the fashion of a duck; and his long beard, being of a greenish tinge, had more the appearance of a tuft of seaweed than of an ordinary beard. Have you never seen a stick of timber that has long been tossed about by the waves, and has got all overgrown with barnacles, and at last, drifting ashore, seems to have been thrown up from the very deepest bottom of the sea? Well, the old man would have put you in mind of just such a wave-tossed spar! But Hercules, the instant he set his eyes on this strange figure, was convinced that it could be no other than the Old One, who was to direct him on his way.

Yes; it was the self-same Old Man of the Sea whom the hospitable maidens had talked to him about. Thanking his stars for the lucky accident of finding the old fellow asleep, Hercules stole on tiptoe towards him and caught him by the arm and leg.

'Tell me,' cried he, before the Old One was well awake, 'which is the way to the garden of the Hesperides?'

As you may imagine, the Old Man of the Sea awoke in a fright. But his astonishment could hardly have been greater than was that of Hercules the next moment. For, all of a sudden, the Old One seemed to disappear out of his grasp, and he found himself holding a stag by the fore and hind leg! But still he kept fast hold. Then the stag disappeared, and in its stead there was a sea-bird, fluttering and screaming, while Hercules clutched it by the wing and claw! But the bird could not get away. Immediately afterwards, there was an ugly three-headed dog, which growled and barked at Hercules, and snapped fiercely at the hands by which he held him! But Hercules would not let him go. In another minute, instead of the three-headed dog, what should appear but Geryon, the six-legged man-monster, kicking at Hercules with five of his legs in order to get the remaining one at liberty! But Hercules held on. By and by no Geryon was there, but a huge snake, like one of those which Hercules had strangled in his babyhood, only a hundred times as big; and it twisted and twined about the hero's neck and body, and threw its tail high in the air, and opened its deadly jaws as if to devour him outright; but Hercules was no whit disheartened, and squeezed the great snake so tightly that he soon began to hiss with pain.

But, as Hercules held on so stubbornly and only squeezed the Old One so much the tighter at every change of shape, and really put him to no small torture, he finally thought it best to reappear in his own figure. So there he was again, a fishy, scaly, web-footed sort of personage, with something like a tuft of seaweed at his chin.

'Pray, what do you want with me?' cried the Old One, as soon as he could take his breath; for it was quite a tiresome affair to go through so many false shapes. 'Why do you squeeze me so hard? Let me go this moment, or I shall begin to consider you an extremely uncivil person!'

'My name is Hercules!' roared the mighty stranger. 'And you will never get out of my clutch until you tell me the nearest way to the garden of the Hesperides!'

When the old fellow heard who it was that had caught him, he saw with half an eye that it would be necessary to tell him everything that he wanted to know. He had often heard of the fame of Hercules, and of the wonderful things that he was constantly performing in various parts of the earth, and how determined he always was to accomplish whatever he undertook. He therefore made no more attempts to escape, but told the hero how to find the garden of the Hesperides, and likewise warned him of many difficulties which must be overcome before he could arrive thither.

'You must go on, thus and thus,' said the Old Man of the Sea, after taking the points of the compass, 'till you come in sight of a very tall giant, who holds the sky on his shoulders. And the giant, if he happens to be in the humour, will tell you exactly where the garden of the Hesperides lies.'

'And if the giant happens not to be in the humour,' remarked Hercules, balancing his club on the tip of his finger, 'perhaps I shall find means to persuade him!'

PART II
Hercules and Atlas

Thanking the Old Man of the Sea, and begging his pardon for having squeezed him so roughly, the hero resumed his journey.

Nothing was before him save the foaming, dashing, measureless ocean. But suddenly, as he looked towards the horizon, he saw something, a great way off, which he had not seen the moment before. It gleamed very brightly, almost as you may have beheld the round, golden disk of the sun when it rises or sets over the edge of the world. It evidently drew nearer; for at every instant this wonderful object became larger and more lustrous. At length it had come so nigh that Hercules discovered it to be an immense cup or bowl, made either of gold or burnished brass. How it had got afloat upon the sea is more than I can tell you. There it was, at all events, rolling on the tumultuous billows, which tossed it up and down and heaved their foamy tops against its sides, but without ever throwing their spray over the brim.

'I have seen many giants in my time,' thought Hercules, 'but never one that would need to drink his wine out of a cup like this!'

And, true enough, what a cup it must have been! It was as large—as large—but, in short, I am afraid to say how immeasurably large it was. To speak within bounds, it was ten times larger than a great mill-wheel; and, all of metal as it was, it floated over the heaving surges more lightly than an acorn-cup adown the brook. The waves tumbled it onward until it grazed against the shore within a short distance of the spot where Hercules was standing.

As soon as this happened, he knew what was to be done; for he had not gone through so many remarkable adventures without learning pretty well how

Right: Hercules holding up the Heavens in place of Atlas *by Heinrich Aldegrever.*

to conduct himself whenever anything came to pass a little out of the common rule. It was just as clear as daylight that this marvelous cup had been set adrift by some unseen power, and guided hitherward, in order to carry Hercules across the sea on his way to the garden of the Hesperides. Accordingly, without a moment's delay, he clambered over the brim and slid down on the inside, where, spreading out his lion's skin, he proceeded to take a little repose. He had scarcely rested until now, since he bade farewell to the damsels on the margin of the river. The waves dashed there with a pleasant and ringing sound against the sides of the hollow cup; it rocked lightly to and fro, and the motion was so soothing that it speedily rocked Hercules into an agreeable slumber.

His nap had probably lasted a good while, when the cup chanced to graze against a rock, and resounded and reverberated through its metal substance a hundred times as loudly as ever you heard a church-bell. The noise awoke Hercules, who instantly started up and gazed around him, wondering whereabouts he was. He was not long in discovering that the cup had floated across a great part of the sea, and was approaching the shore of what seemed to be an island. And on that island, what do you think he saw? It was a giant!

But such an intolerably big giant! A giant as tall as a mountain; so vast a giant, that the clouds rested about his midst like a girdle, and hung like a hoary beard from his chin, and flitted before his huge eyes, so that he could neither see Hercules nor the golden cup in which he was voyaging. And, most wonderful of all, the giant held up his great hands and appeared to support the sky, which, so far as Hercules could discern through the clouds, was resting upon his head!

Meanwhile the bright cup continued to float onward, and finally touched the strand. Just then a breeze wafted away the clouds from before the giant's visage, and Hercules beheld it, with all its enormous features: eyes, each of them as big as yonder lake, a nose a mile long, and a mouth of the same width.

Poor fellow! He had evidently stood there a long while. An ancient forest had been growing and decaying round his feet; and oak trees, of six or seven centuries old, had sprung from the acorn, and forced themselves between his toes.

The giant now looked down from the far height of his great eyes, and

perceiving Hercules, roared out in a voice that resembled thunder proceeding out of the cloud that had just flitted away from his face:

'Who are you down at my feet there? And whence do you come in that little cup?'

'I am Hercules!' thundered back the hero, in a voice pretty nearly or quite as loud as the giant's own. 'And I am seeking the garden of the Hesperides!'

'Ho! ho! ho!' roared the giant, in a fit of immense laughter. 'That is a wise adventure, truly!'

'And why not?' cried Hercules, getting a little angry at the giant's mirth. 'Do you think I am afraid of the dragon with a hundred heads!'

Just at this time, while they talking together, some black clouds gathered about the giant's middle and burst into a tremendous storm of thunder and lightning, causing such a pother that Hercules found it impossible to distinguish a word. Only the giant's immeasurable legs were to be seen, standing up into the obscurity of the tempest; and now and then a momentary glimpse of his whole figure mantled in a volume of mist. He seemed to be speaking most of the time; but his big, deep, rough voice chimed in with the reverberations of the thunder-claps, and rolled away over the hills, like them.

At last the storm swept over as suddenly as it had come. And there again was the clear sky, and the weary giant holding it up, and the pleasant sunshine beaming over his vast height, and illuminating it against the background of the sullen thunder-clouds. So far above the shower had been his head, that not a hair of it was moistened by the raindrops!

When the giant could see Hercules still standing on the sea-shore, he roared out to him anew.

'I am Atlas, the mightiest giant in the world! And I hold up the sky upon my head!'

'So I see,' answered Hercules. 'But can you show me the way to the garden of the Hesperides?'

'What do you want there?' asked the giant.

'I want three of the golden apples,' shouted Hercules, 'for my cousin, the king.'

'There is nobody but myself,' quoth the giant, 'that can go to the garden of the Hesperides and gather the golden apples. If it were not for this little business of holding up the sky, I would make half a dozen steps across the sea and get them for you.'

'You are very kind,' replied Hercules. 'And cannot you rest the sky upon a mountain?'

'None of them are quite high enough,' said Atlas, shaking his head, 'But if you were to take your stand on the summit of that nearest me, your head would be pretty nearly on a level with mine. You seem to be a fellow of some strength. What if you should take my burden on your shoulders while I do your errand for you?'

Hercules, as you must be careful to remember, was a remarkably strong man; and though it certainly requires a great deal of muscular power to uphold the sky, yet, if any mortal could be supposed capable of such an exploit, he was the one. Nevertheless, it seemed so difficult an undertaking that, for the first time in his life, he hesitated.

'Is the sky very heavy?' he inquired.

'Why, not particularly so, at first,' answered the giant, shrugging his shoulders. 'But it gets to be a little burthensome after a thousand years!'

'And how long a time,' asked the hero, 'will it take you to get the golden apples?'

'Oh, that will be done in a few moments,' cried Atlas. 'I shall take ten or fifteen miles at a stride, and be at the garden and back again before your shoulders begin to ache.'

'Well, then,' answered Hercules, 'I will climb the mountain behind you there and relieve you of your burden.'

The truth is, Hercules had a kind heart of his own, and considered that he should be doing the giant a favor by allowing him this opportunity for a ramble. And besides, he thought that it would be still more for his own glory, if he could boast of upholding the sky, than merely to do so ordinary a thing as to conquer a dragon with a hundred heads. Accordingly, without more words, the sky was shifted from the shoulders of Atlas and placed upon those of Hercules.

When this was safely accomplished, the first thing that the giant did was to stretch himself; and you may imagine what a prodigious spectacle he was then. Next, he slowly lifted one of his feet out of the forest that had grown up around it; then the other. Then, all at once he began to caper, and leap, and dance for joy at his freedom; flinging himself nobody knows how high into the air, and floundering down again with a shock that made the earth tremble. Then he laughed—Ho! ho! ho!—with a thunderous roar that was echoed from the mountains, far and near, as if they and the giant had been so many rejoicing brothers. When his joy had a little subsided, he stepped into the sea; ten miles at the first stride, which brought him mid-leg deep; and ten miles at the second, when the water came just above his knees; and ten miles more at the third, by which he was immersed nearly to his waist. This was the greatest depth of the sea.

Hercules watched the giant, as he still went onward; for it was really a wonderful sight, this immense human form, more than thirty miles off, half hidden in the ocean, but with his upper half as tall, and misty, and blue, as a distant mountain. At last the gigantic shape faded entirely out of view. And now Hercules began to consider what he should do, in case Atlas should be drowned in the sea, or if he were to be stung to death by the dragon with the hundred heads which guarded the golden apples of the Hesperides. If any such misfortune were to happen, how could he ever get rid of the sky? And, by the by, its weight began already to be a little irksome to his head and shoulders.

'I really pity the poor giant,' thought Hercules. 'If it wearies me so much in ten minutes, how must it have wearied him in a thousand years?'

I know not how long it was before, to his unspeakable joy, he beheld the huge shape of the giant, like a cloud, on the far-off edge of the sea. At his nearer approach, Atlas held up his hand, in which Hercules could perceive three magnificent golden apples, as big as pumpkins, all hanging from one branch.

'I am glad to see you again,' shouted Hercules, when the giant was within hearing. 'So you have got the golden apples?'

'Certainly, certainly,' answered Atlas; 'and very fair apples they are. I took the finest that grew on the tree, I assure you. Ah! it is a beautiful spot, that garden of

the Hesperides. Yes; and the dragon with a hundred heads is a sight worth any man's seeing. After all, you had better have gone for the apples yourself.'

'No matter,' replied Hercules. 'You have had a pleasant ramble, and have done the business as well as I could. I heartily thank you for your trouble. And now, as I have a long way to go and am rather in haste—and as the king, my cousin, is anxious to receive the golden apples—will you be kind enough to take the sky off my shoulders again?'

'Why, as to that,' said the giant, chucking the golden apples into the air twenty miles high, or thereabouts, and catching them as they came down—'as to that, my good friend, I consider you a little unreasonable. Cannot I carry the golden apples to the king, your cousin, much quicker than you could? As his majesty is in such a hurry to get them, I promise you to take my longest strides. And besides, I have no fancy for burdening myself with the sky just now.'

Here Hercules grew impatient, and gave a great shrug of his shoulders. It being now twilight, you might have seen two or three stars tumble out of their places. Everybody on earth looked upward in affright, thinking that the sky might be going to fall next.

'Oh, that will never do!' cried Giant Atlas, with a great roar of laughter. 'I have not let fall so many stars within the last five centuries. By the time you have stood there as long as I did, you will begin to learn patience!'

'What!' shouted Hercules very wrathfully, 'do you intend to make me bear this burden for ever?'

'We will see about that, one of these days,' answered the giant. 'At all events, you ought not to complain, if you have to bear it the next hundred years, or perhaps the next thousand. I bore it a good while longer, in spite of the back-ache. Well, then, after a thousand years, if I happen to feel in the mood, we may possibly shift about again. You are certainly a very strong man, and can never have a better opportunity to prove it. Posterity will talk of you, I warrant it!'

'Pish! a fig for its talk!' cried Hercules, with another hitch of his shoulders. 'Just take the sky upon your head one instant, will you? I want to make a cushion of my lion's skin for the weight to rest upon. It really chafes me, and will cause

unnecessary inconvenience in so many centuries as I am to stand here.'

'That's no more than fair, and I'll do it!' quoth the giant; for he had no unkind feeling toward Hercules, and was merely acting with a too selfish consideration of his own ease. 'For just five minutes, then, I'll take back the sky. Only for five minutes, recollect! I have no idea of spending another thousand years as I spent the last. Variety is the spice of life, say I.'

Ah, the thick-witted old rogue of a giant! He threw down the golden apples, and received back the sky from the head and shoulders of Hercules upon his own, where it rightly belonged. And Hercules picked up the three golden apples, that were as big or bigger than pumpkins, and straightway set out on his journey homeward, without paying the slightest heed to the thundering tones of the giant, who bellowed after him to come back. Another forest sprang up around his feet, and grew ancient there; and again might be seen oak trees of six or seven centuries old, that had waxed thus aged betwixt his enormous toes.

And there stands the giant to this day; or, at any rate, there stands a mountain as tall as he, and which bears his name; and when the thunder rumbles about its summit, we may imagine it to be the voice of Giant Atlas bellowing after Hercules!

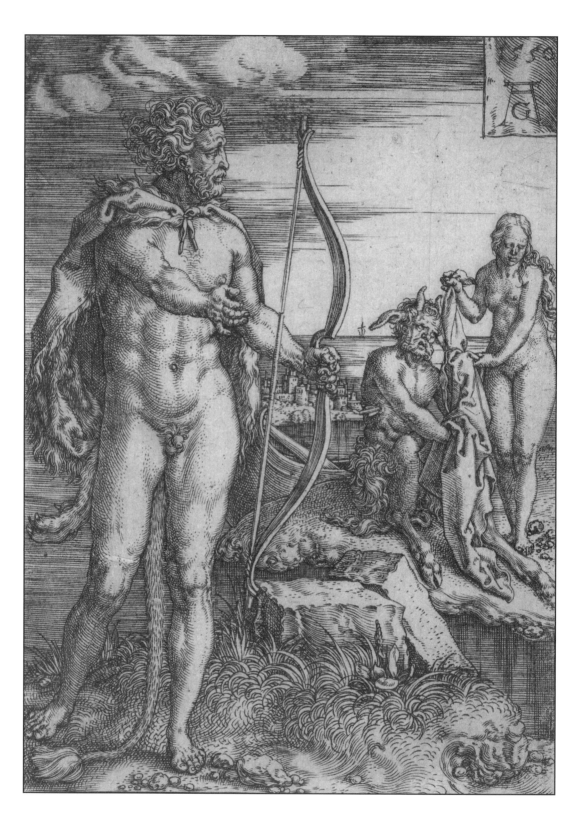

Hercules and Nessus

H.P. Maskell

Fairest among the maidens of Ætolia was Deianira, daughter of Oeneus, King of Calydon. From far and wide came suitors seeking her hand in marriage, but her father promised to give her only to him who could prove his strength and courage above all others. What lover, however ardent his desire, dare venture to try his skill against Hercules? And when the hero came to court only Achelous the river-god would enter the lists against him.

Long and fierce was the battle between these two as they rushed together, grasping each other foot to foot, fingers pressed upon fingers, and forehead to forehead. For some time they seemed equal in strength, but Hercules pressed harder, and seizing his enemy by the shoulders threw him to the earth. In vain Achelous changed himself into a serpent; his throat was grasped with a grip that would strangle him in spite of all his lithe, winding folds, and the hissing as he darted forth his forked tongue. In vain, too, he sought to change the issue of the fight in the form of a wild bull. The hero took him by the horns, and held him to the ground. One of the horns he tore off by main force. The Naiads took this horn, filled it with fruit and flowers, and offered it to the goddess of Plenty.

Left: Engraving by Heinrich Aldegrever showing Hercules killing Nessus the Centaur with a poisoned arrow. Nessus is handing his blood-stained tunic to Deianira.

So Hercules was victor in the lists of love, and won for prize the king's fair daughter. Many years the happy pair abode in Calydon, and children were born to them. Deianira was a happy wife, and her only grief was that her lord was so often absent from home, for Hercules would never rest from his toils. On one of these adventures he had been persuaded by his wife to take her with him, and on their way home they came to a broad and rapid river. The stream was swollen with winter rains, and the eddies were deep and dangerous. Nessus the Centaur, who lived in a cavern close by, offered to carry Deianira over on his back. He knew the fords, and his strength was as the strength of ten. So Hercules trusted his wife to the Centaur, although she was almost as much afraid of Nessus as she was of the dark roaring torrent. He himself threw his club and crooked bow across, and plunged boldly into the stream.

Just as he reached the farther bank and was taking up his bow he heard a scream. Nessus had betrayed his trust, and was about to carry off Deianira in the very sight of her husband. Swiftly flew an arrow from the bow, which pierced the traitor's back. It was tinged with poison from the hydra, and the wound was mortal. Nessus, as he drew the barbed steel from his body, muttered to himself, 'I will not die unavenged.' Then handing his blood-stained tunic to Deianira, he cried, 'I have sinned, and am justly punished. Pardon a dying man, and in token of forgiveness accept from me a dying gift. Keep this tunic as a talisman. If ever thy lord's love should wax cold, or he should look upon another woman to love her more than thee, give him this charmed tunic to wear, and it will rekindle his old passion.'

Time passed by, and the feats of the mighty Hercules were known all over the world. Returning victorious from battle he was preparing a sacrifice vowed to Jupiter on Mount Oeta, when he found he lacked the proper dress, and sent a messenger to Deianira for a robe. Meanwhile rumor had been busy, and a tale had reached the ears of Deianira that Hercules was in love with Iole, daughter of Eurytus, whom he had lately vanquished and slain. As she loved him, she believed it, and alarmed with the story burst into a torrent of grief. But soon she took comfort. 'Why these tears? They will only flatter my rival. I must seek

some means to keep my husband for myself.' And then she bethought herself of the tunic that Nessus had given her. What if she gave this tunic to the messenger, so that Hercules should wear it, and so by its virtue her husband be restored to her again?

The fatal gift was sent. Hercules, not knowing whose it had been, put it on as he went to sacrifice. As he was pouring wine on the altars the venom from the garment began to work. He tried to tear the tunic from him, but it clung to him like a coat of pitch. He rolled in agony on the ground, he tore away his very flesh, he roared in agony like a wounded bull, and the hollows of Oeta reverberated his groans. At last he fell exhausted, and his comrades bore him on a litter to the ships. Then Hercules knew that his end was come, and, preparing himself to die as a hero should, he gave his last injunctions to his son.

A pile was built with trees at the top of the mountain. To his friend Philoctetes he gave the famous bow and quiver. Then, when the fire had been kindled, he spread over all the skin of the Nemæan lion, and laid himself down upon it, with his head resting on his club, as calmly as a guest resting after the banquet.

Jupiter, looking down from heaven, saw the hero thus peaceful amid the flames of the burning pile. 'He who has conquered all men,' he cried, 'shall conquer also these fires. Only that which is mortal and which he received from his mother can perish there. His immortal part I will receive into the realms above.' And the other gods assented. Even Juno, who had pursued the hero so cruelly during his life, had no word to urge against their decision. The burning pile was shrouded in a mist of dark smoke; and while the mortal body of Hercules fell into ashes, him the great father, taking up among circling clouds, bore aloft to the glittering stars in his chariot drawn by four fiery steeds.

The Quest of the Golden Fleece

M.M. Bird

The great hall was decked for a banquet. Revelers sat round the laden board and feasted and sang and quaffed rich wines from silver goblets. The king on his daïs toyed with his jeweled wine-cup and gazed down the length of the hall at the flushed faces of the feasters, and heard their gay laughter peal up to the vaulted roof. Yet the eyes of Pelias, the king, were dark, and a settled scowl was on his brow. Terror of Heaven's vengeance still haunted him. He had commanded this festival in honour of Neptune, and yet he knew that the anger of Jupiter was unappeased while the Golden Fleece still hung in the wood at Colchis.

For Phrixus, son of Æolus, had fled on the Sacred Ram with the Fleece of Gold, to Æetes, King of Colchis, who had protected him and given him his daughter Chalciope to wife. Though Phrixus was now dead, Æetes still held the Fleece in Colchis, and the line of Æolus languished under the wrath of Jupiter till such time as it was restored to Greece.

This was the subject of the king's meditations as he looked down on the gay company assembled at his feast. And of a sudden his eyes lighted on a travel-stained figure making his way up the long hall to the steps of his throne, in spite of the soiled and tattered weeds. He recognized his royal kinsman. It was Jason son of Æson, his own nephew, who, determined to have speech with his uncle

the king, had now dared the crossing of the river Anaurus, although swollen by winter rains, and had hardly won through. Till he entered the palace he did not know of the great feast that was being held, but he stood not on ceremony, and made his way to the foot of the throne, just as he was. One of his sandals had stuck in the mire and been left in the river bed.

Now an oracle had come to the king but a short time before, warning him to beware of a man coming in from the field with one sandal lacking. And King Pelias shrank from the sight of the innocent youth who stood before him; and in the dark depths of his heart devised a cruel plot for his destruction, whereby he might rid himself of the menace and, at the same time, be restored to the favour of Jupiter.

Undaunted by the tyrant's frown, Jason stood before him and asserted his claim to the throne. 'I, Jason, son of Æson, of the line of Æolus, live as a peasant among peasants on the banks of Anaurus,' he cried, in his brave young voice. 'Restore me to my rightful place as son of the late king.'

The king dared not openly dispute the claim, but with a feigned smile he answered: 'Fetch hither the Golden Fleece held by Æetes in Colchis, that you may thus prove worthy to boast yourself of the proud line of Æolus. Deliver your father's house from the wrath of Jupiter, and then come to claim your birthright!'

He devised this task, thinking that even could Jason perchance overcome the Colchians, he must assuredly be slain by enemies or lost in the sea ere ever he won home again. For it was well known that Æetes had hung the Golden Fleece in an enchanted wood, and set a sleepless serpent to guard the treasure against any who should pass his men-at-arms.

At first Jason was cast into despair at the greatness of this task, but strong in his own innocence and determined to vindicate his rights, he took up the challenge. 'I go,' he cried, 'at the ruthless behest of a tyrannous king and the doom of a god! Who will go in my company—who?'

And from east and west and south the heroes of a hundred deeds came hasting to join him on his quest, for all had heard of the Golden Fleece and its theft by the Colchian men.

And the fame of its quest was noised abroad so that all who loved a bold venture came to proffer Jason their aid; and with others it was the lust of gold that drew them; and with others, again, love of justice and pity for the youth robbed of his birthright by an unjust king. Thus there came to Iolcus the mighty Hercules, and the twin sons of Jupiter, Castor and Pollux, Orpheus with his magic lute, Idmon the seer, and Tiphys the steersman, and others all famous for their prowess in war, the sons of gods and heroes, too many to name.

Then Jason set himself to prepare for his great enterprise, gathering stores and arms, and eagerly seeking information of those who had traveled afar off of the Colchians and their king Æetes, and the famed Fleece of Gold, while the good ship Argo was daily growing under the fashioning hands of Argus and his men, who, instructed by Minerva, built so gallant a ship as had never before sailed the seas. And daily there were added to Jason's company valiant warriors and men of renown, young and old, till at last the day came when the Argo was launched for her great enterprise, and the last sacrifices were paid to the protecting gods, and the last feast was eaten on the Pagasæan shore. Then the heroes cast lots for their places at the oars—for all but the place of honor at the middle thwart, which was given to Hercules and his companion Ancæus. Tiphys,

Jason confronting the dragon guarding the Golden Fleece, from 'Histoire de Jason et de la conquête de la toison d'or' by René Boyvin.

by common consent, was set at the helm, while Jason was proclaimed captain and chief, in peace and in war, of all the goodly band.

And thus it came that such a company of heroes as had never before been gathered together on one quest sailed forth from Iolcus in the Argo in search of the Golden Fleece.

For many days they pursued their way, braving the storms of those dangerous seas, landing on strange coasts where sometimes they found shelter and kindness, but oftener had to fight for life and honour. But ever the glorious quest inspired them, the Golden Fleece brightened their dreams, and they strove loyally together to win through all temptations and dangers. But not all of them survived to reach their goal. Great Hercules was left on the Mysian hills seeking his lost armor-bearer Hylas; and Idmon the seer, faring across a marshy plain, was suddenly attacked by a wild boar and so wounded that he died. For three whole days the heroes mourned his loss; and while they mourned, Tiphys the steersman fell sick, and his sickness was unto death. For grief then the band had gone no farther on the quest had not Ancæus rekindled their courage with brave words and offered himself as their steersman. And by general acclamation he was elected to the post, and they set forth on their way with renewed faith.

But at last the gallant Argo won through the Pontus Sea and the dreadful Dark Blue Crags, and the voyagers knew themselves to be near to Colchis and the end of their journeying. Picture to yourselves the storm-tossed Argo flying over the seas, and great eagles swooping and wheeling overhead, by which Jason, the captain, knew that they approached the island of Mars, where those winged messengers of the gods were wont to attack any who dared effect a landing. But by his command the heroes armed themselves, and the oarsmen were protected by the shields of their comrades from the feathered darts rained down upon them by the furious birds. And with loud clashing and clanging of their harness the creatures were scared away. So the heroes reached the shore and rested there in peace after their battling with the storm. And as they lay on the shore they saw in the waves a great spar, and four young men clinging to it, tossed hither and thither, till at length it was cast up on to the beach. These proved to be the four

sons of Phrixus, who had been thrust out of Colchis by their stern grandsire Æetes, and sent away in a little boat. Their skiff had been too frail to withstand the storm that the good ship Argo had outlived.

When these heard of the quest, they offered Jason their allegiance, and begged him to accept their aid in his perilous venture, which he gladly did. So, in calm weather, they sailed gaily on to Colchis, elated to have thus escaped all the perils and to be within sight of their goal.

The Golden Fleece burned ever brighter before the longing eyes of that hero band; courage and loyalty inspired each heart and nerved each arm; they were ready to give life itself, if need be, to achieve their task and bring again the miraculous Fleece to Greece—and such a spirit is unconquerable.

Now Æetes, King of Colchis, dwelt in his city by the sea. He had but two daughters; the elder, Chalciope, was the widow of that Phrixus who had come hither riding on the Golden Ram, while the younger was Medea, a sorceress. She was a priestess of Hecate, and served the dreadful mysteries of the goddess. She was versed in all poisons and philters, and would wander out into wild places beyond the city to gather herbs for the brewing of her mystic potions. She lived with her brothers, the sons of Æetes, and Chalciope her sister, in a palace in the city, and beside it stood a temple to Hecate.

It happened on a certain day that Medea, as was her wont, went into the hall of the temple, and as she stood there she saw a crowd approaching up the street. Foremost in the throng she saw her sister's four sons, who had been mourned as lost for ever. She cried aloud, and the waiting-women in the palace heard her cry and dropped their broideries, and with Chalciope her sister came running to learn the cause of her fear. And Chalciope saw her sons and clasped them to her with tears of joy. But Medea stood gazing at the splendid strangers who came with them—Jason and his two friends, Telamon and Augias. And as she gazed, Cupid let fly one of his burning shafts, and it pierced the maiden's bosom and there burned with a dull flame. And her eyes were fastened on Jason's comely face, and the conscious blushes flamed in the whiteness of her cheeks, and she stood as if bound by one of her own spells.

Hearing the commotion, the king and queen inquired the cause; and when they saw the handsome strangers they gave them fair welcome, and invited them to join their banquet. Though Æetes looked sourly on the sons of Phrixus, of whom he had thought to have rid himself for ever, he was constrained to receive them also with their rescuers.

When seated at the banquet, Argus, one of Phrixus' sons, explained to the king all the circumstances of Jason's coming, and the quest on which he came. 'Not to take the Fleece by force he comes,' pleaded Argus, 'but is minded to pay a fair price for thy gift. He has heard of the bitter enmity of the Sauromatæ: these rebels he will subdue for thee, and put them under thy sway.'

The king's wrath waxed hot, and chiefly with his daughter's sons, for he deemed that they had stirred up Jason to this quest. 'Not for the Fleece come ye!' he cried; 'but my scepter and my kingly honour ye come to steal! Now, if ye had not broken bread at my table before ye spoke, your tongues had I surely cut out, and had hewn your hands from your wrists, and had sent you forth with naught but your feet to fare through the land! So should ye refrain hereafter from coming on such like quest.'

But Jason made gentle answer to the angry king, assuring him that no such wild dream had brought him to this land, but the ruthless behest of a tyrannous king and the doom of a god.

Then the king inly pondered whether to fall on the heroes and do them to death or put their might to the test. And this he decided to be the better way, for they were mighty men and renowned for valor, and he saw that he should have to overcome them by subtlety. So he set Jason this impossible task: On the plain of Mars were two brazen-hoofed bulls, breathing flames of fire; these Jason must yoke, and by them drive four plowshares across the plain from dawn to dusk. And in the furrows sow the teeth of a dragon, from which out of the earth armed warriors should spring, and these he must smite and conquer!

The hero sat speechless in his despair, for he deemed no man sufficient for so terrible a task. But Argus went out with him, and knowing his own and his brothers' fate to hang on him, implored him to consult his mother's sister, Medea, the sorceress. Jason, for kindness, consented, but with little hope of the issue.

So Argus returned to his mother, to beg her to intercede with Medea.

Medea, torn with love for Jason, spent the night in mourning over his certain fate unless he craved her aid in his gigantic task, and was longing, yet ashamed, to proffer it. It was, therefore, to the relief of her indecision that her sister Chalciope came to her at length, and begged her to interfere to save her four sons from the doom that threatened them. Medea was glad, for she was thus enabled to save her dignity, and in obeying the dictates of her heart seem only to be concerned with the safety of her sister's sons.

Next morning, therefore, she called her maidens and went out in her chariot to the fane of Hecate on the plain beyond the city, a place where she was often wont to go to gather herbs. There Jason met her, and he sacrificed his pride to beg her assistance. She was torn between love for him and a sense of duty to her father; but yet love was the stronger, and she promised him her aid. Long they talked together in that wilderness till the shades of evening fell and her attendants became uneasy at her long tarrying. She gave him a magic drug that would render his body and arms invulnerable against all attack, and gave him also minute directions for his guidance in his dreadful conflict. And Jason saw how beautiful and tender she was, and love for her awoke in his heart, and he wooed her with gentle words, and vowed that if she would go with him to Greece she should there be made his honored wife.

Evening drew on, and Medea went sadly back to her night of anguished vigil in her palace in the city, while Jason prepared himself for his doubtful conflict. At midnight he bathed alone in the sacred river. Then he digged a pit in the plain as Medea had directed him, and offered a lamb by the pit's brink, and kindled a pyre and burned the carcase. Mingled libations he also poured, and then, calling on Hecate, drew back and strode from the place, and looked not once behind him at the awful queen he had invoked, nor the shapes of fear that accompanied her, nor turned at the wild baying of the hounds of hell.

Then he sprinkled his corslet, his helm, and his arms with the drug Medea gave him, and his comrades proved his harness with all their might and main, whose ringing blows fell harmless upon it. Then he sprinkled his own limbs with the magic drug and fared forth invincible.

At dawn, the heroes sailed in the Argo up the river till they came near to the plain of Mars, and there anchored. King Æetes came out from the city in procession to the lists, and all the men of Colchis were gathered on the one hand and the heroes on the other to watch the outcome of this terrible strife.

So Jason set to his task. Bearing with him his helm full of the dragon's teeth he crossed the field, and there saw the brazen yoke lying, and the plow of massive stone. Suddenly, from their lair, the bulls rushed out together and bore down upon him. Jason, setting his feet wide, caught their charge on his shield and withstood the shock. Mightily he seized the horn of one of the monsters, haled with all his strength, and striking its hoof with his foot cast it down on its knees. And, to the amazement of all, he did likewise to its fellow. Then he cast away his shield, and holding them down set the brazen yoke on their necks. All marveled at his superhuman strength. The brow of Æetes was black, but the heroes rejoiced and cheered their leader right lustily.

Then he took with him the helm full of dragon's teeth, and his spear for a goad, and forced those frantic beasts to draw the massive plow across the plain, and sowed his baneful seed as he went. All day long he drove his resisting team across the stony plain; and as the granite plowshare tore its way through the earth he cast the dragon's teeth among the upturned clods.

And at length the evening fell, and he unloosed the yoke, and with smiting and shouting scared the bulls across the plain to their caves. Then he gladly returned to the Argo, plunged his helm into the river, and was about to slake his terrible thirst, when he turned to see the whole earth bristling with armed warriors, row on row of shields and spears and helms. The words of Medea came to his remembrance then, and ere he fell upon them he took up from the earth a great round boulder such as four strong men of today scarce could move, and flung it in their midst.

Loudly the Colchians shouted, but speechless fear seized on their king when he saw the flight of that massive crag and beheld the earthborn slaying each other.

And among them stood Jason, beautiful as a god, hewing them down with his sword, till not one was left alive.

Then the night fell and Jason slept, for he knew that his task was accomplished. Æetes and his princes went silently back to their city, for the superhuman power of the hero inspired them with nameless fears.

And in the palace Medea was smitten with terror, for she knew that it must come to the ears of the king her father, that by her arts Jason had been helped to victory, and she dreaded his vengeance. She knew not where to turn for aid but to Jason himself; so she veiled herself, and thrusting her secret drugs and poisons into her bosom, she fled in the darkness from her palace. Through the night she hastened, weeping piteously, torn between love and duty to her parents and her passion for the man her spells had helped, till she saw the gleam of the fire where the heroes were feasting on the river bank. And through the noise of their revelry and the ringing of their gay laughter a bitter cry was heard—a woman's cry. And the sons of Phrixus, her nephews, and Jason, her lover, knew her voice, and they hastily thrust out from the bank and rowed to the place where she stood, and Jason leaped to the bank beside her.

Then Medea clung to his knees and besought him to carry her away lest her father's vengeance should fall heavy upon her. Therefore, before them all, he swore to take her to Greece and wed her there.

Then she adjured them to go in haste, wasting no more precious hours in revelry, to fetch the Golden Fleece before Æetes came in pursuit of them. 'Speed,' she cried, 'while darkness covers your deeds!'

So they went in all haste, till they came to the enchanted wood where the Fleece was hanging on an oak tree. And Medea landed there with Jason, and together they sped through the wood till they saw the Fleece shining like flame through the dusk, while before it, in coil on coil, loathsome, with open, watchful eyes, the awful serpent reared its head.

Then Medea called the magic of sleep to her aid. She anointed the serpent's head with her drugs, and rained her spells on its unsleeping eyes, and it sank down upon the earth in lazily undulating folds, until at length it slept.

Then Jason cast the great Fleece across his shoulder, and it fell down all his height and trailed upon the ground. And he caught it up about him and hastened from the spot. The Argonauts, watching anxiously, saw it come flaming through the trees. They greeted the achieving of their quest with shouts of joy, and strove among themselves to touch the glorious Fleece. But Jason was seized with fear lest some god or man should arrive to wrest his treasure from him, so he covered the shimmering Fleece with a mantle, and it lay in the stern of the Argo, with the maiden beside it, and Jason stood above them with his harness on his back and his great sword in his hand.

And the rowers bent to their oars, and the strong blades beat the waves, and swifter than a flying bird the good ship sped down the tide.

By this King Æetes and the Colchians knew of Medea's love and her deeds of rebellion. They swarmed on the river banks, and Æetes on his white charger pursued the flying boat. But he could not reach his disobedient daughter nor stay the flight of the hero band who had escaped the death he plotted, by the aid of love. And in his wrath the king sent ships after them and charged his captains: 'Except ye lay hands on the maiden and bring her so that I may pour the fury with which I burn upon her, on your heads shall all these things light, and ye shall learn the full measure of my wrath.'

But far across the seas the good ship Argo flew, and though the Colchians pursued, Medea was never taken, but after all adventure reached Iolcus with Jason, her lover and her lord.

For it was ordained of the high gods that the Golden Fleece should be brought back to Greece by the might of Jason and his brotherhood of heroes, that the wrath of Jupiter might be appeased. For the heroes went on the quest armed with the strength of innocence, and love fought on their side that they might prove mightier than a ruthless king or the doom of an offended god.

How Theseus Found his Father

Nathaniel Hawthorne

In the old city of Troezene, at the foot of a lofty mountain, there lived, a very long time ago, a little boy named Theseus. His grandfather, King Pittheus, was the sovereign of that country, and was reckoned a very wise man; so that Theseus, being brought up in the royal palace, and being naturally a bright lad, could hardly fail of profiting by the old king's instructions. His mother's name was Æthra. As for his father, the boy had never seen him. But, from his earliest remembrance, Æthra used to go with little Theseus into a wood, and sit down upon a moss-grown rock, which was deeply sunken into the earth. Here she often talked with her son about his father, and said that he was called Ægeus, and that he was a great king, and ruled over Attica, and dwelt at Athens, which was as famous a city as any in the world. Theseus was very fond of hearing about King Ægeus, and often asked his good mother Æthra why he did not come and live with them at Troezene.

'Ah, my dear son,' answered Æthra, with a sigh, 'a monarch has his people to take care of. The men and women over whom he rules are in the place of children to him; and he can seldom spare time to love his own children as other parents do. Your father will never be able to leave his kingdom for the sake of seeing his little boy.'

'Well, but, dear mother,' asked the boy, 'why cannot I go to this famous city

of Athens, and tell King Ægeus that I am his son?'

'That may happen by and by,' said Æthra. 'Be patient, and we shall see. You are not yet big and strong enough to set out on such an errand.'

'And how soon shall I be strong enough?' Theseus persisted in inquiring.

'You are but a tiny boy as yet,' replied his mother. 'See if you can lift this rock on which we are sitting.'

The little fellow had a great opinion of his own strength. So, grasping the rough protuberances of the rock, he tugged and toiled amain, and got himself quite out of breath, without being able to stir the heavy stone. It seemed to be rooted into the ground. No wonder he could not move it; for it would have taken all the force of a very strong man to lift it out of its earthy bed.

His mother stood looking on, with a sad kind of a smile on her lips and in her eyes, to see the zealous and yet puny efforts of her little boy. She could not help being sorrowful at finding him already so impatient to begin his adventures in the world.

'You see how it is, my dear Theseus,' said she. 'You must possess far more strength than now before I can trust you to go to Athens, and tell King Ægeus that you are his son. But when you can lift this rock, and show me what is hidden beneath it, I promise you my permission to depart.'

Often and often, after this, did Theseus ask his mother whether it was yet time for him to go to Athens; and still his mother pointed to the rock, and told him that, for years to come, he could not be strong enough to move it. And again and again the rosy-cheeked and curly-headed boy would tug and strain at the huge mass of stone, striving, child as he was, to do what a giant could hardly have done without taking both of his great hands to the task. Meanwhile the rock seemed to be sinking farther and farther into the ground. The moss grew over it thicker and thicker, until at last it looked almost like a soft green seat, with only a few gray knobs of granite peeping out. The overhanging trees, also, shed their brown

Left: Theseus Finding his Father's Arms *by Giovanni Benedetto Castiglione.*

leaves upon it, as often as the autumn came; and at its base grew ferns and wild flowers, some of which crept quite over its surface. To all appearance the rock was as firmly fastened as any other portion of the earth's substance.

But difficult as the matter looked, Theseus was now growing up to be such a vigorous youth that, in his own opinion, the time would quickly come when he might hope to get the upper hand of this ponderous lump of stone.

'Mother, I do believe it has started!' cried he, after one of his attempts. 'The earth around it is certainly a little cracked!'

'No, no, child!' his mother hastily answered. 'It is not possible that you can have moved it, such a boy as you still are!'

Nor would she be convinced, although Theseus showed her the place where he fancied that the stem of a flower had been partly uprooted by the movement of the rock. But Æthra sighed and looked disquieted; for, no doubt, she began to be conscious that her son was no longer a child, and that, in a little while hence, she must send him forth among the perils and troubles of the world.

It was not more than a year afterwards when they were again sitting on the moss-covered stone. Æthra had once more told him the oft-repeated story of his father, and how gladly he would receive Theseus at his stately palace, and how he would present him to his courtiers and the people, and tell them that here was the heir of his dominions. The eyes of Theseus glowed with enthusiasm, and he would hardly sit still to hear his mother speak.

'Dear mother Æthra,' he exclaimed, 'I never felt half so strong as now! I am no longer a child, nor a boy, nor a mere youth! I feel myself a man! It is now time to make one earnest trial to remove the stone.'

'Ah, my dearest Theseus,' replied his mother, 'not yet! not yet!'

'Yes, mother,' he said resolutely, 'the time has come!'

Then Theseus bent himself in good earnest to the task, and strained every sinew, with manly strength and resolution. He put his whole brave heart into the effort. He wrestled with the big and sluggish stone, as if it had been a living enemy. He heaved, he lifted, he resolved now to succeed, or else to perish there and let the rock be his monument forever! Æthra stood gazing at him, and clasped her hands, partly with a mother's pride and partly with a mother's sorrow. The great rock stirred! Yes; it was raised slowly from the bedded moss and earth, uprooting the shrubs and flowers along with it, and was turned upon its side. Theseus had conquered!

While taking breath he looked joyfully at his mother, and she smiled upon him through her tears.

'Yes, Theseus,' she said, 'the time has come, and you must stay no longer at my side! See what King Ægeus, your royal father, left for you, beneath the stone, when he lifted it in his mighty arms and laid it on the spot whence you have now removed it.'

Theseus looked, and saw that the rock had been placed over another slab of stone, containing a cavity within it; so that it somewhat resembled a roughly made chest or coffer, of which the upper mass had served as the lid. Within the cavity lay a sword, with a golden hilt, and a pair of sandals.

'That was your father's sword,' said Æthra, 'and those were his sandals. When he went to be King of Athens, he bade me treat you as a child until you should prove yourself a man by lifting this heavy stone. That task being accomplished, you are to put on his sandals, in order to follow in your father's footsteps, and to gird on his sword, so that you may fight giants and dragons, as King Ægeus did in his youth.'

'I will set out for Athens this very day!' cried Theseus.

But his mother persuaded him to stay a day or two longer, while she got ready some necessary articles for his journey. When his grandfather, the wise King Pittheus, heard that Theseus intended to present himself at his father's palace, he earnestly advised him to get on board of a vessel, and go by sea; because he might thus arrive within fifteen miles of Athens, without either fatigue or danger.

'The roads are very bad by land,' quoth the venerable king; 'and they are terribly infested with robbers and monsters. A mere lad like Theseus is not fit to be trusted on such a perilous journey all by himself. No, no; let him go by sea!'

But when Theseus heard of robbers and monsters, he pricked up his ears and was so much the more eager to take the road along which they were to be met with. On the third day, therefore, he bade a respectful farewell to his grandfather,

thanking him for all his kindness; and, after affectionately embracing his mother, he set forth, with a good many of her tears glistening on his cheeks, and some, if the truth must be told, that had gushed out of his own eyes. But he let the sun and wind dry them, and walked stoutly on, playing with the golden hilt of his sword and taking very manly strides in his father's sandals.

I cannot stop to tell you hardly any of the adventures that befell Theseus on the road to Athens. It is enough to say that he quite cleared that part of the country of the robbers about whom King Pittheus had been so much alarmed. One of these bad people was named Procrustes, and he was indeed a terrible fellow, and had an ugly way of making fun of the poor travelers who happened to fall into his clutches. In his cavern he had a bed, on which, with great pretense of hospitality, he invited his guests to lie down; but if they happened to be shorter than the bed, this wicked villain stretched them out by main force; or, if they were too tall, he lopped off their heads or feet, and laughed at what he had done as an excellent joke. Thus, however weary a man might be, he never liked to lie in the bed of Procrustes. Another of these robbers, named Sinis, must likewise have been a very great scoundrel. He was in the habit of flinging his victims off a high cliff into the sea; and in order to give him exactly his deserts, Theseus tossed him off the very same place. But if you will believe me, the sea would not pollute itself by receiving such a bad person into its bosom, neither would the earth, having once got rid of him, consent to take him back; so that, between the cliff and the sea, Sinis stuck fast in the air, which was forced to bear the burden of his naughtiness.

Thus, by the time he reached his journey's end, Theseus had done many valiant feats with his father's golden-hilted sword, and had gained the renown of being one of the bravest young men of the day. His fame traveled faster than he did, and reached Athens before him. As he entered the city, he heard the inhabitants talking at the street corners and saying that Hercules was brave, and Jason too, and Castor and Pollux likewise, but that Theseus, the son of their own king, would turn out as great a hero as the best of them. Theseus took longer strides on hearing this, and fancied himself sure of a magnificent reception at his father's court, since he came thither with Fame to blow her trumpet before him, and cry to King Ægeus, 'Behold your son!'

Theseus and the Witch Medea

Nathaniel Hawthorne

Theseus little suspected, innocent youth that he was, that here in this very Athens, where his father reigned, a greater danger awaited him than any which he had encountered on the road. Yet this was the truth. You must understand that the father of Theseus, though not very old in years, was almost worn out with the cares of government, and had thus grown aged before his time. His nephews, not expecting him to live a very great while, intended to get all the power of the kingdom into their own hands. But when they heard that Theseus had arrived in Athens, and learned what a gallant young man he was, they saw that he would not be at all the kind of person to let them steal away his father's crown and scepter, which ought to be his own by right of inheritance. Thus these bad-hearted nephews of King Ægeus, who were the own cousins of Theseus, at once became his enemies. A still more dangerous enemy was Medea, the wicked enchantress; for she was now the king's wife, and wanted to give the kingdom to her son Medus, instead of letting it be given to the son of Æthra, whom she hated.

Left: Copper engraving showing the wicked enchantress Medea riding a dragon.

It so happened that the king's nephews met Theseus, and found out who he was, just as he reached the entrance of the royal palace. With all their evil designs against him, they pretended to be their cousin's best friends, and expressed great joy at making his acquaintance. They proposed to him that he should come into the king's presence as a stranger, in order to try whether Ægeus would discover in the young man's features any likeness either to himself or his mother Æthra, and thus recognize him for a son. Theseus consented, for he fancied that his father would know him in a moment, by the love that was in his heart. But while he waited at the door, the nephews ran and told King Ægeus that a young man had arrived in Athens, who, to their certain knowledge, intended to put him to death and get possession of his royal crown.

'And he is now waiting for admission to your Majesty's presence,' added they.

'Aha!' cried the old king, on hearing this. 'Why, he must be a very wicked young fellow, indeed! Pray, what would you advise me to do with him?'

In reply to this question, the wicked Medea put in her word. You have heard already of this enchantress, and the wicked arts that she practiced upon men. Amongst a thousand other bad things, she knew how to prepare a poison, that was instantly fatal to whomsoever might so much as touch it with his lips.

So when the king asked what he should do with Theseus, this naughty woman had an answer ready at her tongue's end.

'Leave that to me, please your Majesty,' she replied. 'Only admit this evil-minded young man to your presence, treat him civilly, and invite him to drink a goblet of wine. Your Majesty is well aware that I sometimes amuse myself with distilling very powerful medicines. Here is one of them in this small phial. As to what it is made of, that is one of my secrets of state. Do but let me put a single drop into the goblet, and let the young man taste it, and I will answer for it, he shall quite lay aside the bad designs with which he comes hither.'

As she said this, Medea smiled; but, for all her smiling face, she meant nothing less than to poison the poor innocent Theseus before his father's eyes. And King Ægeus, like most other kings, thought any punishment mild enough for a person who was accused of plotting against his life. He therefore made little or no

objection to Medea's scheme, and as soon as the poisonous wine was ready, gave orders that the young stranger should be admitted into his presence. The goblet was set on a table beside the king's throne, and a fly, meaning just to sip a little from the brim, immediately tumbled into it, dead. Observing this, Medea looked round at the nephews and smiled again.

When Theseus was ushered into the royal apartment, the only object that he seemed to behold was the white-bearded old king. There he sat on his magnificent throne, a dazzling crown on his head, and a scepter in his hand. His aspect was stately and majestic, although his years and infirmities weighed heavily upon him, as if each year were a lump of lead and each infirmity a ponderous stone, and all were bundled up together and laid upon his weary shoulders. The tears, both of joy and sorrow, sprang into the young man's eyes; for he thought how sad it was to see his dear father so infirm, and how sweet it would be to support him with his own youthful strength, and to cheer him up with the alacrity of his loving spirit. When a son takes his father into his warm heart, it renews the old man's youth in a better way than by the heat of Medea's magic caldron. And this was what Theseus resolved to do. He could scarcely wait to see whether King Ægeus would recognize him, so eager was he to throw himself into his arms.

Advancing to the foot of the throne, he attempted to make a little speech, which he had been thinking about as he came up the stairs. But he was almost choked by a great many tender feelings that gushed out of his heart and swelled into his throat, all struggling to find utterance together. And therefore, unless he could have laid his full, over-brimming heart into the king's hand, poor Theseus knew not what to do or say. The cunning Medea observed what was passing in the young man's mind. She was more wicked at that moment than ever she had been before; for (and it makes me tremble to tell you of it) she did her worst to turn all this unspeakable love with which Theseus was agitated to his own ruin and destruction.

'Does your Majesty see his confusion?' she whispered in the king's ear. 'He is so conscious of guilt that he trembles and cannot speak. The wretch lives too long! Quick; Offer him the wine!'

Now King Ægeus had been gazing earnestly at the young stranger as he drew near the throne. There was something, he knew not what, either in his white brow, or in the fine expression of his mouth, or in his beautiful and tender eyes, that made him indistinctly feel as if he had seen this youth before; as if, indeed, he had trotted him on his knee when a baby, and had beheld him growing to be a stalwart man, while he himself grew old. But Medea guessed how the king felt, and would not suffer him to yield to these natural sensibilities, although they were the voice of his deepest heart, telling him, as plainly as it could speak, that here was his dear son, and Æthra's son, coming to claim him for a father. The enchantress again whispered in the king's ear, and compelled him, by her witchcraft, to see everything under a false aspect.

He made up his mind therefore to let Theseus drink of the poisoned wine.

'Young man,' said he, 'you are welcome! I am proud to show hospitality to so heroic a youth. Do me the favor to drink the contents of this goblet. It is brimming over, as you see, with delicious wine, such as I bestow only on those who are worthy of it! None is more worthy to quaff it than yourself!'

So saying, King Ægeus took the golden goblet from the table and was about to offer it to Theseus. But, partly through his infirmities and partly because it seemed so sad a thing to take away this young man's life, however wicked he might be, and partly, no doubt, because his heart was wiser than his head, and quaked within him at the thought of what he was going to do—for all these reasons the king's hand trembled so much that a great deal of the wine slopped over.

In order to strengthen his purpose, and fearing lest the whole of the precious poison should be wasted, one of his nephews now whispered to him: 'Has your Majesty any doubt of this stranger's guilt? There is the very sword with which he meant to slay you. How sharp, and bright, and terrible it is! Quick!—let him taste the wine, or perhaps he may do the deed even yet.'

At these words Ægeus drove every thought and feeling out of his breast, except the one idea of how justly the young man deserved to be put to death. He sat erect on his throne, and held out the goblet of wine with a steady hand, and bent on Theseus a frown of kingly severity; for, after all, he had too noble a spirit

to murder even a treacherous enemy with a deceitful smile upon his face.

'Drink!' said he, in the stern tone with which he was wont to condemn a criminal to be beheaded. 'You have well deserved of me such wine as this!'

Theseus held out his hand to take the wine. But before he touched it, King Ægeus trembled again. His eyes had fallen on the gold-hilted sword that hung at the young man's side. He drew back the goblet.

'That sword!' he cried. 'How came you by it?'

'It was my father's sword,' replied Theseus, with a tremulous voice. 'These were his sandals. My dear mother (her name is Æthra) told me his story while I was yet a little child. But it is only a month since I grew strong enough to lift the heavy stone and take the sword and sandals from beneath it and come to Athens to seek my father.'

'My son! my son!' cried King Ægeus, flinging away the fatal goblet and tottering down from the throne, to fall into the arms of Theseus. 'Yes, these are Æthra's eyes; it is my son.'

I have quite forgotten what became of the king's nephews. But when the wicked Medea saw this new turn of affairs she hurried out of the room, and going to her private chamber, lost no time in setting her enchantments at work. In a few moments she heard a great noise of hissing snakes outside of the chamber window; and behold! there was her fiery chariot and four huge winged serpents, wriggling and twisting in the air, flourishing their tails higher than the top of the palace, and all ready to set off on an aërial journey. Medea stayed only long enough to take her son with her, and to steal the crown jewels, together with the king's best robes and whatever other valuable things she could lay hands on; and getting into the chariot, she whipped up the snakes and ascended high over the city.

The king, hearing the hiss of the serpents, scrambled as fast as he could to the window and bawled out to the abominable enchantress never to come back. The whole people of Athens too, who had run out of doors to see this wonderful spectacle, set up a shout of joy at the prospect of getting rid of her. Medea, almost bursting with rage, uttered precisely such a hiss as one of her own snakes, only

ten times more venomous and spiteful; and glaring fiercely out of the blaze of the chariot, she shook her hands over the multitude below, as if she were scattering a million of curses among them. In so doing, however, she unintentionally let fall about five hundred diamonds of the first water, together with a thousand great pearls and two thousand emeralds, rubies, sapphires, opals, and topazes, to which she had helped herself out of the king's strong-box. All these came pelting down, like a shower of many-colored hailstones, upon the heads of grown people and children, who forthwith gathered them up and carried them back to the palace. But King Ægeus told them that they were welcome to the whole, and to twice as many more, if he had them, for the sake of his delight at finding his son and losing the wicked Medea. And, indeed, if you had seen how hateful was her last look, as the flaming chariot flew upward, you would not have wondered that both king and people should think her departure a good riddance.

A 17th-century etching showing Theseus using his sword and shield to fight the Minotaur, by Wilhelm Janson and Antonio Tempesta.

Theseus Goes to Slay the Minotaur

Nathaniel Hawthorne

And now Prince Theseus was taken into great favor by his royal father. The old king was never weary of having him sit beside him on his throne (which was quite wide enough for two), and of hearing him tell about his dear mother, and his childhood, and his many boyish efforts to lift the ponderous stone. Theseus, however, was much too brave and active a young man to be willing to spend all his time in relating things which had already happened. His ambition was to perform other and more heroic deeds, which should be better worth telling in prose and verse. Nor had he been long in Athens before he caught and chained a terrible mad bull, and made a public show of him, greatly to the wonder and admiration of good King Ægeus and his subjects. But pretty soon he undertook an affair that made all his foregone adventures seem like mere boy's play. The occasion of it was as follows:

One morning, when Prince Theseus awoke, he fancied that he must have had a very sorrowful dream, and that it was still running in his mind, even now that his eyes were open. For it appeared as if the air was full of a melancholy wail; and when he listened more attentively, he could hear sobs, and groans, and screams of woe, mingled with deep, quiet sighs, which came from the king's palace, and from the streets, and from the temples, and from every habitation in the city.

And all these mournful noises, issuing out of thousands of separate hearts, united themselves into the one great sound of affliction which had startled Theseus from slumber. He put on his clothes as quickly as he could (not forgetting his sandals and gold-hilted sword), and hastening to the king, inquired what it all meant.

'Alas! my son,' quoth King Ægeus, heaving a long sigh, 'here is a very lamentable matter in hand! This is the woefullest anniversary in the whole year. It is the day when we annually draw lots to see which of the youths and maidens of Athens shall go to be devoured by the horrible Minotaur!'

'The Minotaur!' exclaimed Prince Theseus; and, like a brave young prince as he was, he put his hand to the hilt of his sword. 'What kind of a monster may that be? Is it not possible, at the risk of one's life, to slay him?'

But King Ægeus shook his venerable head, and to convince Theseus that it was quite a hopeless case, he gave him an explanation of the whole affair. It seems that in the island of Crete there lived a certain dreadful monster, called a Minotaur, which was shaped partly like a man and partly like a bull, and was altogether such a hideous sort of a creature that it is really disagreeable to think of him. If he were suffered to exist at all, it should have been on some desert island, or in the duskiness of some deep cavern, where nobody would ever be tormented by his abominable aspect. But King Minos, who reigned over Crete, laid out a vast deal of money in building a habitation for the Minotaur, and took great care of his health and comfort, merely for mischief's sake. A few years before this time there had been a war between the city of Athens and the island of Crete, in which the Athenians were beaten, and compelled to beg for peace. No peace could they obtain, however, except on condition that they should send seven young men and seven maidens, every year, to be devoured by the pet monster of the cruel King Minos. For three years past this grievous calamity had been borne. And the sobs, and groans, and shrieks with which the city was now filled were caused by the people's woe, because the fatal day had come again when the fourteen victims were to be chosen by lot; and the old people feared lest their sons or daughters might be taken, and the youths and damsels dreaded lest they themselves might be destined to glut the ravenous maw of that detestable man-brute.

But when Theseus heard the story, he straightened himself up, so that he seemed taller than ever before; and as for his face, it was indignant, despiteful, bold, tender, and compassionate, all in one look.

'Let the people of Athens this year draw lots for only six young men, instead of seven,' said he. 'I will myself be the seventh; and let the Minotaur devour me if he can!'

'Oh, my dear son!' cried King Ægeus, 'why should you expose yourself to this horrible fate? You are a royal prince, and have a right to hold yourself above the destinies of common men.'

'It is because I am a prince, your son, and the rightful heir to your kingdom, that I freely take upon me the calamity of your subjects,' answered Theseus. 'And you, my father, being king over this people, and answerable to Heaven for their welfare, are bound to sacrifice what is dearest to you, rather than that the son or daughter of the poorest citizen should come to any harm.'

The old king shed tears, and besought Theseus not to leave him desolate in his old age, more especially as he had but just begun to know the happiness of possessing a good and valiant son. Theseus, however, felt that he was in the right, and therefore would not give up his resolution. But he assured his father that he did not intend to be eaten up unresistingly, like a sheep, and that, if the Minotaur devoured him, it should not be without a battle for his dinner. And finally, since he could not help it, King Ægeus consented to let him go. So a vessel was got ready, and rigged with black sails; and Theseus, with six other young men and seven tender and beautiful damsels, came down to the harbor to embark. A sorrowful multitude accompanied them to the shore. There was the poor old king, too, leaning on his son's arm, and looking as if his single heart held all the grief of Athens.

Just as Prince Theseus was going on board his father bethought himself of one last word to say.

'My beloved son,' said he, grasping the prince's hand, 'you observe that the sails of this vessel are black, as indeed they ought to be, since it goes upon a voyage of sorrow and despair. Now, being weighed down with infirmities, I know not whether I can survive till the vessel shall return. But as long as I do live, I shall creep daily to the top of yonder cliff, to watch if there be a sail upon the sea. And, dearest Theseus, if by some happy chance you should escape the jaws of the Minotaur, then tear down those dismal sails, and hoist others that shall be bright as the sunshine. Beholding them on the horizon, myself and all the people will know that you are coming back victorious, and will welcome you with such a festal uproar as Athens never heard before.'

Theseus promised that he would do so. Then, going on board, the mariners trimmed the vessel's black sails to the wind, which blew faintly off the shore, being pretty much made up of the sighs that everybody kept pouring forth on this melancholy occasion. But by and by, when they got fairly out to sea, there came a stiff breeze from the north-west, and drove them along as merrily over the white-capped waves as if they had been going on the most delightful errand imaginable. And though it was a sad business enough, I rather question whether fourteen young people, without any old persons to keep them in order, could continue to spend the whole time of the voyage in being miserable. There had been some few dances upon the undulating deck, I suspect, and some hearty bursts of laughter, and other such unseasonable merriment among the victims, before the high, blue mountains of Crete began to show themselves among the far-off clouds. That sight, to be sure, made them all very grave again.

No sooner had they entered the harbor than a party of the guards of King Minos came down to the waterside and took charge of the fourteen young men and damsels. Surrounded by these armed warriors, Prince Theseus and his companions were led to the king's palace and ushered into his presence. Now Minos was a stern and pitiless king. He bent his shaggy brows upon the poor Athenian victims. Any other mortal, beholding their fresh and tender beauty and their innocent looks, would have felt himself sitting on thorns until he had made every soul of them happy by bidding them go free as the summer wind. But this immitigable Minos cared only to examine whether they were plump enough to satisfy the Minotaur's appetite. For my part, I wish he himself had been the only victim; and the monster would have found him a pretty tough one.

One after another, King Minos called these pale, frightened youths and sobbing maidens to his footstool, gave them each a poke in the ribs with his scepter (to try whether they were in good flesh or no), and dismissed them with a nod to his guards. But when his eyes rested on Theseus, the king looked at him more attentively, because his face was calm and grave.

'Young man,' asked he, with his stern voice, 'are you not appalled at the certainty of being devoured by this terrible Minotaur?'

'I have offered my life in a good cause,' answered Theseus, 'and therefore I give it freely and gladly. But thou, King Minos, art thou not thyself appalled, who, year after year, hast perpetrated this dreadful wrong, by giving seven innocent youths and as many maidens to be devoured by a monster? Dost thou not tremble, wicked king, to turn thine eyes inward on thine own heart? Sitting there on thy golden throne and in thy robes of majesty, I tell thee to thy face, King Minos, thou art a more hideous monster than the Minotaur himself!'

'Aha! do you think me so?' cried the king, laughing in his cruel way. 'Tomorrow, at breakfast time, you shall have an opportunity of judging which is the greater monster, the Minotaur or the king! Take them away, guards; and let this free-spoken youth be the Minotaur's first morsel!'

Theseus and Ariadne, from 'Game of Mythology', etched by Stefano della Bella. Ariadne waves farewell as Prince Theseus and his companions sail homeward.

Theseus and Ariadne

Nathaniel Hawthorne

Near the king's throne stood his daughter Ariadne. She was a beautiful and tender-hearted maiden, and looked at these poor doomed captives with very different feelings from those of the iron-breasted King Minos. She really wept, indeed, at the idea of how much human happiness would be needlessly thrown away by giving so many young people, in the first bloom and rose-blossom of their lives, to be eaten up by a creature who, no doubt, would have preferred a fat ox, or even a large pig, to the plumpest of them. And when she beheld the brave-spirited figure of Prince Theseus bearing himself so calmly in his terrible peril, she grew a hundred times more pitiful than before. As the guards were taking him away, she flung herself at the king's feet and besought him to set all the captives free, and especially this one young man.

'Peace, foolish girl!' answered King Minos. 'What hast thou to do with an affair like this? It is a matter of state policy, and therefore quite beyond thy weak comprehension. Go water thy flowers, and think no more of these Athenian caitiffs, whom the Minotaur shall as certainly eat up for breakfast as I will eat a partridge for my supper.'

So saying, the king looked cruel enough to devour Theseus and all the rest of the captives himself, had there been no Minotaur to save him the trouble. As he would not hear another word in their favour, the prisoners were now led away and clapped into a dungeon, where the jailer advised them to go to sleep as soon

as possible, because the Minotaur was in the habit of calling for breakfast early. The seven maidens and six young men soon sobbed themselves to slumber. But Theseus was not like them. He felt conscious that he was wiser and braver and stronger than his companions, and that therefore he had the responsibility of all their lives upon him, and must consider whether there was no way to save them, even in this last extremity. So he kept himself awake, and paced to and fro across the gloomy dungeon in which they were shut up.

Just before midnight the door was softly unbarred, and the gentle Ariadne showed herself, with a torch in her hand.

'Are you awake, Prince Theseus?' she whispered.

'Yes,' answered Theseus. 'With so little time to live, I do not choose to waste any of it in sleep.'

'Then follow me,' said Ariadne, 'and tread softly.'

What had become of the jailer and the guards Theseus never knew. But however that might be, Ariadne opened all the doors and led him forth from the darksome prison into the pleasant moonlight.

'Theseus,' said the maiden, 'you can now get on board your vessel and sail away for Athens.'

'No,' answered the young man; 'I will never leave Crete unless I can first slay the Minotaur, and save my poor companions, and deliver Athens from this cruel tribute.'

'I knew that this would be your resolution,' said Ariadne. 'Come, then, with me, brave Theseus. Here is your own sword which the guards deprived you of. You will need it; and pray Heaven you may use it well.'

Then she led Theseus along by the hand until they came to a dark, shadowy grove, where the moonlight wasted itself on the tops of the trees, without shedding hardly so much as a glimmering beam upon their pathway. After going a good way through this obscurity, they reached a high marble wall, which was overgrown with creeping plants, that made it shaggy with their verdure. The wall seemed to have no door, nor any windows, but rose up, lofty and massive and mysterious, and was neither to be clambered over nor, so far as Theseus could perceive, to be

passed through. Nevertheless, Ariadne did but press one of her soft little fingers against a particular block of marble and, though it looked as solid as any other part of the wall, it yielded to her touch, disclosing an entrance just wide enough to admit them. They crept through, and the marble stone swung back into its place.

'We are now,' said Ariadne, 'in the famous labyrinth which Dædalus built before he made himself a pair of wings and flew away from our island like a bird. That Dædalus was a very cunning workman, but of all his artful contrivances this labyrinth is the most wondrous. Were we to take but a few steps from the doorway, we might wander about all our lifetime and never find it again. Yet in the very center of this labyrinth is the Minotaur, and, Theseus, you must go thither to seek him.'

'But how shall I ever find him?' asked Theseus, 'if the labyrinth so bewilders me, as you say it will?'

Just as he spoke they heard a rough and very disagreeable roar, which greatly resembled the lowing of a fierce bull, but yet had some sort of sound like the human voice. Theseus even fancied a rude articulation in it, as if the creature that uttered it were trying to shape his hoarse breath into words. It was at some distance, however, and he really could not tell whether it sounded most like a bull's roar or a man's harsh voice.

'That is the Minotaur's noise,' whispered Ariadne, closely grasping the hand of Theseus, and pressing one of her own hands to her heart, which was all in a tremble. 'You must follow that sound through the windings of the labyrinth, and, by and by, you will find him. Stay! take the end of this silken string; I will hold the other end; and then, if you win the victory, it will lead you again to this spot. Farewell, brave Theseus.'

So the young man took the end of the silken string in his left hand, and his gold-hilted sword, ready drawn from its scabbard, in the other, and trod boldly into the inscrutable labyrinth. How this labyrinth was built is more than I can tell you, but so cunningly contrived a mizmaze was never seen in the world before nor since. Theseus had not taken five steps before he lost sight of Ariadne; and in five more his head was growing dizzy. But he still went on, now creeping through a low arch, now ascending a flight of steps, now in one crooked passage, and now in another, with here a door opening before him, and there one banging behind, until it really seemed as if the walls spun round and whirled him along with them. And all the while, through these hollow avenues, now nearer, now farther off again, resounded the cry of the Minotaur; and the sound was so fierce, so cruel, so ugly, so like a bull's roar, and withal so like a human voice, and yet like neither of them, that the brave heart of Theseus grew sterner and angrier at every step; for he felt it an insult to the moon and sky, and to our affectionate and simple Mother Earth, that such a monster should have the audacity to exist.

As he passed onward, the clouds gathered over the moon, and the labyrinth grew so dusky that Theseus could no longer discern the bewilderment through which he was passing. He would have felt quite lost, and utterly hopeless of ever again walking in a straight path, if every little while he had not been conscious of a gentle twitch at the silken cord. Then he knew that the tender-hearted Ariadne was still holding the other end, and that she was fearing for him, and hoping for him, and giving him just as much of her sympathy as if she were close by his side. But still he followed the dreadful roar of the Minotaur, which now grew louder and louder, and finally so very loud that Theseus fully expected to come close upon him, at every new zigzag and wriggle of the path. And at last, in an open space, in the very center of the labyrinth, he did discern the hideous creature.

Sure enough, what an ugly monster it was! Only his horned head belonged to a bull; and yet, somehow or other, he looked like a bull all over, preposterously waddling on his hind legs; or, if you happened to view him in another way, he seemed wholly a man, and all the more monstrous for being so. And there he was, the wretched thing, with no society, no companion, no kind of a mate, living only to do mischief, and incapable of knowing what affection means. Theseus hated him, and shuddered at him, and yet could not but be sensible of some sort of pity; and all the more, the uglier and more detestable the creature was. For he kept striding to and fro in a solitary frenzy of rage, continually emitting a hoarse roar, which was oddly mixed up with half-shaped words; and, after listening awhile, Theseus understood that the Minotaur was saying to himself how miserable he

was, and how hungry, and how he hated everybody, and how he longed to eat up the human race alive.

Was Theseus afraid? By no means, my dear auditors. What! a hero like Theseus afraid! Not had the Minotaur had twenty bull heads instead of one. Bold as he was, however, I fancy that it strengthened his valiant heart, just at this crisis, to feel a tremulous twitch at the silken cord, which he was still holding in his left hand. It was as if Ariadne were giving him all her might and courage; and, much as he already had, and little as she had to give, it made his own seem twice as much. And to confess the honest truth, he needed the whole; for now the Minotaur, turning suddenly about, caught sight of Theseus, and instantly lowered his horribly sharp horns, exactly as a mad bull does when he means to rush against an enemy. At the same time he belched forth a tremendous roar, in which there was something like the words of human language, but all disjointed and shaken to pieces by passing through the gullet of a miserably enraged brute.

Theseus could only guess what the creature intended to say, and that rather by his gestures than his words; for the Minotaur's horns were sharper than his wits, and of a great deal more service to him than his tongue. But probably this was the sense of what he uttered:

'Ah, wretch of a human being! I'll stick my horns through you, and toss you fifty feet high, and eat you up the moment you come down.'

'Come on, then, and try it!' was all that Theseus deigned to reply; for he was far too magnanimous to assault his enemy with insolent language.

Without more words on either side, there ensued the most awful fight between Theseus and the Minotaur that ever happened beneath the sun or moon. I really know not how it might have turned out, if the monster, in his first headlong rush against Theseus, had not missed him, by a hair's-breadth, and broken one of his horns short off against the stone wall. On this mishap he bellowed so intolerably that a part of the labyrinth tumbled down, and all the inhabitants of Crete mistook the noise for an uncommonly heavy thunder-storm. Smarting with the pain, he galloped around the open space in so ridiculous a way that Theseus laughed at it long afterwards, though not precisely at the moment. After this the two antagonists stood valiantly up to one another, and fought sword to horn, for a long while. At last, the Minotaur made a run at Theseus, grazed his left side with his horn, and flung him down; and thinking that he had stabbed him to the heart, he cut a great caper in the air, opened his bull mouth from ear to ear, and prepared to snap his head off. But Theseus by this time had leaped up, and caught the monster off his guard. Fetching a sword-stroke at him with all his force, he hit him fair upon the neck, and made his bull head skip six yards from his human body, which fell down flat upon the ground.

So now the battle was ended. Immediately the moon shone out as brightly as if all the troubles of the world, and all the wickedness and the ugliness that infest human life, were past and gone forever. And Theseus, as he leaned on his sword, taking breath, felt another twitch of the silken cord; for all through the terrible encounter he had held it fast in his left hand. Eager to let Ariadne know of his success, he followed the guidance of the thread, and soon found himself at the entrance of the labyrinth.

'Thou hast slain the monster,' cried Ariadne, clasping her hands.

'Thanks to thee, dear Ariadne,' answered Theseus, 'I return victorious.'

'Then,' said Ariadne, 'we must quickly summon thy friends, and get them and thyself on board the vessel before dawn. If morning finds thee here, my father will avenge the Minotaur.'

To make my story short, the poor captives were awakened, and hardly knowing whether it was not a joyful dream, were told of what Theseus had done, and that they must set sail for Athens before daybreak. Hastening down to the vessel, they all clambered on board, except Prince Theseus, who lingered behind them, on the strand, holding Ariadne's hand clasped in his own.

'Dear maiden,' said he, 'thou wilt surely go with us. Thou art too gentle and sweet a child for such an iron-hearted father as King Minos. He cares no more for thee than a granite rock cares for the little flower that grows in one of its crevices. But my father, King Ægeus, and my dear mother, Æthra, and all the fathers and mothers in Athens, and all the sons and daughters too, will love and honour thee as their benefactress. Come with us, then; for King Minos will be

very angry when he knows what thou hast done.'

Now, some low-minded people, who pretend to tell the story of Theseus and Ariadne, have the face to say that this royal and honourable maiden did really flee away, under cover of the night, with the young stranger whose life she had preserved. They say, too, that Prince Theseus (who would have died sooner than wrong the meanest creature in the world) ungratefully deserted Ariadne on a solitary island, where the vessel touched on its voyage to Athens. But had the noble Theseus heard these falsehoods, he would have served their slanderous authors as he served the Minotaur! Here is what Ariadne answered, when the brave Prince of Athens besought her to accompany him:

'No, Theseus,' the maiden said, pressing his hand and then drawing back a step or two, 'I cannot go with you. My father is old, and has nobody but myself to love him. Hard as you think his heart is, it would break to lose me. At first King Minos will be angry; but he will soon forgive his only child; and, by and by, he will rejoice, I know, that no more youths and maidens must come from Athens to be devoured by the Minotaur. I have saved you, Theseus, as much for my father's sake as for your own. Farewell! Heaven bless you!'

All this was so true, and so maiden-like, and was spoken with so sweet a dignity, that Theseus would have blushed to urge her any longer. Nothing remained for him, therefore, but to bid Ariadne an affectionate farewell, and go on board the vessel and set sail.

In a few moments the white foam was boiling up before their prow, as Prince Theseus and his companions sailed out of the harbor, with a whistling breeze behind them.

On the homeward voyage the fourteen youths and damsels were in excellent spirits, as you will easily suppose. They spent most of their time in dancing, unless when the sidelong breeze made the deck slope too much. In due season they came within sight of the coast of Attica, which was their native country. But here, I am grieved to tell you, happened a sad misfortune.

You will remember (what Theseus unfortunately forgot) that his father, King Ægeus, had enjoined it upon him to hoist sunshiny sails, instead of black ones, in case he should overcome the Minotaur, and return victorious. In the joy of their success, however, and amidst the sports, dancing, and other merriment with which these young folks wore away the time, they never once thought whether their sails were black, white, or rainbow colored, and, indeed, left it entirely to the mariners whether they had any sails at all. Thus the vessel returned, like a raven, with the same sable wings that had wafted her away. But poor King Ægeus, day after day, infirm as he was, had clambered to the summit of a cliff that overhung the sea, and there sat watching for Prince Theseus, homeward bound; and no sooner did he behold the fatal blackness of the sails, than he concluded that his dear son, whom he loved so much, and felt so proud of, had been eaten by the Minotaur. He could not bear the thought of living any longer; so, first flinging his crown and scepter into the sea (useless baubles that they were to him now!) King Ægeus merely stooped forward, and fell headlong over the cliff, and was drowned, poor soul, in the waves that foamed at its base!

This was melancholy news for Prince Theseus, who, when he stepped ashore, found himself king of all the country, whether he would or no; and such a turn of fortune was enough to make any young man feel very much out of spirits. However, he sent for his dear mother to Athens, and, by taking her advice in matters of state, became a very excellent monarch, and was greatly beloved by his people.

Paris and Oenone

V.C. Turnbull

Hither came at noon
Mournful Oenone, wandering forlorn
Of Paris, once her playmate on the hills.

Alfred, Lord Tennyson (1809–1892): 'Oenone'

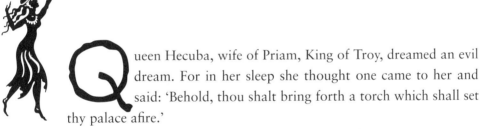

Queen Hecuba, wife of Priam, King of Troy, dreamed an evil dream. For in her sleep she thought one came to her and said: 'Behold, thou shalt bring forth a torch which shall set thy palace afire.'

Not many days afterwards, therefore, when the Queen bore a son, Priam, to whom she had told her dream, ordered his slaves to destroy the child. But before his cruel order could be carried out, Hecuba contrived to steal away the babe and place it with certain shepherds—kindly folk, who cared for it as their own child—on Mount Ida, over against the city of Troy. And they called the child Paris.

Now Paris, though reared among rude shepherd folk, soon showed that royal blood ran in his veins, and he won great praise from the shepherds for his skill in

Left: Paris and Oenone from 'The Greek Heroines' by Georg Pencz.

tending the sheep upon the mountain, and for the daring with which he pursued and slew the wild beasts who sought to devour them.

So Paris grew to man's estate, and in all the land was none fairer than he, or more gracious withal. No marvel, then, that the mountain maid Oenone, whose home was in the vale of Ida, should be smitten by his beauty; and he loving her with equal warmth, they were wedded and lived together in that pleasant land with the happiness of simple folk.

Together they shared the pleasures of the chase, and Oenone was not less skilled than Paris in cheering on the hounds and in spreading the nets. In quieter moods they would wander together by the river or in the woods, and Paris would carve their names upon the gray boles of the beeches. And on one poplar that grew on the banks of the river Xanthus, he carved these words:

'Back to its source thy stream shall start, Ere Paris from Oenone part.'

But even then the gods were preparing a bitter sorrow for Paris, for Oenone, and for countless generations of mortals otherwise.

Across the sea, in Thessaly, a great feast was being held to celebrate the wedding of Peleus and Thetis. And because the bride was no maiden born of woman, but an immortal Nereid, all the gods and goddesses were bidden to the banquet. All were bidden save one, Eris by name, the Goddess of Strife, most hateful of the immortals. So she, full of rage at the slight, cast on the board where all the guests were feasting a golden apple bearing the legend To the Fairest.

Then ensued, as Eris had intended, great strife among the goddesses, and, in especial, Juno, Minerva, and Venus claimed each the golden fruit. So the gods, not willing themselves to settle the dispute, bade the three goddesses betake themselves to Mount Ida, there to seek the judgment of Paris and to abide by his decision.

So on a day before the lowly bower of Paris and Oenone stood the three great goddesses. Naked they came, clad in celestial radiance, as with a garment, and at their feet violets and crocuses pushed upward through the grass, and hovering round them were the peacock of Juno, the owl of Minerva, and the doves of Venus.

Then when Paris faltered, not knowing which to choose when all were so fair,

Juno, Queen of Heaven, said: 'Choose me, and I will give thee the kingdoms of the world.'

Then Minerva, the wise Virgin goddess, said: 'Choose me, and I will give thee wisdom.'

Last of all, Venus, the sea-born Goddess of Love, whispered: 'Choose me, and I will give thee to wife the fairest woman in Greece.'

Smiling, she stretched forth her hand and the golden apple was hers, and the three goddesses vanished in a cloud, and with them vanished all happiness from the heart of Oenone.

Not long after this, Priam, King of Troy, proposed a contest in arms among his sons and other princes, promising to the winner the finest bull on the pastures of Mount Ida. And Paris, grieving to see the bull driven off by the messengers of Priam, determined that he too would strive with the sons of Priam, whom as yet he knew not for his brothers.

So on the day fixed for the contests, Paris strove with Priam's sons Polites, Helenus, and Deiphobus, and with other princes, and worsted them all. Yea, and he strove also with the strongest of the king's sons, great Hector himself, and for him too was he a match. But Hector, enraged, turned and pursued Paris as he would kill him, so that Paris fled to the temple of Jupiter for refuge. In this temple he was met by Cassandra, the daughter of Priam, to whom Apollo had granted knowledge of things to come. And marking in Paris the very mold and features of her own brothers, she drew from him all he knew of his story. So, adding thereto of her own knowledge, Cassandra knew that this was indeed her brother who was put away while a baby, and taking him by the hand she led him back to the household of Priam and Hecuba, bidding all embrace their brother and son. Then Priam and Hecuba and all their sons very gladly took Paris to their hearts, for they forgot the dismal prophecy of his birth, noting only his modest courtesy, his beauty, and his strength.

Paris, therefore, remained a while in the royal household, and all made him great cheer. Yet was he not wholly happy in the palace of Priam. Not, alas! that his thoughts turned often to Oenone whom he had left on Mount Ida, but evermore

there sounded in his ears the low voice of Venus, saying: 'The fairest woman in Greece shall be thy wife.'

And Paris would muse, saying to himself: 'Helen, wife of Menelaus, King of Sparta, is the fairest of all the daughters of men. All the princes of Greece sought her hand in marriage, and when those who have seen her try to tell of her beauty, speech fails them, for she is more fair than man can tell or poet can sing.'

Then, pursuing his thought, he would ponder: 'Am not I, Paris, no more a shepherd on Mount Ida, but now a prince in a royal palace and son of the King of Troy? Surely the word that Venus spake will yet be fulfilled!'

Now Priam's sister, Hesione, had been carried off and wedded against her will, and this thing was a bitterness to Priam. So Paris, perceiving this, set himself and his fellows to build and man a fleet, declaring that he would bring back Hesione, but thinking in his heart not of Hesione, but of Helen. To obtain wood for his ships he returned to Mount Ida to cut down the tallest pines that crowned the craggy ledges where the winds of the sea sighed through the branches, as it were, indeed, the soughing of another sea through the melancholy tree-tops.

Oenone received her lord with gladness on his return; but when she knew that his thought was but to fashion ships for a voyage, the spirit of prophecy came upon her, and she cried to him, as one inspired: 'A bitter thing is this that thou doest, O Paris, my husband! For behold, thou farest to Greece to fetch hither the ruin of thy country and thy kindred. Yea, and to me shalt thou come at the last, stricken unto death, beseeching the aid of my leechcraft . . .' At this place the gift failed her as suddenly as it had come, and she fell to weeping.

But Paris, kissing her, bade her put away her fears and look out over the sea for his return. And when he had fashioned his ships and rigged them with tall masts and calked them with pitch, he set sail across the seas, leaving Oenone to watch for his homeward sails.

Many days did she sit upon a cliff that overlooked the blue waters, watching for the ship's return. One night, as in a vision, she saw, or seemed to see, a white sail on the marge, and it sped before the wind and passed close beneath the cliff where she stood at gaze. And as she looked down, her heart turned sick within

her; for on the deck stood a lady. A daughter of the gods she seemed, divinely fair, and her arms were round the neck of Paris, while her head lay upon his breast. And Oenone saw Paris spring to shore bearing this lady in his arms; she saw him lead her to the city of Troy; she saw the gates flung open and all the people come forth to meet the pair; and she knew that this was Helen, the fairest of women, who had fled with Paris from Menelaus, her husband. She knew, too, that she, Oenone, would be left lonely till she died.

Now followed that great siege of Troy of which poets will sing till the end of time. For Menelaus, the husband of Helen, and his brother Agamemnon, the great general, stirred up all the princes of Greece who had been the suitors of Helen and, on her marriage with Menelaus, had bound themselves in a solemn league to protect her from all manner of violence. So all the princes and captains of Greece came with a great host and many ships, and laid siege to Troy; and many battles were fought upon the plains outside the city walls. And to Oenone, wandering widowed upon Mount Ida, the sound of the strife rolled up, and from afar she perceived the confused struggle of chariots and horses and men; but she heard and saw these things as one who marked them not, for it was as if her heart had died, and her life had ended.

Now when the war had lasted for a space of years, Paris, although constantly protected by the goddess Venus, received a wound from the poisoned arrow of one Philoctetes. Then in his anguish he remembered his deserted Oenone, and her great skill at leechcraft, and he said to his attendants: 'Carry me out of the city to Mount Ida, that I may look once more on the face of my wife Oenone, and beseech her pardon for the great wrong she has endured at my hands. And haply, when she seeth my grievous state, her pitiful heart will be moved with compassion, and she will heal me with her leechcraft, for naught else may avail.'

So they carried Paris in a litter up the slopes of Mount Ida. And Oenone, seeing them approach, went down swiftly to meet them. And Paris, when he saw her coming, stretched out his arms a little and let them fall, for they were very weak; and Oenone, uttering a lamentable cry, like a bird who sees her nestling slain, flew to meet his embrace. But in that moment Paris had breathed his last.

The eyes, once so bright, were fixed in a stony stare, and the dews of death were on that marble brow. Then Oenone, forgetting all the wrongs she had suffered, remembering only the morning light of happy marriage and that he had come back to her at the last, fell down upon his breast embracing him and bathing him with her tears. Then, crying aloud with a great and exceeding bitter cry, she plucked a dagger from her girdle and plunged it into her heart, falling dead upon the breast which had pillowed her head in other years. So died Oenone, faithful to the faithless, the most innocent of all who perished for the sin of Paris, the son of Priam.

Iphigenia

Mrs. Guy E. Lloyd

Menelaus, brother of the King of Mycenæ, had for his wife the most beautiful woman in the world, whose name was Helen; but she was stolen from him by a treacherous guest, Paris, the son of Priam, King of Troy, who carried her away with him to his home far over the sea.

Then Menelaus, in his anger and sorrow, asked all his friends to help him to bring back his wife, and to punish his treacherous guest, and all the chieftains of Greece came to his aid, for Troy was a wondrous strong city, and its walls had been built by Neptune, the god of the sea.

Foremost of all the chieftains was Agamemnon, King of Mycenæ, the elder brother of Menelaus; he was chosen to be the head of the whole array, and under him served Ulysses, the wise king of Ithaca, and Achilles, chief of the Myrmidons, whom no weapon could wound save in the heel; and many more of fame throughout the whole world.

The fleet came together at Aulis in the land of Boeotia; all were ready and eager to fare forth over the sea and fight against Troy; and a goodly sight it was to see the brass-beaked vessels and the brave warriors who crowded thick upon them.

Left: A 17th-century pen and ink drawing showing The Sacrifice of Iphigenia *by Gerard de Lairesse. Diana can be seen at the top of the picture, laying a hart (male deer) upon the altar.*

But day after day passed by and the fleet lay still in harbor, for no breeze came to fill the sails. And all the chieftains were dumfounded, for their valor was of no avail, and their hearts were heavy within them; for they knew not wherefore their ships lay thus becalmed, and they feared lest the immortal gods did not will that Troy should fall.

At last they sent for Calchas, the wise seer, and asked if he could tell them the will of the gods.

And Calchas made answer: 'The winds are withheld from you, O chieftains, by the will of Diana, the huntress of the woods. For King Agamemnon, once on a day, slew a stag within her sacred grove, and ever since she has hated him sore, and therefore she will not let you sail till her anger is appeased by rich offerings.'

Then said King Agamemnon; 'Since mine is the blame, let the expiation be mine also. Speak, Calchas: what offering will content the goddess, that the winds may come forth from their prison-house and our ships spread their sails and fare over the sea to Troy?'

All hearkened eagerly, for the face of Calchas was dark and terrible, so that every man feared to hear his answer.

'The goddess asks of thee the best and most beautiful of all that is thine,' said the stern seer; 'she asks the life of thy daughter Iphigenia.'

A shudder ran through all who heard the fearful words. Menelaus, with a cry of sorrow and terror, came close to his brother and laid his hand on his arm, and Agamemnon the king stood in a tumult of agony, speaking no word for some little space.

At length the chieftain looked round upon his comrades, saying: 'A hard fate is upon me, ye leaders of the Greeks. For either I must shed blood that is dearer to me than my own, or else our great array must lie here idle till the ships are rotten or the captains desert and leave us stranded.'

Then said Menelaus to Calchas: 'Is there no other way? Cannot the great goddess be appeased without this innocent victim?'

And Calchas made answer: 'There is no other way.'

Agamemnon, with bowed head, climbed slowly to his tent upon the hillside,

and the rumor ran quickly through the camp that the wrath of Diana could only be turned away by the death of the fair and innocent maiden Iphigenia, the daughter of the king.

Then Agamemnon despatched a guileful message to his wife Clytemnestra, praying her to send their daughter Iphigenia quickly to Aulis, since Achilles, the noble chief of the Myrmidons, had asked leave to wed the maiden, and it must be done in haste, for the fleet was on the point of sailing.

When Clytemnestra heard her husband's message she was glad at heart, for the fame of Achilles was great, and he was brave and strong and beautiful as the immortal gods.

In haste was the maiden decked for her wedding and sent with the messengers of Agamemnon to the camp at Aulis.

And as Iphigenia was led into the camp she marveled greatly, for all who looked upon her were filled with pity, and cold fear touched the heart of the maiden as she passed through the silent and sorrowful host. The warriors were moved at the sight of her youth and innocence; but no man strove to save her from her fate, for without her death all their gathering together would be for naught. Within the tent of Agamemnon the stern seer Calchas awaited the destined victim. All was prepared for the sacrifice, and Agamemnon and Menelaus already stood by the altar. In haste was the maiden decked out—not for her bridal, but for her death.

Then they led her forth into the sunshine again, and she looked round upon the hillside and the blue sea where lay the idle ships; and when she saw her father standing by the altar she would have cried out to him and begged for mercy, but those who led her laid their hands upon her mouth. The poor child tried to win from her father one pitying glance, but Agamemnon hid his face in his mantle; he could not look upon the face of the child who was to be slain to expiate his sin. So there was no help for the beautiful and innocent maiden, and she was led to her death. But so great was the ruth of the Greeks that no man save the stern Calchas dared witness the terrible deed; and because they could not bear to believe afterwards that the maiden had indeed been slain there upon the altar, the tale went forth that at the last moment Diana had laid a hart upon the altar and had borne the maiden safely away to Tauris.

But in truth the cruel sacrifice was completed, and even as the flame leapt up on the altar the tree-tops swung and swayed, and ripples coursed over the glassy surface of the sea; the breeze for which the host had waited so long had been set free, and the warriors joyfully hoisted their sails and stood out of the harbor of Aulis on their way to the siege of Troy.

But now was Diana well avenged for Agamemnon's profanation of her grove. For, from the innocent blood of Iphigenia, uprose an avenger, destined to follow King Agamemnon and all his family till the dark deed had been expiated.

Long and grievous was the warfare before the walls of Troy; and it was not till the tenth year after his setting forth that tidings came that King Agamemnon was on his way home. All through those years his wife had nourished the hope of vengeance in her heart, both for the death of Iphigenia and for the falsehood that had made her send the maiden to the camp. So the king came home only to his grave. His wife received him with gracious words and with every sign of rejoicing; but ere night fell Agamemnon lay slain in his bath, where the dagger of Clytemnestra had smitten him down.

Next the Avenger of Blood put into the heart of Orestes, son of Agamemnon and Clytemnestra, a great hatred for the mother who had slain his father. He was far from home when the cruel deed was done, and it was long ere he returned; but when at last he came he smote his own mother and slew her.

After this deed of awe and terror the Avenger of Blood pursued Orestes, and drove him, a branded outlaw, from land to land. At length he fled to the sanctuary of the great goddess Minerva, and was at last permitted to expiate his guilt.

He had to seek a piece of land that was not made when he killed his mother, so he went to the mouth of a river where fresh soil was being formed by the sand that was brought down by the rushing flood. And here he was allowed to purify himself, and the Avenger of Blood left him, at last, at peace.

Plaque with Cavalry Battle between Greeks and Trojans *by Master KIP. The monogram 'KIP' is thought to be that of Jean Poillevé. One of the commanding figures in the picture is Hector, the most valiant of the Trojans in 'The Iliad'.*

Protesilaus

Mrs. Guy E. Lloyd

 Protesilaus, King of Thessaly, was a happy and a fortunate man. A beautiful and fertile kingdom was his, left to him by his father, the fleet-footed Iphicles, and his wife Laodamia, a fair and gracious queen, was very dear to his heart.

But the call of honour came, and all Greece was arming to revenge upon the false Paris the wrong he had done to his host Menelaus in carrying off his wife, the beauteous Helen. Then Protesilaus donned his armor with the rest, and forty goodly vessels sailed from the coast of Thessaly, and joined the assembled fleet of the Greeks at Aulis in Boeotia.

Sad was the parting with the fair Queen Laodamia, and many bitter tears she wept when her husband's ships had sailed away and she was left alone. Her whole life was bound up in him, and when he was gone everything that was left to her seemed empty and worthless. Often would she climb the rocks and look forth over the sun-lit waters for hours dreaming and dreaming of the day when Protesilaus should come back to her again to reign over his people in peace and safety.

For many days the Greek ships lay wind-bound at Aulis, because their leader, King Agamemnon, had offended the great goddess Diana. At length (as the preceding story told) he was forced to expiate his guilt by the sacrifice of his innocent daughter Iphigenia. As soon as the offering was completed the goddess, appeased, let loose the imprisoned winds, and the great fleet set sail for Troy.

Most of the warriors on those bounding ships were eager and happy; their waiting was over, the delight of battle was close before them.

But Protesilaus was silent and thoughtful; he would stand for hours on the deck of his vessel looking down upon the lines of foam that it left in its wake, and ever his thoughts were the same.

He was not mourning for his beloved wife, nor for the happy home he had left. He was not sad to think of all the perils and hardships that awaited the Greeks at Troy. He was thinking and thinking of the words spoken by the oracle of Apollo at Delphi. The first man to leap ashore, so the oracle had said, should be slain; and even as he had first heard the stern sentence the heart of Protesilaus had beat high with the determination that he himself would be that man. He would crowd all sail on his swift ship, and waiting on the prow would spring on shore through the breakers, and so fulfil the will of the gods.

All through the voyage this one thought filled the mind of Protesilaus. He grieved, it is true, that he should never again see his dearly loved wife, Laodamia, nor the beautiful palace they had been building for themselves, wherein they had hoped to be happy together for many years, after the war was over. And sometimes a passionate regret would overcome the warrior when he remembered that the war must all be fought out without his having any share in the famous battles that were before his comrades. His brother would lead the men of Thessaly to the strife, and would return with them in triumph to their homes when, as Calchas had foretold, in the tenth year the city of King Priam should fall.

So, undaunted in courage, steadfast in resolution though sad at heart, Protesilaus sailed on to his chosen fate, and even the immortal gods were stirred with wonder and admiration when they saw his ship shoot forth before all the rest as soon as the land of Troy came in sight. Tall and stately on the prow stood the figure of Protesilaus, clad in glittering armor, and with sword and spear and shield all ready for the combat. The helmsman steered straight for a little sandy spit that rose from the water's edge, and Protesilaus sprang ashore long before the rest of the Greek array had neared the Trojan strand. Then the words of the oracle were fulfilled. Some say it was the spear of Hector, some that of Æneas that struck the hero down. Foremost of all the mighty army of King Agamemnon he fell, honored and mourned by all his comrades.

Queen Laodamia waited impatiently in the peaceful land of Thessaly, longing for tidings from her lord. She had heard of the long waiting at Aulis, she shuddered when the words of Calchas were repeated to her; in sight of all the host a serpent devoured first nine sucklings and then the mother sow, and when Calchas saw it he said that this was a sign that in the tenth year the city of Priam should fall before the attacks of the Greeks.

Ten years seemed a long, long time to the eager queen before she should see her dear lord home again. She would wake up suddenly in the night, and stare into the darkness, thinking with terror of the months and months of hopeless waiting that lay before her.

Then tidings came to Thessaly of the sailing of the fleet, and as men told over the names of the mighty heroes who had gone forth to fight with Agamemnon, they forgot the words of the wise seer Calchas, and hoped that this brave array must soon return in triumph.

Not many weeks later Laodamia was seated at her loom weaving a robe for her warrior to wear on his return in triumph when there came to her, white and trembling, her favourite of all her maidens.

The queen looked up in alarm. 'What ails thee, child?' she asked. 'Why dost thou stand there pale and silent? Is aught amiss?'

The maiden tried in vain to frame words to answer. Covering her face with her hands she sank upon her knees and burst into tears.

And the queen, with a great terror at her heart, went forth into a house full of tears and lamentations, for the tidings had come, over the sea, of the death of the noble Protesilaus.

Then Laodamia went back into her inner chamber, and covering her head she flung herself prone upon the ground, and lay there all through the day, while her maidens wept and wailed without the door, and none dared enter or attempt to comfort her.

But at nightfall the queen arose, and passing from her chamber to the temple,

she begged the priest to instruct her what sacrifice to offer to the gods of the world of spirits, that they might allow her but once more to look upon her lord.

Then the priest prepared in haste the sevenfold offering due to the great gods of the under-world, and told her the vows and prayers that she must offer, and then left her alone in the temple.

Then, standing erect and stretching her suppliant hands towards the heavens, the queen flung her whole soul into the impassioned entreaty that she might see her dear lord once again.

No door opened, no curtain was lifted, but on a sudden two forms appeared before the startled suppliant. One she saw at once, by his winged helmet and his rod encircled by snakes, must be the swift messenger of the gods, Mercury; the other, she recognized with a thrill of terror and joy, was the husband for a sight of whom she had just been praying so earnestly.

Then Mercury touched Laodamia with his rod, and at the touch all her fear fell from her at once.

'Great Jupiter has heard thy prayer,' said Mercury. 'Behold, thy husband is with thee once more, and he shall tarry with thee for the space of three hours.'

Having thus spoken Mercury vanished from sight, and Protesilaus and Laodamia stood alone together.

Then the queen sprang forward and tried to fling her arms round her dear husband; but though he stood there before her in form and features unchanged, it was but the ghost of her lost lord. Thrice she essayed to embrace him, and thrice her arms clasped nothing but the empty air.

Then she cried out in anguish: 'Alas! have the gods mocked me after all? Is this not Protesilaus, then, who seems to stand before me?'

Then the shade of the warrior made answer: 'Nay, dear wife, the gods do not mock thee, and it is indeed Protesilaus who stands before thee. Yet am I no living man; for the oracle had foretold that the first of the Greek host to leap ashore should be slain; therefore, seeing that the immortal gods asked a life, I gave them mine, and steering to the shore before all the other ships, I sprang on land the first of all the host, and fell, slain by the spear of the enemy.'

Then the queen made answer: 'Noblest and best of warriors! even the gods are filled with admiration for thy courage, for they have allowed thee to come back to thy wife and to thy home. Surely they will go on to give thee even a greater gift. As I look upon thee I see no change in thee; thou art fair and young as when we said farewell. Doubtless the gods will give thee back to me wholly again, and naught shall ever more divide us.'

But even as she spoke the queen shrank back in dread, for the face of the vision changed and became like that of a dead man, while Protesilaus made answer: 'Short is my sojourn upon earth, soon must I leave thee again. But be brave and wise, dear love; give not thy whole life over unto mourning, but be patient; and though I must pass from thee now, some day we shall meet once more; and though our earthly love is ended, yet may we joy for ever in faithful companionship one with another.'

'Ah! wherefore shouldst thou leave me?' cried the queen; 'the gods have already wrought wonders, why should they not give thee back thy life? If thou goest from me again, I will follow thee, for I cannot stay alone.'

Then Protesilaus tried to soothe and calm his wife, that she might give up the vain hope of living again together as they once had done, and might look forward instead to a pure and happy life beyond the grave. The gods had already given her much, he said, and she ought to strive to be worthy of their mercy, and by her courage and self-control win for herself eternal peace.

While her husband was speaking his face lost its ghastly look, and he seemed even more beautiful and gracious than when he was alive. And Laodamia watched him, and was calmed and cheered at the sight; but she hardly marked his words, so sure was she that the gods would relent when the end of the three hours was come, and would allow him to stay with her once more a living man.

But even while the hero urged his wife to be patient and courageous, even while she looked for the gods to restore him to her, lo! the three hours were past, and Mercury stood once more within the temple.

Then, Laodamia understood that her hopes were vain, and that Protesilaus was doomed to leave her. She tried to hold that dear form fast, but she grasped a shadow; her empty fingers closed helplessly as Protesilaus vanished from her sight.

With a shriek she fell prone on the temple floor, and the priests who hurried to their queen's assistance raised a lifeless corpse.

True to her lord, if ever yet was wife, she had followed him to the Shades; yet alas! in death they were not reunited. The gods are just, and Laodamia had not yet learnt the lesson of Protesilaus, that there is a higher and nobler thing even than human love—self-sacrifice and duty. Therefore she is doomed for a set time to wander in the Mourning Fields apart from happy ghosts, till her spirit raised and solemnized by suffering is worthy to meet her lord who walks with the heroes of old in the dwellings of the blest.

Hector's last visit, before his death, with his wife, Andromache, and his infant son, Astyanax,
from Iliad Stories Retold for Boys and Girls *by Agnes Spofford Cook Gale.*

The Death of Hector

V.C. Turnbull

Of all the Trojan warriors none could be compared with their leader, Hector, the son of Priam. Terrible was he in battle, as the Greeks had known to their cost; but within the walls of Troy none was more loved than he; for towards all he was gracious and kindly. To Priam and Hecuba a dutiful son; aye, even to Paris and Helen, the guilty cause of unnumbered woes, he showed a brother's spirit. But none knew the depth of his love and gentleness as did his wife, Andromache, and their little son, Astyanax. These, in the pauses of the strife around the walls of Troy, he would seek out, comforting his wife with tender words and dandling the young child in his strong hands. Such was Hector, greatest of the Trojans.

Of the Greeks, the greatest in strength and terrible might of battle was Achilles, son of Peleus and the divine Thetis. A mightier warrior was he even than Hector himself, and no man unaided of the gods might fight against him and live.

And when Troy had been besieged for nine long years, and countless brave warriors had fallen on either side, these two champions of the Greek and Trojan hosts met face to face. And this is how they came to fight and how they fared.

Achilles, in high dudgeon with King Agamemnon over what he deemed an unfair division of spoil, had suddenly withdrawn to his tent and left the rest to fight on without his aid. But his young comrade in arms and dearest friend, Patroclus, the son of Menoetius, he at length permitted to return to the fight, arming him with his own armor. But him Hector slew, stripping off from his body the armor of Achilles and donning it himself.

Now, when Achilles heard that Patroclus was dead, his grief was so terrible that he could scarce be held from laying hands on himself. But his wrath was stronger than his grief, and he swore to slay the slayer of his friend. Therefore, forgetting his old quarrel, he hastened to make peace with Agamemnon. And since his own armor had been taken by Hector, his mother, Thetis, prevailed upon Vulcan, the god-smith, to fashion him a corslet, a helmet, and a mighty shield wrought all round with strange devices. Armed in this panoply of the god and towering over the heads of all the Greeks, he strode shouting into the fray.

And indeed the Greeks needed all the help that he could bring; for Hector had driven them down to their very ships, and scarcely had they been able to rescue the body of Patroclus. And now Hector, seeing Achilles, would have rushed to meet him, had not Apollo forbade. But the youngest and dearest of Priam's fifty sons, dying to flesh his maiden sword (for the fond father had forbidden him to fight), sprang forward in his brother's place, and fell transfixed at the first encounter; no match, rash boy, for the divine Achilles. At this sight, not Apollo himself could restrain the wrath of Hector, who bounded over the plain and, bestriding his brother's corpse, hurled his spear. But though his aim was true, Minerva turned the spear aside, and when Achilles charged, Hector too was snatched away by his guardian Apollo.

But upon the other Trojans Achilles fell with terrible fury. Many he drove into the river Scamander that flowed by the walls of Troy, slaying them, as a great dolphin of the sea might devour the small fishes; and twelve Trojans he took alive that he might sacrifice them at the funeral of his friend Patroclus. None indeed could stand before him, and those who escaped his fury fled back to the city, where Priam had ordered the gate to be opened to receive the fugitives.

At last all were within the walls save only Hector, who stood by the Scæan gate alone. Achilles, afar on the plain, was hotly pursuing one whom he believed to be the Trojan Agenor, whose shape, however, Apollo had taken to draw Achilles from the walls. Now, however, the son of Peleus discovered his mistake, and, turning, he came raging across the plain in his glittering armor towards the Scæan gate. And Hector stood and waited for him there.

While he waited, King Priam, his old father, many of whose sons Achilles had already slain, came out and entreated him to enter the city. And his mother Hecuba implored him, in pity for her gray hairs not to give battle to Achilles, but to enter while there was yet time.

But Hector was deaf to all prayers. It was foolhardiness in not ordering an earlier retreat that had brought dire misery upon the Trojans, and should he enter the city to meet the reproaches of all? No; better stay there single-handed, either to slay Achilles or by him be honourably slain.

While he thus pondered Achilles was upon him, brandishing a great spear, his armor flashing like fire. And so terrible was the aspect of this warrior, larger than mortal and clad in the mail of Vulcan, that, for the first time, the heart of even Hector failed, and he turned and fled. Fast he fled, and, as a hawk chases a dove, Achilles pursued. Past the watch-tower they ran, along the wagon-road about the walls, and on to the twofold spring of Scamander. Thrice they ran round the city, and in Olympus the high gods looked down, and the heart of Jupiter himself was moved to pity, and he cried to the other gods: 'Shall we save Hector, or let him fall by the hand of Achilles?'

Then Minerva answered: 'Wilt thou, great sire, rescue a man whom Fate has appointed to die? This thing is not well pleasing in our eyes.'

Jupiter answered: 'Fain would I have it otherwise, but it shall be as thou wilt.'

Then Minerva came down swiftly from Olympus to aid Achilles. Nevertheless, Apollo was already with the two putting strength and swiftness into the limbs of Hector, who sought always the shelter of the towers, hoping that those who stood upon them might defend him with their spears; but always Achilles would force him outward, driving him towards the plain.

Now, for the fourth time, Achilles the pursuer and Hector the pursued had reached the springs of Scamander, and Jupiter held out the scales of doom, weighing the fates of the two men. And the scale of Hector sank, and Apollo left him.

Then Minerva, cruelly deceiving, bethought her by evil guile to end the fray, and took on the shape of Hector's brother Deiphobus, saying, 'Come, my brother, let us make a stand against Achilles and flee from him no more.'

And Hector, suspecting no guile, answered gratefully: 'O, ever dearest of all my brothers, dearer still art thou now to me, for thou alone hast ventured to stand by my side in this perilous hour.'

Then, as Achilles came upon them, Hector cried with a strong voice:

'Great Achilles, I fear thee now no more. Only let this be agreed between us: that whichever of us shall fall, his body shall not be dishonored, but shall be given back for burial rites.'

But Achilles scowled and answered: 'No covenant be there between thee and me. Fight! for the time is come to pay the penalty for all my comrades whom thou hast slain.'

Thus speaking, he hurled his spear, but Hector bowed his head and the weapon passed, and touched him not. And Hector wot not that Minerva had caught it as it flew and restored it to Achilles' hand. Confident of victory, he hurled his spear, striking the very middle of Achilles' shield. But the handiwork of Vulcan was proof even against the spear of Hector. And Hector, perceiving this, turned to Deiphobus for another spear. But no Deiphobus was there. Then, indeed, Hector knew that Minerva had deceived him, and that he stood there godforsaken, a doomed man. He knew he must perish; but he resolved to perish gloriously.

Drawing, therefore, his great sword, he rushed upon Achilles. But ere he could strike a blow the spear of Achilles pierced him where the neck joins the shoulder, and Hector fell.

And Achilles, triumphing over him, cried aloud: 'Slayer of Patroclus, despoiler of his arms, the dogs and vultures shall devour thy carcase!'

But the dying Hector answered: 'Nay, great Achilles, let not this shame be. Take rather the ransom that my parents shall bring thee, and suffer me to be buried in Troy.'

For he knew that while his body remained unburied his spirit would know no rest in the lower world.

But Achilles, savage as a wild beast, cried to him: 'No ransom shall buy back thy body; no, nor shall thy weight in gold save thy flesh from the dogs.'

Hector answered with his last breath: 'Oh, heart of iron! But on thee, too,

shall fall vengeance, in that day when Paris and Apollo shall slay thee by the Scæan gate.'

With this dying curse the spirit of Hector fled.

Then Achilles, stripping off the armor of Patroclus, pierced the ankle bones of the dead man, binding them with thongs to the chariot, and letting the head that was once so fair drag in the dust. Thus dragged he Hector to the ships. And Andromache, beholding this from the city wall, swooned as one dead.

And on each following day Achilles dragged the body of Hector round the bier of Patroclus. Yet was it not in any way defiled, for Venus and Apollo preserved it in all its beauty as when Hector was alive.

At last Priam rose up, and, taking with him a great ransom, drove unscathed to the Grecian camp (for Mercury was his guide), and, falling on his knees and kissing the murderous hands of Achilles, besought him to restore the body of Hector. And Achilles, touched with ruth by the old man's tears and prayers, consented, and himself lifted the body into the litter.

So Priam bore back his dead son to Troy. And they who so often had gone forth to hail Hector returning victorious from the field, now flocked round to greet him with tears. The first to wail over him was Andromache, his wife. Then came Hecuba, his mother. Last of all came Helen, who cried: 'Never did I hear thee utter one bitter word. And if any spake harshly to me, thou would'st check them with thy kind and gentle words. Therefore I weep for thee, I, friendless now in all Troy.'

On the tenth day after this the Trojans burned the body of Hector on a great pile, quenching the embers with wine. And the ashes they laid in a golden chest and wrapped it in purple robes and laid it in mother earth, and over it they raised a mighty cairn.

Thus did men bury Hector, captain of the hosts of Troy.

The Wooden Horse

F. Storr

hrice three years had passed, and it seemed to the Greek leaders that they were no nearer the capture of Troy than when they had first landed in the Troad, a gallant company, fired with hope and the promise of an easy victory. Since then the tide of battle had ebbed and flowed with alternate fortunes. Many a Trojan chieftain had fallen, but no breach had been made in the walls, and they seemed to have gained no painful inch. There was mutiny in the Grecian host, and they clamored to be led home again.

But the crafty Ulysses summoned the mutineers to an assembly, and addressed them in honeyed words: 'My friends,' he said, 'we have all endured hardships, I no less than you. Have patience yet a while. Have we labored for nothing these nine weary years? Will ye leave your quarry when it is at the last gasp? Know ye not the prophecy of Calchas, that in the tenth year, and not before, Troy was destined to fall? Trust to me, for to me the gods have revealed a cunning stratagem whereby of a surety ye shall take and sack the city.' Thus Ulysses persuaded them to stay on, for not only was he the most persuasive of orators, but none had ever known his wisdom at fault.

Left: A 16th-century illustration based on Virgil's epic poem 'Aeneid', printed by Johannes Grüninger. Pandemonium is breaking out around the Wooden Horse in the town of Troy.

Nor had they long to wait for the fulfilment of his promise. The very next day came an order that all should strike their tents and embark forthwith. Before night-fall the whole host had gathered on the shore; the beached ships had been hauled down, and away they sailed. Westward they sailed, but not to Greece. No sooner were they to the leeward of a small rocky island in the offing then they tacked, and came to anchor in a sandy cove well hidden from the mainland by jutting cliffs.

Great was the rejoicing in Troy town at their departure. The gates were flung wide open, and the townsfolk, so long pent up within the walls, streamed out as for a holiday, to visit the battlefield and view the spots where so many famous forays and single combats had taken place. But of all the sights that attracted the crowd, the most popular was a strange object that no one had observed before. It was a Wooden Horse on rollers, in build and shape not unlike one of those toys that children love to drag about by a string; but this horse was huge as a mountain, and ribbed with solid beams of fir. Long and eagerly they debated for what purpose it had been built, and why the Greeks had left it behind them. Some were for burning it as an uncanny thing that could bode them no good. Others cried: ''Tis a votive offering to Minerva; let us drag it within the walls and set it up in the citadel as a memorial of our deliverance.'

While this dispute was hotly raging, Laocoön, in his priestly robes, rushed into the throng. 'Fools,' he cried, 'will ye let yourselves be cheated? Are ye so slow of heart as not to detect Greek subtlety or the guile of Ulysses? The Greeks, I tell you, have not gone, and either this Horse is an engine of war to overtop our battlements, or Greek warriors are hidden in its womb.' And as he spoke he hurled a mighty spear against the Horse, and the cavernous depths reverberated with the shock, and from within there came a rattle as of clashing arms. But the multitude heeded not the warning, for fate had sealed their ears.

While this was going on outside the walls, there was scarcely less excitement in the city. Certain shepherds had surprised a young Greek, and were dragging their captive before King Priam, with a hooting and jeering crowd at their heels. 'Woe is me!' cried the youth as he came into the king's presence; 'have I escaped

from the Greeks, my bitter foes who sought my life, only to fall among Trojans from whom I can expect no mercy?' But the king bade him fear nothing, and tell his tale.

It was an artful tale concocted for him by Ulysses, how to the Greeks, desirous of sailing home and detained by contrary winds, an oracle had come—'To speed you here a virgin maid was slain, Blood must be spilt to speed you home again'— how he had been pointed out by Calchas as the destined victim, and had escaped even as he was being led in bonds to the altar.

His tattered dress and bleeding wrists bore out this plausible tale. The king ordered his captors to free him from his manacles, and assuring the prisoner that he need fear nothing, begged him to tell them what was the design of the Greeks in building and leaving behind them the Wooden Horse.

Sinon (for that was the name that the pretended deserter took) first invoked on his head the direst curses if he failed to reveal to his deliverers the whole truth, and then repeated the lesson in which his cunning master Ulysses had drilled him. 'You must know,' he said, 'that all the hopes of Greece lay in the favor and protection of their patron goddess, Minerva. But the wrath of the goddess was kindled against the host, for the son of Tydeus, at the prompting of Ulysses—that godless knave who sticks at no crime—had invaded her shrine, slain her custodians, and snatched therefrom the Palladium, the sacred image of the goddess, deeming it a charm that would bring them certain victory. And the goddess showed by visible signs her displeasure. In each encounter our forces were routed; around the carven image now set up in the camp lightnings played, and thrice amid the lightning and thunder the goddess herself was seen with spear at rest and flashing targe. And Calchas, of whom we sought counsel in our terror, bade us sail back to Argos, and when in her great temple we had shriven us, with happier auspices renew the fray; but first in her honor we must erect a Wooden Horse, so huge that it could not pass your gates or be brought within your walls. Moreover, Calchas told us that if any man were rash enough to lay sacrilegious hands on the votive Horse, he would straightway be smitten by the vengeful goddess!'

And lo! even as he spoke a strange portent was seen to confirm his words.

The Trojans Pull the Wooden Horse into the City *by Giulio di Antonio Bonasone and Francesco Primaticcio.*

Laocoön, the high priest of Neptune—he who had hurled his spear at the Wooden Horse—was sacrificing to the sea god a mighty bull at the altar, when far away in the offing two leviathans of the deep were seen approaching from Tenedos. They looked like battleships as they plowed the waves, but as they drew nearer you could mark the blood-beclotted mane and ravenous jaws of the sea-serpent, while behind lay floating many a rood coil upon coil like some huge boa-constrictor's.

The crowd fled in terror, but the sea-serpents passed through the midst and made straight for the altar of Neptune. First they coiled themselves round the two sons of Laocoön, who were ministering to their father as he sacrificed, and squeezed the life out of the miserable boys. Then, as Laocoön rushed to release his sons and sought to pierce the scaly monsters with his sacrificial knife, they wound their folds twice about his middle and twice about his neck, and high above his head they towered with blood-shot eyes and triple-forked tongues. And Laocoön, like the bull he had immolated at the altar, bellowed aloud in his dying agony. But the sea-serpents slowly unwound themselves and glided out of sight beneath the pediment of Diana's statue.

This seemed to all a sign from heaven to confirm what Sinon had told them. No more doubt was possible, and a universal clamor arose: 'To the Horse! to the Horse!' Out rushed the crowd; ropes were fastened to its neck and legs, and soon half the city was tugging at them might and main, while the sappers made a breach in the walls to let it in, and by help of levers and pulleys it mounted the steep escarpment, and as it passed down the street a joyous troop of boys and girls followed, struggling to take hold of the taut ropes and chanting snatches of pæans and songs of victory.

Thus did the gods send on the Trojans a strong delusion that they should believe a lying tale; and what ten long campaigns and a thousand brass-beaked ships, what all the might of Agamemnon, king of men, and the prowess of Achilles, goddess-born, had failed to accomplish, was brought to pass by the guile and craft of one man.

DICTYS et DARES,

cum Notis
ANNÆ DACERIÆ
et Variorum
integris.

The Sack of Troy

F. Storr

The Wooden Horse was set up in the citadel, and after a night of feasting and carousal, the Trojan warriors had all retired to rest from their labors, and deep slumber sealed their weary eyes, for now they feared no nightly alarms, no réveillé before break of day.

But with night-fall the Greek fleet at Tenedos had loosed their moorings, and were making full sail for the Trojan shore.

When all slept the traitor Sinon slipped out from the turret of the palace where the king had assigned him a lodging, and crouching in the shadow climbed the hill of the citadel. There stood the Wooden Horse, weird and ghostly in the moonlight, not a sentinel to guard it. Leaning on the parapet he watched the white sails of the fleet as it sped landward, and soon he saw the preconcerted signal—a flaming torch at the masthead of the admiral ship. Then by the ropes still left hanging from the Horse's neck, he swarmed up and opened a secret panel in the side. One by one the mailed warriors let themselves down: first Ulysses, the arch-plotter, then Neoptolemus, Achilles' son, Menelaus, Epeos, the architect of the Horse, and other chieftains too many to name. They made straight for the city gates, and despatching the sentinels before any had time to give the alarm, let in

Left: The frontispiece of Dictys, Dares and Joseph of Exeter *(1702) depicts Venus and Cupid witnessing the destruction of Troy.*

195

the serried battalions who were waiting outside.

Like the rest of the Trojan warriors Æneas slept, but his sleep was disturbed by a vision of the night. At his bedside stood a ghostly form. His visage was marred, his locks and beard were clotted with gouts of blood, his breast was slashed and scarred, and his feet were pierced and livid with the marks of cords. Yet, though thus defaced and maimed, Æneas knew at once the godlike Hector, and cried to him, 'Light of Troy, our country's hope and stay, thou com'st much looked for. Where hast thou tarried this long, long while? Why is thy visage thus marred? What mean those hideous scars?'

The ghost answered nothing but gazed down on Æneas with sad, lack-luster eyes. Only as it vanished it spoke. 'Fly, goddess-born; save thyself from the flames. The foe is within the gates. Troy topples to its fall. Could faith and courage have availed, this right hand had saved it. To thee Troy now commends her household gods. Take them with thee in thy flight, and with them to guide and guard thee found beyond the seas a new and mightier Troy.'

The ghost had vanished; but when Æneas woke he found at his bedside the household gods and the fillets of Vesta and her fire that is never quenched.

From without there came a confused sound of hurrying feet, the tramp of armed men, the clash of arms, and mingled shouts and groans. He climbed to the roof to see what it all meant. Volumes of smoke like a mountain torrent were rolling over the city, and from the murk there leapt tongues of flame. In desperate haste he donned his arms and went forth, bewildered and not knowing which way to turn. At his threshold he met Panthus, high priest of Apollo and custodian of the citadel, and asked him what was happening.

'All is over,' cried the priest; 'the gods have deserted us; Greece has triumphed; Troy is no more—a name, a city of the past.'

Horror-stricken but undeterred, Æneas hurried on to where the fray seemed the hottest, and gathering round him some score of trusty comrades, he thus addressed them: 'Friends and brothers in arms, all is not lost; let us take courage from despair, and at worst die like men with our breasts to the foe.'

They all rushed into the mellay, and at first fortune favored the brave.

Androgeus, the captain of a picked corps of Greeks, hailed them; and mistaking them in the darkness for fellow-countrymen, twitted them on their tardiness, and bade them hurry on to share in the loot. Too late he perceived his mistake. Before they had time to unsheath a sword or unbuckle a shield, Æneas and his comrades were on them and not one escaped.

Flushed with their first success, Coroebus, one of the forlorn hope, cried: 'Hark ye, comrades, I have bethought me of a glorious stratagem; let us exchange arms and scutcheons with our dead foemen. All is fair in war.' No sooner said than done; and great was the havoc they wrought at the first by this disguise, but in the end it cost them dear.

As they passed by the temple of Minerva they were arrested by a piteous spectacle. Cassandra, the prophetic maid, was being dragged from the altar by the rude soldiery, her hair disheveled, her arms pinioned, and her eyes upturned to heaven. Coroebus' high spirit could not brook the sight, and he hurled himself on the ruffians, the rest following his lead. Though outnumbered they held, and more than held, their own, till from the pinnacles of the temple a whole battery of rocks and missiles rained down on their devoted heads. Their disguise had too well deceived the defenders of the temple, and soon the assailants were reinforced by the main body of the Greeks, with Ajax and the two Atridæ at their head, who soon penetrated their disguise. Coroebus was the first to fall; then Ripeus, the justest ruler in all Troy; nor did his gray hairs and the fillet of Apollo that he wore save Panthus from the common fate.

Æneas, with two wounded comrades, all that was left of that devoted band, made his way to the palace of Priam, where it looked as if the whole Greek force had gathered. Part were working battering-rams against the solid masonry, others planting scaling ladders against the walls, up which the boldest, with shields held high above their heads, were already swarming, while the garrison hurled down on them stones, tiles, whatever came to hand; even the gilded beams of the royal chambers.

At the rear of the palace was a postern gate leading to a covered passage that connected the house of Hector and Andromache with the palace. By this Æneas entered and climbed to a watch-tower that commanded the whole city, the plain with the Greek encampments, and beyond, the sea, now studded with ships. At his bidding the guards set to work, and soon, with axes and crow-bars, they had loosened the foundations of the turret. It tottered, it toppled, and fell with a mighty crash, burying hundreds of the besiegers beneath its ruins. But what were they among so many?

At the main entrance of the palace stood Neoptolemus in his glittering armor, like a snake who has lost its winter weeds, and snatching a double-headed ax from a common soldier, he battered in the panels and wrenched the massive door from its brass hinges. Through the long corridors and gilded ante-chambers, like a river that has burst its dam, the flood of armed Greeks swept on, and from the inner chambers there came a long-drawn wail of women's voices that shivered to the golden stars. On came Neoptolemus, sweeping before him the feeble palace guards. The cedarn doors gave way like match-wood, and there, huddled on the floor or clinging to the pillars of the tapestried chamber, he beheld, like sheep led to the slaughter, the queen and the princesses, the fifty daughters and fifty daughters-in-law of King Priam. But where was Priam the while?

In the center of the palace was a court open to the sky, and in the center of the court was a great altar over-shadowed by an immemorial bay-tree. Hither Hecuba and her kinswomen had fled for refuge when the rabble of soldiers burst in on them, and in the court she espied her aged husband girt in armor that ill-fitted his shrunken limbs, and she called to him, 'What madness hath seized thee thus to rush to certain death? Hector himself could not save us now; what can thy feeble arms avail? Take sanctuary with us. Either this altar shall protect us or here we shall all perish together!'

The feeble old king yielded to his wife's entreaties, but hardly had he reached the altar when he beheld Polites, the child of his old age, whom he loved most now Hector was dead, limping towards them like a wounded hare, and close behind him in hot pursuit Neoptolemus with outstretched lance; and a moment after the son fell transfixed at his father's feet. 'Wretch,' he cried, beside himself with righteous wrath, 'more fell than dire Achilles! He gave me back my son's

198

corpse, but thou hast stained my gray hairs and god's altar with a son's blood.' He spake, and hurled at Neoptolemus with nerveless arm a spear that scarce had force to pierce the outmost fold of the targe.

With a scornful laugh Neoptolemus turned on him, and dragged him by his long white beard from the altar. 'Die, old dotard,' he cried, 'and in the shades be sure thou tell my sire Achilles what a degenerate son is his.' So saying, he drove his sword to the old king's heart.

'Such was the end of Priam, such his fate, To see in death his house all desolate, And Troy, whom erst a hundred states obeyed, A heap of blackened stones in ruin laid. A headless corpse washed by the salt sea tide, Not e'en a stone to show where Priam died.'

The Death of Ajax, *from Ovid's 'Metamorphoses', by Antonio Tempesta. Ajax killed himself by falling on his own sword.*

The Death of Ajax

F. Storr

Of all the Greek knights who fought against Troy the boldest and most chivalrous was Ajax, son of Telamon. But his fiery temper oft proved his bane, and in the end it led him to ruin and death.

When Achilles died he left his arms to be awarded by the captains of the host to him whom they should pronounce the bravest of the Greeks, and the prize fell to Ulysses.

Ajax took this award in high dudgeon, and, knowing himself the better man, affirmed that this judgment could have been procured only by fraud and corruption, and swore that he would be avenged of his crafty rival. He challenged his enemy to single combat, but Ulysses was too wary to risk his life against such a swordsman, and the chiefs who heard of the quarrel interfered, saying that Greek must not take the blood of Greek. Thus balked, Ajax raged more furiously, and swore that if Ulysses would not fight he would slay him in his tent.

So Ulysses went about in fear of his life, and he appealed to his patron goddess to defend him. Minerva heard his prayer, and promised her favourite warrior that he should suffer no harm. She kept her word by sending on Ajax a strong delusion, whereby in his frenzy he mistook beasts for men.

The Greeks found the herds and flocks that had been taken in raids, and were kept in pound as a common stock to feed the army, hacked and hewn in the night, as though a mountain lion had been ravaging them; and they suspected Ajax,

whose strange behavior none could fail to notice, as the offender, but they had no certain proof, and Ulysses, the man of many wiles, was by common consent deputed to search into the matter.

So the next night he stole forth from the camp alone, and in the early light of dawn he espied a solitary figure hurrying over the plain, and he followed the trail like a bloodhound till it led him to the tent of Ajax.

He paused uncertain, for he dared not venture farther, and was about to return and report to the commanders what he had seen, when he heard a voice saying, 'Ulysses, what dost thou here?' and he knew it could be none other than the voice of his own goddess Minerva.

He told her the case and craved her aid in his perplexity, and the goddess gently upbraided him. 'Thou wert no coward soul, Ulysses, when I chose thee as my favoured knight, and now dost thou fear a single unarmed man, and one by me bereft of his wits?' And Ulysses answered, 'Goddess, I am no coward, but the bravest may quail before a raving madman.' But Minerva replied, 'Be of good heart, and trust as ever to me. Lo, I will show thee a sight whereon thou mayst glut thine eyes.' Thereupon she opened the flap of the tent, and within stood Ajax, wild and haggard, his hands dripping with gore, and all around him were sheep and oxen, some beheaded, some ripped up, and some horribly mutilated—a very shambles. At the moment Ajax was belaboring a huge ram that he had strapped up to a pillar of the tent, and, as each blow of the double thong descended he shouted, 'Take that, Ulysses; that's for thy knavery, that for thy villainy, that for thy lies, thou white-livered rogue.' Ulysses could not but smile as he saw himself scourged and cursed in effigy, but he was touched by a thought of human infirmity and the ruin of a noble soul, and he prayed the goddess to avert from him such a calamity.

In the women's tent hard by sat Tecmessa, the captive wife of Ajax, weeping and wringing her hands. His tender love had made her forget her desolate home and slaughtered brethren, and she had borne him a son, the pride and joy of both parents. But ever since he had lost the prize for bravery she had noted a growing estrangement. He avoided her, meeting her advances with cold looks, and the night before, when she asked him why he was girding on his armor at that hour, he had answered her, 'Silence, woman; women should be seen, not heard.' And then he had gone forth and returned with these beeves and sheep that he was now hacking to pieces like a madman. Their boy she had sent away with his nurse to be out of harm's way, and she sat cowering in her tent.

As she sat, half dazed with grief and watching, she heard her name called. Trembling she arose and met her lord at the tent door. Again he called her, but now his voice was tender and low, and he gazed at her with a look of mingled pity and love. And her heart rejoiced, for she saw that his madness had passed, that her old Ajax was restored to her. 'Tecmessa,' he asked, 'where is our boy?' And Tecmessa hastened and brought back their child Eurysaces. Ajax took him from his nurse's arms, and he kissed the innocent brow and spoke: 'My boy, may thy lot in life be happier than thy father's; but in all else be like unto me, and thou shalt prove no base man.' Then he passed with Tecmessa into her tent, and flung himself down on the bed and lay there as a sick man who has scarce recovered from a grievous illness. She would fain have ministered to him, but he refused all meat and drink, and lay for long hours holding her hand. Ever and anon he would ask, 'Where is Teucer? Is not Teucer returned? I would fain speak with my brother.'

As the sun was setting he rose from his bed and took his sword, telling his wife that he must leave her for a while, but would soon return. She, fearing another fit of madness, sought with tears to detain him, but he gently put her aside and told her what his errand was. He must needs go to the sea-baths, and with pure ablution wash away his stains and make him clean. And he gently unwound her clinging arms, closed her lips with a kiss, and went on his way.

When he reached the river, he drew his sword from the scabbard and planted it firm in earth. 'Fatal blade,' he cried, 'once the sword of Hector, then a foeman's gift to his arch-enemy, a bane to each who owned thee; but to me, thy last master, a friend at need. I have had my day, and for me there is living none. My sword, go with me to the shades.' Therewith he hurled himself upon the naked steel and gave up the ghost.

Fishermen dragging their nets at dawn found the body, and brought it back to camp. Teucer, warned by the seer Calchas that unless his brother could be kept within doors for that day some dread calamity awaited him, had hurried to warn and save him from his doom; but as he reached the tent he was met by the bearers bringing home his brother's corpse.

There was mourning in the Grecian camp. A great man had fallen that day; for his brief madness the gods alone were to blame; and his long years of service, his gallant deeds, his fearless courage, his noble generosity, were alone remembered. So they decreed for him a public funeral with all the pomp and ceremony that befitted a great chieftain.

Already they had begun to raise a huge funeral pile and to deck the sacrificial altar, when Menelaus, who shared with Agamemnon the chief command, rode up in hot haste to forbid the public burial. 'No man,' he declared, 'who had defied his authority and done such injury to the common cause should be honored.' But Ulysses with a soft answer turned away his wrath: 'True, he hath sinned against thee, O king, and in life he hated me, but death is the great atoner. Honor the fearless knight. Let his ashes rest in peace.'

A 16th-century engraving by Agostino Carracci after a painting by Federico Barocci showing Æneas and his family fleeing in haste from the flames of Troy.

The Flight of Aeneas from Troy

F. Storr

Æneas, standing on the battlements of the palace, had beheld the heartrending scene of Troy's destruction, horror-stricken and unable to help. All his comrades were dead or had fled, and he alone was left. As he looked on Priam's bleeding corpse the face of his own father Anchises, as old and as defenseless, flashed across his fancy, and he saw in vision his desolate home, his wife Creusa, and Iulus clinging to his mother's knees.

He stole out of the palace by the same covered way that had let him in, and was hurrying home when he passed the shrine of Vesta, and cowering behind the altar, by the glare of the conflagration that still raged, he espied Helen, the prime cause of all their woes. His soul burned with righteous indignation. 'What,' he cried to himself, 'shall this cursed woman, the bane both of Greece and of Troy, shall she alone escape scot-free; shall she return to Greece a crowned queen with our captive sons and daughters in her train? No,' he cried, as he drew his sword; 'to slay a woman is no knightly deed, but men will approve me as the minister of God's vengeance.'

But of a sudden, effulgent in the heavens like her own star, he beheld his goddess-mother, and she laid a hand on his outstretched arm in act to strike, and whispered in his ear: 'My son, why this empty rage? Dost thou forget thy mother and all her care for thee and thine? Think of thine aged sire, thy loving wife, thy little son. But for me they had all perished by the sword and flames. 'Tis not Paris, 'tis not that Spartan woman who hath wrought this ruin, but the gods who were leagued against Troy. Lo, I will take the scales from thine eyes, and for a moment thou shalt behold as one of themselves the immortals at work. Look yonder, where walls and watch-towers are crashing down, as though upheaved by an earthquake, Neptune is up-prizing with his dread trident the walls that he helped to build. There at the Scæan gates stands Juno in full mail crying Havoc! and hounding on the laggard Greeks. Look backward at the citadel; above it towers Minerva, wrapt in a storm-cloud, and flashing her Gorgon shield. Nay more, on far Olympus (but this thou canst not see) the Almighty Father is heartening those gods who are banded for the ruin of Troy. Save thyself, my son, while yet there is time. Let adverse gods rage; I, thy mother, will never leave thee nor forsake thee.'

The goddess vanished, and as by a flash of lightning he beheld for an instant the grim visages of the Powers of Darkness.

Under the tutelage of Venus, Æneas reached his home without adventure and found all safe, as she had promised. He was preparing for his flight to the neighboring hills when an unforeseen impediment arose. No persuasions would induce Anchises to accompany him. 'Ye are young and lusty,' cried his sire, 'fly for your lives and leave me, a poor old man tottering on the brink of the grave. All I ask is that ye repeat over me the ritual for the dead. The Greeks, when they find me, will grant me sepulture.'

No prayers or arguments could move the old man from his obstinate resolution, and Æneas, in desperation, was again girding on his armor, choosing to perish with wife and child in single-handed fight rather than desert his aged parent, when a sign from heaven was given that first amazed and then filled all hearts with joy. On the head of the child Iulus there appeared a tongue of fire that spread among his curly locks, and played round his smooth brow, crowning him like the aureole of a saint. In horror his mother sought to extinguish the flames, but the water she poured made them only burn the brighter. But Anchises knew the heavenly sign, and with uplifted palms he prayed that Jupiter would confirm his good will by some more certain augury. And straightway on the left (the lucky side) a clap of thunder was heard, and from the zenith there fell a meteor that left a long trail of light as it fell to earth on the pine-clad slopes of Mount Ida.

Then at last Anchises yielded, and Æneas, stooping down, lifted the old man on his shoulder. By his side, holding his right hand, was Iulus, bravely trying to keep pace with his father's long strides, and last came Creusa, with a train of household slaves. As trysting-place, in case they should get separated in the crowd and confusion, Æneas assigned to them a deserted shrine of Vesta, near to a solitary cypress tree which would serve them as a landmark. They were well on their way, and had escaped the worst perils, when Anchises cried out, 'Hist! I hear the tramp of armed men, and see the glint of armor.' And Æneas, who never before had quailed in the storm of battle, now trembled like an aspen leaf, and snatching up the boy he ran for his life, and never drew breath till he had reached the deserted shrine. Then he looked back, and to his horror Creusa was nowhere to be seen.

Had she missed the road, or had she fainted on the way? He questioned his household who had by now arrived, but none had seen their mistress since they left the city. Again he donned his arms and rushed back by the way he had come. Not a trace of his wife could he find. He re-entered the city by the same gate, and rethreaded the same dark alleys. He sought his home, but it was now a mass of smoldering ruins. As a last desperate hope he sought the Royal Treasure House, if haply she might there have found a hiding-place, but at the entrance stood Phoenix and Ulysses, the captains told off to guard the loot. There lay, piled in a confused heap, all the wealth of Troy that the flames had not consumed—purple robes, coverlets and tapestries, armlets and anklets of wrought gold, jeweled drinking-bowls, and the sacred vessels from the temples.

Reckless of the risks he ran he shouted from street to street, 'Creusa! Creusa!' when at last a familiar voice replied, and before him he saw, not, alas! Creusa,

but her ghost, larger than human, gazing down on him with eyes of infinite pity. 'Why,' it whispered, 'this wild grief? Nothing, dear lord, is here for tears. 'Twas not the will of heaven that I should share thy wanderings and toils. Be of good heart. In the far west, so fate ordains, where Tiber rolls his yellow tide, thou shalt found a new empire and espouse a princess of the land. Nor need'st thou pity my less fortunate lot. I have known all the joys of married bliss, and my body shall rest in the soil that gave me birth. No proud Greek will boast that he bears home in his captive train her who was the wife of Æneas, the daughter-in-law of Venus. And now, fare thee well. Forget not our sweet child, and her who bore him.'

'Thrice he essayed with arms outstretched to clasp Her shade, and thrice it slipped from his fond grasp, Like frolic airs that o'er a still lake play, Or dreams that vanish at the break of day.'

Aeneas and Dido

V.C. Turnbull

Hardly less renowned than the wanderings of crafty Ulysses, after the fall of Troy, are those of pious Æneas, the Trojan. Many were his adventures and heavy his losses, for he was pursued evermore by the hatred of Juno, who detested all Trojans, and but for the protecting care of his mother Venus he must have perished.

On the Sicilian shore he had lost his aged father, Anchises, and Æneas mourned his good old sire, whom he had carried on his shoulders from burning Troy.

Thence he set sail with his son Iulus to Italy. But when they had put forth to sea, Juno smote them with a terrible storm, so that Æneas lost all but seven ships of his fleet and not a few of his comrades perished. He himself, with his son Iulus and his friend Achates, was driven out of his course and carried to the shores of Libya. Here the Trojans disembarked and thankfully rested their brine-drenched limbs on the beach. And when they had feasted off the grain brought from their ships, and the venison procured for them by their captain's bow, Æneas, taking with him only Achates, set forth to survey this unexplored country.

On their way through a forest they met a fair maid in the garb of a huntress, and of her they inquired what land this might be and who dwelt therein. She told them they had come to the land and city of Carthage, over which ruled the Tyrian Queen Dido. She told them, moreover, that the Queen had once ruled in Tyre, the consort of Sichæus, a Phoenician prince, and that when her lord had been murdered by his cruel brother Pygmalion, she had fled to Libya, where even now she was rearing the stately city of Carthage. And she bade them seek the Queen and throw themselves on her protection. Æneas had gazed in wonder and admiration at the maiden, deeming her some nymph of Diana's train, and he was about, on bended knee, to give her thanks when she turned on him a parting glance. And lo! the goddess stood revealed, radiant in celestial beauty; and as he recognized his mother, she had vanished from his sight.

Cheered by this vision, Æneas and Achates pressed forward, and, that none might molest them, Venus wrapped them in a thick mist. Emerging from the forest they climbed a hill overlooking the city of Carthage, where skilled workmen were on all sides busied rearing stately buildings. In the midst of the city, with a flight of marble stairs and surrounded by a grove of trees, stood a temple to Juno, its gates of brass glittering in the morning sun. And Æneas, drawing near, marveled to find the walls of this temple painted with pictures of the Trojan War—aye, and himself he saw portrayed fighting against the Grecian leaders.

Whilst Æneas and Achates were still gazing, Queen Dido drew near with a great retinue of maidens and youths. She seated herself on a throne under the dome of the temple, for here it was her custom to deal justice and apportion work to her subjects, urging forward with cheerful words the building of her city. Among the first to appear before the Queen, Æneas and Achates saw with astonishment certain of their own friends—Ilioneus, Antheus, Sergestus, and Cloanthus, whom they had supposed to have been drowned in the storm. These, coming before Dido, told her of their sufferings and entreated her protection in that strange country.

'We had for our king Æneas,' said Ilioneus, the spokesman, 'than whom none was more pious and brave. If he yet lives we shall not despair, neither shalt thou, O Queen, repent thee of thy hospitality.'

Queen Dido answered the Trojans graciously, promising them all they asked and more.

'And would,' she added, 'that your prince Æneas too were here! But my messengers shall search the Libyan coasts, and if he has been cast ashore he shall be found.'

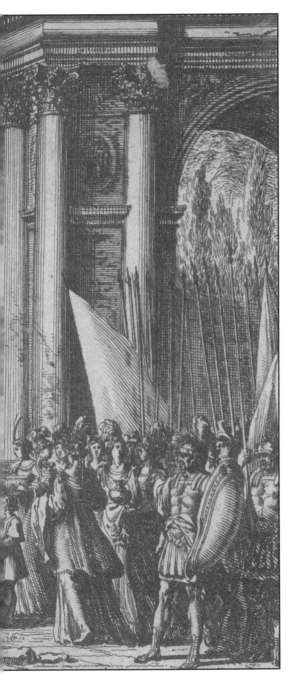

Even as she spoke, the mist that hid Æneas and Achates suddenly parted, and Æneas stood forth in the bright light like a god; and, joyfully embracing his friends, poured out his gratitude to Dido.

The voice of the Queen was even gentler than before as she replied: 'I too have been tossed by fortune on the high seas; I too came to these shores a stranger. What sorrow was myself have known, and learnt to melt at others' woe.'

Then Dido bade Æneas and Achates to a feast in her palace, and to their followers on the shore she sent bulls, lambs, and wine to provide a banquet. Æneas also despatched Achates to the beach to bring therefrom the young Iulus, and with him presents for the Queen— a mantle stiff with gold, a scepter, a necklace of pearls, and a crown set with double rows of gems and gold.

The gifts made and his son embraced, Æneas was led into the great hall of the palace, where the guests reclined on purple couches. In the midst Queen

Æneas's Farewell to Dido by Jean Le Pautre.
The unhappy event brought despair and
thoughts of death to Dido, Queen of Carthage.

Dido reclined on a golden couch under a rich canopy, and beside her lay the boy Iulus. So they feasted and were merry, and after the banquet Dido pledged her guest in a loving cup and invited him to tell her all that had befallen him since the fall of Troy.

And he told her the long tale of his perils by land and sea, and of the shipwreck which had landed him upon the hospitable shores of Carthage.

And, as Queen Dido listened, the memory of her dead husband Sichæus was no longer first in her thoughts, for a great love sprang up for this princely stranger who had endured so much and had followed his star, true to his country and his country's gods. Far into the night the Queen sat listening to the tale, and in the night watches the image of the hero haunted her fevered sleep. At the first dawn she sought her sister Anna, and poured into sympathetic ears the trouble of her heart, confessing with shame her fears lest she should prove faithless to the memory of her dead lord.

But Anna bade her mourn no more for the unheeding dead, wasting her youth and beauty.

'Surely,' said she, 'it was Juno who sent the Trojans to this shore. Think, sister, how your city will flourish, how your kingdom will wax great from such an alliance! How will the Carthaginian glory be advanced by Trojan arms!'

That day she invited her guest to view all the wonders of Carthage. She showed him her rising quays and forts, her palace and its treasures; but even as they conversed her voice would falter, and her silence and blushes were tell-tales and betrayed her growing love. When the evening feast was ended she asked again to hear the tale of Troy, and hung again on his lips.

For the next day, to divert her guest, the Queen ordered a great hunt, and an army of beaters was sent to scour the hills and drive in the game. At dawn a gallant company—all the proud lords of Carthage and the comrades of Æneas—gathered at the palace gates and waited for the Queen. At length she descended from her chamber, robed in gold and purple, and the long cavalcade rode forth headed by Dido and Æneas. When they reached the hills they scattered far and wide in the ardor of the chase, and the royal pair found themselves alone. On a sudden the

heavens were darkened and the rain descended in torrents, and Dido and Æneas betook themselves for shelter to a mountain cave. Thus had Juno planned it, for she hated the Trojans and would have kept Æneas in Carthage. There, in the dark cavern, the Trojan plighted his troth to the Carthaginian Queen. That day the tide of death set in. The heavens thundered and the mountain nymphs wailed over their bridal.

But the triumph of Juno was short-lived, for Jupiter, from his throne on Olympus, beheld the founder of the Roman race forgetful of his destiny and sunk in soft dalliance. He called to him his son Mercury, and bade him bind on his winged sandals, and bear to Carthage this stern reproof: 'Shame on thee, degenerate hero, false to thy mother and thy son, thus sunk in luxury and ease! Set sail and leave this fatal shore.'

The heart of the hero, when he heard this message, was torn in twain. How could he disobey the voice of the god? How could he bring himself to desert the Queen whose heart he had won, and break his troth?

But what were the closest of human ties when the god had spoken? So he called to him his comrades and bade them in secret make ready the ships for departure. But lovers' ears are keen, and rumors of the preparation reached the Queen in her palace. She raved like a madwoman, and called down curses on the perjured traitor. Grown calmer, she sought Æneas and, with mingled reproaches and appeals to his pity, besought him at least to delay his departure. The lover's heart was touched, but the hero was unmoved; and with the gentlest words he could frame, he told the Queen that he had no choice but to follow his weird as Heaven ordained. He could never forget her lovingkindness, and would cherish her memory to his dying day.

Then the Queen knew that she was betrayed, and flatteries and soft words served but to rekindle her rage. She bade the perjured wretch begone; she cursed his false gods and their lying message, and swore that she would pursue him with black flames, and that after death her ghost would haunt him in every place. This said, she turned and left him, and he saw her nevermore.

Æneas would fain have stayed to calm her grief and soothe her rage, but duty bade him go, and he urged on his men to equip the fleet for departure. They, nothing loath, set to, and the harbor was like an ant-hill, with the sailors shaping new oars and loading the beached vessels. Soon the black keels rode the waters all along the shore. Dido, perceiving this from her tower, sent her sister Anna with a last message imploring Æneas yet a little to delay. But Æneas, steadfast as a rock, turned to her a deaf ear, and into the heart of the unhappy Dido came despair and thoughts of death.

To death, indeed, dark omens turned her mind. For when she offered sacrifice, the wine which she poured upon the smoking incense turned to blood; and at night, when kneeling before the shrine of her dead husband, she heard his voice bidding her arise and come to him.

So the Queen, interpreting these dark signs as her sick heart dictated, made ready to die.

Calling her sister Anna, she declared that she would now make use of a magic charm given to her by a priestess to bring back faithless lovers or make the love-sick whole. To work this spell it was necessary to collect and burn all tokens of the light of love.

'Do you, therefore,' said Dido to Anna, 'gather together the arms and garments which Æneas in his haste to be gone has left behind him, and lay these upon a vast funeral pile, which I beseech you to erect secretly in the inner court of the palace, under the open sky.'

As she spoke, a deadly pallor overspread the face of Dido. But her sister Anna, suspecting nothing, made haste to obey the Queen. The great pile was quickly erected, with torches and fagots of oak, and crowned with funeral boughs. On it were placed the weapons and raiment of Æneas, while the Queen offered sacrifices, and herbs cut by moonlight with brazen sickles.

Next morning, before daybreak, Æneas called upon his comrades to set sail. With his own sword he cut the hawsers, and his men, pushing off, smote the sounding waves with their oars, and the wind filling their unfurled sails, they swept out into the open sea as the sun rose over the waters.

From the tower of her palace Queen Dido saw them depart. And lifting up her

voice she laid a curse upon them, prophesying that for ages to come dire enmity should rage between the race of Æneas and the Carthaginian people.

Then, very pale, she entered the inner court and mounted the funeral pile. A little while she paused, musing and shedding her last tears.

Anon she spoke, and bade farewell to the light of the sun: 'I have lived my life; I have finished the course ordained to me by Fate. I have raised a glorious city. I descend illustrious to the shades below.'

She paused, and her voice fell to a low wail as she added: 'Happy, ah, too happy, my lot had the Trojan ships never touched my shores!'

Then, unsheathing the sword, she plunged it into her bosom and fell down upon the pyre.

Her handmaidens, seeing her fall, rent the air with their cries. And Anna, rushing in, raised her dying sister in her arms, striving in vain to stanch the flowing blood, and crying with tears: 'Oh, sister, was it for this that you bade me raise the pyre? Ah, would that you had let me be your companion in death!'

But the last words of Dido, Queen of Carthage, had been spoken.

Far out at sea, Æneas saw a great smoke rising from Carthage, as it were from a funeral pyre. And a sore pang smote him, and bitterly he divined what had passed. But he held upon his destined way, nor looked he back again, but turned his eyes towards the promised land of Latium.

Aeneas in Hades

V.C. Turnbull

The journey down to the abyss
Is prosperous and light;
The palace gates of gloomy Dis
Stand open day and night;
But upward to retrace the way,
And pass into the light of day,—
There comes the stress of labor—this
May task a hero's might.

Virgil (Conington's translation)

neas, in the course of his wanderings, landed on the shores of Cumæ in Italy. Here he sought out the Sibyl, the inspired prophetess who dwelt in a cave behind the temple of Apollo, and gave forth to inquirers the answers of the god. High destinies she promised Æneas, but not without many further trials.

Æneas, undismayed, besought the Sibyl to guide him on his way: 'O Priestess, it has been told that here are the gates of the lower world. Open for me, I beg of you, that portal, for I long greatly to speak once more with my dear father. I bore him on my shoulders from flaming Troy, and in all my voyages he accompanied me, facing, though infirm, the terrors of sea and sky. Nay, more, it was at his bidding that I came a suppliant to thy temple. Have pity upon us both, O Sybil, and enable us to meet once more.'

Then the Sibyl, in reply, warned Æneas that though many went down with ease into the Abode of the Dead, few—very few, and they the specially favored of the gods—returned therefrom. 'But if,' she went on, 'you are determined to dare the desperate enterprise, seek out in this dark wood a tree that hides one branch all golden. This bough is sacred to Proserpine, Queen of the Lower World, and to her must you bear it as a gift. Without it no living being may enter the Lower World. Pluck it, and if the Fates have willed it so, it will yield at a touch, else no mortal force can wrest it from its parent stem.'

So Æneas and Achates plunged into the primeval forest near which the Sibyl dwelt. They had not gone far when two doves alighted on the sward hard by. Then Æneas was glad, for he knew them to be the birds of his mother Venus, and he besought his mother that her messengers might guide him on his way. And the doves flitted on before them till they lighted at last on a lofty tree, amid the boughs of which Æneas discerned the gleam of gold. This was the Golden Bough, growing like mistletoe from the oak, and there was a tinkle in the air as the breeze rustled the golden foil. Joyfully Æneas broke it from the trunk, and bore it back to the dwelling of the Sibyl.

Then the priestess led the way back into the gloomy wood, halting before a cavern, vast and hideous with its yawning black mouth, from which exhaled so poisonous a breath that no bird could cross it unhurt. Here Æneas and the Sibyl offered sacrifices to the Gods of the Lower World. At sunrise the ground began to rumble beneath their feet, and a baying of hell-dogs rolled up from the chasm.

'Avaunt, ye profane!' cried the priestess, 'and, Æneas, do thou draw thy sword and march boldly forward; now is the hour to try thy mettle.'

So saying, she plunged into the dark cavern, and Æneas, following, entered the world of the dead.

In a desolate country on the outskirts of the spirit-world they saw the forms of Grief and vengeful Cares; here dwelt disconsolate Old Age, Fear, Famine, Death, and Toil. Murderous War was here, and frantic Discord, whose viperous locks are bound with bloody fillets.

All these they passed, coming to the turbid flood Acheron, on which the ferryman Charon, a grisly, unkempt graybeard, with eyes of flame, plied to and fro.

On the banks of the river stood a great company of ghosts, matrons and men, boys and maidens, numerous as swallows flying south, or leaves before the autumn wind. They stood praying to be taken into the boat, and stretching their hands towards the farther shore; but the sullen boatman would take only a few, choosing whom he would. Then, in reply to his questions, the priestess told Æneas that the bodies of those whom the boatman refused had been left unburied upon earth, wherefore these ghosts were doomed to flutter for a hundred years along the shores of Acheron before Charon would consent to ferry them across.

By this time they had reached the landing-stage, and the priestess beckoned to Charon; he refusing at first to carry a mortal across that river till she showed him the Golden Bough. At the sight of this Charon came at once with his boat, pushing out the ghosts that sat therein to make room for Æneas. Groaning beneath the weight of a mortal the boat was well-nigh swamped, but at length the priestess and the hero were safely landed on the farther shore.

But now at the gate stood Cerberus, the three-headed dog, making those

realms resound with his barking. To him the priestess threw an opiate of honey-cakes, and he, snatching at it with his three mouths, lay down to sleep, thus permitting them to pass.

Now to their ears came the wails of infants, ghosts of those who had been bereft of sweet life even at their mother's breast. Next came those who had been condemned to death unheard or falsely charged. Full justice they now received; Minos the judge metes out to each his proper sentence.

After these Æneas came upon a group of those unhappy ones who with their own hands had destroyed their lives. Ah, gladly now would they endure poverty and toil could they but revisit the kindly light of the sun!

Now Æneas entered a region named the Fields of Mourning, inhabited by the ghosts of those who had died for love. And among them, in a wood, Æneas saw, or deemed he saw, dim as the new moon in a cloudy sky, the form of Dido, still pale from her death-wound. Tears in his eyes, he addressed her sad ghost with loving words as of old: 'So, as I feared, it was true, the message of those funeral fires. And was I, alas! the cause of your death? O Queen, believe that it was against my will that I left thy coasts! Unwilling, I swear, by the behest of the gods did I leave thee, even as now, by the same behest, I tread the land of darkness and despair. Ah, tarry but a little! 'Tis our last farewell.'

So he spoke, seeking to soothe the injured shade. But she, with averted eyes, stood still as a statue of stone. Then in silent scorn she fled to seek her first lord, Sichæus, who answers sorrow with sorrow.

Thence to the farthest fields they passed the haunts of heroes slain in battle; and here Æneas greeted many comrades of early days. But when the ghosts of Agamemnon's Greek army beheld the mighty hero, his arms gleaming through the shades, they quaked, and many fled as erstwhile before to their ships, while others, trying to raise the war-cry, could utter only 'the bat-like shrilling of the dead.'

A pitiful shade, with marred visage and mangled body, approached them, and Æneas recognized the ghost of Deiphobus, son of Priam, and asked of his cruel fate; and Deiphobus poured forth the long tale of his wife's treachery, and how he had been foully slaughtered in his sleep. Long had they thus conversed, but the Sibyl plucked Æneas by the robe and warned him: 'Night falls apace; 'tis time to go. Thou hast come to the parting of the ways. Here lie Elysium and the fields of the blessed, and there, to the left, Tartarus and the tortures of the damned.' And even now Æneas descried vast prisons inclosed with a triple wall, round which the river Phlegethon rolled its threefold floods of flame, while rocks whirled roaring down the stream. Over against the stream stood a massive gateway, whose adamantine columns defied all force of men or gods, and above the gate rose a tower of iron. Here sat the Fury Tisiphone, watching all who entered. And from within the gate came groans and the whistling of scourges and the clanking of chains.

Æneas asked what meant this woeful wailing, and the Sibyl replied:

'None innocent may cross that threshold. There Rhadamanthus judges the dead, and avenging Tisiphone scourges the guilty. Within the gate rages the Hydra with fifty gaping mouths. Downward sinks the pit, twice as deep as the heavens are high. In it groan the Titans, hurled down with thunderbolts, and the giants, Otus and Ephialtes, who strove to overturn the throne of Jupiter himself. There lies Tityus, o'er nine roods outstretched, and eternally does a vulture tear his liver with her beak. Over some hangs a rock threatening ever to fall; before others a bounteous banquet is continually spread, but the hands that they stretch to take the food are evermore struck back by the Furies. Some roll a huge stone, others are bound to the revolving wheel. Here lie they who heaped up riches for themselves, an unnumbered multitude; here also they who hated their brothers or lifted cruel hands against their parents. Take warning by their fate, and ask no further concerning their awful doom.'

Thus warned, Æneas went forward in silence, and at the direction of the Sibyl he offered the Golden Bough at the gate.

Now came they at length to the regions of joy, the green retreats and happy groves of Elysium. An ampler ether and a purer light invest these fields, for the blessed have their own sun and stars. In jousts and races, in dance and song, they fleet the golden hours, a blessed company of bards and patriots, paladins

and victors in the races. Among them Æneas marked Ilus, a former king of Troy, and Dardanus, that city's founder. Their chariots were empty, their spears stood fixed in the ground, their horses fed at large throughout the plain, for the ruling purpose in life survives the grave.

There, in a sequestered dale, stood Anchises surveying the souls that were to revisit earth once more, among them his own offspring yet unborn. But when he saw Æneas moving to meet him, with outstretched arms and tearful eyes he cried: 'O my son, my son, hast thou come to me indeed? Am I permitted to see thy face and hear thy well-known voice once more?' And Æneas answered, weeping also: 'Give me thy hand, my father, and take me to thy breast.' Thrice he strove to throw his arm round his father, thrice the phantom slipped from his embrace, thin as the fluttering breeze or like a dream of the night. Gazing around him he saw in a wooded glade numberless peoples and tribes, hovering above the brakes like bees in summer-time, and he inquired of his sire what these might be.

Then Anchises taught Æneas many wonderful things concerning the state of departed souls in Elysium and the future of the Trojan race. And touching the first, he said that after suffering many things the evil of their natures was washed or burned away, and they passed to Elysium, there to dwell for a thousand years. 'All these,' he continued, 'are then summoned forth by the gods in a great body to the river Lethe, wherein they leave all memory of the past and again become willing to return into mortal bodies.'

Saying this, he led Æneas to the summit of a hill from which they who were to be born could be seen passing in an endless file before them.

'See you,' he said, 'that youth leaning on a pointless spear? He shall be Silvius, the child of thy old age, and shall reign over Alba Longa. Behold there Romulus, the founder of Rome, the city of the seven hills, he shall rule the world. The graybeard behind him is Numa, the lawgiver, and next comes Tullus, the warrior. Those that follow are the proud Tarquins. There, too, is Brutus, unhappy man, who shall give liberty to Rome; and, unhappy father! whose inflexible justice shall doom to death his guilty sons.'

All these and many others who sprang from Æneas' loins, did Anchises point out, crying as he ended: 'To you, O Romans, be it given to rule the nations, to dictate terms of peace, to spare the humbled, and to crush the proud.'

Last they watched the great Marcellus, the terror of the Gauls, the conqueror of Carthage.

Then Æneas asked: 'What youth is he, O father, who walks by his side in shining armor; but his countenance is sad, his eyes fixed upon the ground? Is he a son, or haply a grandson?'

And Anchises wept as he replied: 'Alas, my son, for the sorrows of thy kindred! Dear child of pity! could'st thou but burst thy fate's invidious bar, our own Marcellus thou! Ah! woful shall be the day of his death! Could he but live none had faced his onset. Bring lilies—lilies in handfuls; let me heap bright flowers on the shade unborn, and pay at least this empty tribute.'[1]

Thus they passed through Elysium, Anchises showing and explaining all to Æneas, firing him with the thoughts of future fame, and instructing him how to act throughout the struggles of his remaining life. Then, when all had been shown and said, Father Anchises sent back his son Æneas and the Sibyl to the mortal world by that shining Ivory Gate where through pass the dreams that visit the slumbers of men.

FOOTNOTE:

[1] The reference is to Marcellus, nephew and son-in-law of Augustus, and his destined heir. He died at the early age of eighteen.

Nisus and Euryalus

F. Storr

Æneas was absent from the camp. Warned by Father Tiber he had gone with a picked band of followers to seek the alliance of his kinsman, King Evander, who with his Arcadians had settled themselves on the seven hills which now are Rome.

Whilst he was away, the camp was left in charge of his son Iulus, and as adjutant and counselor to the young prince he appointed his most experienced general, old Aletes.

But Juno, the implacable foe of Troy, had despatched to Turnus, the Rutulian Prince, her messenger Iris to tell him of Æneas' absence and bid him seize the occasion to storm the Trojan camp. So all day long the garrison, reduced in numbers and without its great captain, saw the tide of horse and foot, Latins, Rutulians, and Etruscans, gathering in the plain and sweeping onward to overwhelm them, like the Nile in full flood. As Æneas had bid them, they retired within their intrenchments, too strong to be carried at the first assault.

At nightfall the enemy withdrew, and the weary defenders lay down to sleep, but in fear of a night attack they ventured not to unbuckle their armor, and at each camp-gate was posted a strong guard of sentinels.

Conspicuous among the captains of the guard was Nisus, whom his mother, Ida, the world-famed huntress, had sent as squire to Æneas, no less skilled than his mother with javelin or with bow. With him as his lieutenant was Euryalus, the fairest youth, save Iulus alone, in all the Trojan host, the down of manhood just

showing on his cheek, elsewise as round and smooth as a girl's.

The two were more than brothers-in-arms, inseparable as twin cherries on a single stalk; the one followed the other as his shadow, and their love was more than the love of man and maid.

And now as they kept watch together they thus conversed:

NISUS. I know not what ails me, brother, but to-night I feel a wild unrest, a strange prompting to be up and doing some doughty deed. What think you, brother? Is it an inspiration of heaven or only my own fiery spirit, pent up within these walls and fretting for the fray? Mark you, brother. The enemy's camp is silent as the tomb. Not a sentinel is stirring, and the rare watch-fires burn low. 'Tis plain to me that the captains, having driven us back to our trenches, have been celebrating their victory and are now buried in drunken slumber. Now I will expound to thee the plan that is working in my brain. At all hazards Æneas must be summoned back from the city of Evander—so our generals and men are all agreed. If only my proposal is accepted, methinks I have discovered a way to bear the message and work our deliverance.

EURYALUS. Verily 'tis a glorious venture and well worth the risk, but thou speakest as if the venture were thine. Can I have heard thee aright? Truly, brother, the plan is thine, but the execution is ours. Thinkest thou, brother, alone to put thy head into the lion's mouth? Shall I not share thy triumph or thy death? In life we have been one, and in death we shall not be divided.

NISUS. Nay, brother, I never doubted thy courage or thy love. This thought alone, perhaps a selfish thought, was mine: if perchance I should fall—and sanguine as I am of success I know 'tis a perilous hazard—I would fain one sure friend survived to lay my body in mother earth, or if that grace is denied, at least to perform due rites at my cenotaph. I thought, moreover, that thou art the younger man and thy mother's only son.

EURYALUS. Out on thy vain excuses! Only if thou takest me with thee will I forgive them. My mind is set. Let us to work.

So they called to the nearest sentinels to relieve them of their guard and hurried to seek Iulus. They found him in his tent presiding over a council of war,

but the sentries let them pass on business that would not wait. It chanced that the captains were at that moment debating how possibly to convey a message to Æneas informing him of their pressing need, and when Nisus expounded to them his plan, assuring them that as a young hunter he had explored every inch of the ground and knew a secret forest path that would lead them to the rear of the enemy's camp, he was welcomed as a messenger sent from heaven. Old Aletes laid his hands on their heads and with tears in his eyes blessed the gods for sending such deliverers. 'Young heroes!' he cried, 'your virtue is its own reward, but Æneas, when he returns, will know how to recompense you.' Iulus, with boyish generosity, promised them his choicest treasures, embossed tankards and two talents of gold, aye and the charger and arms of Turnus, whose fall was certain when Æneas returned; and he put his arms round Euryalus' neck (the youth was scarce older than himself) and called him his brother-in-arms.

Boldened by this signal favor of the prince, Euryalus, on bended knee, besought one parting boon. 'Prince,' he cried, 'I have an aged mother who for my sake left her native home and the court of King Acestes to accompany me to the wars. I may not stay to bid her farewell and receive her blessing, nor could I dare confide to her our perilous errand. Thou hast deigned to call me brother: O prince, be to her a son. To know that thou wilt be here to solace and comfort her will give me fresh confidence.' The prince swore to love and cherish her no less than his own lost mother, Creusa, and wishing him Godspeed he girt on his shoulder the sword of that famous Cretan swordsman, Lycaon, with hilt of wrought gold and scabbard of ivory. To Nisus, Achates gave his own helmet, that had borne the brunt of many a shrewd blow.

Thus armed and charged with many messages from Iulus to his father they left the camp, and the captains sent after them a parting cheer.

The night was dark, but Nisus could almost have found his way blindfolded through the familiar forest. In a short hour they had reached the camp unperceived, and then, as Nisus had anticipated, they found a scene of barbarous revelry. Amongst tilted war-chariots, tethered horses, and empty wine-jars men lay stretched in drunken slumber.

'Follow me,' whispered Nisus, 'and keep an open eye lest any attack me from behind. I will hew thee anon a path of blood by which we can both pass to our goal.'

With drawn sword he rushed on Rhamnes, who lay snoring on a pile of broidered coverlets: an augur was he of royal blood, but little did his augury avail him that day. His three attendants soon followed their master to the shades. Like a ravening wolf who has leapt into the sheepfold he dealt havoc right and left, and all that Nisus spared the sword of Euryalus despatched.

'Enough,' cried Nisus, at length sated with carnage; 'our way through the enemy is clear, and the tell-tale morn is nigh at hand.' Much rich spoil they left behind—flagons of gold and silver, gemmed goblets and broideries; but Euryalus cast longing eyes on a huge baldrick with bosses of gold, an heirloom of the dead augur, and he strapped it round his shoulder; nor could he resist (proud youth) the temptation to try on a bright helmet with flaming crest of Messapus, the Tamer of Steeds. With these spoils to attest their glorious raid, the pair left the camp and gained in safety the open.

Their task seemed well-nigh accomplished, but it chanced that a troop of three hundred horse, despatched from the Latin capital as an advanced guard for Turnus, were just then approaching the camp from the opposite direction, and espying in the twilight the glint of the helmet they challenged the pair. No answer was returned, and Nisus, who was leading, quickened his pace to gain the shelter of the forest. The horsemen wheeled round and sought to cut off their retreat, but they were too late, and Nisus was already speeding down a winding bypath that he knew full well, when he looked back, and to his horror perceived that Euryalus was not following. 'Euryalus!' he shouted, but no answer came. He turned and painfully retraced his steps. Soon he heard the tramp of horses among the brushwood and broken branches, and guided by the sound in a clearing of the forest he saw Euryalus, his back against an oak, like a stag at bay, facing a

Right: Nisus Slaying Volscens *by Wenceslaus Hollar. This 17th-century etching is an illustration accompanying Virgil's 'Aeneid'.*

ring of horsemen. What was he to do? To save himself by flight was unthinkable, but should he rush at once on certain death? In desperation he breathed a prayer to his patron goddess Diana. 'Queen of the woods,' he cried, 'by the gifts I have offered on thine altar, by the vows I have daily paid, help me now in my utmost need and guide my aim!' So praying, he hurled with all his might a spear, and so straight and swift it flew that Sulmo was transfixed from back to breast, and the shaft snapped off short as the barbed head quivered in the wound. A second spear buried itself in Tagus's brain, and he too bit the dust. Volscens, the captain of the troop, saw his two comrades struck down as by a bolt from the blue, and with drawn sword he turned on Euryalus crying, 'If I cannot reach the fiend who hurled those spears, thy blood at least shall atone the bloody deed.'

At this Nisus could no longer restrain himself, and leaping from the covert he shouted, 'I, none but I, am the guilty cause. Oh, spare this innocent boy and turn your swords on me! To love his friend too well, this was his only crime!' But his words were vain; while yet he spoke the sword of Volscens had pierced the boy's heart and stained with gore his white side, and he drooped his head like a poppy drenched with rain, or a harebell upturned by the plowshare.

At the sight Nisus hurled himself into the thick of his foes, scattering them right and left with the lightnings of his glaive, till he forced his way to Volscens, and with a dying effort smote the murderer of his sweet friend. Pierced with a hundred wounds he fell upon Euryalus' prostrate corpse, and a smile was on his lips, for in death they were not divided.

Such was the tale that Virgil sang, and the prophecy that he uttered nigh upon two thousand years ago has been fulfilled:

> 'O happy pair, if aught my verse avail, Your memory through the ages shall not fail, While on the Capitol Rome's flag is seen And Rome holds sway, Italia's Empress Queen.'

Ulysses in Hades

M.M. Bird

Before he left fair Circe's isle Ulysses reminded the goddess of her promise to speed them on their homeward way. This, she assured him, not she but the Fates refused. Nor could they hope to breathe their native air till a long and toilsome journey had been taken, a journey that would lead them down even to the dread realms of Death. 'But there,' she said, 'you shall seek out blind Tiresias, the Theban bard; though his eyes be blind his mind is filled with prophetic light. He will tell you all you seek to know of your future and the fate of those you love.'

Brave as he was, Ulysses shuddered at the awful road he had to tread, and appealed to Circe for further aid in this adventure. So she told him the landmarks to guide him on his way, and instructed him what to do when he reached the realms of Tartarus. And when morn broke he summoned his companions to set forth. They came in haste and joy.

But one was missing. Elpenor, the youngest of the band, a wild and senseless youth, had climbed to the housetop to breathe the cold air after a debauch lasting far into the night. At the sudden tumult of departure he was roused, and hastening down he missed the ladder and fell headlong from the roof and broke his neck.

Ignorant of his fate, the rest crowded eagerly round their leader, till his few and sober words told them that not yet the joys of homecoming awaited them, but it was decreed that first they should seek the awful shade of Tiresias in the dark and dreary realms of Death. Sadly then upon that shore they made their sacrifices

to the immortal gods, and sadly embarked in the waiting ship and spread their sails to the freshening breeze.

As the sun sank, and all the ways were darkened, they reached the utmost bounds of Ocean, a lonely land, where the sun never shines, where darkness broods perpetually over bare and rocky crags, the abode of the Cimmerians. Off their desolate shore Ulysses cast anchor, and leaping from his ship, descried the awful chasm that leads to the realms of the dead.

His two companions bore with them the black sheep as Circe had bidden, and Ulysses drew his shining sword and carved a great trench, a cubit long and wide, in the black earth. This was filled with wine, milk, and honey, and the blood of the newly offered sacrifices. Thus, with solemn rites and holy vows, they invoked the nations of the dead. And lo! among the frowning caverns and all along the dusky shores appeared the phantom shapes of unsubstantial ghosts. Old and young, warriors ghastly with wounds, matrons and maids, rich and poor, they crowded about the trench filled with the reeking blood of sacrifice. But Ulysses in terror brandished his sword above the flowing blood, and the pale throngs started back and stood silently about him.

Then he saw Elpenor, new to the realms of Death. Astonished, he demanded of the shade how it was that he had outrun their swift sail, and was found wandering with the dead. To which the youth replied that his feet, unsteady through excess of wine, had betrayed him and sent him headlong from the tower, and as he fell his neck was broken and his soul plunged in Hell.

But he implored Ulysses, by all he held most dear, to give his unburied limbs a peaceful grave, and set up a barrow, and on it plant his oar to show that he had been one of Ulysses' crew. And Ulysses granted the boon, and the spirit of Elpenor departed content.

Then, as Ulysses sat watching the trench, he saw the shade of his royal mother, Anticlea, approach; but though the tears bedewed his cheek at the sight, the pale shade stood regardless of her son.

Next came the mighty Theban, Tiresias, bearing a scepter of gold; and he knew him and spake: 'Why, son of Laertes, wanderest thou from cheerful day to

tread this sorrowful path? What angry gods have led thee, alive, to be companion of the dead? If thou wilt sheathe thy sword I will relate thy future and the high purposes of Heaven towards thee.'

Ulysses sheathed his glittering blade, and the seer bent down and drank of the dark blood. Then he foretold all the strange disasters that would threaten and detain Ulysses on his homeward way. He told how at length he alone of all his crew would survive to reach his country—there to find his labors not yet at an end, with foes in power at his court, lordly suitors besieging his wife, and wasting his substance in riot and debauch. But a peaceful end to his long and toilsome life should come at last, and see him sink to the grave blessed by all his people. 'This is thy life to come, and this is Fate,' said the seer.

To whom Ulysses, unmoved, made answer: 'All that the gods ordain the wise endure.'

So the prophet went his way, and Ulysses waited on for his mother to come. And anon, Anticlea came and stooped and drank of the dark blood, and straightway all the mother in her soul awoke, and she addressed her son, asking whence he came and why.

'To seek Tiresias, and learn my doom,' Ulysses answered, 'for I have been a roamer and an exile from home ever since the fall of Troy.' Then he asked her how her own death had happened, whether his good father Laertes still lived, if Telemachus his son ruled in Ithaca, and if Penelope yet waited and watched for her absent lord, or if she had taken a new mate.

To all his questions Anticlea made answer with tender pity. Penelope, his faithful wife, still mourned for him uncomforted; Telemachus, now almost grown to manhood, ruled his realm; and old Laertes, bowed with grief, only waited in sorrow for the release of the tomb, since his son Ulysses returned no more. She herself, his mother, had died of a broken heart; for him she lived, and when he came not, for love of him she died.

Ulysses, deeply moved, strove thrice to clasp her in his arms, and thrice she slipped from his embrace, like a shadow or a dream. In vain he begged that his fond arms might enfold the parent so tenderly loved, that he might know it was she herself and no empty image sent by Hell's queen to mock his sorrow. But the pensive ghost admonished him that such were all spirits when they had quit their mortal bodies. No substance of the man remained, said she: all had been devoured by the funeral flames and scattered by the winds to the empty air. It was but the soul that flew, like a dream, to the infernal regions. 'But go,' she adjured him; 'haste to climb the steep ascent; regain the day and seek your bride, to recount to her the horrors and the laws of Hell.'

As she ceased and disappeared, a cloud of phantoms, wives and daughters of kings and heroes, flitted round the visitant of earth. Dauntless he waved his sword; the ghostly crew shrank away and dared not drink of the wine in the trench at his feet. They passed, and to each other Ulysses heard them recount their names and needs. There he saw Alcmena, mother of Alcides; Megara, wife of Hercules, who was slain by him in his madness; the beautiful Chloris, Antiope, and Leda, mother of the deathless twins Castor and Pollux, who live and die alternately, the one in Heaven and the other in Hell, the favored sons of Jove.

There walked Phædra, shedding unceasing tears of remorse for her slain love, and near her mournful Ariadne. All these, and many more, Ulysses recognized in that pale procession of departed spirits. When they had been summoned back to the black halls of Proserpine, the forms of the heroes slain by the foul Ægisthus came in sight. High above them all towered great Agamemnon. He drank the wine and knew his friend; with tears Ulysses greeted him and inquired what relentless doom, what fate of war, or mischance upon the ocean, had thrust his spirit into Hell? And Agamemnon told him all the dreadful story of his return from Troy, and the treachery of his wife Clytemnestra and her lover, who slew him as he feasted, and with him all his friends; most pitiful of all, the voice of the dying Cassandra, slain at his side as he himself lay dying, still rang in his ears.

And Ulysses answered him: 'What ills hath Jupiter wreaked on the house of Atreus through the counsels of women!'

'Be warned,' replied Agamemnon, 'and tell no woman all that is in thy heart; not even Penelope, though she is discreet and true above all other women and will not plot thy death.' And he grieved for his own son Orestes, on whom he

had never looked, envying his friend an heir so wise and brave as the young Telemachus.

Then he saw Achilles and Patroclus, approaching through the gloom. Achilles knew his friend and hastened to his side. 'Oh mortal, overbold,' he asked, 'how durst thou come down living to the realms of the dead?' Ulysses told him how he had come, though living, to seek counsel of the dead.

But Achilles made answer:

'Rather would I, in the sun's warmth divine, Moil as a churl, who drags his days in grief, Than the whole lordship of the dead were mine.'

Then, like Agamemnon, he demanded news of his son, and Ulysses charmed the father's heart by telling of the gallant deeds of Neoptolemus at Troy town, and how he had escaped unscathed from the fight.

Achilles glowed with pride and delight; and as he joined the illustrious shades of the warriors about him, Ulysses sought the side of Ajax, whom he perceived standing apart in gloom and sullenness. His lost honours perpetually stung his mind, though the fight had been fair and Ulysses had been judged the victor by the Trojans. Ulysses seeing him stand thus mournfully aloof, addressed him with tender sorrow. 'Still burns thy rage? Can brave souls bear malice e'en after death?' he asked him sadly. But for all his appeals the resentful shade turned from him with disdain, and silently stalked away. Touched to the depths of a generous heart Ulysses started in pursuit through the black and winding ways of Death, to find and force him to reply to his earnest questioning, but on the way such strange and awful scenes met his astonished eyes as caused him to pause and turn aside.

There was huge Orion, whirling aloft his ponderous mace of brass to crush his savage prey.

There was Tityus, the son of Earth, who for offering violence to the goddess Latona was shot dead by her children, and lay forever in Hell in fetters while vultures gnawed at his liver.

Again he looked, and beheld Tantalus, whose awful groans echoed through the roofless caverns. When to the stream that rippled past him he applied his parched lips, it fled before he could taste of it. Fruit of all kinds hung round him—pomegranates, figs, and ripening apples; but if he strove to seize the fruit, the baffling wind would toss the branch high out of his reach.

When in horror at the sight of these torments, Ulysses turned aside, he saw a labouring figure, Sisyphus, who with weary steps up a high hill was heaving a huge round stone. When, with infinite straining, he reached at length the summit, the boulder, poising but an instant, bounded down the steep again with a wild impetuous rush, and dragged with it Sisyphus into the depths of an awful cavern. Thence once again, with sweat and agony, he must renew his toil and creep with painful labor up the slope, thrusting the rock before him. This the punishment for a life of avaricious greed, devoted to a pitiless unassuageable lust for gold and power.

And farther on great Hercules was seen, a towering specter of gigantic form. Gloomy as night he stood, in act to shoot an arrow from his monstrous bow. With grim visage and terrible look he lamented his wrongs and woes, and then abruptly turning, strode away.

When Ulysses, curious to view the kings of ancient days and all the endless ranks of the mighty dead, would have stood strong in this resolve to watch them, a great swarm of specters rose from deepest Hell. With hideous yells they flew at him; they gaped at him and gibbered in such menacing tones that his blood froze in his veins. In fear lest the Gorgon, rising from the depths of the infernal lake, with her crown of hissing snakes about her brow, should transfix him to stone, he turned and fled.

He climbed the steep ascent and joined his waiting shipmates. They set sail with all haste to leave the dread Cimmerian shore, and a fair wind sped them on their backward way.

Circe's Palace

Nathaniel Hawthorne

After escaping from the Cyclopes, and enduring many other perils by land and sea in the course of his weary voyage to Ithaca, Ulysses arrived at a green island, the name of which was unknown to him, and was glad to moor his tempest-beaten bark in a quiet cove. But he had encountered so many dangers from giants, and one-eyed Cyclopes, and monsters of the sea and land, that he could not help dreading some mischief, even in this pleasant and seemingly solitary spot. For two days, therefore, the poor weather-worn voyagers kept quiet, and either stayed on board of their vessel, or merely crept along under the cliffs that bordered the shore; and to keep themselves alive, they dug shell-fish out of the sand, and sought for any little rill of fresh water that might be running towards the sea.

Before the two days were spent, they grew very weary of this kind of life; for the followers of King Ulysses were terrible gormandizers, and pretty sure to grumble if they missed their regular meals, and their irregular ones besides. Their stock of provisions was quite exhausted, and even the shell-fish began to get scarce, so that they had now to choose between starving to death or venturing into the interior of the island, where perhaps some huge three-headed dragon, or other horrible monster, had his den.

But King Ulysses was a bold man as well as a prudent one; and on the third morning he determined to discover what sort of a place the island was, and whether it were possible to obtain a supply of food for the hungry mouths of his companions. So, taking a spear in his hand, he clambered to the summit of a cliff and gazed round about him. At a distance, towards the center of the island, he beheld the stately towers of what seemed to be a palace, built of snow-white marble, and rising in the midst of a grove of lofty trees. The thick branches of these trees stretched across the front of the edifice, and more than half concealed it, although, from the portion which he saw, Ulysses judged it to be spacious and exceedingly beautiful, and probably the residence of some great nobleman or prince. A blue smoke went curling up from the chimney, and was almost the pleasantest part of the spectacle to Ulysses. For, from the abundance of this smoke, it was reasonable to conclude that there was a good fire in the kitchen, and that, at dinner-time, a plentiful banquet would be served up to the inhabitants of the palace, and to whatever guests might happen to drop in.

With so agreeable a prospect before him, Ulysses fancied that he could not do better than to go straight to the palace gate, and tell the master of it that there was a crew of poor shipwrecked mariners, not far off, who had eaten nothing for a day or two save a few clams and oysters, and would therefore be thankful for a little food. And the prince or nobleman must be a very stingy curmudgeon, to be sure, if, at least, when his own dinner was over, he would not bid them welcome to the broken victuals from the table.

Pleasing himself with this idea, King Ulysses had made a few steps in the direction of the palace, when there was a great twittering and chirping from the branch of a neighboring tree. A moment afterwards a bird came flying towards him, and hovered in the air, so as almost to brush his face with its wings. It was a very pretty little bird, with purple wings and body, and yellow legs, and a circle of golden feathers round its neck, and on its head a golden tuft, which looked like a king's crown in miniature. Ulysses tried to catch the bird. But it fluttered

Right: The Magic of Circe *by Friedrich Preller, from* Die Gartenlaube *(The Garden Arbour).*

nimbly out of his reach, still chirping in a piteous tone, as if it could have told a lamentable story, had it only been gifted with human language. And when he attempted to drive it away, the bird flew no farther than the bough of the next tree, and again came fluttering about his head, with its doleful chirp, as soon as he showed a purpose of going forward.

'Have you anything to tell me, little bird?' asked Ulysses.

'Peep!' said the bird, 'peep, peep, pe—weep!' And nothing else would it say, but only, 'Peep, peep, pe—weep!' in a melancholy cadence, and over and over and over again. As often as Ulysses moved forward, however, the bird showed the greatest alarm, and did its best to drive him back with the anxious flutter of its purple wings. Its unaccountable behavior made him conclude, at last, that the bird knew of some danger that awaited him, and which must needs be very terrible, beyond all question, since it moved even a little fowl to feel compassion for a human being. So he resolved, for the present, to return to the vessel, and tell his companions what he had seen.

This appeared to satisfy the bird. As soon as Ulysses turned back, it ran up the trunk of a tree, and began to pick insects out of the bark with its long, sharp bill; for it was a kind of woodpecker, you must know, and had to get its living in the same manner as other birds of that species. But every little while, as it pecked at the bark of the tree, the purple bird bethought itself of some secret sorrow, and repeated its plaintive note of 'Peep, peep, pe—weep!'

On his way to the shore, Ulysses had the good luck to kill a large stag. Taking it on his shoulders he lugged it along with him, and flung it down before his hungry companions.

But the next morning their appetites were as sharp as ever. They looked at Ulysses, as if they expected him to clamber up the cliff again and come back with another fat deer upon his shoulders. Instead of setting out, however, he summoned the whole crew together, and told them it was in vain to hope that he could kill a stag every day for their dinner, and therefore it was advisable to think of some other mode of satisfying their hunger.

'Now,' said he, 'when I was on the cliff yesterday, I discovered that this island

is inhabited. At a considerable distance from the shore stood a marble palace, which appeared to be very spacious, and had a great deal of smoke curling out of one of its chimneys.'

'Aha!' muttered some of his companions, smacking their lips. 'That smoke must have come from the kitchen fire. There was a good dinner on the spit; and no doubt there will be as good a one today.'

'But,' continued the wise Ulysses, 'you must remember, my good friends, our misadventure in the cavern of one-eyed Polyphemus, the Cyclops! To tell you the truth, if we go to yonder palace, there can be no question that we shall make our appearance at the dinner-table; but whether seated as guests, or served up as food, is a point to be seriously considered.'

'Either way,' murmured some of the hungriest of the crew, 'it will be better than starvation; particularly if one could be sure of being well fattened beforehand, and daintily cooked afterwards.'

'That is a matter of taste,' said King Ulysses, 'and, for my own part, neither the most careful fattening nor the daintiest of cookery would reconcile me to being dished at last. My proposal is, therefore, that we divide ourselves into two equal parties, and ascertain, by drawing lots, which of the two shall go to the palace and beg for food and assistance. If these can be obtained, all is well. If not, and if the inhabitants prove as inhospitable as Polyphemus, or the Læstrygons, then there will but half of us perish, and the remainder may set sail and escape.'

As nobody objected to this scheme, Ulysses proceeded to count the whole band, and found that there were forty-six men including himself. He then numbered off twenty-two of them, and put Eurylochus (who was one of his chief officers, and second only to himself in sagacity) at their head. Ulysses took command of the remaining twenty-two men in person. Then, taking off his helmet, he put two shells into it, on one of which was written, 'Go,' and on the other, 'Stay.' Another person now held the helmet, while Ulysses and Eurylochus drew out each a shell; and the word 'Go' was found written on that which Eurylochus had drawn. In this manner it was decided that Ulysses and his twenty-two men were to remain at the seaside until the other party should have found out what sort of treatment they might expect at the mysterious palace. As there was no help for it, Eurylochus immediately set forth at the head of his twenty-two followers, who went off in a very melancholy state of mind, leaving their friends in hardly better spirits than themselves.

No sooner had they clambered up the cliff than they discerned the tall marble towers of the palace, ascending, as white as snow, out of the lovely green shadow of the trees which surrounded it. A gush of smoke came from a chimney in the rear of the edifice. The vapor rose high in the air, and, meeting with a breeze, was wafted seaward, and made to pass over the heads of the hungry mariners. When people's appetites are keen, they have a very quick scent for anything savory in the wind.

'That smoke comes from the kitchen!' cried one of them, turning up his nose as high as he could, and snuffing eagerly. 'And, as sure as I'm a half-starved vagabond, I smell roast meat in it.'

'Pig, roast pig!' said another. 'Ah, the dainty little porker! My mouth waters for him.'

'Let us make haste,' cried the others, 'or we shall be too late for the good cheer!'

But scarcely had they made half a dozen steps from the edge of the cliff, when a bird came fluttering to meet them. It was the same pretty little bird, with the purple wings and body, the yellow legs, the golden collar round its neck, and the crown-like tuft upon its head, whose behavior had so much surprised Ulysses. It hovered about Eurylochus, and almost brushed his face with its wings.

'Peep, peep, pe—weep!' chirped the bird.

So plaintively intelligent was the sound, that it seemed as if the little creature were going to break its heart with some mighty secret that it had to tell, and only this one poor note to tell it with.

'My pretty bird,' said Eurylochus—for he was a wary person, and let no token of harm escape his notice—'my pretty bird, who sent you hither? And what is the message which you bring?'

'Peep, peep, pe—weep!' replied the bird, very sorrowfully.

Then it flew towards the edge of the cliff, and looked round at them, as if

exceedingly anxious that they should return whence they came. Eurylochus and a few others were inclined to turn back. They could not help suspecting that the purple bird must be aware of something mischievous that would befall them at the palace, and the knowledge of which affected its airy spirit with a human sympathy and sorrow. But the rest of the voyagers, snuffing up the smoke from the palace kitchen, ridiculed the idea of returning to the vessel. One of them (more brutal than his fellows, and the most notorious gormandizer in the whole crew) said such a cruel and wicked thing, that I wonder the mere thought did not turn him into a wild beast, in shape, as he already was in his nature.

'This troublesome and impertinent little fowl,' said he, 'would make a delicate titbit to begin dinner with. Just one plump morsel, melting away between the teeth. If he comes within my reach, I'll catch him, and give him to the palace cook to be roasted on a skewer.'

The words were hardly out of his mouth, before the purple bird flew away, crying, 'Peep, peep, pe—weep!' more dolorously than ever.

'That bird,' remarked Eurylochus, 'knows more than we do about what awaits us at the palace.'

'Come on, then,' cried his comrades, 'and we'll soon know as much as he does.'

The party, accordingly, went onward through the green and pleasant wood. Every little while they caught new glimpses of the marble palace, which looked more and more beautiful the nearer they approached it.

At one place they came to a crystal spring, and paused to drink at it for want of liquor which they liked better. Looking into its bosom, they beheld their own faces dimly reflected, but so extravagantly distorted by the gush and motion of the water, that each one of them appeared to be laughing at himself and all his companions. So ridiculous were these images of themselves, indeed, that they did really laugh aloud, and could hardly be grave again as soon as they wished. And after they had drank, they grew still merrier than before.

'It has a twang of the wine-cask in it,' said one, smacking his lips.

'Make haste!' cried his fellows; 'we'll find the wine-cask itself at the palace; and that will be better than a hundred crystal fountains.'

Then they quickened their pace, and capered for joy at the thought of the savory banquet at which they hoped to be guests. But Eurylochus told them that he felt as if he were walking in a dream.

'If I am really awake,' continued he, 'then, in my opinion, we are on the point of meeting with some stranger adventure than any that befell us in the cave of Polyphemus, or among the gigantic man-eating Læstrygons, or in the windy palace of King Æolus, which stands on a brazen-walled island. This kind of dreamy feeling always comes over me before any wonderful occurrence. If you take my advice, you will turn back.'

'No, no,' answered his comrades, snuffing the air, in which the scent from the palace kitchen was now very perceptible. 'We would not turn back, though we were certain that the king of the Læstrygons, as big as a mountain, would sit at the head of the table, and huge Polyphemus, the one-eyed Cyclops, at its foot.'

At length they came within full sight of the palace, which proved to be very large and lofty, with a great number of airy pinnacles upon its roof. Though it was now midday, and the sun shone brightly over the marble front, yet its snowy whiteness, and its fantastic style of architecture, made it look unreal, like the frostwork on a window pane, or like the shapes of castles which one sees among the clouds by moonlight. But, just then, a puff of wind brought down the smoke of the kitchen chimney among them, and caused each man to smell the odor of the dish that he liked best and, after scenting it, they thought everything else moonshine, and nothing real save this palace, and save the banquet that was evidently ready to be served up in it.

So they hastened their steps towards the portal, but had not got halfway across the wide lawn, when a pack of lions, tigers, and wolves came bounding to meet them. The terrified mariners started back, expecting no better fate than to be torn to pieces and devoured. To their surprise and joy, however, these wild beasts merely capered around them, wagging their tails, offering their heads to be stroked and patted, and behaving just like so many well-bred house-dogs, when they wish to express their delight at meeting their master or their master's friends. The biggest lion licked the feet of Eurylochus; and every other lion, and every

wolf and tiger, singled out one of his two-and-twenty followers, whom the beast fondled as if he loved him better than a beef-bone.

But, for all that, Eurylochus imagined that he saw something fierce and savage in their eyes; nor would he have been surprised, at any moment, to feel the big lion's terrible claws, or to see each of the tigers make a deadly spring, or each wolf leap at the throat of the man whom he had fondled. Their mildness seemed unreal, and a mere freak; but their savage nature was as true as their teeth and claws.

Nevertheless, the men went safely across the lawn with the wild beasts frisking about them, and doing no manner of harm; although, as they mounted the steps of the palace, you might possibly have heard a low growl, particularly from the wolves, as if they thought it a pity, after all, to let the strangers pass without so much as tasting what they were made of.

Eurylochus and his followers now passed under a lofty portal, and looked through the open doorway into the interior of the palace. The first thing that they saw was a spacious hall, and a fountain in the middle of it, gushing up towards the ceiling out of a marble basin, and falling back into it with a continual plash. The water of this fountain, as it spouted upward, was constantly taking new shapes, not very distinctly, but plainly enough for a nimble fancy to recognize what they were. Now it was the shape of a man in a long robe, the fleecy whiteness of which was made out of the fountain's spray; now it was a lion, or a tiger, or a wolf, or an ass, or, as often as anything else, a hog, wallowing in the marble basin as if it were his sty. But, before the strangers had time to look closely at this wonderful sight, their attention was drawn off by a very sweet and agreeable sound. A woman's voice was singing melodiously in another room of the palace, and with her voice was mingled the noise of a loom, at which she was probably seated, weaving a rich texture of cloth, and intertwining the high and low sweetness of her voice into a rich tissue of harmony.

By and by the song came to an end; and then, all at once, there were several feminine voices, talking airily and cheerfully, with now and then a merry burst of laughter, such as you may always hear when three or four young women sit

at work together.

'What a sweet song that was!' exclaimed one of the voyagers.

'Too sweet, indeed,' answered Eurylochus, shaking his head. 'Yet it was not so sweet as the song of the Sirens, those bird-like damsels who wanted to tempt us on the rocks so that our vessel might be wrecked, and our bones left whitening along the shore.'

'But just listen to the pleasant voices of those maidens, and that buzz of the loom as the shuttle passes to and fro,' said another comrade. 'What a domestic, household, homelike sound it is! Ah, before that weary siege of Troy, I used to hear the buzzing loom and the women's voices under my own roof. Shall I never hear them again? nor taste those nice little savory dishes which my dearest wife knew how to serve up?'

'Tush! we shall fare better here,' said another. 'But how innocently those women are babbling together, without guessing that we overhear them! And mark that richest voice of all, so pleasant and familiar, but which yet seems to have the authority of a mistress among them. Let us show ourselves at once. What harm can the lady of the palace and her maidens do to mariners and warriors like us?'

'Remember,' said Eurylochus, 'that it was a young maiden who beguiled three of our friends into the palace of the king of the Læstrygons, who ate up one of them in the twinkling of an eye.'

No warning or persuasion, however, had any effect on his companions. They went up to a pair of folding doors at the farther end of the hall, and throwing them wide open, passed into the next room. Eurylochus, meanwhile, had stepped behind a pillar. In the short moment, while the folding doors opened and closed again, he caught a glimpse of a very beautiful woman rising from the loom, and coming to meet the poor weather-beaten wanderers, with a hospitable smile, and her hand stretched out in welcome. There were four other young women, who joined their hands and danced merrily forward, making gestures of obeisance to the strangers. They were only less beautiful than the lady who seemed to be their mistress. Yet Eurylochus fancied that one of them had sea-green hair, and that the close-fitting bodice of a second looked like the bark of a tree, and that both the others had something odd in their aspect, although he could not quite determine what it was, in the little while that he had to examine them.

The folding doors swung quickly back, and left him standing behind the pillar, in the solitude of the outer hall. There Eurylochus waited until he was quite weary, and listened eagerly to every sound, but without hearing anything that could help him to guess what had become of his friends. Footsteps, it is true, seemed to be passing and repassing in other parts of the palace. Then there was a clatter of silver dishes, or golden ones, which made him imagine a rich feast in a splendid banqueting hall. But by and by he heard a tremendous grunting and squealing, and then a sudden scampering, like that of small, hard hoofs over a marble floor, while the voices of the mistress and her four handmaidens were screaming all together, in tones of anger and derision. Eurylochus could not conceive what had happened, unless a drove of swine had broken into the palace, attracted by the smell of the feast. Chancing to cast his eyes at the fountain, he saw that it did not shift its shape as formerly, nor looked either like a long-robed man, or a lion, a tiger, a wolf, or an ass. It looked like nothing but a hog, which lay wallowing in the marble basin, and filled it from brim to brim.

But we must leave the prudent Eurylochus waiting in the outer hall, and follow his friends into the inner secrecy of the palace. As soon as the beautiful woman saw them, she arose from the loom, as I have told you, and came forward smiling, and stretching out her hand. She took the hand of the foremost among them, and bade him and the whole party welcome.

'You have been long expected, my good friends,' said she. 'I and my maidens are well acquainted with you, although you do not appear to recognize us. Look at this piece of tapestry, and judge if your faces must not have been familiar to us.'

So the voyagers examined the web of cloth which the beautiful woman had been weaving in her loom; and, to their vast astonishment, they saw their own figures perfectly represented in different colored threads. It was a life-like picture of their recent adventures, showing them in the cave of Polyphemus, and how they had put out his one great moony eye; while in another part of the tapestry they were untying the leathern bags, puffed out with contrary winds; and farther on they beheld themselves scampering away from the gigantic king of the Læstrygons, who had caught one of them by the leg. Lastly, there they were, sitting on the desolate shore of this very island, hungry and downcast, and looking ruefully at the bare bones of the stag which they devoured yesterday. This was as far as the work had yet proceeded; but when the beautiful woman should again sit down at her loom, she would probably make a picture of what had since happened to the strangers, and of what was now going to happen.

'You see,' she said, 'that I know all about your troubles; and you cannot doubt that I desire to make you happy for as long a time as you may remain with me. For this purpose, my honoured guests, I have ordered a banquet to be prepared. Fish, fowl, and flesh, roasted and in luscious stews, and seasoned, I trust, to all your tastes, are ready to be served up. If your appetites tell you it is dinner-time, then come with me to the festal saloon.'

At this kind invitation the hungry mariners were quite overjoyed; and one of them, taking upon himself to be spokesman, assured their hospitable hostess that any hour of the day was dinner-time with them, whenever they could get flesh to put in the pot, and fire to boil it with. So the beautiful woman led the way; and the four maidens (one of them had sea-green hair, another a bodice of oak bark, a third sprinkled a shower of water drops from her fingers' ends, and the fourth had some other oddity, which I have forgotten), all these followed behind, and hurried the guests along until they entered a magnificent saloon. It was built in a perfect oval, and lighted from a crystal dome above. Around the walls were ranged two-and-twenty thrones, overhung by canopies of crimson and gold, and provided with the softest of cushions, which were tasseled and fringed with gold cord. Each of the strangers was invited to sit down; and there they were, two-and-twenty storm-beaten mariners, in worn and tattered garb, sitting on two-and-twenty cushioned and canopied thrones, so rich and gorgeous that the proudest monarch had nothing more splendid in his stateliest hall.

Then you might have seen the guests nodding, winking with one eye, and leaning from one throne to another, to communicate their satisfaction in hoarse whispers.

'Our good hostess has made kings of us all,' said one. 'Ha! do you smell the feast? I'll engage it will be fit to set before two-and-twenty kings.'

But the beautiful woman now clapped her hands; and immediately there entered a train of two-and-twenty serving-men, bringing dishes of the richest food, all hot from the kitchen fire, and sending up such a steam that it hung like a cloud below the crystal dome of the saloon. An equal number of attendants brought great flagons of wine of various kinds, some of which sparkled as it was poured out, and went bubbling down the throat; while of other sorts, the purple liquor was so clear that you could see the wrought figures at the bottom of the goblet. While the servants supplied the two-and-twenty guests with food and drink, the hostess and her four maidens went from one throne to another, exhorting them to eat their fill, and to quaff wine abundantly, and thus to recompense themselves at this one banquet for the many days when they had gone without a dinner. But, whenever the mariners were not looking at them (which was pretty often, as they looked chiefly into the basins and platters), the beautiful woman and her damsels turned aside and laughed. Even the servants, as they knelt down to present the dishes, might be seen to grin and sneer while the guests were helping themselves to the offered dainties.

And once in a while the strangers seemed to taste something that they did not like.

'Here is an odd kind of a spice in this dish,' said one. 'I can't say it quite suits my palate. Down it goes, however.'

'Send a good draught of wine down your throat,' said his comrade on the next throne; 'that is the stuff to make this sort of cookery relish well. Though I must needs say, the wine has a queer taste, too. But the more I drink of it the better I like the flavor.'

Whatever little fault they might find with the dishes, they sat at dinner a prodigiously long while. They forgot all about their homes, and their wives and children, and all about Ulysses, and everything else, except this banquet, at which they wanted to keep feasting forever. But at length they began to give over, from mere incapacity to hold any more.

'That last bit of fat is too much for me,' said one.

'And I have not room for another morsel,' said his next neighbor, heaving a sigh. 'What a pity! My appetite is as sharp as ever.'

In short, they all left off eating, and leaned back on their thrones, with such a stupid and helpless aspect as made them ridiculous to behold. When their hostess saw this, she laughed aloud; so did her four damsels; so did the two-and-twenty serving-men that bore the dishes, and their two-and-twenty fellows that poured out the wine. And the louder they all laughed, the more stupid and helpless did the two-and-twenty gormandizers look. Then the beautiful woman took her stand in the middle of the saloon, and stretching out a slender rod (it had been all the while in her hand, although they never noticed it till this moment), she turned it from one guest to another, until each had felt it pointed at himself. Beautiful as her face was, and though there was a smile on it, it looked just as wicked and mischievous as the ugliest serpent that ever was seen; and fat-witted as the voyagers had made themselves, they began to suspect that they had fallen into the power of an evil-minded enchantress.

'Wretches,' cried she, 'you have abused a lady's hospitality; and in this princely saloon your behavior has been suited to a hog-pen. You are already swine in everything but the human form, which you disgrace, and which I myself should be ashamed to keep a moment longer, were you to share it with me. But it will require only the slightest exercise of magic to make the exterior conform to the hoggish disposition. Assume your proper shapes, gormandizers, and begone to the sty!'

Uttering these last words, she waved her wand; and stamping her foot imperiously, each of the guests was struck aghast at beholding, instead of his comrades in human shape, one-and-twenty hogs sitting on the same number of golden thrones. Each man (as he still supposed himself to be) essayed to give a cry of surprise, but found that he could merely grunt, and that, in a word, he was just such another beast as his companions. It looked so intolerably absurd to see hogs on cushioned thrones, that they made haste to wallow down upon all fours, like other swine. They tried to groan and beg for mercy, but forthwith emitted the

most awful grunting and squealing that ever came out of swinish throats. They would have wrung their hands in despair, but, attempting to do so, grew all the more desperate for seeing themselves squatted on their hams, and pawing the air with their fore-trotters. Dear me! what pendulous ears they had! what little red eyes, half buried in fat! and what long snouts, instead of Grecian noses!

'Begone to your sty!' cried the enchantress, giving them some smart strokes with her wand; and then she turned to the serving-men—'Drive out these swine, and throw down some acorns for them to eat.'

Meantime Eurylochus had waited, and waited, and waited in the entrance hall of the palace, without being able to comprehend what had befallen his friends. At last, when the swinish uproar sounded through the palace, and when he saw the image of a hog in the marble basin, he thought it best to hasten back to the vessel and inform the wise Ulysses of these marvelous occurrences. So he ran as fast as he could down the steps, and never stopped to draw breath till he reached the shore.

'Why do you come alone?' asked King Ulysses, as soon as he saw him. 'Where are your two-and-twenty comrades?'

At these questions Eurylochus burst into tears.

'Alas!' cried he, 'I greatly fear we shall never see one of their faces again.'

Then he told Ulysses all that had happened, as far as he knew it; and added that he suspected the beautiful woman to be a vile enchantress, and the marble palace, magnificent as it looked, to be only a dismal cavern in reality. As for his companions, he could not imagine what had become of them, unless they had been given to the swine to be devoured alive. At this intelligence all the voyagers were greatly affrighted. But Ulysses lost no time in girding on his sword, and hanging his bow and quiver over his shoulders, and taking a spear in his right hand. When his followers saw their wise leader making these preparations, they inquired whither he was going, and earnestly besought him not to leave them.

'You are our king,' cried they; 'and what is more, you are the wisest man in the whole world, and nothing but your wisdom and courage can get us out of this danger. If you desert us, and go to the enchanted palace, you will suffer the same fate as our poor companions, and not a soul of us will ever see our dear Ithaca again.'

'As I am your king,' answered Ulysses, 'and wiser than any of you, it is therefore the more my duty to see what has befallen our comrades, and whether anything can yet be done to rescue them. Wait for me here until tomorrow. If I do not then return, you must hoist sail and endeavor to find your way to our native land. For my part, I am answerable for the fate of these poor mariners, who have stood by my side in battle, and been so often drenched to the skin, along with me, by the same tempestuous surges. I will either bring them back with me or perish.'

Had his followers dared, they would have detained him by force. But King Ulysses frowned sternly on them, and shook his spear, and bade them stop him at their peril. Seeing him so determined they let him go, and sat down on the sand, as disconsolate a set of people as could be, waiting and praying for his return.

It happened to Ulysses, just as before, that, when he had gone a few steps from the edge of the cliff, the purple bird came fluttering towards him, crying, 'Peep, peep, pe—weep!' and using all the art it could to persuade him to go no farther.

'What mean you, little bird?' cried Ulysses. 'You are arrayed like a king in purple and gold, and wear a golden crown upon your head. Is it because I too am a king, that you desire so earnestly to speak with me? If you can talk in human language, say what you would have me do.'

'Peep!' answered the purple bird, very dolorously. 'Peep, peep, pe—we—ep!'

Certainly there lay some heavy anguish at the little bird's heart; and it was a sorrowful predicament that he could not at least have the consolation of telling what it was. But Ulysses had no time to waste in trying to get at the mystery. He therefore quickened his pace, and had gone a good way along the pleasant wood-path, when there met him a young man of very brisk and intelligent aspect, and clad in a rather singular garb. He wore a short cloak, and a sort of cap that seemed to be furnished with a pair of wings; and from the lightness of his step, you would have supposed that there might likewise be wings on his feet. To enable him to walk still better (for he was always on one journey or another), he carried a winged staff, around which two serpents were wriggling and twisting. In

short, I have said enough to make you guess that it was Quicksilver[2]; and Ulysses (who knew him of old, and had learned a great deal of his wisdom from him) recognized him in a moment.

'Whither are you going in such a hurry, wise Ulysses?' asked Quicksilver. 'Do you not know that this island is enchanted? The wicked enchantress (whose name is Circe, the sister of King Æetes) dwells in the marble palace which you see yonder among the trees. By her magic arts she changes every human being into the brute beast or fowl whom he happens most to resemble.'

'That little bird, which met me at the edge of the cliff,' exclaimed Ulysses; 'was he a human being once?'

'Yes,' answered Quicksilver. 'He was once a king, named Picus, and a pretty good sort of a king too, only rather too proud of his purple robe, and his crown, and the golden chain about his neck; so he was forced to take the shape of a gaudy-feathered bird. The lions, and wolves, and tigers, who will come running to meet you, in front of the palace, were formerly fierce and cruel men, resembling in their dispositions the wild beasts whose forms they now rightfully wear.'

'And my poor companions,' said Ulysses, 'have they undergone a similar change through the arts of this wicked Circe?'

'You well know what gormandizers they were,' replied Quicksilver; and, rogue that he was, he could not help laughing at the joke. 'So you will not be surprised to hear that they have all taken the shapes of swine! If Circe had never done anything worse, I really should not think her so very much to blame.'

'But can I do nothing to help them?' inquired Ulysses.

'It will require all your wisdom,' said Quicksilver, 'and a little of my own into the bargain, to keep your royal and sagacious self from being transformed into a fox. But do as I bid you, and the matter may end better than it has begun.'

While he was speaking, Quicksilver seemed to be in search of something; he went stooping along the ground, and soon laid his hand on a little plant with a snow-white flower, which he plucked and smelt. Ulysses had been looking at that very spot only just before; and it appeared to him that the plant had burst into full flower the instant when Quicksilver touched it with his fingers.

'Take this flower, King Ulysses,' said he. 'Guard it as you do your eyesight; for I can assure you it is exceedingly rare and precious, and you might seek the whole earth over without ever finding another like it. Keep it in your hand, and smell of it frequently after you enter the palace, and while you are talking with the enchantress. Especially when she offers you food or a draught of wine out of her goblet, be careful to fill your nostrils with the flower's fragrance. Follow these directions, and you may defy her magic arts to change you into a fox.'

When Ulysses reached the lawn in front of the palace, the lions and other savage animals came bounding to meet him, and would have fawned upon him and licked his feet. But the wise king struck at them with his long spear, and sternly bade them begone out of his path; for he knew that they had once been bloodthirsty men, and would now tear him limb from limb, instead of fawning upon him, could they do the mischief that was in their hearts. The wild beasts yelped and glared at him, and stood at a distance while he ascended the palace steps.

On entering the hall, Ulysses saw the magic fountain in the center of it. The up-gushing water had now again taken the shape of a man in a long, white, fleecy robe, who appeared to be making gestures of welcome. The king likewise heard the noise of the shuttle in the loom, and the sweet melody of the beautiful woman's song, and then the pleasant voices of herself and the four maidens talking together, with peals of merry laughter intermixed. But Ulysses did not waste much time in listening to the laughter or the song. He leaned his spear against one of the pillars of the hall, and then, after loosening his sword in the scabbard, stepped boldly forward and threw the folding doors wide open. The moment she beheld his stately figure standing in the doorway, the beautiful woman rose from the loom and ran to meet him, with a glad smile throwing its sunshine over her face and both her hands extended.

'Welcome, brave stranger!' cried she. 'We were expecting you. Your companions have already been received into my palace, and have enjoyed the hospitable treatment to which the propriety of their behavior so well entitles them. If such be your pleasure, you shall first take some refreshment, and then join them

in the elegant apartments which they now occupy. See, I and my maidens have been weaving their figures into this piece of tapestry.'

She pointed to the web of beautifully woven cloth in the loom. Circe and the four nymphs must have been very diligently at work since the arrival of the mariners; for a great many yards of tapestry had now been wrought, in addition to what I before described. In this new part Ulysses saw his two-and-twenty friends represented as sitting on cushioned and canopied thrones, greedily devouring dainties and quaffing deep draughts of wine. The work had not yet gone any farther. Oh, no, indeed. The enchantress was far too cunning to let Ulysses see the mischief which her magic arts had since brought upon the gormandizers.

'As for yourself, valiant sir,' said Circe, 'judging by the dignity of your aspect, I take you to be nothing less than a king. Deign to follow me, and you shall be treated as befits your rank.'

So Ulysses followed her into the oval saloon where his two-and-twenty comrades had devoured the banquet which ended so disastrously for themselves, but all this while he had held the snow-white flower in his hand, and had constantly smelt of it while Circe was speaking; and as he crossed the threshold of the saloon, he took good care to inhale several long and deep snuffs of its fragrance. Instead of two-and-twenty thrones, which had before been ranged around the wall, there was now only a single throne in the center of the apartment. But this was surely the most magnificent seat that ever a king or an emperor reposed himself upon, all made of chased gold, studded with precious stones, with a cushion that looked like a soft heap of living roses, and overhung by a canopy of sunlight which Circe knew how to weave into drapery. The enchantress took Ulysses by the hand, and made him sit down upon this dazzling throne. Then, clapping her hands, she summoned the chief butler.

'Bring hither,' said she, 'the goblet that is set apart for kings to drink out of. And fill it with the same delicious wine which my royal brother, King Æetes, praised so highly when he last visited me with my fair daughter Medea. That good and amiable child! Were she now here, it would delight her to see me offering this wine to my honoured guest.'

But Ulysses, while the butler was gone for the wine, held the snow-white flower to his nose.

'Is it a wholesome wine?' he asked.

At this the four maidens tittered; whereupon the enchantress looked round at them with an aspect of severity.

'It is the wholesomest juice that ever was squeezed out of the grape,' said she; 'for, instead of disguising a man, as other liquor is apt to do, it brings him to his true self and shows him as he ought to be.'

The chief butler liked nothing better than to see people turned into swine, or making any kind of beast of themselves; so he made haste to bring the royal goblet, filled with a liquid as bright as gold, and which kept sparkling upward and throwing a sunny spray over the brim. But, delightful as the wine looked, it was mingled with the most potent enchantments that Circe knew how to concoct. For every drop of the pure grape juice there were two drops of the pure mischief; and the danger of the thing was, that the mischief made it taste all the better. The mere smell of the bubbles, which effervesced at the brim, was enough to turn a man's beard into pig's bristles, or make a lion's claws grow out of his fingers, or a fox's brush behind him.

'Drink, my noble guest,' said Circe, smiling as she presented him with the goblet. 'You will find in this draught a solace for all your troubles.'

King Ulysses took the goblet with his right hand, while with his left he held the snow-white flower to his nostrils, and drew in so long a breath that his lungs were quite filled with its pure and simple fragrance. Then, drinking off all the wine, he looked the enchantress calmly in the face.

'Wretch,' cried Circe, giving him a smart stroke with her wand, 'how dare you keep your human shape a moment longer? Take the form of the brute whom you most resemble. If a hog, go join your fellow-swine in the sty; if a lion, a wolf, a tiger, go howl with the wild beasts on the lawn; if a fox, go exercise your craft in stealing poultry. Thou hast quaffed off my wine, and canst be man no longer.'

But such was the virtue of the snow-white flower, instead of wallowing down from his throne in swinish shape, or taking any other brutal form, Ulysses looked

even more manly and king-like than before. He gave the magic goblet a toss, and sent it clashing over the marble floor to the farthest end of the saloon. Then, drawing his sword, he seized the enchantress by her beautiful ringlets, and made a gesture as if he meant to strike off her head at one blow.

'Wicked Circe,' cried he, in a terrible voice, 'this sword shall put an end to thy enchantments. Thou shalt die, vile wretch, and do no more mischief in the world by tempting human beings into the vices which make beasts of them.'

The tone and countenance of Ulysses were so awful, and his sword gleamed so brightly and seemed to have so intolerably keen an edge, that Circe was almost killed by the mere fright, without waiting for a blow. The chief butler scrambled out of the saloon, picking up the golden goblet as he went; and the enchantress and the four maidens fell on their knees, wringing their hands, and screaming for mercy.

'Spare me!' cried Circe. 'Spare me, royal and wise Ulysses. For now I know that thou art he of whom Quicksilver forewarned me, the most prudent of mortals, against whom no enchantments can prevail. Thou only couldst have conquered Circe. Spare me, wisest of men. I will show thee true hospitality, and even give myself to be thy slave, and this magnificent palace to be henceforth thy home.'

The four nymphs, meanwhile, were making a most piteous ado; and especially the ocean nymph, with the sea-green hair, wept a great deal of salt water, and the fountain nymph, besides scattering dewdrops from her fingers' ends, nearly melted away into tears. But Ulysses would not be pacified until Circe had taken a solemn oath to change back his companions, and as many others as he should direct, from their present forms of beast or bird into their former shapes of men.

'On these conditions,' said he, 'I consent to spare your life. Otherwise you must die upon the spot.'

With a drawn sword hanging over her, the enchantress would readily have consented to do as much good as she had hitherto done mischief, however little she might like such employment. She therefore led Ulysses out of the back entrance of the palace, and showed him the swine in their sty. There were about fifty of these unclean beasts in the whole herd; and though the greater part were hogs by birth

and education, there was wonderfully little difference to be seen betwixt them and their new brethren who had so recently worn the human shape.

The comrades of Ulysses, however, had not quite lost the remembrance of having formerly stood erect. When he approached the sty, two-and-twenty enormous swine separated themselves from the herd and scampered towards him with such a chorus of horrible squealing as made him clap both hands to his ears. And yet they did not seem to know what they wanted, nor whether they were merely hungry, or miserable from some other cause. It was curious, in the midst of their distress, to observe them thrusting their noses into the mire in quest of something to eat. The nymph with the bodice of oaken bark (she was the hamadryad of an oak) threw a handful of acorns among them; and the two-and-twenty hogs scrambled and fought for the prize, as if they had tasted not so much as a noggin of sour milk for a twelvemonth.

'These must certainly be my comrades,' said Ulysses. 'I recognize their dispositions. They are hardly worth the trouble of changing them into the human form again. Nevertheless, we will have it done, lest their bad example should corrupt the other hogs. Let them take their original shapes, therefore, Dame Circe, if your skill is equal to the task. It will require greater magic, I trow, than it did to make swine of them.'

So Circe waved her wand again, and repeated a few magic words, at the sound of which the two-and-twenty hogs pricked up their pendulous ears. It was a wonder to behold how their snouts grew shorter and shorter, and their mouths (which they seemed to be sorry for, because they could not gobble so expeditiously) smaller and smaller, and how one and another began to stand upon his hind-legs, and scratch his nose with his fore-trotters. At first the spectators hardly knew whether to call them hogs or men, but by and by they came to the conclusion that they rather resembled the latter. Finally, there stood the twenty-two comrades of Ulysses, looking pretty much the same as when they left the vessel.

You must not imagine, however, that the swinish quality had entirely gone out of them. When once it fastens itself into a person's character, it is very difficult getting rid of it. This was proved by the hamadryad, who, being exceedingly

fond of mischief, threw another handful of acorns before the twenty-two newly restored people; whereupon down they wallowed, in a moment, and gobbled them up in a very shameful way. Then recollecting themselves, they scrambled to their feet, and looked more than commonly foolish.

'Thanks, noble Ulysses!' they cried. 'From brute beasts you have restored us to the condition of men again.'

'Do not put yourselves to the trouble of thanking me,' said the wise king. 'I fear I have done but little for you.'

To say the truth, there was a suspicious kind of a grunt in their voices, and for a long time afterwards they spoke gruffly, and were apt to set up a squeal.

'It must depend upon your own future behavior,' added Ulysses, 'whether you do not find your way back to the sty.'

At this moment the note of a bird sounded from the branch of a neighboring tree.

'Peep, peep, pe—weep—ep!'

It was the purple bird who, all this while, had been sitting over their heads, watching what was going forward, and hoping that Ulysses would remember how he had done his utmost to keep him and his followers out of harm's way. Ulysses ordered Circe instantly to make a king of this good little fowl, and leave him exactly as she found him. Hardly were the words spoken, and before the bird had time to utter another 'Pe—weep,' King Picus leaped down from the bough of the tree, as majestic a sovereign as any in the world, dressed in a long purple robe and gorgeous yellow stockings, with a splendidly wrought collar about his neck and a golden crown upon his head. He and King Ulysses exchanged with one another the courtesies which belong to their elevated rank. But from that time forth, King Picus was no longer proud of his crown and his trappings of royalty, nor of the fact of his being a king; he felt himself merely the upper servant of his people, and that it must be his lifelong labor to make them better and happier.

As for the lions, tigers, and wolves (though Circe would have restored them to their former shapes at his slightest word), Ulysses thought it advisable that they should remain as they now were, and thus give warning of their cruel dispositions, instead of going about under the guise of men and pretending to

 261

human sympathies, while their hearts had the blood-thirstiness of wild beasts. So he let them howl as much as they liked, but never troubled his head about them. And when everything was settled according to his pleasure, he sent to summon the remainder of his comrades, whom he had left at the sea-shore. These being arrived, with the prudent Eurylochus at their head, they all made themselves comfortable in Circe's enchanted palace until quite rested and refreshed from the toils and hardships of their voyage.

FOOTNOTE:

[2] The Romans called him Mercury, and the Greeks Hermes.

Ulysses and the Cyclops

Hope Moncrieff

Many a year did the much-enduring Ulysses sail unknown seas, on his way back from Troy to Ithaca, his island home. Beset by such mishaps and enchantments that for long he seemed little like to see again his faithful wife Penelope and his son Telemachus, he escaped from one perilous adventure after another, but none more fearsome than when he came to the smoking mountain-land of the Cyclops. So were named a cruel race of one-eyed giants, wild as the rocky heights on which they fed their flocks of sheep and goats, knowing not to plant corn or fruit, and holding no commerce with kindly men, nor reverencing the lords of heaven.

The very danger of venturing into such a land was lure enough for this hero, when from his ship he sighted a huge cave opening high above the beach, its mouth half hidden by a tangle of dark wood. Here lived alone one of these monsters, Polyphemus by name, a savage so churlish of nature that he kept aloof even from his fierce fellows. Eager to explore that gloomy lair, Ulysses picked out twelve of his boldest men, with whom he landed, leaving the vessel moored by the shore to await their return. On reaching the cave they found its master absent, but that he would soon return they might guess from the flocks of bleating lambs and kids penned up within, along with great piles of cheeses, vats of curd, and rows of milking vessels, the giant's household goods. The sailors, their hearts chilled by its damp shades, were not for staying long in this vast and deep-sunk hollow.

'Let us begone,' they urged their leader, 'back to the ship with a load of cheeses and a drove of lambs and kids to mend our fare on the salt waves! It were better to help ourselves behind the back of such a host, who may soon come to catch us in his den.'

But Ulysses let curiosity get the better of prudence. He had a mind at all risks to know what manner of creature this was that lived in so strange an abode; and he kept his companions in the cave, with a venturesomeness that cost them dear. They even made bold to light a fire and to refresh themselves from the giant's store of milk and cheese; and thus were they caught, taking their ease, when Polyphemus came home at evening, driving before him his full-uddered flock.

Above their bleating and scurrying was heard the heavy tramp of that monster, and the earth shook as from his shoulders he flung down a crashing stack of firewood, gathered in the forests through which he stalked like a moving mountain. The flock driven inside, he closed the entrance of the cave by dragging across it a mighty boulder that would have made a load for twenty wagons. Having thus shut out the fading light, he knelt down to milk his ewes and goats, as yet unaware what uninvited guests were straining their eyes at his black bulk from the deepest and darkest recess into which they had shrunk before his coming. But when he went on to light a fire, the flickering flames showed them his hideous face with its one broad red eye, that glowed in sudden anger when it fell upon the strangers; and through the smoky vaults echoed the blood-curdling roar with which he greeted them.

'Who, and whence are ye?' he thundered forth. 'Pirates, doubtless, who peril your own lives to rob other men!'

'Nay,' answered Ulysses, who of all the trembling band alone found voice to speak. 'We are men of famous race, the Greeks who at last overcame Troy, and now, sailing home, have been driven by winds and waves upon this coast. As helpless suppliants we fall before thee, seeking the hospitality due to misfortune

from all who fear the gods.'

'Ho, ho!' bellowed Polyphemus, in gigantic laughter. 'Stranger, thou art strange indeed to this land, and a fool to boot, if thou think'st a Cyclops owns any law but his own will. For gods we care not, nor yet for men, whoever they boast themselves! But say, how and where came ye on our shore?'

So he asked cunningly, hoping to make prize of their ship if anchored near at hand; but Ulysses was no less wily than bold, and took heed not to tell the truth.

'Our vessel, alas! was dashed to pieces on the cliff, and, of all the crew, we only have saved nothing but our lives.'

Now the men saw with what an inhuman monster they had to do. The savage giant, wasting no more time in parley, caught up the first two that came to his hands, dashed their brains out against the stony floor, then greedily devoured their flesh before the eyes of the survivors, shuddering to think how soon they might meet the same fate. Ulysses alone, undaunted and indignant, laid hands on his sword, but forebore to draw it. Even when, having ended his horrid meal and washed it down with large draughts of milk, Polyphemus laid himself carelessly to sleep among his flocks, the hero saw it was vain to strike, for though he might slay their fearsome foe, he knew that the strength of all together could not roll away that rocky barrier from the cave mouth. There was nothing for it but to remain patient, watching a chance to overcome the giant by craft rather than by force.

Through the night the poor sailors took such rest as they could, and the glimmering dawn brought fresh terror. As soon as the giant had risen and stretched his knotty limbs, he first set the lambs to the ewes, then snatched up two more of the hapless men, taken at random, to glut his taste for blood. When he turned out the flock to pasture, he neglected not to roll back the great rock that sealed up the cave, thus turned into a prison for these rash strangers, and soon like to be their tomb.

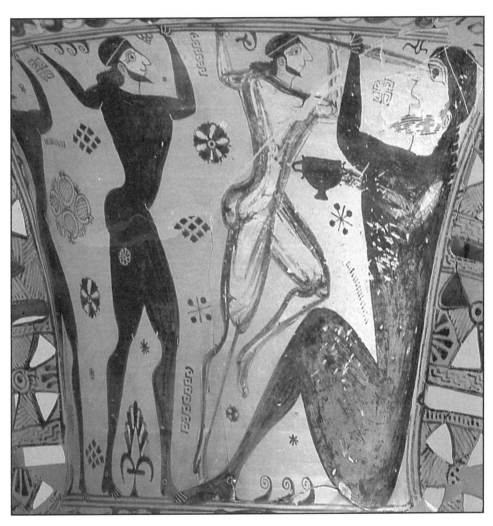

The blinding of the cyclops. Detail of a Proto-Attic amphora, circa 650 BC, currently held in Eleusis, Archaeological Museum.

But through the day their shrewd captain set his wits to work on a plot for escape. By good chance they had brought on shore with them a goat-skin full of strong wine, that now might serve to dull the giant's senses. In the cave they found a tree trunk he had plucked up by the root to make a club such as only so huge a monster could wield, for it was longer than the mast of their ship. This Ulysses had sharpened to a point and hardened in the fire before hiding it away among the dust and dirt that littered the cave. He explained to his comrades how he meant to use this enormous weapon, bidding them draw lots who should bear a hand with himself in the attempt; and, to his secret satisfaction, the lot fell on the very men he would have chosen for a daring deed.

Polyphemus duly returned at night-fall and again, when he had closed the entrance and seen to his flocks, he caught up two more of the Greeks to make his supper. Half of his twelve men having thus been devoured, Ulysses brought to the blood-stained monster a milk-pail filled from the wine-skin.

'Deign, O Cyclops,' he cried on bended knee, 'to taste this precious blood of the grape that rightly crowns a Greek banquet. It is well we have saved from our wreck one skin to offer thee, that may move thy heart to send us on our way unhurt, and not without some friendly boon. Else thy thirst for human blood will scare all men from this hateful shore, and never again canst thou come by such noble drink. Taste and know!'

The greedy giant snatched up the bowl and drained it to the bottom; then, smacking his lips for delight, he held it out to be refilled.

'Truly, it is noble drink, such as was never known in our land! Speak, stranger. Who art thou that bringest the nectar of the gods? Thy name?'

'My name is Noman,' quoth the crafty Ulysses, as he refilled the bowl.

'Then, Noman, I grant thee a boon,' hiccoughed the giant in boisterous glee, the fumes of the wine already mounting to his head. 'In reward for the drink, I will eat up all thy companions before thee; and Noman shall be the last of all to die. So fill once more!'

Again was poured the dark wine; and when Polyphemus had tossed off three brimming bowls, his brain began to reel, while his limbs failed him as well as his

voice, with which he would have roared out brutal jests mixed with praises of this magic liquor. Staggering here and there, he stumbled and sprawled helplessly on the ground, and soon his snoring re-echoed through the cave like rolling thunder, as he sank into drunken slumber.

When all else was still, Ulysses whispered the word to his wakeful crew. From the litter they silently dragged out that huge stake he had made ready: and blowing up the fire, heated its point till the green wood had almost burst into flame. It was all they could do to bear it along to the side of the sleeping giant. When their leader gave the signal, they plunged that red-hot spit into his eye, and, turning it like an awl, they bored a hole so deep and so wide that a torrent of blood gushed out to quench the fiery brand.

The drunken giant started to his feet with a roar which sent them quailing backwards. But when he had torn the tormenting brand from his forehead, all he could do was to grope blindly around him, stamping and howling for pain and for rage against those puny enemies that in the dim firelight could take heed to keep out of his reach. So furious was the alarm he raised, that it woke his neighbor giants, who presently came hurrying along to the cave's mouth, and shouted to him:

'What ails thee, Polyphemus, that thus our rest is disturbed? Who breaks upon thy sleep? Has any man found means to hurt thee? Or has someone been robbing thee by force or fraud?'

'Noman has hurt me!' yelled back the blind giant. 'Noman is robbing my flock! Noman, I say, has played a cruel trick upon me!'

'Then if no man does thee harm, why these complaints?' grumbled his neighbors, while Ulysses chuckled over his sly device, all the more as he heard the giants tramping away to their own lairs with a parting word of mockery for the victim of a nightmare, as they took it to be. 'If the gods send thee pain, take to prayer, and rouse us no more to give help against no man in mortal flesh!'

Thus left to himself, the blinded monster, pouring out his rage in tears of blood, found it hopeless to lay hands on the silently exulting foes, who all night long remained shut up with him in the cave; yet more fiercely his dark mind was

bent on revenge against that insolent Noman and the rest of his crew. Fumbling about till he touched the rock that barred the entrance, he heaved it away; then there sat down with his hands stretched out before him, to make sure that none of the men should slip through among the flock when the rosy dawn called them forth to their pasture.

But again Ulysses was too wily for the thick-headed giant. Through the night he had been busy lashing the biggest rams together, three and three; and each midmost beast bore a man bound to it by osier twigs. The largest of all he kept for himself, creeping beneath it, and clinging to the thick fleece below its belly. On this strange steed he would come forth last of all.

So, when the sheep poured out into the dewy uplands, the Cyclops, handling each as it slipped past him, felt nothing but their fleecy backs. Blind as he was, he knew the tread of that big ram, the pride of the flock, under which lay Ulysses, holding his breath, as its master stopped the beast to growl out:

'Why com'st thou last who wert wont to lead the way, like a chief among thy fellows? Can it be that a dumb creature mourns for what Noman and his hateful band have done to its lord? Ah! could'st thou but speak to tell me in what corner the wretch lurks within, trembling for the moment when at last I shall dash out his brains and warm my heart with his blood!'

With this he let the ram go, still sitting watchful at the entrance barred by his huge hands. But as he sat muttering threats, to his strained ears came a mocking cry from without, where now Ulysses had unbound his men, and the whole band were hurrying down to their ship, driving before them the pick of the giant's flock.

Heartily the crew hailed their captain's return, and eagerly they would have known how it had fared with him. But this was no time for words. Ulysses bid them push off in haste, taking to their oars as soon as they had heaved the sheep on board. Scarcely indeed had they launched when the stumbling and shouting giant appeared upon the rocky heights above the shore.

'Ha, ungracious host!' cried Ulysses; 'didst thou think to gorge thyself on me, whom the gods have made an instrument to punish thy churlish manners?'

No longer able to see his exultant enemies, the raging Cyclops plucked up a

great rock to hurl after them, guided by the sound of that mocking voice. So near it fell that it had almost smashed the rudder, and raised such a wave as would have washed the galley back on shore had not Ulysses pushed it off again with all his strength, while the rowers bent their backs as for their lives. Though they begged him to be silent, their bold captain could not refrain from once more raising his voice in boastful taunts of the baffled monster.

'Hear, Cyclops! Should men ask who blinded thee and made thy face more hideous than before, say not it was Noman, but Ulysses of Ithaca, victor at the walls of Troy!'

Again the giant hurled a mighty rock that, had it struck fair, would have crushed their ship like an eggshell. Drenched by the splash, they rowed with might and main, and were soon out of reach; but so long as they could hear his voice, the raging giant's curses drove them onward across the bounding seas.

Thus did Ulysses, by his cunning, prevail over the brute force of the Cyclops, for Minerva, goddess of Wisdom, inspired and guided him. Then soon, with a hungry heart craving for more adventures, he sailed to further wondrous lands and gathered fresh knowledge year by year.

The Sirens

V.C. Turnbull

Circe, when her spell was broken and she could no longer hope to keep Ulysses in her toils, repented her of the mischief she had done to his companions, and in a sudden fit of generosity (for though fickle and froward she was not wholly bad or heartless) determined to speed her parting guest. Not only did she know the power of herbs that could turn men into beasts, but as a goddess she could see into the future and foretell what should come to pass.

So on the day of his departure she made a great feast and bade Ulysses and his crew. And they ate and drank to their hearts' content, and had no fear that they should suffer the fate of their companions. But Ulysses she took aside and revealed to him all that should befall him on his homeward voyage, and instructed him how he should avoid the perils that would beset him on the way. And first of all she bade him beware of the Sirens—sea maidens, whose song is more musical than is Apollo's lute; no mortal can resist its ravishment, and he who listens is lost.

But Ulysses, whose soul still hungered for new adventures, said: 'To hear such music, a man might well choose to die. Let me at any risk hear the song of the Sirens!'

Then the goddess instructed him how, if he followed her precepts, he might hear the song of the Sirens and yet live. What the instructions were there is no need to tell, for Ulysses did all that the goddess had bidden him, and all that

Left: Illustration of sirens from Imagines deorum *by Vincenzo Cartari and Antoine Du Verdier.*

she foretold came to pass.

So on the morrow the crew embarked, and Circe sending them a fair wind they were carried swiftly upon their way. But the heart of Ulysses was heavy as he pondered the counsels of the goddess and thought on the Sirens who had drawn so many men to their death. So he stood up and spoke to all his men, saying:

'Friends, it is well I should declare to you the oracles of Circe, that with foreknowledge we may shun death—for she bade us shun the sound of the voices of the Sirens, and me only she bade listen to their song. Bind me, therefore, in a hard bond, that I may remain unmoved in my place, upright in the mast-stead, and from the mast let rope-ends be tied; and if I entreat and command you to set me free, then do ye bind me with yet more bonds.'

The men gave good heed, promising to obey in all things the commands of their wise leader.

Meanwhile, land was spied ahead, and, Circe's wind still speeding the ship, she was borne swiftly towards the shore. Suddenly the wind ceased and there was a dead calm. No sea-bird cried, and the very waves seemed spell-bound. Then Ulysses knew that they were approaching the perilous Isle of the Sirens. So while his men were furling in the idle sails and plying the oars once more, he drew his sharp sword and, cutting in pieces a great cake of wax, kneaded it with his strong hands. Then, when the wax was soft, he anointed therewith the ears of his men as they sat at their oars, that they might not hear the voices of the Sirens. And the men in their turn bound their leader hand and foot upright in the mast-stead, and from the mast they fastened rope-ends. Having done this, they sat down to their oars and smote the level waters.

Fast sped the ship across the bay, and now they were within hailing distance of the land. And there on the shore stood the Sirens, lovely as goddesses, singing and striking their golden lyres. Round about them was a green meadow, very sweet to the eyes of those sea-worn warriors, for the white bones with which it was strewn appeared but as lilies such as they remembered in their fields at home.

Nearer sped the ship, and now the Sirens, seeing the far-famed Ulysses on board, sang yet more sweetly, in this fashion:

'O hither, come hither and furl your sails,
Come hither to me and to me:
Hither, come hither and frolic and play;
Here it is only the mew that wails;
We will sing to you all the day:
Mariner, mariner, furl your sails,
For here are the blissful downs and dales,
And merrily, merrily carol the gales,
And the spangle dances in bight and bay,
And the rainbow forms and flies on the land
Over the islands free;
And the rainbow lives in the curve of the sand;
Hither, come hither and see;
And the rainbow hangs on the poising wave,
And sweet is the color of cove and cave,
And sweet shall your welcome be:
O hither, come hither, and be our lords,
For merry brides are we:
We will kiss sweet kisses and speak sweet words:
O listen, listen, your eyes shall glisten
With pleasure and love and jubilee:
O listen, listen, your eyes shall glisten
When the sharp clear twang of the golden chords
Runs up the ridged sea.
Who can light on as happy a shore
All the world o'er, all the world o'er?
Whither away? listen and stay: mariner, mariner, fly no more.'[3]

So they sang, waving their white arms, beckoning with smiles and twanging their
golden lyres. And their voice floating over the waters was sweet in the ears of

travel-worn Ulysses—so sweet indeed, that forgetting the wise counsels of Circe, he called to his company to unbind him. But they, having their ears stopped with wax, could hear neither him nor the Sirens, and rowed more swiftly than before. So Ulysses made signs to them, nodding and frowning, whereupon two of them, Perimedes and Eurylochus, remembering his former words, rose and bound him yet faster to the mast. And bending their backs the rowers pulled their hardest, the curved keel shooting past the perilous shore. Fainter and fainter grew the song of the Sirens as now they were left behind, and their white arms could hardly be seen beckoning. And anon a breeze broke once more upon the deadly calm, and the sails being hoisted the ship was swept out to sea and the Isle of the Sirens became but a speck upon the horizon and was lost to view.

So, by following the wise counsels of Circe of the braided tresses, the much-experienced Ulysses and all his comrades escaped the wiles of the Sirens who had enticed many to their death.

But when the Sirens saw themselves at last defeated, their song was turned into a wail and their white robes seemed like wind-swept foam as they plunged beneath the wave. But the Sirens are immortal, and though no men can now behold their white bosoms pressing golden harps, yet their voices are still heard and still they sing the same song that they sang to Ulysses:

> 'Surely, surely, slumber is more sweet than toil, the shore
> Than labor in the deep mid-ocean, wind and wave and oar;
> O rest ye, brother mariners, we will not wander more.'[4]

FOOTNOTES:

[3] Alfred, Lord Tennyson, 'The Sea Fairies.'
[4] Alfred, Lord Tennyson, 'The Lotos-Eaters.'

The Story of Nausicaa

M.M. Bird

One night, Nausicaa, sole daughter of Alcinous, the Phæacian King, had a dream. She dreamt that the daughter of Dymas, her favourite playmate, stood at her bedside and gently chid her. 'Shame upon thee, lie-a-bed,' she cried, 'to waste the shining hours. 'Twill soon be thy wedding-day, and thy bridal robe and the garments for thy bridesmaids have still to be washed and bleached. Get up and ask thy father to order for thee the wain and mules to draw it, and we'll all go a-washing, thou and I and our favourite playmates, to that clear pool where the river pauses before it plunges into the sea.'

At dawn Nausicaa awoke, but daylight did not dispel the dream, for it was Minerva herself who sent it. She waylaid her father as he went to the Council of the Elders and cried to him: 'Father dear, may I have the high wain and the mules today? There is much soiled raiment to be washed—mine and thine and that of my three brothers who dwell with me in the palace.' But of the bridal of her dream she said nothing, for she was a bashful maiden.

And her father, smiling at her strange eagerness, said, 'My darling child may take the car; whate'er our daughter asks, we give.'

Swiftly her attendants prepared the wain and harnessed the mules. They loaded it with the soiled robes and dresses that the maiden brought from her

bower, and the good mother put on top a basket filled with cates and dainties, and a wine-skin, and a cruse of olive oil wherewith to anoint the maidens after their bath.

Nausicaa climbed into the wain, and away they sped with laughter and with song, this bright bevy of maidens. When they reached the spot where all the falling streams emptied their waters into a wide basin, they unharnessed the mules and let them loose to graze on the plain, while all the girls set gayly to their task.

At length they had finished their toil; every garment had been steeped and trodden with their dainty feet, and rinsed and spread out to dry on the hot sands, which sparkled in the sunlight. Then the maidens undressed and dabbled and splashed one another, and frolicked in the crystal pool. Tired with work and play they anointed their dripping limbs with the olive oil and sat down to rest in the shade. And Nausicaa unpacked the basket, and they ate and drank of the good things that the Queen had provided. This done, and while the clothes were yet drying in the sun, they played ball in the meadow, tossing it from one to another; and all the while Nausicaa guided their movements, keeping time with a rustic ballad measure.

Meanwhile, all unknown to these merry maidens, deep in the shelter of a low-branched tree, Ulysses lay asleep. A tempest had wrecked his ship and robbed him of all his companions, and he had only the day before, by help of the goddess Leucothea, been saved, and hardly saved, from the devouring sea. Clinging to a spar he had been cast upon the Phæacian shore after many hours in the storm-tossed deep. Worn and bruised by battling with the breakers, he had sought shelter under the drooping branches of two ancient olive trees. Beneath this covert he made a great bed of fallen leaves, and heaping them above him, soon fell into a deep slumber sent in mercy to restore him by the ever-watchful Minerva.

It chanced that in their game a girl missed the ball that Nausicaa threw, and it fell into the rapid stream, and was lost. The girls all shrieked, and the piercing cry waked the sleeping Ulysses.

'Alas!' he lamented, 'upon what inhospitable coast have I been cast? Is it possessed by fierce barbarians who will slay, or by men who will prove pitiful? Do

I hear the voices of nymphs, or dryads, or of human maids?'

The hero rose straightway from his leafy bed, and tearing off a green bough to hide his nakedness, he stepped forth to discover his fate. When the affrighted maidens saw this wild and savage man advancing, they fled and hid themselves among the rocks and caves of the broken shore. Not so Nausicaa. Inspired by Minerva with a boldness not her own, she stood and watched this strange interloper. He was now close to her, but he dared not clasp her knees, as suppliants are wont to do, for fear of alarming her, but, keeping his distance, he told her of his perils by sea. For twenty nights he had been wrestling with the waves, and had hardly reached this present haven. Now, famished and exhausted, he waited anxiously to learn where he stood, and only begged some garment to clothe his nakedness.

'Lady,' he added, with cunning flattery, 'I know not whether thou art mortal or divine, so fair a maiden I now behold. Only once in Delos I saw so goodly a thing as thou—the sapling of a palm tree that sprung from the altar of Apollo.'

The fair Nausicaa was touched by his courtly words and bearing, and, marred as he was by the salt sea-foam, she marked his noble features. She answered his questions with graceful sweetness, telling with whom he had found refuge and assuring him of their hospitality. She called her girls and blamed them for their idle fears. Obedient to her directions they led Ulysses to the secret pool where he might bathe, they gave him of the oil to anoint himself, and laid ready for him one of the shining garments that they had just washed and dried in the sun.

The maidens surveyed with wonder the majestic figure of the stranger when he returned to them, bathed and anointed, and clad in the pomp of royal vesture. And Nausicaa, gazing with admiration on him, whispered a prayer to Heaven that some such noble spouse might fall to her happy lot.

They hastened then to serve him, setting before him food and wine, and he ate and drank eagerly, for he was half starved. Then, as evening approached, Nausicaa's cares were directed to their return to her father's palace. The mules were harnessed to the car, and she then turned to the stranger and gave him instructions how to reach the palace. For fear of slanderous tongues, she would

not permit him to accompany her train, but caused him to follow at a seemly distance. She promised to go to her royal father and intercede with him for the stranger, whom she directed to follow her to the palace with all reasonable haste. There she advised that he should seek the Queen, Arete, whom he would find at that hour busied with her weaving. If he disclosed his mournful tale to her sympathetic ear, he would be assured of assistance, and doubtless live to see his native land once again.

Thereon she whipped up her team of mules, and they started at a canter, but she was careful soon to rein them in that Ulysses might keep pace with them. But when they neared the town he stayed awhile in a sacred grove while Nausicaa went on her way through the crowded streets, where all turned to gaze at the princess, and thought she had never looked so beautiful. At the palace gates her brothers gathered round and received from her hands the garments she had washed for them. Then she hastened to her mother's chamber.

Ulysses slowly approached the famous city of the Phæacians. Lest the lordly mien and regal robes of the stranger should attract the attention of the low-born crowd, Minerva spread a mist about her hero wherein he could walk unperceived and unmolested. When he had passed the walls of the city, he saw a girl carrying a pitcher (it was his goddess in disguise). He accosted her and begged her to show him the palace of Alcinous. This she did, and only left him at the gates, telling him that Arete was a gracious Queen, and if he won her favor, she might speed him on his homeward way. She vanished, leaving the hero to admire the beauties of the royal gates. These were of massive brass; a high cornice was reared above them, rich plates of gold overlaid the folding doors, and the pillars were of silver. Two rows of sculptured dogs in gold and silver, formed by Vulcan with divine art, stood guardian at Alcinous' gate, and within was a pleached garden, planted with fruit trees of all kinds, whose fruit faileth not, winter and summer alike. Pear ripens on pear, apple on apple, fig upon fig, and new grapes redden on the vine while the old grapes are treading in the wine-press.

Long while Ulysses gazed and wondered. Then he crossed the threshold, and passing unperceived through the banqueting hall, he sought the inner chamber where sat the royal pair. And he cast his hands about the knees of Arete, and besought her pity, and that of the King, for a wretched exile worn with griefs and long toil. Then he sat him down among the ashes of their hearth.

The King was moved with compassion. He raised the suppliant to a seat beside his own, and bade him share the feast. After pouring a due libation to Jupiter, the god of suppliants, Alcinous summoned his captains and princes to meet in council the following day to debate the cause of the stranger and devise proper means to transport him safe to the distant shore he designed to reach.

When all had taken their departure and Ulysses was left alone with the King and Queen, Arete asked him who he was, whence he came, and who had given him that robe? For well she knew the garments her own hands had fashioned.

Ulysses answered with the tale of his shipwreck and the gentle ministrations of her fair daughter, but his name he did not reveal. But Alcinous answered: 'My daughter was much to blame in that she brought thee not to our house. Gladly would I give her to a man so goodly as thou, and I would bestow on thee lands and wealth if thou would'st stay. But no man will I detain against his will; and if thou would'st depart I will furnish thee with ships and an escort to speed thee on the way.'

Next day there was feasting in the hall to entertain the guest, and Demodocus the famous minstrel was there, and he sang the Song of Troy, of Agamemnon and Hector, aye, and of the feud 'twixt Achilles and Ulysses. And Ulysses, as he listened, drew his cloak over his head to hide his tears.

After the feast there were games—racing, wrestling, and throwing the discus; and when the stranger was invited to make trial of his strength he hurled a huge rock that flew twice as far as the farthest quoit; and to this day the islanders point out to travelers Ulysses' stone.

Again at evening there was feasting in the hall. And Ulysses, as he came from the bath, anointed with oil and clad in the royal mantle that Alcinous had given him, on his way to join the feast, met the white-armed Nausicaa standing in the doorway. 'Farewell, stranger,' she whispered; 'depart in peace; and in thy far home think sometimes on the little maid who saved thee from the sea.'

And Ulysses answered: 'Nausicaa, to thee I owe my life, and if God grants me to reach my home, all my days I will do worship to thee, as to a god.'

Then he hastened to join the feasters, and set him in the seat assigned to him at Alcinous' right hand. Noticing Demodocus, the sweet minstrel, standing by a pillar alone, he called a henchman and said, 'Take from me this mess of wild boar, and when he has eaten thereof and drunk, bid him sing me, as he will, the lay of the Wooden Horse.' And the inspired minstrel brought back to him so vividly that tale of fire and carnage that Ulysses was moved to tears; and Alcinous asked him whether he had lost some kinsman in the fray, or some friend dearer than a brother. Then Ulysses disclosed his name, and gave the King the full and true story of all his wanderings from the fall of Troy to the shipwreck that landed him on this friendly shore.

When the long tale was ended Alcinous spake to his lordly company. 'Let us speed our parting guest, the bravest and the noblest that has ever visited our land. With raiment and gold have I myself furnished him, but each of you give him a tripod or a caldron for a keepsake.'

As the King said so was it done, and Alcinous himself saw all the precious gifts safely stowed in the ship he had provided. Then they pledged one another in a parting cup, and Ulysses bade farewell to his generous and great-hearted hosts. Worn out with the emotions of those crowded hours he wrapped himself in his mantle and lay down to sleep in the stern, while the spread sails caught the freshening breeze and the galley flew over the waters.

When the morning star shone bright in the heavens, the hills of Ithaca appeared like a cloud upon the horizon, and as day broke the ship drew into a little bay and grounded on the sands. Seeing that Ulysses was still wrapped in unbroken slumber, the sailors took him gently upon his couch and placed him on the rocky shore of his own Ithaca. Alcinous' royal gifts they placed beside him in the shade of a wild olive tree. Then they relaunched their bark and sped back across the main.

Thus Ulysses reached once more his native land, but the end of his perils was not yet.

The Homecoming of Ulysses

M.M. Bird

After ten long years of fighting Troy had fallen and the kings and captains had sailed away bearing home to Greece the spoils of the sacked city. Among these chieftains was Ulysses, lord of the small and rocky island of Ithaca, and none more famous than he for prowess in arms and yet more for the spirit of wisdom that the wise goddess Minerva put into the heart of her favored warrior.

But while the other leaders straightway sought their homes, Ulysses roamed the seas for another ten years. The goddess Juno loved him not, and often drove him from his course; and he, ever yearning to gain knowledge of lands and men, encountered the strangest adventures in his wanderings, some of which you have already heard. But it is of his homecoming that I have now to tell.

His perils and adventures were not ended yet, and without Minerva's aid he must surely have perished.

When he landed on the rocky coast of Ithaca he found himself a complete stranger in his own land after twenty years of absence, so by Minerva's advice he disguised himself as a beggar that he might discover something of the state of his kingdom before making himself known. His queen, Penelope, had suffered great troubles and perplexities all these years. She had the care of all the lands and vast herds of cattle that made up the riches of the kingdom; many of her servants

proved both dishonest and rebellious; and now a number of the neighboring princes had come seeking her hand in marriage. For all men held that Ulysses must have perished or he would surely have returned ere this. Telemachus, her young son, had just reached manhood, but was not yet strong enough unaided to drive out his mother's bold and shameless suitors and restore order to his realm. So the suitors continued to live in the palace, feasting daily and wasting Ulysses' goods and cattle with their wanton extravagances, while they continually urged Penelope to marry one of their number and give him the right to rule her kingdom for her. To this she would not give consent, for she loved Ulysses, and wept in secret over his absence and longed for his return, though she scarcely dared to hope for it after so many years had passed without news of his safety.

At length Telemachus was inspired by Minerva to set out on a journey to seek his father. The goddess accompanied him in the guise of a wise old man named Mentor, to assist him in his search. After adventurous wanderings he reached the city of Sparta, where King Menelaus reigned, who gave him news of Ulysses and counseled him to return at once to Ithaca since his father was on his way thither. Telemachus hastened back, and, arriving before he was expected, went secretly to the house of Eumaeus, a faithful servant of the King, who for many years had filled the post of chief herdsman and keeper of the royal swine. This was an office of trust, for much of the wealth of the kingdom was in these herds of swine, which were required as sacrifices to the gods as well as for human food.

Ulysses by this time had reached the house of Eumaeus, who had received him with kindness, and fed him, although he did not recognize his King in the aged beggar he found at his door. To this beggar he made complaint of the King's wasted substance, and the insufferable behavior of these suitors of the Queen. His tales of their doings made Ulysses' blood boil. He could hardly contain his indignation sufficiently to sustain the character of a wandering beggar whom these things did not concern. But he succeeded so well that Eumaeus had no suspicion who his strange guest could be.

When Telemachus appeared, Eumaeus greeted him with the tenderness of a father, for he loved the young man dearly, and at once hastened to announce the joyful news of his safe return to his mother Penelope. When thus left alone, Ulysses threw off his disguise and declared himself to his son. Long time they discussed how best to take vengeance on these wicked and insolent princes who were plotting to deprive them of their kingdom; and they decided that as they were many and powerful it was needful to exercise caution and overcome them by cunning. Therefore Telemachus departed to the palace and disclosed to no one the news of Ulysses' return, not even to the Queen his mother.

The wicked suitors had planned an ambush to slay the young prince as he made his way home from his journey in search of his father, but thanks to his secret and unexpected arrival, he had escaped their clutches.

According to their daily custom they sat down to a feast in the hall of the palace, where Telemachus, putting on an appearance of great friendliness, joined them. Thither Eumaeus persuaded his aged guest to accompany him. In fluttering rags and leaning on his staff as though weighed down by age and weakness, Ulysses passed along the road to the palace that was his own. Outside the gate they were met by Melanthius, the faithless steward, whose own ill deeds made him show spite and jealousy to the blameless Eumaeus. He rated the old beggar soundly and ordered him away, and when he protested, cursed him and muttered a prayer that some suitor's sword might pierce the heart of Telemachus and rid them of a son no better than his dead father. Ulysses stood a moment in speechless rage, doubting whether to strike the wretch to earth with one blow of his mighty arm; but wiser counsels prevailed, and he curbed his anger and bore all affronts and insults with a noble fortitude that steadfastly awaited the right moment to strike.

Passing the insolent Melanthius with disdain they approached the door. Lying on a dunghill beside the way Ulysses beheld his aged hound Argus, the hero of many a gallant chase. Now neglected, starved, forlorn, he had crept forth to die. But at the sound of his master's voice he strove in vain to raise the wasted body that was too weak to move from the dunghill where it lay. But with tail and ears and eyes he proclaimed his joy. A tear stole unperceived down Ulysses' cheek. He questioned Eumaeus about the hound, and as he paused, the noble creature, to whom fate had granted a sight of his master after twenty years of patient waiting, took one last look and died.

When Eumaeus introduced the old beggar into the banqueting hall, true to the character he had adopted Ulysses went round to each reveler in turn and begged for food. Some carelessly flung him a few scraps, giving away readily what was not their own, but Antinous, the most lawless and violent of all the suitors, abused him and threw a footstool at him, striking him on the shoulder. Telemachus indignantly protested against this act of violence, and Ulysses was permitted to sit down by the door, with his scrip full of scraps from the princes' well-filled table.

Presently there entered another beggar, a surly vagrant of great stature, named Irus, well known at the tables of the rich. He was enraged to find that another had been before him, and attacked the old man with loud abuse, finally challenging him to a fight, thinking him too weak with age to defend himself.

The princes applauded him and urged on the fight between the two beggars. Ulysses pretended to fear, but when he threw off his rags and displayed his well-knit limbs and great muscles, all gazed at him astonished, and Irus tried to escape. He was caught and dragged before Ulysses and forced to engage in the combat he had provoked. Ulysses, knowing his own strength to be invincible, did not strike with more than half his force, but the first blow broke the sturdy beggar's jaw and flung him to the ground, from whence he was unable to rise. Ulysses was then given as the prize of victory a stew of savory meat.

When the revelers were deep in their cups Ulysses and his son Telemachus stole away from the hall and conferred together in secret. They gathered all the best of the weapons in the armory and hid them in a convenient chamber, to be at hand in case of need.

Telemachus then introduced Ulysses to the chamber of his mother Penelope, who failed to pierce his disguise, but listened with eagerness to the account the beggar gave of his wanderings and adventures. He claimed to have formerly entertained her husband in Crete, described his appearance exactly, and declared to her joy that his return within a month was certain. She then sent him to the bath, and bade Euryclea wait upon him. It happened that Euryclea was his old nurse, and her heart went out to the stranger, for in his look and voice there was something that reminded her of her absent lord. Gladly she fetched water to refresh him and knelt before him to bathe his feet. He remembered the long scar on his thigh, made by the tusk of a wild boar when as a youth he had hunted on Parnassus, and he strove to keep it concealed. But the loving eyes of his faithful nurse pierced the tattered rags that he wore, and she knew him for her lord and master. 'My son—my King!' she cried. He laid his hand on her lips to stay the cry of joy that broke from her, and gravely warned her not to betray his return.

When he returned from his bath, the Queen, still more impressed by his noble presence, though yet she knew him not, confided to him a design she had planned to assist her choice among these suitors who were all distasteful to her. She proposed to set them a superhuman task—to bend the great bow of Ulysses and perform the feat in which he used to excel. Two rows of beams, six in each row, should be set at equal distances apart, to support twelve silver ax rings, and through each line of six rings the archer must let fly his arrow straight and true. And the noble archer who should perform this feat should be rewarded by her hand.

Ulysses applauded this design, urging her not to fear to name herself the prize, since Ulysses himself would enter the lists before the trial was over, win the prize, and claim her for his own.

The following day another great feast was set, and the princes sat down to their feasting. Ulysses by this time had watched the behavior of his people, and now understood who were faithful to him and who deserved no trust. Into this scene of revelry Penelope entered with her maidens, bearing the great bow and arrows of Ulysses, and challenged the princes to bend this bow and shoot the arrow through the silver rings as her lord Ulysses had been used to do, promising that he who could accomplish this should be her husband.

The beams were already set in place, and Telemachus claimed his right to try his skill first among the suitors, since victory meant to him the safeguarding of a kingdom already his by right of descent. He set the axes in line upon the beams,

with the rings ready for the flight of his arrow. Three times his young arm tried to bend the bow, three times he failed.

Then all the princes in order, from right to left, took up the bow in turn and tried their skill. In vain they strained their muscles; they rubbed the bow with fat; they warmed it at the flame to make it supple; they tried every device to bend it. The tough bow bent not in their impious hands!

While they strove Ulysses took aside Eumaeus, and Philaetus a herdsman and one who had remained faithful to him, and revealed himself to them. He then ordered that every door of the palace should be guarded by a trusty matron, and the main gate secured by a cable, and bade them then attend on him in the hall. Telemachus had sent his mother and her maids away to their own apartments, and asserting his authority now directed Eumaeus to bear the bow to the disguised beggar, that he might try his skill and strength. All the suitors were furious at this strange favor shown to a common beggar, and it was amidst a scene of tumult and confusion that Ulysses, without rising from his seat, bent the bow and sent his arrow straight and true through the silver rings. There was a moment of silent astonishment. Telemachus hastened to gird on his sword and, taking his javelin in his hand, stood by his father's side. Ulysses cried aloud to the suitors that he had won the first game he had tried today, and was ready to play a second with them. And another arrow winged its way straight at the throat of Antinous, who had raised a golden bowl and was drinking deep of the wine. The arrow pierced his neck and he dropped the goblet and fell lifeless on the marble floor.

There was panic in the hall; the princes looked in vain for weapons or a way of escape from the doom that menaced them. 'Aimest thou at princes?' they cried to Ulysses in their terror.

'Dogs! ye have had your day!' cried he, and declared his name and estate to them. Some drew their swords and rushed on him, but the flying arrows pinned them, and they fell dead in heaps, while the sword and javelin of young Telemachus did good service. At length every suitor lay dead. The hall was like a shambles.

Then the unfaithful servants were made to purify the palace and afterwards paid with their lives for their misdeeds, while those who had been true to their lord crowded around him with joy.

Euryclea flew to summon the sleeping Penelope. She was unable to believe the glad news. 'Ulysses comes! The suitors are no more!' She could not think it true. At last she stood trembling before her lord, still afraid to believe it was he, age and time seemed to have made him so strange to her eyes.

Then Minerva crowned her watchful care of the hero by restoring to him the beauty of his youth; but still the Queen hesitated. Ulysses therefore described to her the marvels of the bridal bed he had contrived for her of the huge olive tree that grew in the courtyard.

Penelope saw then that it was indeed the King, who alone could have known the secret of the bed. She fell fainting into his arms in a transport of joy, and Ulysses once more resumed his sway over the kingdom.

Jupiter and Mercury with Philemon and Baucis, *after Peter Paul Rubens.*

Baucis and Philemon

H.P. Maskell

On the slopes of the Phrygian hills there once dwelt a pious old couple named Baucis and Philemon. They had lived all their lives in a tiny cottage of wattles thatched with straw, cheerful and contented in spite of their poverty. Servants never troubled them, because they waited on themselves, and they never had to consider the whims of other people, because they were their own masters.

As this worthy old couple sat dozing by the fireside one evening in the late autumn, two strangers came and begged a shelter for the night. They had to stoop to enter the humble doorway, where the old man welcomed them heartily and bade them rest their weary limbs on the settle. Meanwhile Baucis stirred the embers, blowing them into a flame with dry leaves, and heaping on fagots and logs to boil the stewing-pot. Hanging from the blackened beams was a rusty side of bacon. Philemon cut off a rasher to roast; and while his guests refreshed themselves with a wash at the rustic trough, he gathered what pot herbs could be culled from his patch of garden. Then the old woman, her hands trembling with age, laid the cloth and spread the board. It was a rickety old table. One leg was too short, and had to be propped up with a potsherd.

It was but a frugal meal, but one that hungry wayfarers could relish. The first course was a sort of omelet of curdled milk and eggs garnished with radishes and candied cornel berries, served on rude oaken platters. The cups of turned beechwood were filled with home-made wine from an earthenware jug. With

the second course there were nuts, dried figs, and dates—plums too, and sweet-smelling apples, grapes, and a piece of clear white honeycomb. What made it the more grateful to the guests was the hearty spirit in which all was offered. Their hosts gave all they had to give without stint or grudging.

But all at once something happened which startled and amazed Baucis and Philemon. They poured out wine for their guests, and lo! each time the pitcher filled itself again to the brim! In alarm they knelt down and implored the pardon of their visitors, for they now saw that these were not mere mortals. They were indeed none other than Jupiter and Mercury, who had come down to earth in disguise. The old couple excused themselves; by reason of their poverty and the lack of time, they had not been able to provide them a better entertainment. And Philemon hurried out and gave chase to their single goose, who served them for a watch-dog, intending to kill it and roast it for their guests. However, these forbade him, saying: 'We are from above, and we have come down to punish the impious dwellers of the plains. In mortal shape we came down, and at a hundred houses asked for lodging and for rest. For answer a hundred doors were locked and barred against us. You alone, the poorest of all, have received us gladly, and given us of your best. Now it is for us to punish those who treat strangers so churlishly, while you shall be spared. Only leave your cottage and follow us to the mountain-top.'

So saying, the deities led the way up the hill, and the two old folk hobbled after them on their crutches. Presently they stopped to take rest, and, looking round, saw all the country round sinking into a marsh, their own hut alone left standing. And while they gazed, before their very eyes their cabin was changed into a temple. The stakes in the porch turned into marble columns, and the door expanded into a great carved and inlaid gate of bronze. The thatch grew yellow, till at last they saw that it had become a roof of gold tiles. Then Jupiter, regarding them with kindly eyes, inquired: 'Tell us, good old man, and you, good wife, well worthy of such a husband, what boon would you crave of us?'

Philemon whispered for a moment with Baucis, and she nodded her approval. 'We desire,' he replied, 'to be your servants, and have the care of this temple. One

other favor only we would ask. From boyhood I have loved only Baucis, and she has lived only for me. Let the same hour take us both away together. Let me never see the tomb of my wife, nor let her suffer the misery of mourning my death.'

The gods willingly granted both these requests, and endowed them with youth and strength as well. So long as their lives lasted Baucis and Philemon were guardians of the temple. And when once more old age and feebleness overtook them, they were standing, one day, in front of the sacred porch and relating to visitors the story of the temple. Baucis happened to turn her gaze on her husband and saw him slowly changing into a gnarled oak. And Philemon, as he felt himself rooted to the ground, saw Baucis at the same time turning to a leafy linden; and as their faces disappeared behind the green foliage, each cried to the other, 'Farewell, dearest love'; and again, 'Dearest love, farewell'; and trunks and branches took the place of their human forms.

For long years these two trees were pointed out to all who came to worship at the temple, and many loved to bring garlands and hang them on the trees, in honour of two souls whose virtue the gods had so signally rewarded.

And still, if you visit the spot, you may see an oak and a linden with branches intertwined. What more proof would you have that this tale is true?

Hypermnestra

V.C. Turnbull

anaüs and Ægyptus, two brothers, ruled together over Egypt. And to Danaüs fifty daughters were born, while Ægyptus begot fifty sons. Yet was not Danaüs happy; nay, he went all day in fear. For the mysterious voice of the Theban oracle had sounded terribly in his ears:

WHEN THY DAUGHTER MARRIETH, DANAÜS, THOU ART DOOMED TO DEATH!

Never could Danaüs put these words from his mind. Walking alone in the gardens of his palace, he started, thinking one whispered them in his ear; at the banquet they sounded like thunder above the singing of the minstrels; and at night he lay trembling on his bed, hearing the doom of the oracle spoken in low tones out of the darkness. So the life of Danaüs became dark and bitter, and his heart grew hard and cruel with fear.

Now the sons of Ægyptus were grown into comely youths, and to their father it seemed but fitting that they should marry their cousins, the daughters of Danaüs, beautiful maidens all. But when he spoke thereon to his brother, a great terror fell on Danaüs. For casting his eyes on the young men as they strove together in their sports, he thought with bitterness: 'Yea, and shall one of these be my murderer?' Then, in fear and rage, he turned to his brother, and, snarling like

a wolf, cried, 'Child of mine weds not child of thine!' Whereat Ægyptus raged mightily, swearing to fulfil his purpose, so that Danaüs, ever cunning rather than valiant, made amends for his hasty words and promised to tell his daughters of their uncle's pleasure.

Howbeit, that night Danaüs gathering together his daughters, his slaves, and his goods, secretly left the palace, and flying northward to the coast of the Great Sea, there took ship and came at length to Argos in Greece. Gelanor, King of Argos, received Danaüs and his daughters with kindness and feasted them with royal cheer. But the heart of Danaüs knew not gratitude, and having left the throne of Egypt, he sought how to take that of Argos. Nor was this difficult, for Gelanor was at strife with his people, who were but too ready to seek a new ruler. Therefore, when Danaüs spoke to them fair words, promising them many things, they gave glad heed, and ere many days had passed Gelanor was driven forth and Danaüs ruled over Argos in his stead.

But not long was he left in peace. For his brother Ægyptus, enraged to find Danaüs forsworn, and hearing of his fortune in Argos, called his sons together and cried to them, saying: 'Sons, will ye suffer yourselves to be fooled? Shall this man snatch from you your brides and rule in peace on the throne which he hath stolen? Nay, if ye be sons of mine, go, gather to yourselves a mighty army and take from him his daughters and his land, and the gods prosper you and protect your rights.'

Then the young men, kindling at their father's words, gathered quickly a great host, and sailing in a fleet to Argos, they harried the country before Danaüs knew of their landing. And when one ran to tell him of their coming, a great fear struck upon his heart, for louder than ever in Egypt sounded in his ear:

WHEN THY DAUGHTER MARRIETH, DANAÜS,
THOU ART DOOMED TO DEATH!

So with fear and hatred in his breast, but with smooth words upon his lips, he went forth to meet the young men and their followers, who were even now at the

palace gates. All that they demanded he promised.

'Take my daughters to wife,' he cried; 'reign over Argos in my stead, for I am old, and weary of ruling a strange people!'

So the young men were admitted into the palace, and the maidens their cousins received them with mirth and feasting, and the day of their nuptials was appointed.

But before the day came, the crafty Danaüs called his daughters to him and commanded them on peril of their lives to slay their husbands so soon as they should be wedded. And to each he gave a sharp dagger to conceal under her wedding robe. These, therefore, the daughters of Danaüs took, purposing to obey their father. For many of them were cruel even as he, while others, caring nothing for their affianced husbands, feared greatly to disobey Danaüs. So it was that as they took counsel together in the women's chamber after leaving their father's presence, there was but one voice among the maidens as to the wisdom of obeying his word.

But the youngest, Hypermnestra, was silent. For her heart was tender and pitiful, and Lynceus, her betrothed, youngest of the sons of Ægyptus and the fairest, had moved her heart to love and tenderness. Like her sisters, she feared her father, and never before had she disobeyed his orders; but love conquered fear, and pity was stronger than filial duty.

Now came the day of the weddings, and at night a great feast was spread. Golden lamps shed their radiance throughout the palace, and clouds of incense rolled up from the altar of Hymen, the god of happy nuptials. But Hypermnestra, heart-sick at the mockery, loathed the rich viands and the fumes of incense seemed to choke her.

The feast was over, and the young bridegrooms, crowned with chaplets of fresh flowers and dressed in wedding robes, had drunk deeply of drugged wine, and were half asleep before they reached their bridal chambers—led like lambs to the slaughter!

Hypermnestra sat up on her couch, listening with straining ears. Surely it was groaning she heard, on this side and on that. Her sisters were obeying their father's command, and dared she alone be disobedient? By her side lay young Lynceus, flushed with wine and sleep, his head thrown back, his breast bare. Nearer and louder sounded the groans, and she knew that Danaüs would speedily be coming to count the dead. In her terror she raised her weapon, and would have stricken first her lover and then herself.

'On earth,' she cried, 'there is no escape. I will die with my love, and we will go together to the realms of Tartarus, I the bride and he the bridegroom of Death.'

But as she bent over the sleeping Lynceus her hot tears awoke him, and he stretched out his arms to embrace her. She started aside like a guilty thing and hid her dagger, and cried to Lynceus: 'Arise, fly hence! else will to-night be to thee an everlasting night!'

'What sayest thou?' he murmured, only half awake. 'Art mocking me? Is that a dagger in thy left hand?'

'Rise and fly, while there is yet time!' she cried again. 'Thy brothers are already dead, treacherously slain by their brides. The dawn is near; soon it will be too late. Leave me; fly! I cannot bear to see thee slain!'

Then Lynceus sprang up and fled, and scarcely had he gone when Danaüs, gloating over his victims, entered to see if Hypermnestra had been obedient as her sisters. But Hypermnestra, fearful no longer, rose and faced him, holding out the bloodless dagger.

'Take back thy weapon, cruel father,' she cried. 'Nay, and if thou wilt, smite me therewith, slaying me with the death I would not bring upon my husband. But not in death itself shalt thou hear me say, "I repent."'

Strong and beautiful she stood there in the dawn, her eyes shining with triumph. But her father, enraged at the escape of one victim, struck her to the ground and ordered slaves to drag her by the hair to the palace dungeon. And not many days after, seated in the city hall of justice, he caused her to be brought before him to be sentenced for her disobedience. So slaves dragged in Hypermnestra, and she stood there before a great multitude, chains on her hands and feet, her white robe besmirched by the dungeon, but with the light of triumph still shining in her eyes. And all the people, seeing her, cried with one voice: 'Spare her, O king!' and as his wrath burned yet fiercer as a fire that meets the blast, the prayer became a threat: 'Spare her, thou cruel king!' But Danaüs, remembering the oracle, gnashed upon them with his teeth and rose as if to smite Hypermnestra with his own hand. But even as he rose a voice like thunder smote upon his ear:

'Hold, thou cursed king!' and the crowd made way for a young warrior to pass. Like a young god, Lynceus rushed upon Danaüs and slew him at a stroke, and all the people hailed him as King over Argos, and his wife Hypermnestra as Queen.

But the guilty sisters of Hypermnestra, seeing what had chanced, fled from Argos, whither none knew or cared. And poets tell that after death their shades in Tartarus were condemned evermore to draw water in bottomless urns, a warning to all false wives and traitors; but Hypermnestra has won for herself a name that will live for all time as a maiden tender and true, who loved greatly and dared greatly.

Oedipus at Colonos

Mrs. Guy E. Lloyd

Not far from the beautiful city of Athens, and within sight of its temple-crowned citadel, the Acropolis, lies the village of Colonos.

Here, on the slope of the hill, once stood a sacred grove of laurel, whose evergreen sprays adorn Apollo's hair; of olive, planted there by the gray-eyed goddess, Minerva, protectress of Athens; and of vine, the gift of Bacchus.

To this grove there came one day an old man, blind and meanly clad, but for all that venerable and noble of aspect, the unfortunate King Oedipus, led by his daughter Antigone, the sole prop and comfort of his old age.

Sad indeed had been the fate of Oedipus. It had been decreed by the immortal gods that he should slay his father, King Laïus, and while he was still a babe in arms Laïus bade his servants take the child and leave him amongst the bare rocks of Cithæron. Here the forsaken infant was found by a shepherd, who bore him far away from his own city of Thebes to Corinth. Merope the queen chanced to see the child, and struck by the likeness to her own child whom she had just lost, she adopted him, and he was brought up in the palace, believing himself to be truly the son of those with whom he dwelt. But having learnt from the oracle of Apollo that he was doomed to slay his own father, he left Corinth in order to escape that doom, and on the road it fell on him without his being aware of it. For he met a choleric old man in a chariot, who tried to thrust him out of the path, and in

301

defending himself against the old man's goad he smote him with his staff and slew him, not knowing who he was. But this was his father, Laïus, King of Thebes.

Oedipus, journeying on, with no thought but to get far from Corinth and avoid all possibility of parricide, came by chance to his own unknown city, Thebes. Here he delivered the people from a monstrous plague, the Sphinx, and they chose him by acclamation for their king. Thereafter he ruled them well and happily till the wrath of the gods fell upon them for the unavenged murder of their late king. Then did Oedipus turn his mind to seek out the slayer of Laïus, and seeking diligently he found, in the end, that he himself had slain the king, and that the king was his own father. In grief and horror at his own unwitting crime, he stabbed and lacerated his own eyes. To crown his cup of sorrows he was driven from his home by his wicked and ambitious sons, and he wandered out into the world a blind beggar, guided and supported by his faithful daughter Antigone.

Far had they wandered, and they were worn with toil and hunger when they sank down to rest beside the sacred grove of Colonos. Antigone guessed that the tower-crowned hill she saw before her in the distance guarded Athens, but she did not know what place this might be where her father rested, and was about to seek some one from whom to inquire, when by chance a man passed by along the road. Oedipus was beginning to ask this stranger to tell them somewhat of the place whither his wanderings had brought him, but the man interrupted his half-spoken question by telling him instantly to leave his seat, for this grove was the home of dread and mighty goddesses, and no man was permitted to set foot within the close, or even to approach the precincts.

Then Oedipus asked the name of these goddesses. The wayfarer himself called them Eumenides, the Gracious Ones; at Athens they were known as the Semnai, or Dread Ladies; but their proper name was the Erinys, or Avengers of Blood.

When Oedipus heard this he was glad, for the oracle had promised that the end of all his woes should come when he reached the shrine of the Dread Goddesses, and that as a sign that his troubles were over there should come a clap of thunder from a cloudless sky. Moreover the oracle foretold a blessing on the land that gave him burial. Therefore Oedipus begged the stranger to go in all haste to summon to him Theseus, the great and just King of Athens. But meanwhile the Thebans also had heard from the oracle that peace and prosperity should be to the last resting-place of the toil-worn Oedipus, and they had sent out to seek him and bring him back to his own city.

It was beside the grove of the Dread Goddesses that the Thebans found their uncrowned king, but he refused to return to a land that had driven him forth from its borders, choosing rather to die where he was, in the land of his adoption, the hospitable state of Athens. But the Thebans were angered at his refusal, and seized and bore off his faithful daughter Antigone. And the old king was in sore distress; but when he appealed to Theseus to help him, Theseus stood his friend and pursued the band that was bearing away Antigone, and brought her back to her father, safe and sound.

Then came to Oedipus yet another to crave the blessing of the uncrowned king, never so powerful as in his last hours. This was Polynices, the elder son of Oedipus. His younger brother had driven him out from Thebes and taken the throne himself, and now Polynices was collecting an army to go back and drive his brother away and make himself king again.

But Oedipus would not help his wicked son, but cursed him instead, foretelling how the two brothers, the last of an accursed house, should fall by each other's hands, and neither of them should ever enjoy the kingdom for which they strove.

Antigone entreated her brother to give up the fatal feud that could profit neither brother, but Polynices said he could not now turn back and desert his sworn allies, and he departed very sorrowful to meet his doom.

And as he went, from the clear sky there came a sudden clap of thunder. Then Oedipus sent in haste for Theseus, for he knew that here was the promised sign, and that his troublous life was all but over.

Theseus came quickly to see what was amiss with his old friend, and found him anxiously waiting, while the thunder roared louder and the forked lightning brought terror to all the beholders.

Then said Oedipus: 'The gods are showing now that the time of my doom is come. Blind though I am, I myself will guide my own steps to the spot where I am doomed to die, but thou alone, O Theseus, shalt know where is my resting-place, and thou shalt tell it to none on earth save when thy death-hour comes, and then shalt thou disclose it to thy eldest born. He in like manner shall hand the secret on, and thus shall peace and prosperity forever dwell in this land. Touch me not. Let me find my hallowed grave myself. Think of me sometimes when I am gone, and thou and all thy state are prosperous.'

Then the old man allowed his weeping daughters to lave his limbs and put on him a garment meet for the grave.

And when this was done, and Antigone still clung weeping to her father, there came first a roll of thunder, and after the thunder a voice that called: 'Ho, Oedipus, why tarriest thou?'

Then the old king arose and called on Theseus and begged him to care for his daughters, and Theseus vowed to be a true friend to the desolate maidens. And Oedipus kissed his daughters and sent them weeping away, and only Theseus saw the blessed end of a man in life more sinned against than sinning, or knew the last resting-place of the body of King Oedipus.

Antigone craved leave to visit her father's sepulcher, but not even she was allowed to know where was the secret burial-place; and when she was told that her father had willed that no mortal save Theseus should know the spot, she submitted, and only begged permission to go back to Thebes and try to save her brothers from their doom. But it was in vain that the gentle maiden strove to bring peace where was nothing but hatred. The two brothers, fighting in single combat, slew each other, and because Polynices had brought a great host against his own city, the Thebans cast his body without their walls and forbade that any man should sprinkle dust upon it, so should its soul never find rest, as a punishment for all its misdeeds. But Antigone would not leave her brother's corpse unburied. Her sister Ismene dared not help in such a deed, so the heroic maiden went alone, poured the three libations due to the dead, and scattered dust upon her brother's body, thus giving rest to his soul.

Then Creon, King of the Thebans, was wroth with the maiden, and he commanded that she should be taken to a cave, and the mouth be barred with

rocks. She should be given just enough food and water to prevent the guilt of her death falling upon the city, and left to pine away in her rocky dungeon. And the guards led her away and did the king's bidding. But when Creon's only son heard what was done he forced his way into that tomb of the living, for he loved Antigone, and would have delivered her at the price of his own life. For this he was too late; the princess had not waited to die by slow starvation within the walled-up cavern, she had strangled herself. The young prince, in his despair, smote himself with his own sword and fell dead beside the body of Antigone. So was the vengeance of the Erinys accomplished, and the work of the Avengers of Blood ended.

Midas

H.P. Maskell

nce upon a time there was born to Gordius, King of Phrygia, a son whom he named Midas. While this son was an infant in his cradle the ants were seen to creep in and put grains of golden wheat into his mouth. From this the wise men foretold that he would be exceeding rich and miserly, and choked with riches.

When Midas grew up to manhood and succeeded his father as king, it was soon proved that the seers were true prophets. He loved wealth and riches for their own sake. Merchants were sent far and wide to trade in all kinds of produce, and brought back their gains to swell his coffers. He caused mines to be dug for the precious metals. As fast as the money came in he invested it again in new ventures, and everything he undertook succeeded. Hence the saying arose: 'All that Midas touches turns into gold.'

Now it happened that Silenus, the foster-father of Bacchus, had wandered into Phrygia, and being an old man and overcome with wine—he was a terrible toper—the rustics used him roughly; and when he was sober they bound him with cords and took him as a prisoner to Midas. The king had been taught the rites of Bacchus, and as soon as he recognized Silenus, he rebuked the ignorant rustics and treated him with great honour, ordaining a special festival of ten days and ten nights to celebrate the visit of his guest. Bacchus, meanwhile, had been mourning the loss of his tutor. In gratitude to Midas for restoring his foster-father and preserving him from insult, he gave Midas the choice of any favor he desired.

'All I desire,' replied Midas, 'is to be the richest king on earth. Make that a truth which men say about me, that everything I touch shall turn to gold.'

'You might have asked for something better,' murmured the god, with a sigh. 'But as you wish, so shall it be.'

Scarcely able to believe it could be true, Midas hurried away to test the reality of his good fortune. An oak grew by the roadside. He took hold of a small twig; it was a twig of gold. He picked up a clod of earth; it was no longer clay, but a huge nugget. Passing through a cornfield, all the ears that brushed against his hand became ears of gold. Plucking an apple from a tree, it was at once like to the golden apple that Paris gave to Venus.

When he reached his palace and put his hand upon the doorpost, the wood turned yellow and glistened at his touch. The basin in which he washed his hands became a golden bowl, filled to the brim with gold-dust.

'Now, indeed,' he cried with joy, 'wealth and power are mine. My riches will be endless. Thanks be given to the gods for this most wonderful and precious of all gifts. What in the world is better than gold?'

While he was thus rejoicing, his servants entered and spread the table for a banquet. He seated himself and took a piece of bread in his hand. But it was no longer bread; it was hard, solid gold. He seized a goblet of wine, but to no purpose; he could not quench his thirst with a stream of gold! Too late he saw his folly. The richest man on earth, he was doomed to die of hunger and thirst. Nothing on earth was so useless to him as his gold!

Raising his hands towards heaven, he implored the pardon of the gods. 'Have mercy on me, for I repent me of my greed; have pity and deliver me from this awful curse!'

Bacchus, seeing that he was cured of his sordid folly, took pity on him, and showed him how the baneful gift could be got rid of. 'Go to Sardis,' said he, 'and track the river to its well-head. Plunge thy head beneath the bubbling spring, and purge thyself from the curse.' The king hastened to bathe in the spring, and so gained relief: the golden virtue left the human body and entered into the water. And even now the sands of Pactolus glitter with grains of gold-dust.

After this stern lesson, Midas no longer cared to go on amassing riches, but turned his attention to country sports and to music. Sad to tell, however, his folly and conceit led to trouble even in this, for he was but a sorry musician, and yet he set up for being a virtuoso. Some nymphs had listened with pleasure to Pan playing on his rustic reeds, and persuaded the minstrel to challenge Apollo, God of Music, to a contest. Old Tmolus, the ruler of the mountain, agreed to act as umpire. Pan's music was rude and uncouth; but when Apollo touched the strings of his lyre his very posture showed the master's skill, and so sweet were the notes that all present agreed with the decision that to Apollo the prize must be given. Midas alone protested that the judgment was unfair, and that Pan's music was superior. As a fit punishment for his crass stupidity Apollo caused his ears to grow longer and longer, with grey hairs all over them,

Apollo and Marsyas and the Judgment of Midas *by Melchior Meier.*

and twitching like the ears of an ass. Midas fled away amid the laughter of the deities and nymphs, and as quickly as possible concealed his disgrace under a thick turban.

None of the people of Phrygia had been present at the musical contest, and for a long time Midas succeeded in hiding the shameful deformity from his subjects. However, the barber who trimmed his hair was obliged to know of it. He did not dare tell anyone what he had seen; yet he found it harder every day to keep such a secret to himself. At last, as the only way he could conceive to relieve his mind of the burden, he went into a distant field, dug a hole in the ground, and whispered into it, 'Midas has ass's ears.' Then he shovelled the earth back, having delivered himself, and yet, as he thought, buried the secret quite safely.

A year passed. A clump of reeds had grown on the spot where the fatal secret lay buried. The reeds rustled gently as they were stirred by the south wind, and the goatherds passing by with their flocks were drawn to the place by the strange sounds that arose. The reeds seemed to be whispering the story one to another: 'Midas has ass's ears.'

And the wind carried the news to the reeds on the thatched sheds of the farm, so that they were soon quivering to tell their tale—when the farmer came in to supper, his goodwife called to him: 'Such a funny saying has been running in my head all day—where it comes from is a mystery: "Midas has ass's ears."'

The flowers told it to the trees, and the trees told it to the birds. Men and women learnt it they knew not how, but all who heard it found themselves forced by some mysterious impulse to repeat it to their neighbors, till all through the land of Phrygia rang the strange tidings: 'Midas has ass's ears!'

The hunger for gold may be cured, if taken in time; but not even a god can cure one who has ass's ears and lets the secret out.

Perseus and Andromeda

V.C. Turnbull

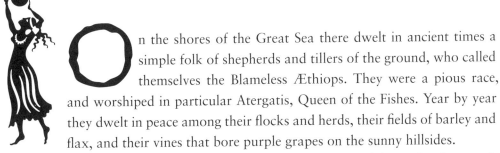

On the shores of the Great Sea there dwelt in ancient times a simple folk of shepherds and tillers of the ground, who called themselves the Blameless Æthiops. They were a pious race, and worshiped in particular Atergatis, Queen of the Fishes. Year by year they dwelt in peace among their flocks and herds, their fields of barley and flax, and their vines that bore purple grapes on the sunny hillsides.

But a great trouble fell upon this happy folk. For the earth heaved and yawned, and the dwellings of the people fell, and the sea poured in on the land, flooding and laying waste the golden harvest fields. Then a greater terror followed, for out of the sea rose a monster huge and terrible, such as never man had seen. Riding on the flood he came, bearing down upon the terrified people, and into his maw he swept their fattest sheep and kine, and also, alas! their fairest sons and daughters. And thus he came night after night, till the people's hearts failed them, and in their utter misery they sought counsel of their king. And King Cepheus spoke unto them, and said: 'Surely, my people, ye have sinned, and offended our great sea-god. Let us go to his temple and offer gifts, and inquire of his priests, and learn which of you has sinned.'

So they went with their King Cepheus to consult the priests of the sea-gods whom they worshiped. And when many sacrifices had been offered, the priests

cast lots to find who it was who had angered the gods and caused them to plague the land. And the lot fell upon Cassiopoeia, the queen.

Then Cassiopoeia stood up before all the people, her ebon hair falling to her feet and her eyes shining with tears, as she cried, and said:

'O my friends, I have sinned in my pride, and brought this evil on your homes. For not many days since my heart was lifted up and I boasted myself fairer than all the Nereids. And they, hearing, have risen in their wrath to avenge the insult. Pardon me, O my friends, for thus have I drawn desolation upon our land.'

And all the people were silent, but the priests made answer: 'Truly hast thou spoken, O Queen, and assuredly has thy boasting been our curse. Now, therefore, take thy daughter Andromeda and bind her to a rock on the seashore, so that when the monster cometh again he shall see that we have given him our best, even our king's daughter. Perchance he will have mercy and spare her when he sees our repentance, but anywise he will depart whence he came and trouble us no more.'

Then King Cepheus and Queen Cassiopoeia rose up and went down to their palace in grief too great for tears. And they took Andromeda, their only

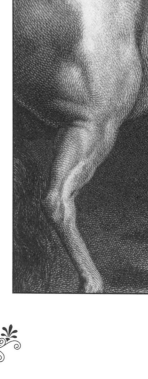

Perseus and Andromeda *by Pierre François Tardieu and Adam Friedrich Oeser, after Peter Paul Rubens.*

child, the fairest maiden in the land, and withal the tenderest and truest, and carried her down to the sea-shore. And all the people followed, weeping bitterly, for to many of them Andromeda had spoken kind words, and to not a few had she done gracious deeds. Yet when they thought on their own desolate homes, where no children played, they told themselves that the young princess must die for the people.

So they led Andromeda to the base of a sea-washed crag, and riveted her white arms with chains of brass to the black rock. And Cassiopoeia, kissing her, cried: 'O child, forgive thy wretched mother!'

And Andromeda answered: 'It is not thou, mother, but the sea-god who hath done me to death.'

And the queen kissed her yet again, and departed weeping. All the people followed, and night fell, and she was left alone. Out of the sky looked down the white moon behind the cloud rack, and not more fair was she than this maiden standing on the black rock like a white statue, half hid by the streaming locks that rippled to her knee.

So all night she stood and waited for her doom, most time mute with terror, but at whiles lamenting, and calling on the gods for pity. But no answer came save the thunder of the sea upon the rocks and the scream of the sea-birds wheeling between earth and sky.

Morning came, flinging roses from her car and scattering gold across the waters, and as those in bitterest pain of heart take strange note of passing things, Andromeda's eyes, dull and despairing, watched the sea-birds at their play. Among them came one flying swifter and greater than osprey or sea-eagle, and the gulls all dived at his approach. As the winged form drew nigh Andromeda was aware that this was no sea-bird; and soon she perceived a youth, godlike and strong, whose plumed sandals carried him over the deep as lightly as if he had been indeed a bird. Blue as the sea were his eyes, and his hair shone in the morning sun like spun gold. From his shoulder floated a goat-skin, on his arm he carried a brazen shield, and on his thigh hung a sword that flashed like diamonds in the sun. Straight to Andromeda he flew, and putting back the hair that covered her face he gazed into her eyes with love and pity, as he cried: 'O maiden, beautiful and pitiful, what cruelty hath brought thee to this pass?'

But Andromeda, wan and weak after the terrors of the night, could only hang her head and weep. So Perseus drew his diamond sword and smote through her chains, and gathered her, set free, to his breast. But when she had wept there a little space Andromeda thrust him away with a sharp cry.

'Oh, leave me!' she wailed, 'for I am the accursed one, the victim offered to the angry gods. Come not between me and my doom, for I suffer in the people's place.'

'Never will I leave thee,' answered Perseus, 'and never shalt thou suffer while I have strength to draw sword in thy defense.'

But Andromeda only wept the more and begged him again to be gone, and he, thinking to calm her, again entreated to hear the story of her sad plight. So Andromeda told him why she was being offered up to the monster, and as she finished speaking, her eyes, wandering seaward, widened with horror, and she shrieked aloud: 'It comes! it comes! Oh, kind and godlike youth, fly ere it is too late! Leave me; let not thine eyes behold my shameful end!'

But Perseus, kissing the tears from her face, laughed aloud and made a mock of the great fish-beast which even now, like a leviathan of the deep, could be seen plowing its way towards them across the sea.

'Shall I flee from a beast of the deep?' he asked. 'Maiden, my father was Jupiter, king of the gods, and the great goddess Minerva hath me under her protection. From her I received this shield, and from Mercury, swiftest of the gods, a cap of darkness, these sandals, and this sword. Then, at Minerva's bidding, I sped northward through regions where man nor beast hath trodden. There found I the Gray Sisters, and snatched from them their one eye, keeping it till they told me the way to the garden of the Hesperides. And from the maidens in that garden I learned the secret dwelling-place of the gorgon Medusa, the very sight of whose face turns all men to stone. Her, at the bidding of Minerva, I slew, using the shield as a mirror and looking not on the gorgon's face as I shore off her viper-crowned head. Seven years have these adventures filled; very far have I traveled and many perils known. And shall I now turn back from a beast of the sea?'

And he laughed again, and his laughter rang so joyously through the morning air that some comfort stole even into the sad heart of Andromeda; but still she besought him to go.

'Many hath the sea-beast slain,' she pleaded; 'and why should he slay thee? Shall two perish instead of one? Strong-limbed art thou and brave; but what mortal shall stand against that strength? Never have I known fairer or gentler man than thou, and why should'st thou die? Seven years hath thy mother awaited thy homecoming, and shall her eyes see thee nevermore?'

And when she had said this, Andromeda hid her face in her hair, sobbing very bitterly as she added: 'Surely some maiden longeth for thee afar; and shall she go longing to her grave?'

But ere Perseus could answer there came a roar from the sea, and looking down they saw that the monster was at hand. His great snout, pouring forth fountains of sea-water, lay already on the rocks, his vast scaly body, shells clinging to its scales and seaweeds dripping down its sides, rolled like some water-logged hulk; his tail, curling, coil upon coil, to the horizon, lashed the waters till they were white with foam, and the sea-birds screamed as before him the fishes fled leaping.

Then Perseus, pausing not an instant, drew forth from under his goat-skin the fatal head of Medusa, the sight of which is death, and gripping it by its viper locks, he swooped like a hawk upon the monster as it rose to clamber up the beach. And the monster's great eyes rolled upward, blinking and wicked; but when they saw the Medusa they became fixed in a ghastly stare. And a great spasm ran through the sea-beast from snout to tail—a shiver, and then no motion or breath or sign of life, for that which had been a monster was now nothing but a long black rock.

Then Perseus went back to Andromeda and showed her that her enemy was indeed dead, and Andromeda, after all her sorrows, was now the happiest maiden in the land. And all the people, hearing what had happened, came down to the shore with laughter and dancing and singing, and carried Andromeda and Perseus to the palace of the king and queen, who sat sorrowing for their daughter, deeming her already dead. And they, when they heard the glad tidings, rose up and embraced their daughter who had come back to them, as it were, from the grave, and gave her to Perseus to wife, begging him to stay with them for a while before he carried home his bride.

So Perseus stayed with Cepheus and Cassiopoeia and their dark-haired Æthiopians for the space of a year, teaching them many things; and after that he built himself a ship of cedar-wood, and in it he sailed with Andromeda to Seriphos among the Isles of Greece, where his mother had waited for him seven years. And after a little while Perseus became King of Argos in the place of his grandfather Acrisius. Long and glorious was his reign, and fair Andromeda bore him four sons and three daughters. And when after many days Perseus died, the gods took him up into the sky. Who has not seen on a starlight night Cassiopoeia seated on her golden throne? There, too, is Perseus, still holding the Medusa's head, and beside him is Andromeda, still stretching out her starry arms to embrace her enstarred deliverer.

Meleager and Atalanta

H.P. Maskell

When Meleager, son of Oeneus, King of Calydon, was born, his mother Althæa dreamed that she had brought forth a burning brand. The three Fates were present at the moment of his birth, and foretold his future greatness. Clotho promised that he should have bravery and courage, Lachesis uncommon strength, and Atropos that he should live as long as the fire-brand on the hearth remained whole and unburnt. Althæa no sooner heard this than she snatched the brand from the fire and quenched it with water. Ever after she kept the brand in a safe place with jealous care, knowing that on this depended the life of her dear son.

Grown to manhood, Meleager soon became famous for his knightly prowess. He sailed with Jason in search of the Golden Fleece, and when rebellious tribes made war against his father, he fought against their army and scattered it.

A year came, long after famous as the harvest year. Never within the memory of man had there been such plenteous crops in the land of Calydon, and Oeneus the king made grateful offerings of first-fruits to the gods: corn to Ceres, wine to Bacchus, and olive oil to Minerva. All the gods received their tribute except Diana. Diana was forgotten, and the goddess was filled with jealousy. She resented the insult to her altars, and in revenge for the neglect sent a wild boar to ravage the kingdom. This boar was huge as a full-grown ox, his eyes were flaming and bloodshot, and the bristles stood up on his neck and flanks like long spikes. It was terrible to see his foaming jaws and large tusks—like an elephant's; when he roared his breath seemed to burn up the very herbage. Wherever he went he destroyed the farmer's hopes, trampling down the young shoots, devouring the corn in the ear, breaking the vines, and stripping the olive trees. Neither dogs nor shepherds could protect the sheep from being gored by his cruel tusks. The country folk had to fly for their lives into the walled cities.

So Meleager invited a choice band of heroes to join him and help to destroy the monster. Nearly all those who had joined in the quest for the Golden Fleece came and brought others with them. But the foremost in Meleager's eyes was the fair huntress Atalanta, daughter of Iasius. Her robe flowed loose to the knee, held up over her left shoulder by one golden brooch, and her hair was gathered into a single knot. At her side hung an ivory quiver. It had been hard to tell whether she were youth or maid, so strong and stalwart were her limbs and so smooth her face. Meleager saw her, and loved her at first sight. 'Here,' he cried, 'is the one maid for me!' But this was no time or place for love-making. The mighty hunt was about to begin.

The monster had been tracked to a dense jungle, and the heroes got ready their nets and slipped the dogs. At length the pack gave tongue, and the hunters raised a shout as the boar came crashing through the wood, scattering the dogs right and left, some barking, some bleeding from ugly wounds. Echion's spear only grazed a maple tree. Jason was next to throw his swift lance, but it overshot the mark. The aim of Alastus was more true, but the iron head snapped off as it hit one of the mighty tusks, and the shaft failed to wound the brute.

Like a stone from a catapult the furious boar rushed madly on among the youths; lightnings flashed from his eyes, and his breath was like a furnace; two of the huntsmen were laid low, and a third received a deadly wound; Nestor saved his life by catching in the nick of time the branch of an oak tree. Having whetted his tusks on the trunk the monster advanced once more, and gored another hero in the thigh. Castor and Pollux, on their white horses, rushed with lances poised to despatch him; they were too late, for the boar had found safe cover in the

Meleager
and Atalanta
*by François
Chauveau,
after Laurent
de La Hyre.*

jungle, where neither horse nor weapon could reach him.

Telamon, in his hot pursuit, was tripped up by a root. While Pelus was helping him to rise, Atalanta fitted an arrow to her bow and let fly. Diana, who loved the maiden, guided her aim. The shaft grazed the ear of the beast, leaving the bristles streaked with red; and Meleager was just as pleased as she herself at her success in drawing the first blood. Pointing it out to his companions, he exclaimed, 'The maid is peerless in archery as in beauty! She puts us men to shame!'

Stung to action by the taunt the heroes bestirred themselves, and shouted to encourage each other, but their very number confused their aim. Ancæus, swinging his battle-ax, rushed madly to his fate, crying, 'Make way for me, and I will show you how much better a man's weapon is than a girl's arrow. Though he bear a charmed life, my right hand shall finish the brute!' As he stood boasting the boar seized him and gored him through and through and through, so that the earth around was soaked with his red life-blood. Theseus stayed his dear friend, Pirithoüs, son of Ixion, who was making straight for the enemy just as rashly. Warning him that it was better to be valiant at a distance, he hurled his heavy lance of cornel-wood pointed with brass. It was well poised, but caught in a beech tree. Jason, too, hurled his javelin again, but by an ill-chance struck an innocent hound and pinned him to the earth.

Meleager's turn had now come, and he used his opportunity to good effect. Of two spears the first only grazed the boar's flank, the second transfixed the beast in the middle of the back. While it was writhing in agony, twisting about, covered with foam and blood, the conqueror lost no time. In a trice he had buried his gleaming blade behind the shoulder. His comrades crowded around him with shouts of joy. They marveled at the huge size of the boar as the carcass lay at full length, scarcely believing it safe even yet to touch, but each dipped his weapon in the blood. Meleager himself, placing his foot on the monster's head, exclaimed, 'Receive, Arcadian nymph, the spoil that is thy right, for thou didst draw first blood! Only let me share thy glory!' So saying, he laid at her feet the skin, thick with stiffened bristles, and the head and monstrous tusks. The maiden was graciously pleased to accept the offering, and the smile that she bestowed on the giver more than repaid him for all his pains and perils.

But his comrades were jealous of the favor bestowed on the young hunter. They murmured amongst themselves, and said, 'Who is this upstart youth who, without asking our leave, bestows on his lady-love the spoils that belong to us all?' And they snatched away the trophy.

This was more than the warlike prince could bear. Mad with anger and indignation, he plunged his sword into the breast of his uncle Plexippus (who had been the moving spirit in the protest), crying, 'This will teach thee not to snatch away another's honors.' And before long his blade was reeking with the blood of Toxeus, who seemed half disposed to avenge his brother's death.

Meanwhile, Queen Althæa had heard of her son's victory over the monster, and was on her way to the temples of the gods with thankofferings, when she beheld the dead bodies of her brothers being borne from the field. All her joy

was turned to sorrow; with a shriek of horror she hastened back home to put on mourning. But when she learnt who was the author of their death, grief vanished and gave place to a thirst for vengeance.

She bethought herself of the brand which the Fates had given her, and which she had kept so carefully, knowing that her son's life depended on it. Now this fatal wood was to be the means of punishing the son for the murder of her brothers.

At her bidding a fire was kindled. Holding the fatal billet in her ruthless hand, she moaned, 'Ye Fates, I both avenge and commit a crime. With death must death be repaid. He deserves to die, and yet the thought of his death appalls me. Oh, that thou hadst been burnt, unnatural son, when an infant, in that first fire!' So saying, with trembling hands, she threw the fatal brand into the midst of the fire. And the brand, as it was caught by the flames, seemed to utter a dying groan.

Meleager, far away, was seized with sudden pains. He felt his entrails scorched by secret fires; bravely he bore the torture. His one regret was that he was doomed to die an inglorious death, and he envied the fate of Ancæus. With his last breath he invoked a blessing on his aged father, his brother, and dear sisters—aye, and on his cruel mother. As the blaze kindled by Althæa rose and fell, so his torments waxed and waned. Both lives flickered out, and his spirit vanished into the light air.

In Calydon, young and old, noble and serf, were all lamenting. The matrons tore their hair as they bewailed the untimely end of their brave young prince. Aged Oeneus abased himself on the ground, with dust on his white locks and wrinkled brow, bemoaning that he had lived to see that day. To the anguished mother, too, came tardy repentance. Natural affection had now gained the mastery over anger and revenge. 'Wretch that I am!' she cried. 'To the loss of my dear brothers, by my own ruthless deed I have added the loss of my dearer son.' Horrified at her act, she could no longer bear to see the sun, and with a sword put an end to her misery and shame.

Dædalus and Icarus *by A.G.L. Desnoyers, after C.P. Landon. The wings were made from the quills of osprey and sea-eagles, bound on a framework of bone using twine and beeswax.*

The Story of Dædalus and Icarus

M.M. Bird

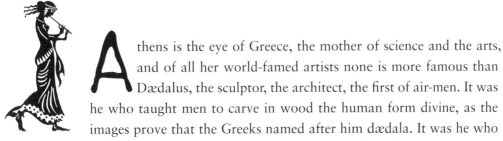

Athens is the eye of Greece, the mother of science and the arts, and of all her world-famed artists none is more famous than Dædalus, the sculptor, the architect, the first of air-men. It was he who taught men to carve in wood the human form divine, as the images prove that the Greeks named after him dædala. It was he who planned for Minos the labyrinth of which you have read elsewhere; and it was he who first made wings that men might fly like birds. Of this, his best and greatest invention, how he came to contrive it, and how disastrously it ended, you shall now hear.

When Theseus had slain the Minotaur, King Minos was exceedingly wrath with his architect for betraying the secret of the labyrinth—a secret that none but the king and its contriver knew. So Dædalus, and with him his young son Icarus, was cast into prison, and there they languished long. But Pasiphaë the queen, who loved not her sovereign lord and loved her favorite artist, contrived their escape and hid them in a sea-cave. Still the cave was little better than a prison. It was dark and dank, and they dared only venture out at night for fear their hiding-place should be discovered.

But though the artist's hands were idle, his busy brain was ever plotting and scheming. One day, as he sat at the cave's mouth watching the seagulls as they

floated past on poised wings or mounted from the waves and with a stroke of their pinions were high in air, there flashed upon his brain the splendor of a sudden thought—With the wings of a bird I too could fly!

At once the father and the son set to work to make themselves wings. The osprey and the sea-eagle, whose aeries were on the rocky heights, the father trapped with cunning snares, and from the combs of the wild bees on the hillside the son collected wax. So with infinite pains, and after endless failures, at last a pair of pinions were made. The upper row of quills were bound together by strong threads of twine on a framework of bone, and to them the bottom feathers were joined by beeswax. Like all great inventors, Dædalus had conquered Nature by imitating her.

At first young Icarus had watched his father with eager curiosity, but like a boy, he had soon grown impatient, and, as Dædalus still persevered, he looked upon him as a harmless lunatic. What, then, were his delight and surprise when, one morning as he awoke, he beheld his father floating in mid-air before the cave's mouth.

'Father,' he cried, embracing him as he alighted, 'what rapture! Let me too try if I can fly. Make me a pair of wings, and together we will escape from this island prison.'

'My boy,' the grave sire replied, 'thou shalt surely try, but flight is no easy matter, and thou must first learn thy lesson. Mark well my words. Steer always a middle flight; there only safety lies. If you fly low the sea spray will wet your flagging feathers, if high the sun will melt the wax. Keep me in sight, and swerve not to the north or south.'

Icarus promised to obey, but so fired was he with the thought of flying that he listened with half an ear, and soon forgot his father's directions.

The second pair of wings were made and strapped with anxious care to the son's shoulder-blades. And, as the parent birds eye their callow nestlings when they essay their first flight, so Dædalus, as he mounted upwards, oft looked back on the boy and again repeated his warnings.

The people were stirring in the towns, the countrymen were out in the fields after their beasts, and all the folk stayed in their morning tasks to gaze at these two strange creatures that floated overhead. 'It is Dædalus and his son,' they cried. 'They have become gods.'

Minos in his palace was told of the strange spectacle. From his terrace he watched in impotent wrath the two dark specks far out to sea, that thus escaped him.

At first Icarus kept close to his father, but soon he had lost all sense of danger, and with the reckless wantonness of youth, determined to go his own way. He reveled in the strong free strokes of his great wings; he mounted ever higher and higher, till the sea was spread below him like a blue plain, and the sandy islands showed like cloths of gold.

Dædalus was winging his careful way lower down, below the scattered clouds, close above the golden islets, and shouted to his son to return. But Icarus, drunk with the delights of flight, mounted ever higher, up into the fierce rays of Phoebus, the Sun-god, who held out burning arms to the adventurous youth, beckoning him to race his fiery car across the heavens.

The horrified father, floating on outspread wings over the Ægean Sea, looked up to see his boy like a tiny speck in the sun's rays. He knew the fierce heat of those rays; he knew that the wings were only fastened on by wax that could not hold against that scorching heat. And lo! as he looked, the speck grew larger and larger, and headlong down the sky he beheld Icarus falling, falling, his limp wings sagging from his shoulders, his frantic arms struggling to spread them and stay his fall. The drooping wings could not uphold him; he came whirling down the hissing air, and his agonized father watched his helpless boy fall into the blue waves beneath. For a moment he saw him struggle feebly, and then, like a bubble, he sank, and the unruffled waters lay calm and smiling as before.

By the sad sea shore of the Ægean, where he landed after that disastrous flight, Dædalus raised a cenotaph to his lost son, and thereon he laid the wings, once the artist's pride, and now the father's bane. 'Icarus, O my Icarus!' he cried; and still those waters echo the name of Icarus.

Scylla Watching Minos from the Castle Walls, *from Ovid's 'Metamorphoses', by Antonio Tempesta.*

Scylla, the Daughter of Nisus

Mrs. Guy E. Lloyd

n Crete, the greatest and most powerful of the isles of Greece and the cradle of Jupiter, there once stood a splendid palace where lived the wealthy King Minos. To this palace came as guests one day Nisus, King of Megara, and his fair daughter Scylla; and there they abode many days, with every day fresh delights sought out by King Minos to give them pleasure. And Scylla, like a fond and foolish maiden, was dazzled by the pomp and by the flattery of King Minos, and he seemed to her the greatest and wisest of living men, and she would fain have tarried there forever, hearkening to his words and admiring all his riches.

But King Nisus would not longer stay, and they departed, bearing with them rich gifts from the generous king, and returned to their own castle at Megara. Very small and mean did her home seem to Scylla now, and often would she climb to the top of a turret that looked over the sea, and thence she would gaze and gaze towards the south, and her thoughts would fly back to the fair island of Crete with its cities and its palaces, and its strong and noble king, till she envied the birds that skimmed past her turret on swift, light wings. They could fly to Crete whenever they would, and settle on the palace eaves; but the princess must sit still in her high turret, and hide even her longing away within her heart.

The days passed by, and Nisus went no more to Crete, but Androgeos, son

of King Minos, came to Megara and abode there some little space, and the king and the princess welcomed him kindly for his father's sake. After his visit Androgeos would not sail back straight to his father's halls; he was minded first to see the great city of Athens, the eye of Greece. King Nisus warned him that the road across the mountains was difficult and dangerous, and that many robbers hid among those hills; but the prince would not be warned. He went his way, and the next news of him that came was that he had been set upon by bandits and murdered.

'He should have hearkened to the counsel of older and wiser men,' said King Nisus. 'I grieve for the youth, but he brought it on himself.'

But when Minos the king heard that his son Androgeos was dead, he was stricken with a great grief, and he sent to King Nisus demanding blood-money, since the prince was slain in the lands of the Megarians. But Nisus refused to pay.

'It was no fault of mine,' he said; 'and I shall make no reparation for the death of one whose blood is on his own head.'

Then was King Minos wroth, and threatened to make good in person his rightful claim.

So it chanced on a day when the Princess Scylla looked forth from her turret over the sea, as her custom was, she saw great ships, with bellying white sails, drawing near from the south; and as they rose upon the heaving billows, the sunbeams glinted back from many a shield and spear, for they carried the mailed warriors of King Minos coming to wrest from King Nisus blood-money for the death of Androgeos, son to King Minos, who had been slain by robbers on the lands of King Nisus.

Then stepped forth from one of the ships the herald of King Minos, and he came into the palace of Megara and proclaimed his master's will to all that stood there.

But Nisus the king frowned upon the herald. 'I will pay no blood-money,' he said. 'Go your ways to your master and tell him so. Better were it for him to be satisfied with this answer of mine and to turn and hie him home. Little use is it for mortal men to strive against those who are protected by the undying gods. I

care not for the wrath of King Minos, and the spears of his warriors have no more power to hurt my people than the bulrushes that children gather in the fields and break in mimic warfare with each other.'

'Thou speakest in riddles, King Nisus,' replied the herald; 'but my master is of kin to the immortals, and it cannot be that they will let him quail before a petty king like thee.'

So the herald turned and went back to his ships; and when King Minos heard that King Nisus refused to pay the blood-money, he made him ready for battle.

Then the men of Crete fought stoutly against the men of Megara, and day after day the tide of battle surged around the walls of the town. But strive as they might the men of Crete won no inch of ground, but the men of Megara drove their foes before them like sheep.

At length the warriors of King Minos began to murmur among themselves and to repeat the words that King Nisus had spoken to the herald.

'If the city of Megara is indeed defended by the deathless gods,' said they, 'what avails it to fight and to strive?'

And Minos knew that his men murmured, and his heart was sore within him.

The Princess Scylla looked forth one day upon the host that was besieging the city of her home, and she chanced to see King Minos pass quite close to her casement. So near was he that she could see his face quite plainly. Pale and sorrowful he looked with grief at the death of his son and disappointment at the failure of his attack. He stood for a moment looking despairingly at the strong walls of his enemy's city, seeking and seeking as often before, and ever in vain, to find some way for his warriors to win passage into the town. At length he passed on his way, sad and dejected, for he saw no way at all of gaining the mastery in the strife.

But the heart of the princess beat fast with love and sorrow. 'Alas!' she thought to herself, 'King Minos is fighting a hopeless battle, for none may gain any advantage over my father, so long as he keeps safe the purple lock of hair that the gods have placed upon his head as a spell against every evil. Vain is the strength of the warriors of Crete, vain the wisdom of their king. The bright lock of King Nisus will hold him and his people safe through every attack.'

The princess covered her face with her hands, and sat for a little space silent and miserable. Then on a sudden she raised her head and a new light was in her eyes. She was the only child of King Nisus, and when he died the city and the palace would be hers. The only man whom she had ever wished to wed was the stately King Minos. If he would but wed her all would be well; he should reign, as her husband, over the city against which he was leading his warriors in vain. And surely King Minos would willingly wed her as a reward if she put within his power the victory he had striven in vain to wrest for himself from the men of Megara.

There was feasting that night in the hall of King Nisus, and the princess herself poured out her father's wine, and he was well pleased that she should wait upon him, for of late she had moped in her chamber and refused to share his feasts. But when the banquet was over a strange drowsiness weighed down the eyelids of King Nisus, for Scylla had mingled the juice of poppy and mandragora with the wine. Then the king sought his bed and lay there as one in a swoon, and his guards, who had drunk of the poppied wine, slept also as they kept watch before the door of Nisus. And when all was dark and still the princess Scylla stole softly to her father's chamber, holding a pair of shears in her hand.

She drew back the heavy purple curtain that the moonlight might stream into the room, and then, kneeling beside the couch, she sought the bright lock on which depended the fortune of Megara, and with her shears she shore it off. Then, drawing the curtain close again that the moonlight might not awake the king, she hid the lock safely in the corner of her veil, and glided silently from the room.

The moon was making a glittering path across the sea that murmured softly on the rocks, and all was still and dark within the city, when the watchman of the Cretan host saw a woman drawing near. Her bent head was shrouded in a dark veil, so that he could see naught of her face as she came, but she called to him in his own tongue, praying to be led forthwith to King Minos.

'Nay, maiden, whosoever thou may'st be,' replied the man. 'The king is asleep in his tent at this hour, and none may have speech with him.'

'I will hold thee blameless, friend,' said the princess; and the man was awed by her imperial speech and manner, and turning he led her to the tent of King Minos, passed within the curtains, roused the king, and brought him forth into the moonlight.

'Who art thou who would'st speak with me?' asked the king, glancing keenly at the veiled woman.

'I must speak with thee alone,' she whispered, for she was now overcome with shame, and her tongue clave to the roof of her mouth.

But the king recognized at once the voice, and bidding the sentinel go back to his post, he asked in amazement: 'What would'st thou with me, Princess Scylla?'

Then the maiden flung back the veil from her head, and taking heart of courage, looked straight into the eyes of King Minos. 'In the days that are gone,' she made answer, 'kind words were spoken between thee and me, O King. Remember now thy past affection, and look upon me gently, for through great peril come I to win happiness for both our peoples, and for thee and me, if thou wilt have it so.'

And King Minos read her love in the eyes of the maiden, but in his own heart was naught but bitterness for the unatoned death of his son and for his many days of fruitless warfare. Nevertheless he spoke gentle words, for he hoped that the love of Scylla might bring him profit.

Then the princess took from her bosom her father's magic lock, and held it out to the king. 'Behold the fortune of my father and of his people,' she said. 'This bright lock was placed on my father's head by the undying gods, and as long as it was safe no evil could befall him or his people; but I have shorn it off and brought it to thee, for peace is better than war, love is stronger than hate; and surely thou wilt look kindly upon her who plucks victory from defeat, and holds it forth for thee and thy warriors to take.'

Then King Minos took the lock, and he smiled upon Scylla as he made answer: 'I take thy gift, fair maiden; when the battle shall be ended we will speak of the requital.'

So, wrapping her veil once more around her head, Scylla passed forth from the tent of King Minos, and took her way, not back to the towers of her home, but down to the sea-shore. Here she found a hidden nook among the rocks where she flung herself down, fordone and distracted by her own fierce hopes and fears.

She had thought to be very happy when she looked once more upon the face of King Minos and heard him speak kindly to her; but there was no joy in her palpitating heart: only a vague dread as she remembered the smile of the king and a vague hope as she repeated to herself his words of promise.

Lulled by the sound of the lapping waves and murmuring over and over to herself, 'When the battle shall be ended we will speak of the requital,' the wearied princess sank at length to sleep.

The sky above her head flushed crimson with the rising of the sun; the warriors of King Minos came forth from their tents and set themselves in battle array. All through that day the princess slept on, while the men of Megara rushed to defend their crumbling walls, and King Nisus, roused from his heavy sleep, discovered his loss and flung himself into the front of the battle, knowing that now he fought in vain, since the magic lock was gone that had brought victory to him and his people.

Sore amazed were the men of Megara to find that their foes were driving them backwards. At first they fought desperately, hoping that the Cretans were gaining the advantage only for a time, but presently it began to be whispered through the ranks that the favour of the immortals had deserted Megara, and men flung down their arms and fled headlong.

The sky was reddened again by the sunset when Scylla was roused from her long slumber of exhaustion by the tramp of armed men close to her hiding-place. Lifting herself up, she peered cautiously between the rocks, and saw the Cretan warriors, bearing the spoils of the plundered city, returning to their ships. For King Minos was in haste to journey on and make Athens share in the punishment of Megara, since it was on a journey from Megara to Athens that his son Androgeos had been slain, and both the cities shared in the guilt of the slayer. Scylla watched the hurrying ranks, at first not understanding what they did. Then, on a sudden, she saw approaching the stately form of King Minos, and she came forth from among the rocks, and waited, hoping he might look upon her. But seeing that he

made as though he would pass by, the princess stood in his path.

Then said King Minos coldly: 'What wilt thou with me, maiden?'

And a great fear caught at the heart of Scylla, and she clasped her hands to her bosom as though she were at her last gasp. Yet with a supreme effort she made her last appeal: 'My home is desolate, my father slain. 'Tis I, his daughter, who gave the battle to thy hands. I come, King Minos, to claim my promised guerdon.'

And King Minos made answer: 'There is no gift in the world precious enough to make requital to a maiden who by her own deed has slain her father and laid her home in ruins and the pride of her people in the dust. I will not mock thee, princess, by striving to equal thy gift.'

And King Minos passed on his way to his ship; and as they followed him his warriors gazed with horror upon the maiden who had given the life of her father into the hand of his enemy; for all men knew by now that the safety of Nisus and his city had depended upon the magic lock, and that his daughter had shorn it from him and given it to King Minos.

But Scylla stood on the rocky pathway where she had hearkened to the mocking words of King Minos, and the blue heavens seemed black above her head, and the silver sea black beneath her feet, and nowhere in the world was there for her any help or comfort.

The troops of warriors passed her by and embarked in the ships that waited for them there below the cliff. The sunlight faded and the moon came out, and still the stricken maiden leant against the rock where Minos had dashed all her hopes to ruin.

At length the song of the mariners came up from the sea, telling that the men were on board and the ships ready to sail, and with a cry of bitter anguish Scylla crept to the top of the rock that overlooked the sea. She saw the ship of King Minos moving slowly from the shore, and clasping her hands above her head, she leapt from the tall cliff.

And men say that the gods had pity on her, and changed her into a sea-lark. But her father was wrath with her even in death, and he craved of the infernal powers the boon of vengeance. Therefore he was turned into a sea-eagle, and still the father, with hooked hands and ravenous beak, watches from his mountain walls to swoop upon his feathered daughter, who flits along the shore and cowers in the crannies of the rocks.

The Story of Pyramus and Thisbe

M.M. Bird

'The most lamentable comedy and most cruel death of Pyramus and Thisby.'

William Shakespeare (1564–1616)

In Babylon of old, where walls were first built of bricks, two houses had been set so close together that they shared one roof. Two families came to dwell in them, and young Pyramus of the one house soon made acquaintance with fair Thisbe of the other. Their friendship grew and ripened into love. But alas! a deathless feud had arisen to separate the two families, and the unhappy lovers were inexorably divided.

Still, though angry parents could forbid their love and could prevent them meeting, all this could not avail to kill their love. The thwarted pair could but gaze upon each other, could only look and sigh: yet that was enough to feed the flame of love. And at last they found a way to reach each other's ears, as lovers will: a chink between two bricks in the wall that divided the two houses—a little chink where the cement had crumbled away, so small it had never been noticed and filled in. Through this friendly chink young Pyramus breathed his vows, and fair Thisbe answered him with tender words. Their eager lips pressed the unresponsive brick, their hands that longed to clasp each other were kept apart by the hard, unfeeling wall. Their sighs and softly spoken words of love alone could pierce the barrier that divided them.

At last they resolved to defy the cruel parents who thus wronged their love; to steal out one night in the concealing darkness, and fly together despite all opposition.

Outside the town, beside a little brook and shaded by a widespread mulberry tree, stood the tomb of Ninus. Here they agreed to meet at nightfall.

Impatiently they watched the sun sink slowly down the western sky and bathe in the western sea. Thisbe, with caution, unbarred her father's door and stole softly forth, veiling her face and hasting through the town to the spot where the tomb stood on the open plain.

But in the darkness other creatures had come forth. A lioness, scouring the plain in search of prey, had slain an ox. Surfeited with flesh and all besmeared with blood, it came swiftly to the brook to slake its thirst. By the light of the moon Thisbe, approaching the trysting-place, saw the fearful beast. She flew trembling across the plain to the neighboring rocks and hid within a cave. And as she fled her floating veil dropped from her shoulders and was left upon the ground.

When the queen of beasts had drunk her fill, she came bounding back across the plain. She found the veil, and this she tore and mouthed with jaws still wet with the blood of the slaughtered ox. And then went on her way.

Young Pyramus, who could not elude his parents so soon, came hastening to the tryst. By the moonlight he noted the footprints of the savage beast beside the brook, and farther on his anguished eyes beheld his loved Thisbe's torn and blood-stained veil. Convinced that the beast had slain his love, he cried in his agony of grief that the fault was his in that he had not been first at the tryst to protect her, and cursed the malevolence of fate that had caused him to fix the spot

Right: Pyramus and Thisbe *by Albrecht Altdorfer.*

where she should meet her death. He kissed the veil so torn, so dear to him. And then, crying that Death should not divide two hearts so fond, he drew his sword and plunged it into his breast. The life-blood spurted from the grievous wound and besprinkled all the white clusters of the mulberry.

Cautiously the trembling Thisbe left her hiding-place among the rocks, fearing lest delay should make her lover think her untrue, and neared the appointed spot. But though the tomb and the brook were there as of old, the tree she could not recognize with its new burden of crimson clusters.

As she gazed in doubt, her eyes fell on a form that lay stretched upon the ground. She saw her lover bathed in his blood.

She shrieked and tore her hair; she raised him, clasped him, bathed with her tears his gaping wound. She cried to him to wake and answer his poor Thisbe. His dying eyes unclosed in one long look of love, and then he died in her arms.

She gazed around, saw her torn veil, and saw his own sword lying, blood-stained and sheathless, by his side. She saw that by his own hand he had inflicted the fatal wound; that, believing her dead, he had not chosen to survive.

Should her love be weaker than his? She it was who had been the innocent cause of his death, and she would share it. One prayer she breathed that their cruel parents would grant them at last to be joined together, and in one urn confine their ashes. Of the drooping mulberry tree, beneath whose kindly shade she made her piteous lament, she begged one boon—that by the purple color of its fruit it would bear perpetual witness to their love and their untimely death.

Then in her bosom she plunged the sword, yet warm with the blood of its slaughtered lord, and fell dead beside him.

The prayer that dying Thisbe breathed was heard by compassionate gods and parents. Their ashes were mixed in one golden urn, and from that sad day the fruit of the mulberry tree has been stained a lustrous purple.

Hero and Leander

Mrs. Guy E. Lloyd

The goddess Venus was the Queen of Love and Beauty, and her worship was spread over all the world, for indeed she was one of the greatest of the immortals, and even the father of gods and of men himself had to own her power.

She had many great and noted temples, and one of these was at Sestos, close by the side of the Hellespont, the sea in which Helle sank and was drowned when the Golden Ram carried off her brother Phrixus and herself.

When this tale begins the priestess of the temple of Venus at Sestos was a very beautiful maiden called Hero. It was her duty to tend the altar of the goddess, to offer sacrifices, to hang up the votive offerings of worshipers round the walls, and to see that the slaves appointed to the work kept the marble steps and pillars always shining and polished.

And many a youth came to worship at the temple, less for the sake of the goddess than for the beautiful priestess; but Hero never gave a glance at any man but carefully fulfilled her daily task, and every night retired to a tall tower on the cliff beside the sea, where she lived alone with an aged nurse who loved her dearly and was ready to do anything for her.

Every year a great festival was held at Sestos, in honour of Adonis, the beautiful boy whom Venus had loved, and who had been slain by a wild boar. To this festival flocked all the countryside. Large-eyed oxen drew the creaking wagons all adorned with flowers and grasses, and crowded with rustics from the

inland farms, and across the narrow strait came gay barges, bringing worshipers from the villages along the opposite shore. In the festal company there came one day from the town of Abydos, a beautiful youth named Leander. He was tall and straight as a young poplar, his bright eyes had a ready smile, his red lips a pleasant word for every one, but no maiden had ever yet won his love.

Leander only laughed at these reproaches, but hidden within his heart was the dream of a maiden fairer and sweeter than any he yet had seen, to whom he would give his whole heart, and who, so he dreamt, would give him love for love.

So it came about that when the yearly feast of Venus at Sestos returned, Leander determined to go and sacrifice at the altar of the goddess and pray to her that he might meet the maiden of his heart's desire.

With the throng of worshipers Leander mounted the hill to the temple of Venus. White marble steps led up to a bright crystal pavement that was called by the citizens of Sestos the glass of Venus. The walls were of veined marble, and on the dome a cunning artist had painted a vine of vivid green, with Bacchus, the friend of Venus, gathering the purple grapes. On the wall behind was Proteus, the changeful god of the changeful sea, whence Venus had arisen. Rich offerings of gold, silver, precious stones, and gorgeous raiment hung on the walls between the carven figures. Leander gazed his fill at all these wonders, till his eyes were caught and held by the statue of the goddess that stood on a pedestal in the middle of the temple. Beneath her feet was a great sea-shell, borne on a breaking wave; in her hands, held close against her breast, a pair of doves; her face, looking out upon her worshipers, was such a miracle of loveliness that the gazer caught his breath in awe and wonder.

Before the statue stood a little silver altar, and at this the priestess was kneeling when Leander came to the temple, for the sacrifice was just about to be consummated. For a while Leander saw nothing but the face of the marble goddess; then the kneeling priestess, robed in her gauzy veil, arose and faced for a moment the congregation of worshipers. Leander's eyes turned from the marble image to the living woman who stood before it, and the eyes of Hero met his. As if fascinated they gazed at one another, while in both their hearts flamed

up the sudden fire of love.

The worshipers all knelt, and Leander knelt with them, but his prayer was not to Venus: his soul was full and overflowing with love for the fair priestess, and it was of her alone he thought.

It seemed as though Hero had read his thoughts, for as one who walks in his sleep she drew nearer to the young man.

He started to his feet, and bending forward grasped her hand. The sacrifice was over, the worshipers were dispersing, the two were left alone, and for a moment they stood motionless, both of them trembling and awed at their own emotion.

But when Hero, as if waking from a dream, strove to free her hand, Leander tightened his hold and whispered eagerly: 'Nay, leave me not, fair maiden, for I love thee. Never before have I cared aught for mortal maid, but now thou art more to me than everything in the world beside.'

Hero flushed a rosy red, and her long eyelashes veiled the light of her eyes.

'I know thee not, kind youth,' she faltered, struggling betwixt love and maiden modesty, abashed at what she had done, and at the thought of how Leander's words had made her heart leap for joy. 'It is not fitting that I should speak with thee—here.' And then, in a lower whisper, turning half away and blushing more deeply than before, the maiden added hastily: 'I dwell alone with my servant in yonder tower by the sea-shore, and when I leave the service of the goddess I ever put a light in the turret at the top, so that those on the sea may know where the haven lies and steer safely home. But thou must not seek me there.'

And snatching her hand from Leander's grasp the affrighted maiden turned and fled, while the tears sprang to her eyes, and as she ran she wept and smiled. As she mounted the slope that led to her tower on the cliff she slackened her pace, and dashing the tears from her eyes, looked back. Leander stood still where she had left him, gazing after her. Flinging her veil back over her shoulder she resumed her homeward way, slowly and with many a backward look.

When she came to her tower Hero told her old servant to lay out all in readiness for the evening meal, and then to retire to her chamber above.

'Thou art overtired, my pretty one,' said the old crone. 'These crowded

festivals and long days of sacrifice are too much for such a tender flower as thou. Never fear, I will leave thee here in peace—and see, I will light thy lamp in the turret above, even now in the daylight, then may I seek the couch whereof my old bones ever are full fain, and thou shalt not need to climb those weary stairs.'

'As thou wilt, good nurse,' answered Hero, turning aside to take off her veil and to hide her blush of pleasure. She had told Leander that the light was the signal that her office was ended for the day—would he notice it? Would he come?

She wandered out in the twilight and broke off branches of roses to deck the room; she put on the table the candied fruits and honey-cakes and wine of Cyprus that the worshipers of Venus offer to her priestess. The heavy footsteps of the old dame sounded as she mounted the stair and came back to her chamber and her wished-for bed. Then silence fell on the tower, and Hero sat with beating heart and waited.

Leander had climbed to the top of the cliff, and there had lain down with his face to the sea, determined to keep his eyes from the tower till there was a reasonable chance of seeing the light.

'When I see it glow,' said Leander to himself, 'then shall I too know where the haven lies, and steer safely home.'

He closed his eyes that he might see once more in fancy the sweet averted face under the fine veil.

A noise below the cliff made him look up; the boat that had come from Abydos in the morning was starting back again. He watched it with a smile. It seemed to him a lifetime since he stepped from its deck upon the quay. Straight across to the other shore of this narrow arm of the sea was but a mile, but the slanting course to Abydos was full three miles' distance. Leander watched the boat as she left the quay with all his friends on board; then he could wait no longer; he looked up at Hero's tower; and there, in the top of the turret, flamed the signal light.

Small pause made Leander when once he had seen that.

Meanwhile, from her casement, Hero too had seen the boat putting out for Abydos, and believing Leander to be on board, gone from Sestos perhaps forever, the maiden sank down beside her open door, and covering her face with

her hands she wept sore.

'Alas,' she murmured, 'he is gone, gone, gone! The boat has sailed away.'

Leander, as he mounted the rocky stairs that led to the turret, overheard the maiden's cry, and, rushing forward, he flung himself on his knees beside her and softly kissed her fingers. Then, looking up with a start, the maiden would fain have seemed wroth at the sight of him, but it was too late. She had yielded at a touch, and Love was lord of all.

But on the morrow Leander must return to his home at Abydos. So he took ship early in the morning, finding a vessel that was sailing thither, and came to his own home again. His father noticed at once that the youth was wearing a sprig of myrtle and a scarf embroidered with the doves of Venus, and he chid him sharply.

'There are plenty of fair maids here, in thy own land,' said he; 'choose one of them and be happy with her, but woo not the priestess of Venus, or harm will come of it.'

Leander made no answer to his father's admonition, but in his heart he knew that no other maiden could ever after content him, and that he must see Hero again, though he died for it.

After his father's admonition he dared not be seen crossing the strait by day, but when night fell he wandered by the sea, looking longingly across the dark water; then, far and faint, like a star through the clear night, he caught the glimmer of Hero's lamp.

'Alas!' cried Leander, 'there lies the haven. Ah, would that I might steer safely home.'

Then with sudden resolution he flung his outer garment from him and plunging into the water oared his way with mighty strokes towards the glimmer of the light, and Hero, combing her long locks in the moonlight and thinking of her lover, was ware that he stood before her, and could hardly believe it was his very self.

So once more they had joy of one another's love until the daybreak appeared in the sky, and then Leander said farewell with many kisses and swam safely home again, and no man the wiser.

The days passed on and the youth's father was pleased at his restored cheerfulness, and thought that Hero must be forgotten, for he never crossed as he had been wont to Sestos.

The summer passed, and one day there swept down from the hills the first of the autumn storms.

Poor Hero, as she set her light in the turret, looked out across the tossing, white-capped waves and sighed as she thought that no swimmer could cross a sea like that. But Leander flinched not, for he plunged, buffeting the angry waves with a good heart, and ever as he rose upon their crests looking out for Hero's light. The fury of the sea could not master him, but the autumn chill struck home to his bones. Long he battled with the rising billows, but the storm waxed fiercer and the farther shore seemed no nearer. Fainter and fainter grew the swimmer, but still he struggled on. When he looked from a crest of the waves his lodestar was gone; a black cloud had hidden the turret lamp. Then at last his heart failed him, and flinging up his arms he sank to his watery grave.

Long did Hero wait that night, hoping and fearing by turns; and when her lover did not come she wept bitter tears. But far worse pain was to come. For on the next day came to her tower the father of Leander.

'Is my son here?' he asked, briefly and sternly.

Hero trembling answered, 'No, fair sir.'

'Is it true that he hath many times swum across the sea and visited thee?'

The maiden hanging her head and blushing deeply answered, 'Yea.'

'Then without doubt my son is drowned, and by thy fault,' said the grief-stricken father, 'for this morning were his garments found near the water's edge, but of him there was no sign.'

Even while he spoke there came from the quay a cry of sorrow and lamentation, and clambering swiftly down the cliff those two saw, laid upon the shore by tender hands, the strong and beautiful body of the dead Leander, whom they both had loved beyond all other living things upon the earth.

Pygmalion, etched by Stefano della Bella, taken from Game of Mythology, *designed by Jean Desmarets de Saint-Sorlin.*

Pygmalion and the Image

(After William Morris)

F. Storr

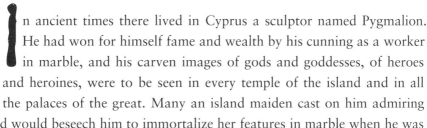

In ancient times there lived in Cyprus a sculptor named Pygmalion. He had won for himself fame and wealth by his cunning as a worker in marble, and his carven images of gods and goddesses, of heroes and heroines, were to be seen in every temple of the island and in all the palaces of the great. Many an island maiden cast on him admiring eyes, and would beseech him to immortalize her features in marble when he was engaged in sculpturing a naiad for a public fountain, or an oread for the shrine of the Great Huntress. Yet, though rich and famous and admired of women, Pygmalion was sad and dissatisfied. The nobles applauded and feasted him, but regarded him as an artisan of low birth and would not admit him to their friendship. The fairest maidens of Crete seemed to him plain and common when he compared them with the godlike forms that his chisel had wrought, and, still more, with the perfect woman whom his imagination pictured but even his hand had not the skill to realize.

So it chanced one day that, after wandering listlessly about the streets, watching the bales of Tyrian purple piled on the quays, and listening to the chaffering of the dark-eyed merchants, he hied him home heavy-hearted, and turned mechanically

349

for relief to the daily work by which he earned his bread.

He had begun rough-hewing a block of Parian marble, uncertain at starting what he should make of it; but as he worked on, the veins in the marble suggested to him a woman's form, and in careless mood he exclaimed, 'Grant, Lady Venus, that this statue may be a fulfilment of my dream, an express image, a reflection on earth of thy celestial beauty. Only grant my prayer and I vow that the maid shall be dedicated to thee, and serve thee in thy myrtle grove.' So he prayed carelessly, but the goddess was by and heard his prayer, and so guided his hand that he wrought more surely and deftly than he had ever wrought before. As the white chips flew beneath his touch, a strange joy thrilled his heart, and withal, a dim sense of trouble, as though he were pursuing his own shadow, a phantom of his brain that still eluded his grasp.

So he worked on hour after hour through the day, and all night he dreamt of his work. So absorbed was he that for a whole month he forgot his morning plunge in the river, forgot his stroll through the woods at sunset, forgot even to water the flowers in his garden close. And yet, so exquisitely delicate were the added touches and the smoothing of the marble, that you could have covered with a penny-piece all that had fallen in the month from his chisel.

And still he seemed no nearer to his goal; so one morning, after a restless night, he arose and said to himself, 'Pygmalion, thou art mad; some witch hath laid her spell upon thee. Rouse thyself while it is yet time; break the wicked spell; live as thou didst before, and seek not to attain that perfect beauty that is laid up in the heavens beyond mortal ken.'

With that he took his bow and quiver, passed through the town and out of the gates to the high woodlands beyond, to see if he had quite forgotten his old woodcraft.

It was a fine summer morning, and the scent of the fields was wafted to him on the west wind. All around him as he passed was astir with life. The tall poplars rippled and quivered in the sunlight; the bees were busy in the clover; the swallows darted overhead, and the swish of the mower's scythe kept time with him as he strode on.

At last he sat him down fordone. 'The sun,' he mused, 'like me, has already passed his zenith and is hurrying to his rest. All nature is stirring, and each living thing is pursuing the daily round, its appointed task. Why am I alone a dreamer of dreams, the idler of an empty day?'

With that he turned, and, goaded on by a wild desire, he knew not for what, found himself before he was aware at his own door.

One moment he lingered at the threshold and said, 'Ah! what should I do if she were gone?' As he uttered the words he turned red at his own madness to dream that the goddess might have wrought a miracle and spirited her away to the myrtle grove, and yet again he turned deadly pale at the very thought of such a marvel. So, sighing, he passed into the house, but paused again before he summoned courage to enter his chamber where the statue stood.

Nothing was changed. He caught up his chisel and tenderly essayed to perfect the marvel of the face that he had wrought. But to touch it now seemed to him a profanation, and flinging down the idle chisel he cried, 'Alas! why have I made thee that thou should'st mock me thus? I know that there are many like unto thee, whose beauty is a snare to draw men into the net; but these the gods made to punish lust. Thee I made with a pure heart to worship and adore, and thou wilt not speak one little word to me.'

So saying, he drew back and gazed on the image through his tears. In truth it was of wondrous beauty, and could you have seen it, you would have said that it lacked little to be a living maid. Her unbound hair half hid the tender curve of her breast; one hand was outstretched as if to greet a lover, and the other held a full-blown rose. There was no smile on the parted lips, and in the wistful eyes there was a look, not of love, but as of one to whom love's mystery and magic were already half revealed.

Thus he stood agaze, ashamed of his infatuate folly, yet with an infinite longing, stronger and stranger than he had ever felt before.

There happened to be passing in the street some sturdy slaves who were bearing bales to the wharf. He hailed them and offered them a rich reward if they would help him to move the ponderous statue and set it in an empty niche beside his bed. When they had departed he searched his coffers to find gems and jewels wherewith to deck his lady of marble, but those he possessed seemed all too poor; so he took with him all his store of gold and bought from the merchants a necklace of pearls, and anklets and bracelets set with rare and precious stones. These he hung upon the cold marble and cast him down like a pilgrim at a shrine, praying his saint to accept his poor offering. So he prayed on till, outworn with passion, he slept at her feet. With the first dawn he awoke and passed into his garden to pick fresh flowers to lay upon her shrine. Then he brought an altar that he had wrought of chased gold for a great lord's hearth, and lit thereon a fire of cedar and sandal-wood, and, as the smoke of cassia and frankincense arose, he prayed and said, 'Thou cold and mute image, not till I die shall I know whether the gods have sent a lying spirit to make me their sport, but this I know, that in life I shall love none but thee alone. Therefore, if thou canst not give me love for love, in pity take my life and let me rest at last.'

Thus he prayed, and the image neither spake nor moved, but the sweet grave eyes his hands had wrought gazed down, as if touched with ruth and tenderness, on his bended head. So all day he worshiped at the shrine; but on the morrow, as the incense-smoke was curling round her head, he heard in the street the sound of minstrelsy, and as if fascinated by the sweet music, he left his prayer half said and went forth and beheld a gay train of men and maidens who bore on a car of gold an image of the Queen of Love that he himself had wrought in the old forgotten days, now draped for her solemn festival in a saffron robe broidered with mystic characters of gold.

So he donned a festal chlamys and joined the glad procession, who led the goddess back to her temple, stripped her reverently of her weeds, and laid at her shrine their offerings of golden grain and honeycomb. By midday the crowd of worshipers had all departed, and he was left alone in the dim-lit temple. He drew near the shrine where stood his masterpiece—how feeble and faulty now it seemed—and casting incense on the altar flame, he prayed with stammering lips to his goddess:

'Queen of Heaven, who didst help me of yore, help me yet again. Have I not

prayed, have I not wept, have I not done thee true service? I have no words to tell thee my need, but thou knowest all my heart's desire. Hear me, O Queen!'

And, as he prayed, suddenly the thin flame on the altar quivered like a live thing, and leapt up till it almost touched the temple dome, sinking once more into a feeble flicker.

At this marvel his heart bounded wildly; but as the flame died down he said to himself, 'Is not this another brain-sick phantom?' and with sad steps and slow he left the temple to seek his loveless home.

As he stood before the door in the broad light of day he seemed like one awaking from a dream, yet the bliss it had brought still lingered on, like the after-glow on an Alpine height, and he blessed the goddess even for his dream. So he entered his chamber, wrapped in memories both sad and sweet, and paused with downcast eyes before they sought again his marble maid. Then he looked up, and lo, the niche was bare! and he cried aloud, bewildered and amazed. A soft, low voice breathed his name. He turned, and there between him and the setting sun stood his marble maid, clad in life and new beauty. The lineaments were the same—the brow, the lips, the tresses unconfined; but she came apparelled in a more precious habit, for over all the goddess had shed the purple light of love, and had clothed her in the shining garment that he had seen that morning laid up in her temple.

Speechless he stood in wonder and amazement, and once again her silver voice rang out clear:

'Wilt thou not come to me, O dear companion of my new-found life, for I am called thy lover and thy wife.'

Still he moved not, and spake no word. Then she reached her hand to him, and looked at him with pleading eyes. The spell that bound him was broken; he caught the outstretched hands and drew her to him, felt the sweet breath he had sought so long in vain, felt the warm life within her heaving breast, and clasped in his arms his living love.

And, as they stood there, cheek touching cheek, he heard her say, 'Why art thou silent, O my love? Dost think, perchance, that this too is a dream? Nay, if thou lov'st me still, I will never leave thee nor forsake thee. Come with me into thy garden close, and there will I tell thee all the comfortable words that the Queen of Love spoke to me, and thou shalt tell me all thy hopes and fears, thy yearning for a beauty not of earth, thy sleepless nights, and all thy pain.'

So they passed into the garden close, and there beneath the whispering trees, by the soft moonlight, those happy lovers told each other the story of their love. What were the words they said I cannot tell again. This happened long ago, when the world was young, and they spoke in a tongue that few if any now can understand. Yet a poet of our own age has understood and translated for us the last word that the Queen of Heavenly Love spoke to her servant Pygmalion:

'Beauty is truth, truth beauty—that is all ye know on earth, and all ye need to know.'

Cephalus and Procris

H.P. Maskell

t was the banqueting-hall of the palace at Ægina. The young prince Phocus had invited his comrades to join him in a hunting party, and now, after dinner, they were gathered round the fire amusing themselves with stories of the chase. Meanwhile Cephalus, gray-headed and stricken in years, more weary than the others, sat silent and apart.

The prince, noticing his moody look, rose and made room for him to join the circle. 'May I ask,' he inquired, 'from what tree the javelin thou art holding was cut? I have been a hunter all my life, yet its texture puzzles me. A wild oak would have been brown in color, a cornel-wood shaft would show the knots. Never yet have I seen so taper and shapely a javelin.'

One of the youths interposed: 'Ah! but as a weapon it is even more wonderful than for its beauty. Whatever it is aimed at it strikes. Chance does not guide its course when thrown; and it flies back of its own accord, stained with the blood of the quarry.'

Then Phocus became more curious still to know its history. Who was the giver of so precious a present?

Cephalus at length consented to tell the story, tears starting to his eyes at the sorrow revived in his heart by the memories it recalled. 'Long as I live,' he

Right: Cephalus Receiving the Spear and Hound from Procris by Laurent de La Hyre.

exclaimed with a sigh, 'this weapon will cause me to weep, for it proved the ruin of myself and my dear wife Procris. Fairer and sweeter was she than even her sister Orithyia, whom Boreas carried off. Her father Erechtheus bestowed her upon me, and for love she chose me for her own. I was considered a lucky man in possessing her, and so I was. In all Greece you could not have found a happier pair of lovers, and the gods themselves were jealous of our bliss—too great for mortals. Before the second month was ended after our marriage feast, Aurora, the goddess of the Dawn, beheld me in the early morn as I was planting nets to trap the deer from the heights of Hymettus, and I followed her against my will. She cast her spell on me, and held me by the witchery of her great eyes and rosy fingers. Fair she is, with a beauty not of earth, but she seemed to me less fair than Procris. Procris was ever in my thoughts, and in my dreams I breathed the name of Procris. Then the goddess cried angrily, "You may keep your Procris. The day will come when you will wish you had never possessed her!"

'Diana had bestowed on Procris, who loved the hunt, Lælaps, the hound whom no wild beast can outrun, and this javelin which nothing can escape, as a token of our reconciliation. These she gave to me.

'Would you like to know the fate of this other present—the dog? When Oedipus had solved that riddle which none other could guess, and the Sphinx who invented it lay a mangled corpse, Themis left her not unavenged. Another plague was sent against Thebes, and a savage monster devoured both the peasants and their cattle. We, the youth of the district, came together and inclosed the fields with nets, but the monster with a light bound leaped over them and escaped. The dogs were loosed, and they followed, but it escaped them as easily as a winged bird. My dog Lælaps—a tempest for speed—was straining at the leash. Eagerly the bystanders begged me to unloose him. Scarcely had I done so when he was lost to our sight. A spear flies not more swiftly, nor pellets from a sling, nor arrows from a Cretan bow. I watched from the hill-top this marvelous chase. At one time the wild beast seemed caught, at another to have clean escaped as it dodged and doubled, so that its enemy could not run full tilt at it. I was now thinking to use my javelin; and while fitting my fingers to the thongs, turned my eyes one

moment from the quarry. When I looked again, I beheld a still more wonderful sight. There were two marble statues in the middle of the plain; you would fancy one was flying and the other barking in pursuit. No doubt some god desired that both should remain unconquered in this test of speed.'

'But why should you complain of the javelin?' interrupted Phocus. 'What fault is there in it?'

'O Son of Æacus,' replied Cephalus, 'my sorrows have yet to be told. For years I was blest in my wife, and she was happy in her husband. None, not even Jupiter himself, could have come between us, nor could Venus have drawn me from my love.

'When the sun was just gilding the hill-tops I was wont to go into the woods to hunt. I wanted no servants, nor horses, nor even keen-scented hounds with me; my sure javelin was enough for me. When I was sated with the slaughter of wild beasts I would betake myself to some cool shady spot, and enjoy the breeze coming gently over the cool valleys, and so refreshing in the noontide heat. While I awaited the rising of the breeze, I would sing a sort of refrain: "Come, gentle Aura, kindly Aura; come to my breast; with thy cool sweetness refresh me, parched by the heat!" Perhaps, as cruel fate might have prompted me, I added other words, such as "Sweet Aura, thou art my delight! Thou dost love and refresh me; thou makest me to seek woods and lonely haunts, and thy breath is pleasant on my face." Some busybody must have heard me; and, imagining that I was in love with some nymph named Aura, carried the story to my wife.

'Love is only too ready to believe the worst. When Procris heard the tale she fell down fainting with sudden grief. Then coming to, she bemoaned her wretched fate, and wept for my faithlessness. She believed that this Aura was a maiden and a rival. Yet, hoping she might be deceived, she would not pass sentence unless she beheld my treachery with her own eyes.

'Next morning, at sunrise, I went out as usual to the woods, and being successful in the chase, lay down to rest myself, murmuring, "Come to me, sweetest Aura." Methought I heard a faint far-distant moan, but I heeded not and said again, "Come, Aura, come!" A rustling of leaves startled me, and, thinking

it was a wild beast, I let fly my javelin.

'Alas! it was Procris. Crying, "Ah, wretched me!" she received the dart in her breast. I ran to the sound of her voice. To my distraction I found her dying, her garments stained with blood, and drawing her own gift, that too-sure javelin, out of her wound. I lifted up her body, dearer to me than my own, in my guilty arms, and bound up the cruel wounds with strips torn from my garments; and I tried vainly to stanch the blood, begging her not to die and leave me desolate.

'With gasping breath and broken utterance she whispered in my ear: "I beseech thee, by the gods above, and by our marriage vows, and by my love even now enduring though I die, not to let that light-of-love, Aura, possess the heart that once was mine!" Then, at last, I saw the mistake of the name, and that her fears were about a shadow. I reassured her. But what availed it? She was sinking, and her little strength faded away with her life-blood. So long as she could look at anything, she gazed on me, and breathed out with a smile her unhappy life. But I like to fancy she died free from care, and with a look of content.

'I still cherish her memory. No mortal maid has since possessed my heart. So have I grown old in the service of Diana, looking to the day which cannot now be long distant when we can meet and renew our love in the Elysian fields.'

Landscape With Narcissus and Echo *by Franciscus de Neve.*

Echo and Narcissus

Thomas Bulfinch

Echo was a beautiful nymph, fond of the woods and hills, where she devoted herself to woodland sports. She was a favorite of Diana, and attended her in the chase. But Echo had one failing; she was fond of talking, and whether in chat or argument, would have the last word. One day Juno was seeking her husband, who, she had reason to fear, was amusing himself among the nymphs. Echo by her talk contrived to detain the goddess till the nymphs made their escape. When Juno discovered it, she passed sentence upon Echo in these words: 'You shall forfeit the use of that tongue with which you have cheated me, except for that one purpose you are so fond of—*reply*. You shall still have the last word, but no power to speak first.'

This nymph saw Narcissus, a beautiful youth, as he pursued the chase upon the mountains. She loved him, and followed his footsteps. O, how she longed to address him in the softest accents, and win him to converse! but it was not in her power. She waited with impatience for him to speak first, and had her answer ready. One day the youth, being separated from his companions, shouted aloud, 'Who's here?' Echo replied, 'Here.' Narcissus looked around, but seeing no one, called out, 'Come.' Echo answered, 'Come.' As no one came, Narcissus called again, 'Why do you shun me?' Echo asked the same question. 'Let us join one another,' said the youth. The maid answered with all her heart in the same words, and hastened to the spot, ready to throw her arms about his neck. He started back, exclaiming, 'Hands off! I would rather die than you should have me!' 'Have me,' said she; but it was all in vain. He left her, and she went to hide her blushes in the recesses of the woods. From that time forth she lived in caves and among the mountain cliffs. Her form faded with grief, till at last all her flesh shrank away. Her bones were changed into rocks, and there was nothing left of her but her voice. With that she is still ready to reply to any one who calls her, and keeps up her old habit of having the last word.

Narcissus' cruelty in this case was not the only instance. He shunned all the rest of the nymphs, as he had done poor Echo. One day a maiden, who had in vain endeavored to attract him, uttered a prayer that he might some time or other feel what it was to love and meet no return of affection. The avenging goddess heard and granted the prayer.

There was a clear fountain, with water like silver, to which the shepherds never drove their flocks, nor the mountain goats resorted, nor any of the beasts of the forest; neither was it defaced with fallen leaves or branches; but the grass grew fresh around it, and the rocks sheltered it from the sun. Hither came one day the youth fatigued with hunting, heated and thirsty. He stooped down to drink, and saw his own image in the water; he thought it was some beautiful water-spirit living in the fountain. He stood gazing with admiration at those bright eyes, those locks curled like the locks of Bacchus or Apollo, the rounded cheeks, the ivory neck, the parted lips, and the glow of health and exercise over all. He fell in love with himself. He brought his lips near to take a kiss; he plunged his arms in to embrace the beloved object. It fled at the touch, but returned again after a moment and renewed the fascination. He could not tear himself away; he lost all thought of food or rest, while he hovered over the brink of the fountain gazing upon his own image. He talked with the supposed spirit: 'Why, beautiful being, do you shun me? Surely, my face is not one to repel you. The nymphs love me, and you yourself look not indifferent upon me. When I stretch forth my arms you do the same; and you smile upon me and answer my beckonings with the like.' His tears fell into the water and disturbed the image. As he saw it depart, he exclaimed, 'Stay, I entreat you! Let me at least gaze upon you, if I may not touch

you.' With this, and much more of the same kind, he cherished the flame that consumed him, so that by degrees he lost his color, his vigor, and the beauty which formerly had so charmed the nymph Echo. She kept near him, however, and when he exclaimed, 'Alas, alas!' she answered him with the same words. He pined away and died; and when his shade passed the Stygian river, it leaned over the boat to catch a look of itself in the waters. The nymphs mourned for him, especially the water-nymphs; and when they smote their breasts, Echo smote hers also. They prepared a funeral pile, and would have burned the body, but it was nowhere to be found; but in its place a flower, purple within, and surrounded with white leaves, which bears the name and preserves the memory of Narcissus.

Milton alludes to the story of Echo and Narcissus in the Lady's song in 'Comus.' She is seeking her brothers in the forest, and sings to attract their attention:

> Sweet Echo, sweetest nymph, that liv'st unseen
> Within thy aëry shell
> By slow Meander's margent green,
> And in the violet-embroidered vale,
> Where the love-lorn nightingale
> Nightly to thee her sad song mourneth well;
> Canst thou not tell me of a gentle pair
> That likest thy Narcissus are?
> O, if thou have
> Hid them in some flowery cave,
> Tell me but where,
> Sweet queen of parly, daughter of the sphere,
> So may'st thou be translated to the skies,
> And give resounding grace to all heaven's harmonies.

Milton has imitated the story of Narcissus in the account which he makes Eve give of the first sight of herself reflected in the fountain:

That day I oft remember when from sleep
I first awaked, and found myself reposed
Under a shade on flowers, much wondering where
And what I was, whence thither brought, and how.
Not distant far from thence a murmuring sound
Of waters issued from a cave, and spread
Into a liquid plain, then stood unmoved
Pure as the expanse of heaven; I thither went
With unexperienced thought, and laid me down
On the green bank, to look into the clear
Smooth lake that to me seemed another sky.
As I bent down to look, just opposite
A shape within the watery gleam appeared,
Bending to look on me. I started back;
It started back; but pleased I soon returned,
Pleased it returned as soon with answering looks
Of sympathy and love. There had I fixed
Mine eyes till now, and pined with vain desire,
Had not a voice thus warned me: 'What thou seest,
What there thou seest, fair creature, is thyself;' &c.

Paradise Lost, Book IV

No one of the fables of antiquity has been oftener alluded to by the poets than that of Narcissus. Here are two epigrams which treat it in different ways. The first is by Goldsmith:

ON A BEAUTIFUL YOUTH, STRUCK BLIND BY LIGHTNING
Sure 'twas by Providence designed,
Rather in pity than in hate,
That he should be like Cupid blind,
To save him from Narcissus' fate.

The other is by Cowper:

ON AN UGLY FELLOW
Beware, my friend, of crystal brook
Or fountain, lest that hideous hook,
Thy nose, thou chance to see;
Narcissus' fate would then be thine,
And self-detested thou would'st pine,
As self-enamored he.'

The Ring of Polycrates

M.M. Bird

Then, would'st thou keep thy happy place,
Beseech the Immortals of their grace
Some bitter with their sweet to blend;
For when the gods on any pour
Of happiness an unmixed store,
Ruin full sure will be his end.

Friedrich Schiller (1759–1805)

Of all earth's monarchs, the lordliest and the proudest was Polycrates, Tyrant of Samos. Whatever he set his hand to had prospered. One by one he had conquered all the isles of Greece, and never had his galleys by sea or his archers on land known defeat. Alone to be compared with him in power was his friend and ally, Amasis, King of Egypt, by whose side he had warred and shared the spoils of victory.

This Polycrates, in his palace on Samos, gazing out across the shining sea and

meditating what new venture should occupy his arms, saw one day a single galley speeding swiftly from the south. It bore the cognizance of the King of Egypt, the watchmen said.

'What message can our good brother Amasis have for us?' mused the King. 'For what new exploit does he demand our aid, what deed does he not dare to venture till he league our charmed fortune with his own?'

The galley flew over the waters; it glided round the outflung arm of the mole, and reached the quay. Messengers bore in haste to the palace a missive sealed with the great seal of Amasis.

Polycrates searched the hieroglyphics in vain for some bold scheme, his share in which shall be more slaves, more land, more gold, more power, and more hate from those he conquers.

For this is what Amasis wrote to his ally:

'It is pleasant to hear of the success of a friend and ally. But thy excessive good fortune doth not please me, knowing as I do that the divinity is jealous. As for me, I would rather choose that both I and my friends should be partly successful in our undertakings, and partly suffer reverses; and so pass life meeting with vicissitudes of fortune than be prosperous in all things. For I cannot remember that I ever heard of any man who, having suffered no reverse, did not at last utterly perish. Be advised therefore by me, and act thus with regard to thy good fortune. Consider well what thou valuest most, and the loss of which would most pain thy soul; this treasure so cast away that it may never more be seen of man.'

Polycrates put down the letter and meditated. He looked round the gorgeous hall wherein he sat, he looked out of the window at the marble terraces, the vines and fruit trees of his palace gardens. Below he saw the crowded streets of his busy town, his quays where ships unloaded their merchandise for his pleasure. There was the harbor where his galleys lay, a hundred of them, each manned by fifty strong oarsmen, slaves. Beyond the great mole that captives of war had built for him lay the crowded islands of the Grecian seas, and they too were his vassals or allies. His power knew no check; the stream of gold flowed unbroken to his shores. He owned to himself with mingled pride and alarm that such prosperity

was a thing to provoke the jealous envy of the immortals.

Amasis had seen this danger, and had sent a kindly warning to his friend. It was well done.

What loss would he most mourn?

Tyrant as he was, Polycrates was a patron of the arts. It was at his court that Anacreon sung of wine and love as none had sung before. Painters and sculptors and musicians were entertained there, and he delighted in their arts. Should he sacrifice his favorite singer, his most gifted painter? Should he obliterate the world-famous fresco of his banquet hall, or slay the most beautiful of his slaves? But a new singer would soon replace the old, another artist would arise and would paint a more enchanting scene, a lovelier slave would fall captive to his arms.

He despaired of selecting among his countless treasures what was most precious, when his eye fell on the great gold signet on his fore-finger. There was the symbol of his power itself, the splendid gold ring, carved by Theodorus, son of Telecles the Samian. There was the emerald engraved by Theodorus with his signet device. The impress of that signet on the pliant wax set the seal of the King's command on every order. His eyes dwelt on the beautiful ring; he turned it on his finger, he marked the cunning work of it, the elegant design. The gold glittered in the sunlight, the heart of the great emerald glowed with green fire.

'This ring,' he cried, 'my dearest treasure, my most valued possession, I will cast into the sea!'

His ministers and courtiers heard him astonished. They spoke among themselves with bated breath of the thing the King proposed to do. How could the business of the realm go on without the King's recognized seal to set upon his ordinances? The news spread through the palace, where astonishment was mingled with consternation, and consternation with admiration of the King who would sacrifice so great a treasure to propitiate the gods for the good of his realm. From the palace the news spread to the town, and men gathered in knots to discuss it, and women ran from house to house to tell and hear it. Then they saw the royal barge of fifty oars being swiftly prepared for sea. The crowds of workers left their toil in the workshops of the town and clustered on the quay. They looked and saw the King coming in procession from the palace, his ministers about him, his courtiers following after. A frown was on his brow and a fierce resolve in his eyes. And as he passed along the gangway they marked that his royal hand was bare; no green fire shone from it like a glow-worm at night.

Out, far out into the sea the rowers drove the swift galley; the water boiled beneath the keel, and fled hissing from the stroke of those fifty oars. At last the silent King made a sign, and the oars flashed out of the water, scattering a silver fountain of spray.

Thrice the King raised his arm in act to throw, and thrice as he eyed the priceless gem he clutched it in his open palm. But the fourth time he closed his dazzled eyes and flung it far from him. And the great emerald, as it fell into the main, flashed like a streamer in the northern sky.

No sign that the gods accepted his sacrifice followed the deed. The sun shone bright overhead, and below was the innumerable laughter of the waves.

The King made a sign with the hand, now so significantly bare, and the galley sped back to the quay. And all the days that followed there was mourning in the palace, the King was wrapped in gloom, the business of the state seemed to have been brought to a standstill.

On the sixth day a humble fisherman climbed to the palace gates, bearing as a gift a royal sturgeon. 'Accept, O King,' he cried, 'an offering worthy of thee. For three-score years have I plied my humble trade, yet never before have my nets brought to land so goodly a fish.'

Polycrates thanked the fisherman and bestowed on him a purse of gold, and the fish he ordered to be served for that night's banquet.

The King was in his chamber, deep in state affairs, when a scullion came running demanding instant audience. In his hand was a jewel that flashed and glowed.

Polycrates stared in amazement, and then stretched forth his hand to seize the ring that had been miraculously restored. For when the fisherman's gift had been cut open the ring had been found in its belly.

The courtiers whispered together in fear: 'What can this mean? Have the jealous gods rejected the sacrifice?'

But Polycrates was beside himself with joy. He wrote in haste to Amasis, King of Egypt, to tell him what had befallen. 'Such good fortune as mine,' he declared, 'is unassailable by gods or men.'

But Amasis was of a different opinion. He felt that no power could avail to save a man so unnaturally fortunate from the vengeance of the jealous gods. He sent his herald to say that he renounced the friendship between them lest, said he, if some dreadful and great calamity befell Polycrates he might himself be involved in it!

Black anger at this desertion filled the heart of Polycrates. He heard that Cambyses, son of Cyrus, King of Persia, was on the point of invading Egypt with a great army, so he offered him help by sea. Cambyses gladly accepted this alliance, and Polycrates despatched forty ships of war.

But in his heaven-sent blindness he manned them with malcontents and men of conquered nations whom he suspected of disloyalty and wished to remove— sending with them secretly a message to Cambyses that he did not wish a man of them to return.

These warriors mutinied before they reached the battle ground, and returned in war array against Samos, but they, too, failed and Polycrates became more powerful than ever. And then it was that Oroetes, the Persian satrap of Sardis, who had conceived a hatred of Polycrates, enticed the fortunate tyrant to visit him and seized upon him treacherously and crucified him, so that men might see how the jealous gods will not suffer a mortal to share immortal bliss, and that soon or late pride has a fall.

Iulio Romano inu:
W. Hollar fecit, 1652,
Ex Collectione S. Nicolai Lennieri

Romulus and Remus

Mrs. Guy E. Lloyd

Every one has heard tell of Rome, that great city, already ancient when Cæsar found on the shores of Britain woad-painted savages living in a swamp where now stands the mightiest city in the world. The story of Romulus and Remus tells of the founding of this ancient city, and how it took its name from its first king.

Older even than Rome was a town built on a hill not far away by Iulus, son of Æneas, of whose wanderings you have heard, and called Alba Longa, the Long White City.

When my story begins it was ruled by King Amulius. He had no right to the throne, but he had seized it by force from his elder brother, Numitor, who was a peace-abiding man, and no match for his ambitious brother.

Amulius had nothing to fear from the gentle Numitor, who abode with his flocks and herds, but his guilty conscience would not let him rest, and he lived in terror lest one day the children of Numitor should avenge their father's wrongs and take the throne that was theirs by right of inheritance.

So he hired assassins to kill the boy, and the girl, Sylvia, he doomed to be a vestal virgin. These were maidens vowed to remain single all their lives, and to watch the ever-burning fire in the shrine of the goddess Vesta; this could only be

Left: Romulus and Remus *from a series of six plates created in the 17th century, etched by Wenceslas Hollar after drawings by Giulio Romano.*

kept alive by spotless virgins, and on its life depended the safety of the city—of Alba first, and afterwards of Rome.

But the god Mars, whom all Romans worship as the leader of their hosts and the founder of their race, looked with pity on the maid, and willed not that the seed of Numitor should perish. So he visited her as she lay asleep in the temple of Vesta, and he sent her a wonderful dream.

She dreamt that as she sat and watched the sacred fire, she dozed, and the fillet slipped from her brow, and from the fillet there sprang two palm trees that grew and spread till their tops reached the heavens, and their branches overspread all the earth. Seven times did she dream the same dream, and she knew at last that it was a message of the god. And lo, in due time there were born to her twin sons of more than mortal beauty.

When Amulius heard of the birth of these twins his wrath was kindled. He commanded that Sylvia should forthwith be buried alive, for that is the punishment appointed for virgins unfaithful to their vows; and himself seizing the wicker cradle in which the babes lay asleep, he flung it into the yellow Tiber.

But Mars was mindful of his own. The mother, Sylvia, was nowhere to be found, for the god had spirited her away in safety, and the helpless babes, still sleeping quietly, floated upon the turbid waters as though their cradle had been a boat, while Father Tiber quelled his raging flood to let them pass unharmed.

On drifted the frail bark down the river till it came to where, at the foot of a hill, stood a great wild fig tree, its gnarled roots laid bare by the wash of the flood. The floating cradle was driven against the roots of this tree and held fast there, for the water had reached its highest level and was beginning now to ebb.

Through all the roaring of the raging river the babes had slept, but now, with a start, they awoke and looked up, expecting to see their mother bending over them and ready to take them to her breast. But over their heads they saw only a glimmer of twilight through the branches of the fig tree, and there was no sound save the sough of the wind and the lapping of the waters, and now and again the distant howl of a wolf seeking its evening meal. Cold and hungry, they cried piteously. Presently, through the gathering darkness, two green eyes stared down

at them. It was a great gray she-wolf, and the hungry babes hushed their cry and gazed in wonder at those lamps of fire.

The wolf sniffed all round the cradle; then she pushed it with her forepaws till it fell right over on its side and the two infants rolled out of it. She licked them gently with her rough tongue, and they cuddled to her warm flanks and clutched instinctively with their tiny fingers at her shaggy fell. She dragged them gently up the hillside, away from the water, to a mossy cavern where she had her lair, and there she gave them milk as though they had been her own cubs, and nestling close against her the babes fell asleep.

It chanced that Faustulus, the chief herdsman of King Amulius, went forth one morning to see if the floods were abated and the pastures once more clear. As he wandered along at the foot of the Palatine hill he saw a cradle lying on its side beneath a fig tree. He went towards it, and as he neared the place his eye was caught by something moving within the dark shadow of an overhanging rock. He bent his steps to the cave to see what might be within it, when on a sudden a she-wolf sprang out and away among the bushes before he could aim a dart at her; and, to his amazement, a green woodpecker, with a piece of bread in its beak, came fluttering forth from the hollow. Both wolf and woodpecker, you must know, are special servants of Mars, and these were doing his pleasure and tending the helpless infants.

Faustulus came to the cave and stooped to look in. There, scrambling over one another on a soft bed of moss and fern, were two beautiful boys; and he marveled greatly, and said to himself: 'These babes were not born of common mortals, but of one of the immortal gods. A naiad, or haply a river-god, must have interposed to save them from the flood, and to feed them with ambrosia, the food of the gods.'

So he took them home to his wife Laurentia, and told her the tale. And when she saw their innocent faces her motherly heart was stirred with love and pity, and she tended them as though they had been her own sons, and called them Romulus and Remus.

The boys grew up brave and strong. When they were old enough they helped the herdsmen of King Amulius; and, because they were ever foremost where there was danger, all the other lads came to look up to them as leaders. It was a life that pleased the twins well. All day they wandered on the slopes of the hills, guarding the grazing cattle from wild beasts or robbers, and at night all the herdsmen would join together and make a camp in some sheltered valley or beneath spreading trees on the mountain side. And here they would build great fires to keep off the wolves, and would lie beside them, singing songs or telling tales to one another.

Sometimes the herdsmen of King Amulius had desperate fights with other herdsmen over good camping-grounds, or fertile pastures, or safe watering-places, or over the ownership of strayed cattle. More especially were their quarrels fierce and frequent with the herdsmen of Numitor, whose grazing-grounds marched with those of King Amulius. Sometimes, after these fights, the herdsmen of Numitor would complain to their master of the two tall striplings who constantly led the herdsmen of Amulius to victory.

At length, one day they laid an ambush and caught Remus, and bore him away to Numitor. As soon as the deposed king saw the lad he was reminded of the face of his long-lost daughter Sylvia, and he eagerly desired to see Romulus also.

Faustulus and his foster-son were wondering what could have befallen Remus, and were preparing to set out in search of him, when they saw a band of youths approaching, with olive boughs in their hands, in token that they came on a peaceful errand.

'Wherefore come you hither, friends?' asked Romulus.

The leader of the band made answer: 'Our master, Numitor, has sent us, Romulus, to pray thee to hasten to his presence.'

'Nay,' answered Romulus, 'I cannot go with you, for I must seek my brother Remus, who is lost.'

Then said the herdsman: 'Fear not for thy brother. He is already with our master Numitor.'

Then Faustulus, who long ago had guessed who the boys must be, said to Romulus: 'Do thou the bidding of Numitor, and go with these youths. I myself will go with thee, and will tell thee on the way certain matters that it much imports thee to know.'

So on the way to the hall of Numitor, Faustulus told Romulus all the tale of the wicker cradle caught beneath the fig tree, and of the wolf and woodpecker that had tended the helpless babes.

When the herd-lads saw Romulus pass by they followed him, armed with staves and slings, to see that no harm should come to him; for they loved him and his brother well, and counted them their leaders.

As soon as Numitor saw the two lads together and heard the tale of their finding, he was sure that they must be the children of his daughter Sylvia.

And Romulus and Remus, when they knew of the evil deeds of their great-uncle Amulius, determined to take vengeance on him.

All the herdsmen were ready to follow wherever the twins might choose to lead, so they set forth at once for the hall of King Amulius, and they overpowered his bodyguard and slew him, and made Numitor king in his stead.

King Numitor was no ungrateful monarch, and he assigned to his grandsons, while yet alive, all the lands beside the Tiber, and here the brothers determined to build a city and to found a kingdom.

And now there came a sharp division between Romulus and Remus. They were of like age, strength, and courage, and of a like high spirit that ill brooked any kind of control. Both wanted to rule, neither was willing to obey; each of the twins was ambitious to be king in the new city, and to call it after his own name.

Then said their grandfather, King Numitor: 'Strive not together over this thing, but let the all-seeing gods decide. Go up, either of you, to the top of one of these mountains, and look abroad upon the earth and sky, and the gods shall send a sign whereby ye may know who is chosen king.'

So Romulus and Remus went each to the top of one of the hills by the Tiber, and they looked abroad upon the earth and sky, all fair and bright in the sunny April weather.

Remus first came back to his grandfather, and he was flushed with triumph.

'Victory!' he cried. 'The gods have chosen me as king, for I have seen six vultures flying in the sky.'

'Wait,' said King Numitor; 'do nothing rashly; let us hear what thy brother hath seen.'

As he spoke Romulus strode into the hall and bowed before his grandfather.

'Speak,' said King Numitor. 'What hast thou seen from thy mountain-top?'

And Romulus made answer: 'I looked abroad upon the earth, and saw no living thing; but when I gazed upwards, lo, I saw twelve vultures flying in the sky.'

Then said Numitor: 'Verily the gods have spoken plainly; here can be no mistaking. Hail, King Romulus! Thy brother saw but six vultures.'

And all the herdsmen cried with a great shout: 'Hail, King Romulus!'

But Remus muttered darkly: 'I saw mine first, and I should be the king.' But no man heeded him.

Then Romulus took a plow with a brazen share and yoked to it a bullock and a heifer, and plowed a deep furrow round the Palatine hill; and all the herdsmen followed after, turning the earth that the share displaced all to the side of the furrow where the city was to stand, so that good fortune might ever follow it and wealth be stored within its walls. But where the gates were to stand, the plow was lifted and carried a little space, for that was the custom of those days, that the gates might not be holy, but that all men might pass through.

The heart of Remus swelled with sullen anger, and he would not help his brother, nor take any part in the building of the city. Romulus would gladly have shared his lands and his wealth, but Remus would take nothing at his hands; if he might not be king he cared for nothing else.

Day by day he loitered about, gloomily watching Romulus and his men as they toiled at the walls of their city. They wrought hard and long each day, for they wished to surround their chosen site with a rampart before any foe came to interrupt their work.

Their first fortification was but a ditch and a mound, neither high nor wide, but enough to serve as a defense while they built better walls behind it at their leisure.

On the day the first wall of his new city was completed, Romulus was filled with joy, and offered sacrifices to the gods, and gave thanks in the presence of all his men.

But Remus thrust rudely in among the throng and laughed aloud in scorn:

'What a wall to make such a pother about!' he cried; and running forward he leaped the ditch and the rampart, and turning leaped back again. 'See how great a defense is your fine wall,' he cried to Romulus, mocking him. 'If a wolf should push against it he would knock it down, and I myself can leap within it whenever I choose.'

And Romulus answered, pale with passion: 'Go thy ways, brother, and leave my wall alone, or I may do thee a mischief.'

'Thy wall!' retorted Remus. 'Scarce can I see where thy wall runs. I thought, verily, some mole must have been rootling here upon the hillside.'

Now it has always been the custom of soldiers to build first with the spade, and the wall that Romulus and his friends had thrown up as they dug their ditch was higher even now than most of the walls that were made in those days.

And Celer, the henchman of Romulus, the youth who had helped him most in his work, was sorely angered when Remus mocked; and when once more he leaped the wall, crying, 'Even so will the enemy enter your city,' Celer made answer fiercely: 'And even thus will we meet the enemy'; and he smote Remus suddenly with the spade that was in his hand, and Remus fell dead at his brother's feet.

And when Celer saw that he had slain the brother of the King he flung down his spade and fled quickly, and being swift of foot he escaped to a far-off land.

And Romulus wept sore for his brother, and they took the body of Remus to the summit of the hill, and there they burnt it upon a great funeral pile.

The newly built city was called Rome; and here for many years Romulus reigned as king, terrible to his foes and just and kindly to all his people.

And when forty years had passed away it chanced that the King called together all his warriors to the Goat's Pool, that he might see and speak with them. They were standing ranged in their ranks while Romulus sat upon a high throne to muster them, when on a sudden there came a great darkness upon the whole assembly so that no man could see the face of him who stood next to him. Then, in the midst of the darkness, came a mighty storm of thunder and lightning. When the storm passed and the sun came out again all gazed in wonder and terror at the throne of Romulus, for the King was gone—he had vanished from their sight.

And there were those who said that they had seen amid the storm a chariot of fire mounting to the heavens, and that the charioteer was none other than Mars himself come to bear away his son Romulus to the abode of the immortal gods.

And while all men doubted and wondered and talked of these things it fell on a day that a friend of Romulus, named Julius Proculus, had a wondrous vision. For it seemed to him as he traveled alone among the mountains, that the King stood before him, great and noble and clad in shining armor.

And Julius cried out: 'Ah, my lord, wherefore hast thou left thy city in such sorrow? Hast thou indeed forsaken forever all those who love thee?'

Then the bright vision made answer: 'For a space have I dwelt with men, and a great and glorious city have I founded. Know me henceforward as Quirinus, one of the immortal gods. And now go back to my people and tell them that if they will follow forever the law that I have given them, suffering neither cowardice nor license among them, but being brave and just and honourable, then will I, Quirinus, ever be at hand to help them in their need, and they shall rule over all the peoples of the world.'

Picture credits

Los Angeles County Museum of Art: 33, 79, 144, 192.

Mary Evans Picture Library: 136.

Metropolitan Museum of Art: 2 and 41 (Gift of Mrs. John Sichel, 1966), 16 (The Elisha Whittelsey Collection, The Elisha Whittelsey Fund, 1949), 24 (Rogers Fund, 1942), 30 (Bequest of Phyllis Massar, 2011), 39 (The Elisha Whittelsey Collection, The Elisha Whittelsey Fund, 1949), 40 (Harris Brisbane Dick Fund, 1917), 42 (The Elisha Whittelsey Collection, The Elisha Whittelsey Fund, 1949), 44 (Bequest of Phyllis Massar, 2011), 50 (Gift of Harry G. Friedman, 1964), 92 (Gift of Henry Walters, 1917), 107 (Bequest of Grace M. Pugh, 1985), 114 (Gift of Felix M. Warburg and his family, 1941), 120–1 (Bequest of Phyllis Massar, 2011), 130 (Purchase, Joseph Pulitzer Bequest, 1917), 150 (Bequest of Phyllis Massar, 2011), 160 (Bequest of Grace M. Pugh, 1985), 168 (Robert Lehman Collection, 1975), 200 (The Elisha Whittelsey Collection, The Elisha Whittelsey Fund, 1949), 206 (Harris Brisbane Dick Fund, 1917), 214–15 (Purchase, Anne and Charles Stern Gift, 1963), 292 (The Elisha Whittelsey Collection, The Elisha Whittelsey Fund, 1949), 308–09 (Gift of Felix M. Warburg and his family, 1941), 312–13 (The Elisha Whittelsey Collection, The Elisha Whittelsey Fund, 1949), 320–21 (Harris Brisbane Dick Fund, 1917), 328 (The Elisha Whittelsey Collection, The Elisha Whittelsey Fund, 1949), 339 (Gift of Felix M. Warburg, 1920), 348 (Bequest of Phyllis Massar, 2011), 356 (Purchase, Fletcher Fund, 1972), 374 (Purchase, Joseph Pulitzer Bequest, 1917).

Wikimedia Commons: 36, 64, 98, 174, 182, 188,194, 220, 231, 241, 267, 272, 324, 362